FORTY SIGNS OF RAIN

Forty Signs of Rain

KIM STANLEY ROBINSON

HarperCollins*Publishers*

Verse from 'The Lockless Door' from 'The Poetry of Robert Frost',
edited by Edward Connery Latham, published by Jonathan Cape.
Reprinted by permission of The Random House Group Ltd.

HarperCollins*Publishers*
77–85 Fulham Palace Road,
Hammersmith, London W6 8JB

www.harpercollins.co.uk

Published by HarperCollins*Publishers* 2004
1 3 5 7 9 8 6 4 2

Copyright © Kim Stanley Robinson 2004

A catalogue record for this title
is available from The British Library

ISBN 0 00 714886 0

Typeset in Sabon by Palimpsest Book Production Limited,
Polmont, Stirlingshire

Printed and bound in Great Britain by
Clays Ltd, St Ives plc

Contents

ONE

The Buddha Arrives

The Earth is bathed in a flood of sunlight. A fierce inundation of photons – on average 342 joules per second per square metre. 4185 joules (one Calorie) will raise the temperature of one kilogram of water by one degree C. If all this energy were captured by the Earth's atmosphere, its temperature would rise by ten degrees C in one day.

Luckily much of it radiates back to space. How much depends on albedo and the chemical composition of the atmosphere, both of which vary over time.

A good portion of Earth's albedo, or reflectivity, is created by its polar ice caps. If polar ice and snow were to shrink significantly, more solar energy would stay on Earth. Sunlight would penetrate oceans previously covered by ice, and warm the water. This would add heat and melt more ice, in a positive feedback loop.

The Arctic Ocean ice pack reflects back out to space a few per cent of the total annual solar energy budget. When the Arctic ice pack was first measured by nuclear submarines in the 1950s, it averaged thirty feet thick in midwinter. By the end of the century it was down to fifteen. Then one August the ice broke up into large tabular bergs, drifting on the currents, colliding and separating, leaving broad lanes of water

1

open to the continuous polar summer sunlight. The next year the break-up started in July, and at times more than half the surface of the Arctic Ocean was open water. The third year, the break-up began in May.

That was last year.

Weekdays always begin the same. The alarm goes off and you are startled out of dreams that you immediately forget. Pre-dawn light in a dim room. Stagger into a hot shower and try to wake up all the way. Feel the scalding hot water on the back of your neck, ah, the best part of the day, already passing with the inexorable clock. Fragment of a dream, you were deep in some problem set now escaping you, just as you tried to escape it in the dream. Duck down the halls of memory – gone. Dreams don't want to be remembered.

Evaluate the night's sleep. Anna Quibler decided the previous night had not been so good. She was exhausted already. Joe had cried twice, and though it was Charlie who had gotten up to reassure him, as part of their behavioural conditioning plan which was intended to convey to Joe that he would never again get Mom to visit him at night, Anna had of course woken up too, and vaguely heard Charlie's reassurances: 'Hey. Joe. What's up? Go back to sleep, buddy, it's the middle of the night here. Nothing gets to happen until morning, so you might as well. This is pointless this wailing, why do you do this, good night damn it.'

A brusque bedside manner at best, but that was part of the plan. After that she had tossed and turned for long minutes, trying heroically not to think of work. In years past she had recited in her head Edgar Allan Poe's poem 'The Raven', which she had memorized in high school and which had a nice soporific effect, but then one night she had thought to

3

herself, 'Quoth the raven, Livermore,' because of work troubles she was having with some people out at Lawrence Livermore. After that the poem was ruined as a sleep aid because the moment she even thought of 'The Raven' she thought about work. In general Anna's thoughts had a tropism towards work issues.

Shower over, alas. She dried and dressed in three minutes. Downstairs she filled a lunch box for her older boy. Nick liked and indeed insisted that his lunch be exactly the same every day, so it was no great trouble to assemble it. Peanut butter sandwich, five carrots, apple, chocolate milk, yogurt, roll of lunch meat, cheese stick, cookie. Two minutes for that, then throw in a freeze pack to keep it chilled. As she got the coldpacks out of the freezer she saw the neat rows of plastic bottles full of her frozen milk, there for Charlie to thaw and feed to Joe during the day when she was gone. That reminded her, not that she would have forgotten much longer given how full her breasts felt, that she had to nurse the bairn before she left. She clumped back upstairs and lifted Joe out of his crib, sat on the couch beside it. 'Hey love, time for some sleepy nurses.'

Joe was used to this, and glommed onto her while still almost entirely asleep. With his eyes closed he looked like an angel. He was getting bigger but she could still cradle him in her arms and watch him curl into her like a new infant. Closer to two than one now, and a regular bruiser, a wild man who wearied her; but not now. The warm sensation of being suckled put her body back to sleep, but a part of her mind was already at work, and so she detached him and shifted him around to the other breast for four more minutes. In his first months she had had to pinch his nostrils together to get him to come off, but now a tap on the nose would do it, for the first breast at least. On the other one he was more recalcitrant. She watched the second hand on the big clock in his room sweep up and around. When they were

4

done he would go back to sleep and snooze happily until about nine, Charlie said.

She hefted him back into his crib, buttoned up and kissed all her boys lightly on the head. Charlie mumbled, 'Call me, be careful.' Then she was down the stairs and out the door, her big work bag over her shoulder.

The cool air on her face and wet hair woke her fully for the first time that day. It was May now and the late spring mornings had only a little bit of chill left to them, a delicious sensation given the humid heat that was to come. Fat grey clouds rolled just over the buildings lining Wisconsin Avenue. Truck traffic roared south. Splashes of dawn sunlight struck the metallic blue sheen of the windows on the skyscrapers up at Bethesda Metro, and as Anna walked briskly along it occurred to her, not for the first time, that this was one of the high points of her day. There were some disturbing implications in that fact, but she banished those and enjoyed the feel of the air and the tumble of the clouds over the city.

She passed the Metro elevator kiosk to extend her walk by fifty yards, then turned and clumped down the little stairs to the bus stop. Then down the big stairs of the escalator, into the dimness of the great tube of ribbed concrete that was the underground station. Card into the turnstile, thwack as the triangular barriers disappeared into the unit, pull her card out and through to the escalator down to the tracks. No train there, none coming immediately (you could hear them and feel their wind long before the lights set into the platform began to flash) so there was no need to hurry. She sat on a concrete bench that positioned her such that she could walk straight into the car of the train that would let her out at Metro Center directly in the place closest to the escalators down to the Orange Line east.

At this hour she was probably going to find a seat on the train when it arrived, so she opened her laptop and began to study one of the jackets, as they still called them: the grant proposals that the National Science Foundation received at a rate of fifty thousand a year. 'Mathematical and Algorithmic Analysis of Palindromic Codons as Predictors of a Gene's Protein Expression'. The project hoped to develop an algorithm that had shown some success in predicting which proteins any given gene sequence in human DNA would express. As genes expressed a huge variety of proteins, by unknown ways and with variations that were not understood, this kind of predicting operation would be a very useful thing if it could be done. Anna was dubious, but genomics was not her field. It would be one to give to Frank Vanderwal. She noted it as such and queued it in a forward to him, then opened the next jacket.

The arrival of a train, the getting on and finding of a seat, the change of trains at Metro Center, the getting off at the Ballston stop in Arlington, Virginia: all were actions accomplished without conscious thought, as she read or pondered the proposals she had in her laptop. The first one still struck her as the most interesting of the morning's bunch. She would be interested to hear what Frank made of it.

Coming up out of a Metro station is about the same everywhere: up a long escalator, towards an oval of grey sky and the heat of the day. Emerge abruptly into a busy urban scene.

The Ballston stop's distinction was that the escalator topped out in a big vestibule leading to the multiple glass doors of a building. Anna entered this building without glancing around, went to the nice little open-walled shop selling better-than-usual pastries and packaged sandwiches, and bought a lunch to eat at her desk. Then she went back outside to make her usual stop at the Starbuck's facing the street.

This particular Starbuck's was graced by a staff maniacally devoted to speed and precision; they went at their work like a drum and bugle corps. Anna loved to see it. She liked efficiency anywhere she found it, and more so as she grew older.

That a group of young people could turn what was potentially a very boring job into a kind of strenuous athletic performance struck her as admirable and heartening. Now it cheered her once again to move rapidly forward in the long queue, and see the woman at the computer look up at her when she was still two back in line and call out to her teammates, 'Tall latte half-caf, non-fat, no foam!' and then, when Anna got to the front of the line, ask her if she wanted anything else today. It was easy to smile as she shook her head.

Then outside again, doubled paper coffee cup in hand, to the NSF building's west entrance. Inside she showed her badge to security in the hall, then crossed the atrium to get to the south elevators.

Anna liked the NSF building's interior. The structure was hollow, featuring a gigantic central atrium, an octagonal space that extended from the floor to the skylight, twelve storeys above. This empty space, as big as some buildings all by itself, was walled by the interior windows of all the NSF offices. Its upper part was occupied by a large hanging mobile, made of metal curved bars painted in primary colours. The ground floor was occupied by various small businesses facing the atrium – pizza place, hair stylist, travel agency, bank outlet.

A disturbance caught Anna's eye. At the far door to the atrium there was a flurry of maroon, a flash of brass, and then suddenly a resonant low chord sounded, filling the big space with a vibrating *blaaa*, as if the atrium itself were a kind of huge horn.

A bunch of Tibetans, it looked like, were now marching into the atrium: men and women wearing belted maroon robes, and yellow winged conical caps. Some played long straight antique horns, others thumped drums or swung censers around, dispensing clouds of sandalwood. It was as if a parade entry had wandered in from the street by mistake. They crossed the atrium chanting, skip-stepping, swirling, all in majestic slow motion.

7

They headed for the travel agency, and for a second Anna wondered if they had come in to book a flight home. But then she saw that the travel agency's windows were empty.

This gave her a momentary pang, because these windows had always been filled by bright posters of tropical beaches and European castles, changing monthly like calendar photos, and Anna had often stood before them while eating her lunch, travelling mentally within them as a kind of replacement for the real travel that she and Charlie had given up when Nick was born. Sometimes it had occurred to her that given the kinds of political and bacterial violence that were often behind the scenes in those photos, mental travel was perhaps the best kind.

But now the windows were empty, the small room behind them likewise. In the doorway the Tibetanesque performers were now massing, in a crescendo of chant and brassy brass, the incredibly low notes vibrating the air almost visibly, like the cartoon soundtrack bassoon in *Fantasia*.

Anna moved closer, dismissing her small regret for the loss of the travel agency. New occupants, fogging the air with incense, chanting or blowing their hearts out: it was interesting.

In the midst of the celebrants stood an old man, his brown face a maze of deep wrinkles. He smiled, and Anna saw that the wrinkles mapped a lifetime of smiling that smile. He raised his right hand, and the music came to a ragged end in a hyperbass note that fluttered Anna's stomach.

The old man stepped free of the group and bowed to the four walls of the atrium, his hands held together before him. His dipped his chin and sang, his chant as low as any of the horns, and split into two notes, with a resonant head tone distinctly audible over the deep clear bass, all very surprising coming out of such a slight man. Singing thus, he walked to the doorway of the travel agency and there touched the door jambs on each side, exclaiming something sharp each time.

'*Rig yal ba! Chos min gon pa!*'

The others all exclaimed, '*Jetsun Gyatso!*'

The old man bowed to them.

And then they all cried '*Om!*' and filed into the little office space, the brassmen angling their long horns to make it in the door.

A young monk came back out. He took a small rectangular card from the loose sleeve of his robe, pulled some protective backing from sticky strips on the back of the card, and affixed it carefully to the window next to the door. Then he retreated inside.

Anna approached the window. The little sign said

EMBASSY OF KHEMBALUNG

An embassy! And a country she had never heard of, not that that was particularly surprising, new countries were popping up all the time, they were one of the UN's favourite dispute-settlement strategies. Perhaps a deal had been cut in some troubled part of Asia, and this Khembalung created as a result.

But no matter where they were from, this was a strange place for an embassy. It was very far from Massachusetts Avenue's ambassadorial stretch of unlikely architecture, unfamiliar flags and expensive landscaping; far from Georgetown, Dupont Circle, Adams-Morgan, Foggy Bottom, east Capitol Hill, or any of the other likely haunts for locating a respectable embassy. Not just Arlington, but the NSF building no less!

Maybe it was a scientific country.

Pleased at the thought, pleased to have something new in the building, Anna approached closer still. She tried to read some small print she saw at the bottom of the new sign.

The young man who had put out the sign reappeared. He had a round face, a shaved head, and a quick little mouth, like Betty Boop's. His expressive black eyes met hers directly.

'Can I help you?' he said, in what sounded to her like an Indian accent.

'Yes,' Anna said. 'I saw your arrival ceremony, and I was just curious. I was wondering where you all come from.'

'Thank you for your interest,' the youth said politely, ducking his head and smiling. 'We are from Khembalung.'

'Yes, I saw that, but . . .'

'Ah. Our country is an island nation. We are living in the Bay of Bengal, near the mouth of the Ganges.'

'I see,' Anna said, surprised; she had thought they would be from somewhere in the Himalayas. 'I hadn't heard of it.'

'It is not a big island. Nation status has been a recent development, you could say. Only now are we establishing a representation.'

'Good idea. Although, to tell the truth, I'm surprised to see an embassy in here. I didn't think of this as being the right kind of space.'

'We chose it very carefully,' the young monk said.

They regarded each other.

'Well,' Anna said, 'very interesting. Good luck moving in. I'm glad you're here.'

'Thank you.' Again he nodded.

Anna did the same and took her leave.

But as she turned to go, something caused her to look back. The young monk still stood there in the doorway, looking across at the pizza place, his face marked by a tiny grimace of distress.

Anna recognized the expression at once. When her older son Nick was born she had stayed home with him, and those first several months of his life were a kind of blur to her. She had missed her work, and doing it from home had not been possible. By the time maternity leave was over they had clearly needed her at the office, and so she had started working again, sharing the care of Nick with Charlie and some babysitters, and eventually a daycare centre in a building in Bethesda, near the Metro stop. At first Nick had cried furiously whenever she left for any reason, which she found excruciating; but then he had seemed to get used to it. And so did she, adjusting as everyone must to the small pains of the daily departure. It was just the way it was.

Then one day she had taken Nick down to the daycare centre – it was the routine by then – and he didn't cry when she said good-bye, didn't even seem to care or to notice. But for some reason she had paused to look back into the window of the place, and there on his face she saw a look of unhappy, stoical determination – determination not to cry, determination to get through another long lonely boring day – a look which on the face of a toddler was simply heartbreaking. It had pierced her like an arrow. She had cried out involuntarily, even started to rush back inside to take him in her arms and comfort him. Then she reconsidered how another goodbye would affect him, and with a horrible wrenching feeling, a sort of despair at all the world, she had left.

Now here was that very same look again, on the face of this young man. Anna stopped in her tracks, feeling again that stab from five years before. Who knew what had caused these people to come halfway around the world? Who knew what they had left behind?

She walked back over to him.

He saw her coming, composed his features. 'Yes?'

'If you want,' she said, 'later on, when it's convenient, I could show you some of the good lunch spots in this neighbourhood. I've worked here a long time.'

'Why, thank you,' he said. 'That would be most kind.'

'Is there a particular day that would be good?'

'Well – we will be getting hungry today,' he said, and smiled. He had a sweet smile, not unlike Nick's.

She smiled too, feeling pleased. 'I'll come back down at one o'clock and take you to a good one then, if you like.'

'That would be most welcome. Very kind.'

She nodded. 'At one, then,' already recalibrating her work

11

schedule for the day. The boxed sandwich could be stored in her office's little refrigerator.

Anna completed her journey to the south elevators. Waiting there she was joined by Frank Vanderwal, one of her programme officers. They greeted each other, and she said, 'Hey I've got an interesting jacket for you.'

He mock-rolled his eyes. 'Is there any such thing for a burnt-out case like me?'

'Oh I think so.' She gestured back at the atrium. 'Did you see our new neighbour? We lost the travel agency but gained an embassy, from a little country in Asia.'

'An embassy, here?'

'I'm not sure they know much about Washington.'

'I see.' Frank grinned his crooked grin, a completely different thing than the young monk's sweet smile, sardonic and knowing. 'Ambassadors from Shangri-La, eh?' One of the UP arrows lit, and the elevator door next to it opened. 'Well, we can use them.'

Primates in elevators. People stood in silence looking up at the lit numbers on the display console, as per custom.

Again the experience caused Frank Vanderwal to contemplate the nature of their species, in his usual sociobiologist's mode. They were mammals, social primates: a kind of hairless chimp. Their bodies, brains, minds and societies had grown to their current state in east Africa over a period of about two million years, while the climate was shifting in such a way that forest cover was giving way to open savannah.

Much was explained by this. Naturally they were distressed to be trapped in a small moving box. No savannah experience could be compared to it. The closest analogue might have been crawling into a cave, no doubt behind a shaman carrying a torch, everyone filled with great awe and very possibly under the influence of psychotropic drugs and religious rituals. An earthquake during such a visit to the underworld would be about all the savannah mind could contrive as an explanation for a modern trip in an elevator. No wonder an uneasy silence reigned; they were in the presence of the sacred. And the last five thousand years of civilization had not been anywhere near enough time for any evolutionary adaptations to alter these mental reactions. They were still only good at the things they had been good at on the savannah.

Anna Quibler broke the taboo on speech, as people would when all the fellow-passengers were cohorts. She said to Frank, continuing her story, 'I went over and introduced myself. They're from an island country in the Bay of Bengal.'

'Did they say why they rented the space here?'

'They said they had picked it very carefully.'

'Using what criteria?'

'I didn't ask. On the face of it, you'd have to say proximity to NSF, wouldn't you?'

Frank snorted. 'That's like the joke about the starlet and the Hollywood writer, isn't it?'

Anna wrinkled her nose at this, surprising Frank; although she was proper, she was not prudish. Then he got it: her disapproval was not at the joke, but at the idea that these new arrivals would be that hapless. She said, 'I think they're more together than that. I think they'll be interesting to have here.'

Homo sapiens is a species that exhibits sexual dimorphism. And it's more than a matter of bodies; the archaeological record seemed to Frank to support the notion that the social roles of the two sexes had diverged early on. These differing roles could have led to differing thought processes, such that it would be possible to characterize plausibly the existence of unlike approaches even to ostensibly non-gender-differentiated activities, such as science. So that there could be a male practice of science and a female practice of science, in other words, and these could be substantially different activities.

These thoughts flitted through Frank's mind as their elevator ride ended and he and Anna walked down the hall to their offices. Anna was as tall as he was, with a nice figure, but the dimorphism differentiating them extended to their habits of mind and their scientific practice, and that might explain why he was a bit uncomfortable with her. Not that this was a full characterization of his attitude. But she did science in a way that he found annoying. It was not a matter of her being warm and fuzzy, as you might expect from the usual characterizations of feminine thought – on the contrary, Anna's scientific work (she still often co-authored papers in

14

statistics, despite her bureaucratic load) often displayed a finicky perfectionism that made her a very meticulous scientist, a first-rate statistician – smart, quick, competent in a range of fields and really excellent in more than one. As good a scientist as one could find for the rather odd job of running the bioinformatics division at NSF, good almost to the point of exaggeration – too precise, too interrogatory – it kept her from pursuing a course of action with drive. Then again, at NSF maybe that was an advantage.

In any case she was so intense about it. A kind of Puritan of science, rational to an extreme. And yet of course at the same time that was all such a front, as with the early Puritans; the hyper-rational co-existed in her with all the emotional openness, intensity and variability that was the American female interactional paradigm and social role. Every female scientist was therefore potentially a kind of Mr Spock, the rational side foregrounded and emphasized while the emotional side was denied, and the two co-existing at odds with one another.

On the other hand, judged on that basis, Frank had to admit that Anna seemed less split-natured than many women scientists he had known. Pretty well integrated, really. He had spent many hours of the past year working with her, engaged in interesting discussions in the pursuit of their shared work. No, he liked her. The discomfort came not from any of her irritating habits, not even the nit-picking or hairsplitting that made her so strikingly eponymous (though no one dared joke about that to her), habits that she couldn't seem to help and didn't seem to notice – no – it was more the way her hyper-scientific attitude combined with her passionate female expressiveness to suggest a complete science, or even a complete humanity. It reminded Frank of himself.

Not of the social self that he allowed others to see, admittedly; but of his internal life as he alone experienced it. He too was stuffed with extreme aspects of both rationality and

15

emotionality. This was what made him uncomfortable: Anna was too much like him. She reminded him of things about himself he did not want to think about. But he was helpless to stop his trains of thought. That was one of his problems.

Halfway around the circumference of the sixth floor, they came to their offices. Frank's was one of a number of cubicles carving up a larger space; Anna's was a true office right across from his cubicle, a room of her own, with a foyer for her secretary Aleesha. Both their spaces, and all the others in the maze of crannies and rooms, were filled with the computers, tables, filing cabinets and crammed bookshelves that one found in scientific offices everywhere. The decor was standard degree-zero beige for everything, indicating the purity of science.

In this case it was all rendered human, and even handsome, by the omnipresent big windows on the interior sides of the rooms, allowing everyone to look across the central atrium and into all the other offices. This combination of open space and the sight of fifty to a hundred other humans made each office a slice or echo of the savannah. The occupants were correspondingly more comfortable at the primate level. Frank did not suffer the illusion that anyone had consciously planned this effect, but he admired the instinctive grasp on the architect's part of what would get the best work out of the building's occupants.

He sat down at his desk. He had angled his computer screen away from the window so that when necessary he could focus on it, but now he sat in his chair and gazed out across the atrium. He was near the end of his year-long stay at NSF, and the workload, while never receding, was simply becoming less and less important to him. Piles of articles and hard-copy jackets lay in stacks on every horizontal surface, arranged in Frank's complex through-put system. He had a lot of work to do. Instead he looked out the window.

The colourful mobile filling the upper half of the atrium

16

was a painfully simple thing, basic shapes in primary colours, very like an infant's scribble. Frank's many activities included rock climbing, and often he had occupied his mind by imagining the moves he would need to make to climb the mobile. There were some hard sections, but it would make for a fun route.

Past the mobile, he could see into one hundred and eight other rooms (he had counted). In them people typed at screens, talked in couples or on the phone, read, or sat in seminar rooms around paper-strewn tables, looking at slide-shows, or talking. Mostly talking. If the interior of the National Science Foundation were all you had to go on, you would have to conclude that doing science consisted mostly of sitting around in rooms talking.

This was not even close to true, and it was one of the reasons Frank was bored. The real action of science took place in laboratories, and anywhere else experiments were being conducted. What happened here was different, a kind of meta-science, one might say, which coordinated scientific activities, or connected them to other human action, or funded them. Something like that; he was having trouble characterizing it, actually.

The smell of Anna's Starbuck's latte wafted in from her office next door, and he could hear her on the phone already. She too did a lot of talking on the phone. 'I don't know, I have no idea what the other sample sizes are like . . . No, not statistically insignificant, that would mean the numbers were smaller than the margin of error. What you're talking about is just statistically meaningless. Sure, ask him, good idea.'

Meanwhile Aleesha, her assistant, was on her phone as well, patiently explaining something in her rich DC contralto. Unravelling some misunderstanding. It was an obvious if seldom-acknowledged fact that much of NSF's daily business was accomplished by a cadre of African-American women

17

from the local area, women who often seemed decidedly unconvinced of the earth-shattering importance that their mostly Caucasian employers attributed to the work. Aleesha, for instance, displayed the most sceptical politeness Frank had ever seen; he often tried to emulate it, but without, he feared, much success.

Anna appeared in the doorway, tapping on the doorjamb as she always did, to pretend that his space was an office. 'Frank, I forwarded that jacket to you, the one about an algorithm.'

'Let's see if it arrived.' He hit CHECK MAIL, and up came a new one from *aquibler@nsf.gov*. He loved that address. 'It's here, I'll take a look at it.'

'Thanks.' She turned, then stopped. 'Hey listen, when are you due to go back to UCSD?'

'End of July or end of August.'

'Well, I'll be sorry to see you go. I know it's nice out there, but we'd love it if you'd consider putting in a second year, or even think about staying permanently, if you like it. Of course you must have a lot of irons in the fire.'

'Yes,' Frank said noncomittally. Staying longer than his one-year stint was completely out of the question. 'That's nice of you to ask. I've enjoyed it, but I should probably get back home. I'll think about it, though.'

'Thanks. It would be good to have you here.'

Much of the work at NSF was done by visiting scientists, who came on leave from their home institutions to run NSF programmes in their area of expertise for periods of a year or two. The grant proposals came pouring in by the thousand, and programme directors like Frank read them, sorted them, convened panels of outside experts, and ran the meetings in which these experts rated batches of proposals in particular fields. This was a major manifestation of the peer review process, a process Frank thoroughly approved of – in principle. But a year of it was enough.

18

Anna had been watching him, and now she said, 'I suppose it is a bit of a rat race.'

'Well, no more than anywhere else. In fact if I were home it'd probably be worse.'

They laughed.

'And you have your journal work too.'

'That's right.' Frank waved at the piles of typescripts: three stacks for *Review of Bioinformatics,* two for *The Journal of Sociobiology.* 'Always behind. Luckily the other editors are better at keeping up.'

Anna nodded. Editing a journal was a privilege and an honour, even though usually unpaid – indeed, one often had to continue to subscribe to a journal just to get copies of what one had edited. It was another of science's many non-compensated activities, part of its extensive economy of social credit.

'Okay,' Anna said. 'I just wanted to see if we could tempt you. That's how we do it, you know. When visitors come through who are particularly good, we try to hold on to them.'

'Yes, of course.' Frank nodded uncomfortably, touched despite himself; he valued her opinion. He rolled his chair towards his screen as if to get to work, and she turned and left.

He clicked to the jacket Anna had forwarded. Immediately he recognized one of the investigators' names.

'Hey Anna?' he called out.

'Yes?' She reappeared in the doorway.

'I know one of the guys on this jacket. The PI is a guy from Caltech, but the real work is by one of his students.'

'Yes?' This was a typical situation, a younger scientist using the prestige of his or her advisor to advance a project.

'Well, I know the student. I was the outside member on his dissertation committee, a few years ago.'

'That wouldn't be enough to be a conflict.'

19

Frank nodded as he read on. 'But he's also been working on a temporary contract at Torrey Pines Generique, which is a company in San Diego that I helped start.'

'Ah. Do you still have any financial stake in it?'

'No. Well, my stocks are in a blind trust for the year I'm here, so I can't be positive, but I don't think so.'

'But you're not on the board, or a consultant?'

'No no. And it looks like his contract there was due to be over about now anyway.'

'That's fine, then. Go for it.'

No part of the scientific community could afford to be *too* picky about conflicts of interest. If they were, they'd never find anyone free to peer-review anything; hyper-specialization made every field so small that within them, everyone seemed to know everyone. Because of that, so long as there were no current financial or institutional ties with a person, it was considered okay to proceed to evaluate their work in the various peer-review systems.

But Frank had wanted to make sure. Yann Pierzinski had been a very sharp young bio-mathematician – he was one of those doctoral students whom one watched with the near certainty that one would hear from them again later in their career. Now here he was, with something Frank was particularly interested in. Frank's curiosity was piqued.

'Okay,' he said now to Anna. 'I'll put in the hopper.' He closed the file and turned as if to check out something else.

After Anna was gone, he pulled the jacket back up. 'Mathematical and Algorithmic Analysis of Palindromic Codons as Predictors of a Gene's Protein Expression.' A proposal to fund continuing work on an algorithm for predicting which proteins any given gene would express.

Very interesting. This was an assault on one of the fundamental mysteries, an unknown step in biology that presented a considerable blockage to any robust biotechnology. The three billion base pairs of the human genome encoded along their way some hundred thousand genes; and most of these genes contained instructions for the assembly of one or more proteins, the basic building-blocks of organic chemistry and life itself. But which genes expressed which proteins, and how exactly they did it, and why certain genes would create more than one protein, or different proteins in different circumstances – all these matters were very poorly understood, or completely mysterious. This ignorance made much of biotechnology an endless and very expensive matter of trial-and-error. A key to any part of the mystery could be very valuable.

Frank scrolled down the pages of the application with practised speed. Yann Pierzinski, PhD bio-maths, Caltech. Still doing post-doc work with his thesis advisor there, a man Frank had come to consider a bit of a credit hog, if not worse. It was interesting, then, that Pierzinski had gone down to Torrey Pines to work on a temporary contract, for a bio-informatics researcher whom Frank didn't know. Perhaps that had been a bid to escape the advisor. But now he was back.

Frank dug into the substantive part of the proposal. The algorithm set was one Pierzinski had been working on even back in his dissertation. Chemical mechanics of protein creation as a sort of natural algorithm, in effect. Frank considered the idea, operation by operation. This was his real expertise; this was what had interested him from childhood, when the puzzles solved had been simple ciphers. He had always loved this work, and now perhaps more than ever, offering as it did a complete escape from consciousness of himself. Why he might want to make that escape remained moot; howsoever it might be, when he came back he felt refreshed, as if finally he had been in a good place.

He also liked to see patterns emerge from the apparent randomness of the world. This was why he had recently taken such an interest in sociobiology; he had hoped there might be algorithms to be found there which would crack the code

of human behaviour. So far that quest had not been very satisfactory, mostly because so little in human behaviour was
susceptible to a controlled experiment, so no theory could
even be tested. That was a shame. He badly wanted some
clarification in that realm.

At the level of the four chemicals of the genome, however
– in the long dance of cytosine, adenine, guanine and thymine
– much more seemed to be amenable to mathematical explanation and experiment, with results that could be conveyed
to other scientists, and put to use. One could test Pierzinski's
ideas, in other words, and find out if they worked.

He came out of this trance of thought hungry, and with a
full bladder. He felt quite sure there was some real potential
in the work. And that was giving him some ideas.

He got up stiffly, went to the bathroom, came back. It was
mid-afternoon already. If he left soon he would be able to
hack through the traffic to his apartment, eat quickly, then
go out to Great Falls. By then the day's blanching heat would
have started to subside, and the river's gorge walls would be
nearly empty of climbers. He could climb until well past
sunset, and do some more thinking about this algorithm, out
where he thought best these days, on the hard old schist walls
of the only place in the Washington DC area where a scrap
of nature had survived.

TWO

In the Hyperpower

Mathematics sometimes seems like a universe of its own. But it comes to us as part of the brain's engagement with the world, and appears to be part of the world, its structure or recipe.

Over historical time humanity has explored further and further into the various realms of mathematics, in a cumulative and collective process, an ongoing conversation between the species and reality. The discovery of the calculus. The invention of formal arithmetic and symbolic logic, both mathematicizing the instinctive strategies of human reason, making them as distinct and solid as geometric proofs. The attempt to make the entire system contained and self-consistent. The invention of set theory, and the finessing of the various paradoxes engendered by considering sets as members of themselves. The discovery of the incompletability of all systems. The step-by-step mechanics of programming new calculating machines. All this resulted in an amalgam of maths and logic, the symbols and methods drawn from both realms, combining in the often long and complicated operations that we call algorithms.

In the time of the development of the algorithm, we also made discoveries in the real world: the double helix within

23

our cells. DNA. Within half a century the whole genome was read, base pair by base pair. Three billion base pairs, parts of which are called genes, and serve as instruction packets for protein creation.

But despite the fully explicated genome, the details of its expression and growth are still very mysterious. Spiralling pairs of cytosine, guanine, adenosine, and thymine: we know these are instructions for growth, for the development of life, all coded in sequences of paired elements. We know the elements; we see the organisms. The code between them remains to be learned.

Mathematics continues to develop under the momentum of its own internal logic, seemingly independent of everything else. But several times in the past, purely mathematical developments have later proved to be powerfully descriptive of operations in nature that were either unknown or unexplainable at the time the math was being developed. This is a strange fact, calling into question all that we think we know about the relationship between maths and reality, the mind and the cosmos.

Perhaps no explanation of this mysterious adherence of nature to mathematics of great subtlety will ever be forthcoming. Meanwhile, the operations called algorithms become ever more convoluted and interesting to those devising them. Are they making portraits, recipes, magic spells? Does reality use algorithms, do genes use algorithms? The mathematicians can't say, and many of them don't seem to care. They like the work, whatever it is.

Leo Mulhouse kissed his wife Roxanne and left their bedroom. In the living room the light was halfway between night and dawn. He went out onto their balcony: screeching gulls, the rumble of the surf against the cliff below. The vast grey plate of the Pacific Ocean.

Leo had married into this spectacular house, so to speak; Roxanne had inherited it from her mother. Its view from the edge of the sea cliff in Leucadia, California, was something Leo loved, but the little grass yard below the second-storey porch was only about fifteen feet wide, and beyond it was an open gulf of air and the grey foaming ocean, eighty feet below. And not that stable a cliff. He wished that the house had been placed a little farther back on its lot.

Back inside, fill his travel coffee cup, down to the car. Down Europa, past the Pannikin, hang a right and head to work.

The Pacific Coast Highway in San Diego County was a beautiful drive at dawn. In any kind of weather it was handsome: in new sun with all the pale blues lifting out of the sea, in scattered cloud when shards and rays of horizontal sunlight broke through, or on rainy or foggy mornings when the narrow but rich palette of greys filled the eye with the subtlest of gradations. The grey dawns were by far the most frequent, as the region's climate settled into what appeared to be a permanent El Niño – the Hyperniño, as people called it. The whole idea of a Mediterranean climate leaving the

25

world, even in the Mediterranean, people said. Here coastal residents were getting sunlight deficiency disorders, and taking vitamin D and anti-depressants to counteract the effects, even though ten miles inland it was a cloudless baking desert all the year round. The June Gloom had come home to roost.

Leo Mulhouse took the coast highway to work every morning. He liked seeing the ocean, and feeling the slight roller-coaster effect of dropping down to cross the lagoons, then motoring back up little rises to Cardiff, Solano Beach and Del Mar. These towns looked best at this hour, deserted and as if washed for the new day. Hiss of tyres on wet road, wet squeak of windshield wipers, distant boom of the waves breaking – it all combined to make a kind of aquatic experience, the drive like surfing, up and down the same bowls every time, riding the perpetual wave of land about to break into the sea.

Up the big hill onto Torrey Pines, past the golf course, quick right into Torrey Pines Generique. Down into its parking garage, descending into the belly of work. Into the biotech beast.

Meaning a complete security exam, just to get in. If they didn't know what you came in with, they wouldn't be able to judge what you went out with. So, metal detector, inspection by the bored security team with their huge coffee cups, computer turned on, hardware and software check by experts, sniff-over by Clyde the morning dog, trained to detect signature molecules: all standard in biotech now, after some famous incidents of industrial espionage. The stakes were too high to trust anybody.

Then Leo was inside the compound, walking down long white hallways. He put his coffee on his desk, turned on his desktop computer, went out to check the experiments in progress. The most important current one was reaching an endpoint, and Leo was particularly interested in the results. They had been using high-throughput screening of some of

26

the many thousands of proteins listed in the Protein Data Bank at UCSD, trying to identify some that would activate certain cells in a way that would make these cells express more high-density lipoprotein than they would normally – perhaps ten times as much. Ten times as much HDL, the 'good cholestorol', would be a life-saver for people suffering from any number of ailments – atherosclerosis, obesity, diabetes, even Alzheimer's. Any one of these ailments mitigated (or cured!) would be worth billions; a therapy that helped all of them would be – well. It explained the high-alert security enclosing the compound, that was for sure.

The experiment was proceeding but not yet done, so Leo went back to his office and drank his coffee and read *Bioworld Today* onscreen. Higher through-put screening robotics, analysis protocols for artificial hormones, proteomic analyses – every article could have described something that was going on at Torrey Pines Generique. The whole industry was looking for ways to improve the hunt for therapeutic proteins, and for ways to get those proteins into living people. Half the day's articles were devoted to one of these problems or the other, as in any other issue of the newszine. They were the recalcitrant outstanding problems, standing between 'biotechnology' as an idea and medicine as it actually existed. If they didn't solve these problems, the idea and the industry based on it could go the way of nuclear power, and turn into something that somehow did not work out. If they did solve them, then it would turn into something more like the computer industry in terms of financial returns – not to mention the impacts on health of course!

When Leo next checked the lab, two of his assistants, Marta and Brian, were standing at the bench, both wearing lab coats and rubber gloves, working the pipettes on a bank of flasks filling a countertop.

'Good morning guys.'

'Hey Leo.' Marta aimed her pipette like a power-point

cursor at the small window on a long low refrigerator. 'Ready to check it out?'

'Sure am. Can you help?'

'In just a sec.' She moved down the bench.

Brian said, 'This better work, because Derek just told the press that it was the most promising self-healing therapy of the decade.'

Leo was startled to hear this. 'No. You're kidding.'

'I'm not kidding.'

'Oh not really. Not really.'

'Really.'

'How *could* he?'

'Press release. Also calls to his favourite reporters, and on his webpage. The chat room is already talking about the ramifications. They're betting one of the big pharms will buy us within the month.'

'Please Bri, don't be saying these things.'

'Sorry, but you know Derek.' Brian gestured at one of the computer screens glowing on the bench across the way. 'It's all over.'

Leo squinted at a screen. 'It wasn't on *Bioworld Today*.'

'It will be tomorrow.'

The company's website *Breaking News* box was blinking. Leo leaned over and jabbed it. Yep – lead story. HDL factory, potential for obesity, diabetes, Alzheimer's, heart disease . . .

'Oh my God,' Leo muttered as he read. 'Oh my God.' His face was flushed. 'Why does he *do* this?'

'He wants it to be true.'

'So *what*? We don't *know* yet.'

With her sly grin Marta said, 'He wants you to make it happen, Leo. He's like the Roadrunner and you're Wile E. Coyote. He gets you to run off the edge of a cliff, and then you have to build the bridge back to the cliff before you fall.'

'But it never works! He always falls!'

28

Marta laughed at him. She liked him, but she was tough. 'Come on,' she said. 'This time we'll do it.'

Leo nodded, tried to calm down. He appreciated Marta's spirit, and liked to be at least as positive as the most positive person in any given situation. That was getting tough these days, but he smiled the best he could and said, 'Yeah, right, you're good,' and started to put on rubber gloves.

'Remember the time he announced that we had haemophilia A whipped?' Brian said.

'Please.'

'Remember the time he put out a press release saying he had decapitated mice at a thousand r.p.m. to show how well our therapy worked?'

'The guillotine turntable experiment?'

'Please,' Leo begged. 'No more.'

He picked up a pipette and tried to focus on the work. Withdraw, inject, withdraw, inject – alas, most of the work in this stage was automated, leaving people free to think whether they wanted to or not. After a while Leo left them to it and went back to his office to check his e-mail, then helplessly to read what portion of Derek's press release he could stomach. 'Why does he *do* this, why why why?'

It was a rhetorical question, but Marta and Brian were now standing in the doorway, and Marta was implacable: 'I tell you – he thinks he can *make* us do it.'

'It's not *us* doing it,' Leo protested, 'it's the gene. We can't do a thing if the altered gene doesn't get into the cell we're trying to target.'

'You'll just have to think of something that will work.'

'You mean like, build it and they will come?'

'Yeah. Say it and they will make it.'

Out in the lab a timer beeped, sounding uncannily like the Roadrunner. *Beep-beep! Beep-beep!* They went to the incubator and read the graph paper as it rolled out of the machine, like a receipt out of an automated teller – like money out of an automated teller, in fact, if the results were good. One very big wad of twenties rolling out into the world from nowhere, if the numbers were good.

And they were. They were very good. They would have to plot it to be sure, but they had been doing this series of experiments for so long that they knew what the raw data would look like. The data were good. So now they *were* like Wile E. Coyote, standing in midair staring amazed at the viewers, because a bridge from the cliff had magically extended out and saved them. Saved them from the long plunge of a retraction in the press and subsequent Nasdaq free-fall.

Except that Wile E. Coyote was invariably premature in his sense of relief. The Roadrunner always had another devastating move to make. Leo's hand was shaking.

'Shit,' he said. 'I would be totally celebrating right now if it weren't for Derek. Look at this –' pointing – 'it's even better than before.'

'See, Derek knew it would turn out like this.'

'The fuck he did.'

'Pretty good numbers,' Brian said with a grin. 'Paper's almost written too. It's just plug these in and do a conclusion.'

Marta said, 'Conclusions will be simple, if we tell the truth.'

Leo nodded. 'Only problem is, the truth would have to admit that even though this part works, we still don't have a therapy, because we haven't got targeted delivery. We can make it but we can't get it into living bodies where it needs to be.'

'You didn't read the whole website,' Marta told him, smiling angrily again.

'What do you mean?' Leo was in no mood for teasing. His stomach had already shrunk to the size of a walnut.

Marta laughed, which was her way of showing sympathy without admitting to any. 'He's going to buy Urtech.'

'What's Urtech?'

'They have a targeted delivery method that works.'

'What do you mean, what would that be?'

'It's new. They just got awarded the patent on it.'

'Oh no.'

'Oh yes.'

'Oh my God. It hasn't been validated?'

'Except by the patent, and Derek's offer to buy it, no.'

'Oh my *God*. Why does he *do* this kind of stuff?'

'Because he intends to be the CEO of the biggest pharmaceutical of all time. Like he told *People* magazine.'

'Yeah right.'

Torrey Pines Generique, like most biotech start-ups, was undercapitalized, and could only afford a few rolls of the dice. One of them had to look promising to attract the capital that would allow it to grow further. That was what they had been trying to accomplish for the five years of the company's existence, and the effort was just beginning to show results with these experiments. What they needed now was to be able to insert their successfully tailored gene into the patient's own cells, so that afterwards it would be the patient's own body producing increased amounts of the needed proteins. If that worked, there would be no immune response from the body's immune system, and with the protein being produced in therapeutic amounts, the patient would be not just helped, but cured.

Amazing.

But (and it was getting to be a big but) the problem of getting the altered DNA into living patients' cells hadn't been solved. Leo and his people were not physiologists, and they hadn't been able to do it. No one had. Immune systems existed precisely to keep these sorts of intrusions from happening. Indeed, one method of inserting the altered DNA into the body was to put it into a virus and give the patient a viral infection, benign in its ultimate effects because the altered

DNA reached its target. But since the body fought viral infections, it was not a good solution. You didn't want to compromise further the immune systems of people who were already sick.

So, for a long time now they had been in the same boat as everyone else, chasing the holy grail of gene therapy, a 'targeted non-viral delivery system'. Any company that came up with such a system, and patented it, would immediately have the method licensed for scores of procedures, and very likely one of the big pharmaceuticals would buy the company, making everyone in it rich, and often still employed. Over time the pharmaceutical might dismantle the acquisition, keeping only the method, but at that point the start-up's employees would be wealthy enough to laugh that off – retire and go surfing, or start up another start-up and try to hit the jackpot again. At that point it would be more of a philanthropic hobby than the cut-throat struggle to make a living that it often seemed before the big success arrived.

So the hunt for a targeted non-viral delivery system was most definitely on, in hundreds of labs around the world. And now Derek had bought one of these labs. Leo stared at the new announcement on the company website. Derek had to have bought it on spec, because if the method had been well-proven, there was no way Derek would have been able to afford it. Some biotech firm even smaller than Torrey Pines – Urtech, based in Bethesda, Maryland (Leo had never heard of it) – had convinced Derek that they had found a way to deliver altered DNA into humans. Derek had made the purchase without consulting Leo, his chief research scientist. His scientific advice had to have come from his vice president, Dr Sam Houston, an old friend and early partner. A man who had not done lab work in a decade.

So. It was true.

Leo sat at his desk, trying to relax his stomach. They would have to assimilate this new company, learn their technique, test it. It *had* been patented, Leo noted, which meant they had it exclusively at this point, as a kind of trade secret – a concept many working scientists had trouble accepting. A secret scientific method? Was that not a contradiction in terms? Of course a patent was a matter of public record, and eventually it would enter the public domain. So it wasn't a trade secret in literal fact. But at this stage it was secret enough. And it could not be a sure thing. There wasn't much published about it, as far as Leo could tell. Some papers in preparation, some papers submitted, one paper accepted – he would have to check that one out as soon as possible – and a patent. Sometimes they awarded them so early. One or two papers were all that supported the whole approach.

Secret science. 'God *damn* it,' Leo said to his room. Derek had bought a pig in a poke. And Leo was going to have to open the poke and poke around.

There was a hesitant knock on his opened door, and he looked up.

'Oh hi, Yann, how are you?'

'I'm good Leo, thanks. I'm just coming by to say goodbye. I'm back to Pasadena now, my job here is finished.'

'Too bad. I bet you could have helped us figure out this pig in a poke we just bought.'

'Really?'

Yann's face brightened like a child's. He was a true mathematician, and had what Leo considered to be the standard mathematician personality: smart, spacy, enthusiastic, full of notions. All these qualities were a bit under the surface, until you really got him going. As Marta had remarked, not unkindly (for her), if it weren't for the head tilt and the speed-talking, he wouldn't have seemed like a mathematician at all. Whatever; Leo liked him, and his work on protein identification had been really interesting, and potentially very helpful.

'Actually, I don't know what we've got yet,' Leo admitted.

33

'It's likely to be a biology problem, but who knows? You sure have been helpful with our selection protocols.'

'Thanks, I appreciate that. I may be back anyway, I've got a project going with Sam's math team that might pan out. If it does they'll try to hire me on another temporary contract, he says.'

'That's good to hear. Well, have fun in Pasadena in the meantime.'

'Oh I will. See you soon.'

And their best biomaths guy slipped out the door.

Charlie Quibler had barely woken when Anna left for work. He got up an hour later to his own alarm, woke up Nick with difficulty, got him to dress and eat, put the still-sleeping Joe in his car seat while Nick climbed in the other side of the car. 'Have you got your backpack *and* your lunch?' – this not always being the case – and off to Nick's school. They dropped him off, returned home to fall asleep again on the couch, Joe never waking during the entire process. An hour or so later he would rouse them both with his hungry cries, and then the day would really begin, the earlier interval like a problem dream that always played out the same.

'Joey and Daddy!' Charlie would say then, or 'Joe and Dad at home, here we go!' or 'How about breakfast? Here – how about you get into your playpen for a second, and I'll go warm up some of *Mom's milk*.'

This had always worked like a charm with Nick, and sometimes Charlie forgot and put Joe down in the old blue plastic playpen in the living room, but if he did Joe would let out a scandalized howl the moment he saw where he was. Joe refused to associate with baby things; even getting him into the car seat or the baby backpack or the stroller was a matter of very strict invariability. Where choices were known to be possible, Joe rejected the baby stuff as an affront to his dignity.

So now Charlie had Joe there with him in the kitchen, crawling underfoot or investigating the gate that blocked the steep stairs to the cellar. Careering around like a human pin-ball. Anna had taped bubblewrap to all the corners; it looked like the kitchen had just recently arrived and not yet been completely unpacked.

'Okay watch out now, don't. Don't! Your bottle will be ready in a second.'

'Ba!'

'Yes, bottle.'

This was satisfactory, and Joe plopped on his butt directly under Charlie's feet. Charlie worked over him, taking some of Anna's frozen milk out of the freezer and putting it in a pot of warming water on the back burner. Anna had her milk stored in precise quantities of either four or ten ounces, in tall or short permanent plastic cylinders that were filled with disposable plastic bags, capped by brown rubber nipples that Charlie had pricked many times with a needle, and topped by snap-on plastic tops to protect the nipples from contamination in the freezer. Contamination in the freezer? Charlie had wanted to ask Anna, but he hadn't. There was a lab book on the kitchen counter for Charlie to fill out the times and amounts of Joe's feedings. Anna liked to know these things, she said, to determine how much milk to pump at work. So Charlie logged in while the water started to bubble, thinking as he always did that the main purpose here was to fulfil Anna's pleasure in making quantified records of any kind.

He was testing the temperature of the thawed milk by taking a quick suck on the nipple when his phone rang. He whipped on a headset and answered.

'Hi Charlie, it's Roy.'

'Oh hi Roy, what's up?'

'Well I've got your latest draft here and I'm about to read it, and I thought I'd check first to see what I should be looking for, how you solved the IPCC stuff.'

'Oh yeah. The new stuff that matters is all in the third

section.' The bill as Charlie had drafted it for Phil would require the US to act on certain recommendations of the Intergovernmental Panel on Climate Change.

'Did you kind of bury the part about us conforming to IPCC findings?'

'I don't think there's earth deep enough to bury that one. I tried to put it in a context that made it look inevitable. International body that we are part of, climate change clearly real, the UN the best body to work through global issues, support for them pretty much mandatory for us or else the whole world cooks in our juices, that sort of thing.'

'Well, but that's never worked before, has it? Come on, Charlie, this is Phil's big pre-election bill and you're his climate guy, if he can't get this bill out of committee then we're in big trouble.'

'Yeah I know. Wait just a second.'

Charlie took another test pull from the bottle. Now it was at body temperature, or almost.

'A bit early to be hitting the bottle, Charlie, what you drinking there?'

'Well, I'm drinking my wife's breast milk, if you must know.'

'Say what?'

'I'm testing the temperature of one of Joe's bottles. They have to be thawed to a very exact temperature or else he gets annoyed.'

'So you're drinking your wife's breast milk out of a baby bottle?'

'Yes I am.'

'How is it?'

'It's good. Thin but sweet. A potent mix of protein, fat and sugar. No doubt the perfect food.'

'I bet.' Roy cackled. 'Do you ever get it straight from the source?'

'Well I try, sure, who doesn't, but Anna doesn't like it. She says it's a mixed message and if I don't watch out she'll wean me when she weans Joe.'

'Ah ha. So you have to take the long-term view.'

'Yes. Although actually I tried it one time when Joe fell asleep nursing, so she couldn't move without waking him. She was hissing at me and I was trying to get it to work but apparently you have to suck much harder than, you know, one usually would, there's a trick to it, and I still hadn't gotten any when Joe woke up and saw me. Anna and I froze, expecting him to freak out, but he just reached out and patted me on the head.'

'He understood!'

'Yeah. It was like he was saying I know how you feel, Dad, and I will share with you this amazing bounty. Didn't you Joe?' he said, handing him the warmed bottle. He watched with a smile as Joe took it one-handed and tilted it back, elbow thrown out like Popeye with a can of spinach. Because of all the pinpricks Charlie had made in the rubber nipples, Joe could choke down a bottle in a few minutes, and he seemed to take great satisfaction in doing so. No doubt a sugar rush.

'Okay, well, you are a kinky guy my friend and obviously deep in the world of domestic bliss, but we're still relying on you here and this may be the most important bill Phil introduces in this session.'

'Come on, it's a lot more than that, young man, it's one of the few chances we have left to avoid complete global disaster, I mean –'

'Preaching to the converted! Preaching to the converted!'

'I certainly hope so.'

'Sure sure. Okay, I'll read this draft and get back to you a.s.a.p., I want to move on with this, and the committee discussion is now scheduled for Tuesday.'

'That's fine, I'll have my phone with me all day.'

'Sounds good, I'll be in touch, but meanwhile be thinking about how to slip the IPCC thing in even deeper.'

'Yeah okay but see what I did already.'

'Sure bye.'

'Bye.'

Charlie pulled off the headset and turned off the stove. Joe finished his bottle, inspected it, tossed it casually aside.

'Man, you are fast,' Charlie said as he always did. One of the mutual satisfactions of their days together was doing the same things over and over again, and saying the same things about them. Joe was not as insistent on pattern as Nick had been, in fact he liked a kind of structured variability, as Charlie thought of it, but the pleasure in repetition was still there.

There was no denying his boys were very different. When Nick had been Joe's age, Charlie had still found it necessary to hold him cradled in his arm, head wedged in the nook of his elbow, to make him take the bottle, because Nick had had a curious moment of aversion, even when he was hungry. He would whine and refuse the nipple, perhaps because it was not the real thing, perhaps because it had taken Charlie months to learn to puncture the bottle nipples with lots of extra holes. In any case he would refuse and twist away, head whipping from side to side, and the hungrier he was the more he would do it, until with a rush like a fish to a lure he would strike, latching on and sucking desperately. It was a fairly frustrating routine, part of the larger Shock of Lost Adult Freedom that had hammered Charlie so hard that first time around, though now he could hardly remember why. A perfect image for all the compromised joys and irritations of Mr Momhood, those hundreds of sessions with reluctant Nick and his bottle.

With Joe life was in some ways much easier. Charlie was more used to it, for one thing, and Joe, though difficult in his own ways, would certainly never refuse a bottle.

Now he decided he would try again to climb the baby gate and dive down the cellar stairs, but Charlie moved quickly to detach him, then shooed him out into the dining room while cleaning up the counter, ignoring the loud cries of complaint.

'Okay okay! Quiet! Hey, let's go for a walk! Let's go walk!'

'No!'

'Ah come on. Oh wait, it's your day for Gymboree, and then we'll go to the park and have lunch, and then go for a walk!'

'NO!'

But that was just Joe's way of saying yes.

Charlie wrestled him into the baby backpack, which was mostly a matter of controlling his legs, not an easy thing. Joe was strong, a compact animal with bulging thigh muscles, and though not as loud a screamer as Nick had been, a tough guy to overpower. 'Gymboree, Joe! You love it! Then a *walk*, guy, a walk to the *park*!'

Off they went.

First to Gymboree, located in a big building just off Wisconsin. Gymboree was a chance to get infants together when they did not have some other daycare to do it. It was an hour-long class, and always a bit depressing, Charlie felt, to be paying to get his kid into a play situation with other kids; but there it was; without Gymboree they all would have been on their own.

Joe disappeared into the tunnels of a big plastic jungle gym. It may have been a commercial replacement for real community, but Joe didn't know that; all he saw was that it had lots of stuff to play with and climb on, and so he scampered around the colourful structures, crawling through tubes and climbing up things, ignoring the other kids to the point of treating them as movable parts of the apparatus, which could cause problems. 'Oops, say you're sorry, Joe. Sorry!'

Off he shot again, evading Charlie. He didn't want to waste any time. Once again the contrast with Nick could not have been more acute. Nick had seldom moved at Gymboree. One time he had found a giant red ball and stood embracing the thing for the full hour of the class. All the moms had stared sympathetically (or not), and the instructor, Ally, had done her best to help Charlie get him interested in something else; but Nick would not budge from his mystical red ball.

Embarrassing. But Charlie was used to that. The problem was not just Nick's immobility or Joe's hyperactivity, but the fact that Charlie was always the only dad there. Without him it would have been a complete momspace, and comfortable as such. He knew that his presence wrecked that comfort. It happened in all kinds of infant-toddler contexts. As far as Charlie could tell, there was not a single other man inside the Beltway who ever spent the business hours of a weekday with preschool children. It just wasn't done. That wasn't why people moved to DC. It wasn't why Charlie had moved there either, for that matter, but he and Anna had talked it over before Nick was born, and they had come to the realization that Charlie could do his job (on a part-time basis anyway) and their infant care at the same time, by using phone and e-mail to keep in contact with Senator Chase's office. Phil Chase himself had perfected the method of working at a distance back when he had been the World's Senator, always on the road; and being the good guy he was, he had thoroughly approved of Charlie's plan. While on the other hand Anna's job absolutely required her to be at work at least fifty hours a week, and often more. So Charlie had happily volunteered to be the stay-at-home parent. It would be an adventure.

And an adventure it had been, there was no denying that. But first time's a charm; and now he had been doing it for over a year with kid number two, and what had been shocking and all-absorbing with kid number one was now simply routine. The repetitions were beginning to get to him. Joe was beginning to get to him.

So now Charlie sat there in Gymboree, hanging with the moms and the nannies. A nice situation in theory, but in practice a diplomatic challenge of the highest order. No one wanted to be misunderstood. No one would regard it as a coincidence if he happened to end up talking to one of the more attractive women there, or to anyone in particular on a regular basis. That was fine with Charlie, but with Joe doing his thing, he could not completely control the situation. There was Joe now, doing it again – going after a black-haired little girl who had the perfect features of a model. Charlie was obliged to go over and make sure Joe didn't mug her, as he was wont to do with girls he liked, and yes, the little girl had an attractive mom, or in this case a nanny – a young blonde *au pair* from Germany whom Charlie had spoken to before. Charlie could feel the eyes of the other women on him; not a single adult in that room believed in his innocence.

'Hi Asta.'

'Hello Charlie.'

He even began to doubt it himself. Asta was one of those lively European women of twenty or so who gave the impression of being a decade ahead of their American contemporaries in terms of adult experiences – not easy, given the way American teens were these days. Charlie felt a little surge of protest: it's not me who goes after the babes, he wanted to shout, it's my son! My son the hyperactive girl-chasing mugger! But of course he couldn't do that, and now even Asta regarded him warily, perhaps because the first time they had chatted over their kids he had made some remark complimenting her on her child's nice hair. He felt himself begin to blush again, remembering the look of amused surprise she had given him as she corrected him.

Singalong saved him from the moment. It was designed to calm the kids down a bit before the session ended and they had to be lassoed back into their car seats for the ride home. Joe took Ally's announcement as his cue to dive into the depths of the tube structure, where it was impossible to follow him or to coax him out. He would only emerge when Ally started 'Ring Around the Rosie', which he enjoyed. Round in circles they all went, Charlie avoiding anyone's eye but Joe's. Ally, who was from New Jersey, belted out the lead, and so all the kids and moms joined her loudly in the final chorus:

'Eshes, eshes, we all, fall, DOWN!'

And down they all fell.

Then it was off to the park.

Their park was a small one, located just west of Wisconsin Avenue a few blocks south of their home. A narrow grassy area held a square sandpit, which contained play structures for young kids. Tennis courts lined the south edge of the park. Out against Wisconsin stood a fire station, and to the west a field extended out to one of the many little creeks that still cut through the grid of streets.

Midday, the sandpit and the benches flanking it were almost always occupied by a few infants and toddlers, moms and nannies. Many more nannies than moms here, most of them West Indian, to judge by their appearance and voices. They sat on the benches together, resting in the steamy heat, talking. The kids wandered on their own, absorbed or bored.

Joe kept Charlie on his toes. Nick had been content to sit in one spot for long periods of time, and when playing he had been pathologically cautious; on a low wooden bouncy bridge his little fists had gone white on the chain railing. Joe however had quickly located the spot on the bridge that would launch him the highest – not the middle, but about halfway down to it. He would stand right there and jump up and down in time to the wooden oscillation until he was catching big air, his unhappy expression utterly different from Nick's, in that it was caused by his dissatisfaction that he could not get higher. This was part of his general habit of using his body as an experimental object, including walking in front of kids on swings, etc. Countless times Charlie had been forced to jerk him out of dangerous situations, and they

43

had become less frequent only because Joe didn't like how loud Charlie yelled afterwards. 'Give me a break!' Charlie would shout. 'What do you think, you're made of steel?'

Now Joe was flying up and down on the bouncy bridge's sweet spot. The sad little girl whose nanny talked on the phone for hours at a time wandered in slow circles around the merry-go-round. Charlie avoided meeting her eager eye, staring instead at the nanny and thinking it might be a good idea to stuff a note into the girl's clothes. '*Your daughter wanders the Earth bored and lonely at age two – SHAME!*'

Whereas he was virtuous. That would have been the point of such a note, and so he never wrote it. He was virtuous, but bored. No that wasn't really true. That was a disagreeable stereotype. He therefore tried to focus and play with his second-born. It was truly unfair how much less parental attention the second child got. With the first, although admittedly there was the huge Shock of Lost Adult Freedom to recover from, there was also the deep absorption of watching one's own offspring – a living human being whose genes were a fifty-fifty mix of one's own and one's partner's. It was frankly hard to believe that any such process could actually work, but there the kid was, out walking the world in the temporary guise of a kind of pet, a wordless little animal of surpassing fascination.

Whereas with the second one it was as they all said: just try to make sure they don't eat out of the cat's dish. Not always successful in Joe's case. But not to worry. They would survive. They might even prosper. Meanwhile there was the newspaper to read.

But now here they were at the park, Joe and Dad, so might as well make the best of it. And it was true that Joe was more fun to play with than Nick had been at that age. He would chase Charlie for hours, ask to be chased, wrestle, fight, go down the slide and up the steps again like a *perpetuum mobile*. All this in the middle of a DC May day, the air going for a triple-triple, the sun smashing down through the wet air and diffusing until its light exploded out of a huge patch of the zenith. Sweaty gasping play, yes, but never a moment spent coaxing. Never a dull moment.

After another such runaround they sprawled on the grass to eat lunch. Both of them liked this part. Fruit juices, various baby foods carefully spooned out and inserted into Joe's baby-bird mouth, apple sauce likewise, a Cheerio or two that he could choke down by himself. He was still mostly a breast-milk guy.

When they were done Joe struggled up to play again.

'Oh God Joe, can't we rest a bit.'

'No!'

Ballasted by his meal, however, he staggered as if drunk. Naptime, as sudden as a blow to the head, would soon fell him.

Charlie's phone beeped. He slipped in an earplug and let the cord dangle under his face, clicked it on. 'Hello.'

'Hi Charlie, where are you?'

'Hey Roy. I'm at the park like always. What's up?'

'Well, I've read your latest draft, and I was wondering if you could discuss some things in it now, because we need to get it over to Senator Winston's office so they can see what's coming.'

'Is that a good idea?'

'Phil thinks we have to do it.'

'Okay, what do you want to discuss?'

There was a pause while Roy found a place in the draft. 'Here we go. Quote, the Congress, being deeply concerned that the lack of speed in America's conversion from a hydrocarbon to a carbohydrate fuel economy is rapidly leading to chaotic climate changes with a profoundly negative impact on the US economy, unquote, we've been told that Ellington is only concerned, not deeply concerned. Should we change that?'

45

'No, we're deeply concerned. He is too, he just doesn't know it.'

'Okay, then down in the third paragraph in the operative clauses, quote, the United States will peg hydrocarbon fuel reductions in a two-to-one ratio to such reductions by China and India, and will provide matching funds for all tidal and wind power plants built in those countries and in all countries that fall under a five in the UN's prospering countries index, these plants to be operated by a joint powers agency that will include the United States as a permanent member; four, these provisions will combine with the climate-neutral power production –'

'Wait, call that power generation.'

'Power generation, okay, such that any savings in environmental mitigation in participating countries as determined by IPCC ratings will be credited equally to the US rating, and not less than fifty million dollars per year in savings is to be earmarked specifically for the construction of more such climate-neutral power plants; and not less than fifty million dollars per year in savings is to be earmarked specifically for the construction of so-called 'carbon sinks', meaning any environmental engineering project designed to capture and sequester atmospheric carbon dioxide safely, in forests, peat beds, oceans, or other locations –'

'Yeah hey you know carbon sinks are *so* crucial, scrubbing CO_2 out of the air may eventually turn out to be our only option, so maybe we should reverse those two clauses. Make carbon sinks come first and the climate-neutral power plants second in that paragraph.'

'You think?'

'Yes. Definitely. Carbon sinks could be the only way that our kids, and about a thousand years' worth of kids actually, can save themselves from living in Swamp World. From living their whole lives on Venus.'

'Or should we say Washington DC.'

46

'Please.'

'Okay, those are flip-flopped then. So that's that paragraph, now, hmm, that's it for text. I guess the next question is, what can we offer Winston and his gang to get them to accept this version.'

'Get Winston's people to give you their list of riders, and then pick the two least offensive ones and tell them they're the most we could get Phil to accept, but only if they accept our changes first.'

'But will they go for that?'

'No, but – wait – Joe?'

Charlie didn't see Joe anywhere. He ducked to be able to see under the climbing structure to the other side. No Joe.

'Hey Roy let me call you back okay? I gotta find Joe he's wandered off.'

'Okay, give me a buzz.'

Charlie clicked off and yanked the earplug out of his ear, jammed it in his pocket.

'JOE!'

He looked around at the West Indian nannies – none of them were watching, none of them would meet his eye. No help there. He jogged south to be able to see farther around the back of the fire station. Ah ha! There was Joe, trundling full speed for Wisconsin Avenue.

'JOE! STOP!'

That was as loud as Charlie could shout. He saw that Joe had indeed heard him, and had redoubled the speed of his diaper-waddle towards the busy street.

Charlie took off in a sprint after him. 'JOE!' he shouted as he pelted over the grass. 'STOP! JOE! STOP RIGHT THERE!' He didn't believe that Joe would stop, but possibly he would try to go even faster, and fall.

No such luck. Joe was in stride now, running like a duck trying to escape something without taking flight. He was on the sidewalk next to the fire station, and had a clear shot at Wisconsin, where trucks and cars zipped by as always.

Charlie closed in, cleared the fire station, saw big trucks bearing down; if Joe catapulted off the kerb he would be right under their wheels. By the time Charlie caught up to him he was so close to the edge that Charlie had to grab him by the back of his shirt and lift him off his feet, whirling him around in a broad circle through the air, back onto Charlie as they both fell in a heap on the sidewalk.

'Ow!' Joe howled.

'WHAT ARE YOU DOING!' Charlie shouted in his face. 'WHAT ARE YOU DOING? DON'T EVER DO THAT AGAIN!'

Joe, amazed, stopped howling for a moment. He stared at his father, face crimson. Then he recommenced howling.

Charlie shifted into a crosslegged position, hefted the crying boy into his lap. He was shaking, his heart was pounding; he could feel it tripping away madly in his hands and chest. In an old reflex he put his thumb to the other wrist and watched the seconds pass on his watch for fifteen seconds. Multiply by four. Impossible. One hundred and eighty beats a minute. Surely that was impossible. Sweat was pouring out of all his skin at once. He was gasping.

The parade of trucks and cars continued to roar by, inches away. Wisconsin Avenue was a major truck route from the Beltway into the city. Most of the trucks entirely filled the right lane, from kerb to lane line; and most were moving at about forty miles an hour.

'Why do you *do* that?' Charlie whispered into his boy's hair. Suddenly he was filled with fear, and some kind of dread or despair. 'It's just crazy.'

'Ow,' Joe said.

Big shuddering sighs racked them both.

Charlie's phone rang. He clicked it on and held an earplug to his ear.

'Hi love.'

'Oh hi hon!'

'What's wrong?'

'Oh nothing, nothing. I've just been chasing Joe around. We're at the park.'

'Wow, you must be cooking. Isn't it the hottest part of the day?'

'Yeah it is, almost, but we've been having fun so we stayed. We're about to head back now.'

'Okay, I won't keep you. I just wanted to check if we had any plans for next weekend.'

'None that I know of.'

'Okay, good. Because I had an interesting thing happen this morning, I met a bunch of people downstairs, new to the building. They're like Tibetans, I think, only they live on an island. They've taken the office space downstairs that the travel agency used to have.'

'That's nice dear.'

'Yes. I'm going to have lunch with them, and if it seems like a good idea I might ask them over for dinner sometime, if you don't mind.'

'No, that's fine, snooks. Whatever you like. It sounds interesting.'

'Great, okay. I'm going to go meet them soon, I'll tell you about it.'

'Okay, good.'

'Okay, bye dove.'

'Bye love, talk to you.'

Charlie clicked off.

After ten giant breaths he stood, lifting Joe in his arms. Joe buried his face in Charlie's neck. Shakily Charlie retraced their course. It was somewhere between fifty and a hundred yards. Rivulets of sweat ran down his ribs, and off his forehead into his eyes. He wiped them against Joe's shirt. Joe was sweaty too. When he reached their stuff Charlie swung

Joe around, down into his backpack. For once Joe did not resist. 'Sowy Da,' he said, and fell asleep as Charlie swung him onto his back.

Charlie took off walking. Joe's head rested against his neck, a sensation that had always pleased him before. Sometimes he would even suckle the tendon there. Now it was like the touch of some meaning so great that he couldn't bear it, a huge cloudy aura of danger and love. He started to cry, wiped his eyes and shook it off, as if shaking away a nightmare. Hostages to fortune, he thought. You get married, have kids, you give up such hostages to fortune. No avoiding it, no help for it. It's just the price you pay for such love. His son was a complete maniac, and it only made him love him more.

He walked hard for most of an hour, through all the neighborhoods he had come to know so well in his years of lonely Mr Momhood. The vestiges of an older way of life lay under the trees like a network of ley lines: railway beds, canal systems, Indian trails, even deer trails, all could be discerned. Charlie walked them sightlessly. The ductile world drooped around him in the heat. Sweat lubricated his every move.

Slowly he regained his sense of normality. Just an ordinary day with Joe and Da.

The residential streets of Bethesda and Chevy Chase were in many ways quite beautiful. It had mostly to do with the immense trees, and the grass underfoot. Green everywhere. On a weekday afternoon like this there was almost no one to be seen. The slight hilliness was just right for walking. Tall old hardwoods gave some relief from the heat; above them the sky was an incandescent white. The trees were undoubtedly second or even third growth, there couldn't be many old-growth hardwoods anywhere east of the Mississippi. Still they were old trees, and tall. Charlie had never shifted out of his California consciousness, in which open landscapes were the norm and the desire, so that on the one hand he found the omnipresent forest claustrophobic – he pined for a pineless view – while on the other hand it remained always exotic and compelling, even slightly ominous or spooky. The dapple of leaves at every level, from the ground to the highest canopy, was a perpetual revelation to him; nothing in his home ground or in his bookish sense of forests had prepared him for this vast and delicate venation of the air. On the other hand he longed for a view of distant mountains as if for oxygen itself. On this day especially he felt stifled and gasping.

His phone beeped again, and he pulled the earplugs out of his pocket and stuck them in his ears, clicked the set on.

'Hello.'

'Hey Charlie, I don't want to bug you, but are you and Joe okay?'

'Oh yeah, thanks Roy. Thanks for checking back in, I forgot to call you.'

'So you found him.'

'Yeah I found him, but I had to stop him running into traffic, and he was upset and I forgot to call back.'

'Hey, that's okay. It's just that I was wondering, you know, if you could finish off this draft with me.'

'I guess.' Charlie sighed. 'To tell the truth, Roy boy, I'm not so sure how well this work-at-home thing is going for me these days.'

'Oh you're doing fine. You're Phil's gold standard. But look, if now isn't a good time . . .'

'No no, Joe's asleep on my back. It's fine. I'm still just kind of freaked out.'

'Sure, I can imagine. Listen we can do it later, although I must say we do need to get this thing staffed out soon or else Phil might get caught short. Dr Strangelove –' this was their name for the President's science advisor '– has been asking to see our draft too.'

'I know, okay talk to me. I can tell you what I think anyway.'

So for a while as he walked he listened to Roy read sentences from his draft, and then discussed with him the whys and wherefores, and possible revisions. Roy had been Phil's chief of staff ever since Wade Norton hit the road and became an advisor *in absentia*, and after years of staffing for the House Resources committee (called the Environment committee until the Gingrich Congress renamed it), he was deeply knowledgeable, and sharp too; one of Charlie's favourite people. And Charlie himself was so steeped now in the climate bill that he could see it all in his head, indeed it helped him now just to hear it, without the print before him to distract him. As if someone were telling him a bedtime story.

Eventually, however, some question of Roy's couldn't be resolved without the text before him. 'Sorry. I'll call you back when I get home.'

'Okay but don't forget, we need to get this finished.'

'I won't.'

They clicked off.

His walk home took him south, down the west edge of the Bethesda Metro district, an urban neighbourhood of restaurants and apartment blocks, all ringing the hole in the ground out of which people and money fountained so prodigiously, changing everything: streets rerouted, neighbourhoods redeveloped, a whole clutch of skyscrapers bursting up through the canopy and establishing another purely urban zone in the endless hardwood forest.

He stopped in at Second Story Books, the biggest and best of the area's several used bookstores. It was a matter of habit only; he had visited it so often with Joe asleep on his back that he had memorized the stock, and was reduced to checking the hidden books in the inner rows, or alphabetizing sections that he liked. No one in the supremely arrogant and slovenly shop cared what he did there. It was soothing in that sense.

Finally he gave up trying to pretend he felt normal, and walked past the auto dealer and home. There it was a tough call whether to take the baby backpack off and hope not to wake Joe prematurely, or just to keep him on his back and work from the bench he had put by his desk for this very purpose. The discomfort of Joe's weight was more than compensated for by the quiet, and so as usual he kept Joe snoozing on his back.

When he had his material open, and had read up on tidal power generation cost/benefit figures from the UN study on same, he called Roy back, and they got the job finished. The revised draft was ready for Phil to review, and in a pinch could be shown to Senator Winston or Dr Strangelove.

'Thanks Charlie. That looks good.'

'I like it too. It'll be interesting to see what Phil says about it. I wonder if we're hanging him too far out there.'

'I think he'll be okay, but I wonder what Winston's staff will say.'

'They'll have a cow.'

'It's true. They're worse than Winston himself. A bunch of Sir Humphreys if I ever saw one.'

'I don't know, I think they're just fundamentalist know-nothings.'

'True, but we'll show them.'

'I hope.'

'Charles my man, you're sounding tired. I suppose the Joe is about to wake up.'

'Yeah.'

'Unrelenting eh?'

'Yeah.'

'But you are the man, you are the greatest Mr Mom inside the Beltway!'

Charlie laughed. 'And all that competition.'

Roy laughed too, pleased to be able to cheer Charlie up. 'Well it's an accomplishment anyway.'

'That's nice of you to say. Most people don't notice. It's just something weird that I do.'

'Well that's true too. But people don't know what it entails.'

'No they don't. The only ones who know are real moms, but they don't think I count.'

'You'd think they'd be the ones who would.'

'Well, in a way they're right. There's no reason me doing it should be anything special. It may just be me wanting some strokes. It's turned out to be harder than I thought it would be. A real psychic shock.'

'Because . . .'

'Well, I was thirty-eight when Nick arrived, and I had been doing exactly what I wanted ever since I was eighteen. Twenty years of white male American freedom, just like what you have, young man, and then Nick arrived and suddenly I was at the command of a speechless mad tyrant. I mean, think about it. Tonight you can go wherever you want to, go out and have some fun, right?'

'That's right, I'm going to go to a party for some new folks at Brookings, supposed to be wild.'

'All right, don't rub it in. Because I'm going to be in the same room I've been in every night for the past seven years, more or less.'

'So by now you're used to it, right?'

'Well, yes. That's true. It was harder with Nick, when I could remember what freedom was.'

'You have morphed into momhood.'

'Yeah. But morphing hurts, baby, just like in *The X-Men*. I remember the first Mother's Day after Nick was born, I was most deep into the shock of it, and Anna had to be away that day, maybe to visit her mom, I can't remember, and I was trying to get Nick to take a bottle and he was refusing it as usual. And I suddenly realized I would never be free again for the whole rest of my life, but that as a non-Mom I was never going to get a day to honour *my* efforts, because Father's Day is not what this stuff is about, and Nick was whipping his head around even though he was in desperate need of a bottle, and I freaked out, Roy. I freaked out and threw that bottle down.'

54

'You threw it?'

'Yeah, I slung it down and it hit at the wrong angle or something and just *exploded*. The baggie broke and the milk shot up and sprayed all over the room. I couldn't believe one bottle could hold that much. Even now when I'm cleaning the living room I come across little white dots of dried milk here and there, like on the mantelpiece or the windowsill. Another little reminder of my Mother's Day freak-out.'

'Ha. The morph moment. Well Charlie, you are indeed a pathetic specimen of American manhood, yearning for your own Mother's Day card, but just hang in there – only seventeen more years and you'll be free again!'

'Oh fuckyouverymuch! By then I won't want to be.'

'Even now you don't wanna be. You love it, you know you do. But listen I gotta go Phil's here bye.'

'Bye.'

After talking with Charlie, Anna got absorbed in work in her usual manner, and might well have forgotten her lunch date with the people from Khembalung; but because this was a perpetual problem of hers, she had set her watch alarm for one o'clock, and when it beeped she saved and went downstairs. She could see through the front window that the new embassy's staff was still unpacking, releasing visible clouds of dust or incense smoke into the air. The young monk she had spoken to and his most elderly companion sat on the floor inspecting a box containing necklaces and the like.

They noticed her and looked up curiously, then the younger one nodded, remembering her from the morning conversation after their ceremony.

'Still interested in some pizza?' Anna asked. 'If pizza is okay?'

'Oh yes,' the young one said. The two men got to their feet, the old man in several distinct moves; one leg was stiff. 'We love pizza.' The old man nodded politely, glancing at his young assistant, who said something to him rapidly, in a language that while not guttural did seem mostly to be generated at the back of the mouth.

As they crossed the atrium to Pizzeria Uno Anna said uncertainly, 'Do you eat pizza where you come from?'

The younger man smiled. 'No. But in Nepal I have eaten pizza in tea houses.'

'Are you vegetarian?'

'No. Tibetan Buddhism has never been vegetarian. There were not enough vegetables.'

'So you are Tibetans! But I thought you said you were an island nation?'

'We are. But originally we came from Tibet. The old ones, like Rudra Cakrin here, left when the Chinese took over. The rest of us were born in India, or on Khembalung itself.'

'I see.'

They entered the restaurant, where big booths were walled by high wooden partitions. The three of them sat in one, Anna across from the two men.

'I am Drepung,' the young man said, 'and the rimpoche here, our ambassador to America, is Gyatso Sonam Rudra Cakrin.'

'I'm Anna Quibler,' Anna said, and shook hands with each of them. The men's hands were heavily callused.

Their waiter appeared. She did not appear to notice the unusual garb of the men, but took their orders with sublime indifference. After a quick muttered consultation, Drepung asked Anna for suggestions, and in the end they ordered a combination pizza with everything on it.

Anna sipped her water. 'Tell me more about Khembalung, and about your new embassy.'

Drepung nodded. 'I wish Rudra Cakrin himself could tell you, but he is still taking his English lessons, I'm afraid. Apparently they are going very badly. In any case, you know that China invaded Tibet in 1950, and that the Dalai Lama escaped to India in 1959?'

'Yes, that sounds familiar.'

'Yes. And during those years, and ever since then too, many Tibetans have moved to India to get away from the Chinese, and closer to the Dalai Lama. India took us in very hospitably, but when the Chinese and Indian governments had their disagreement over their border in 1960, the situation became very awkward for India. They were already in a bad way with Pakistan, and a serious controversy with China would have been . . .' He searched for the word, waggling a hand.

'Too much?' Anna suggested.

'Yes. Much too much. So, the support India had been giving to the Tibetans in exile –'

Rudra Cakrin made a little hiss.

'Small to begin with, although very helpful nevertheless,' Drepung added, 'shrank even further. It was requested that the Tibetan community in Dharamsala make itself as small and inconspicuous as possible. The Dalai Lama and his government did their best, and many Tibetans were relocated to other places in India, mostly in the far south. But elsewhere as well. Then some more years passed, and there were some, how shall I say, arguments or splits within the Tibetan exile community, too complicated to go into, I assure you. I can hardly understand them myself. But in the end a group called the Yellow Hat School took the offer of this island of ours, and moved there. This was just before the India–Pakistan war of 1970, unfortunately, so the timing was bad, and everything was on the hush-hush for a time. But the island was ours from that point, as a kind of protectorate of India, like Sikkim, only not so formally arranged.'

'Is Khembalung the island's original name?'

'No. I do not think it had a name before. Most of our sect lived at one time or another in the valley of Khembalung. So that name was kept, and we have shifted away from the Dalai Lama's government in Dharamsala, to a certain extent.'

At the sound of the words 'Dalai Lama' the old monk made a face and said something in Tibetan.

'The Dalai Lama is still number one with us,' Drepung clarified. 'It is a matter of some religious controversies with his associates. A matter of how best to support him.'

Anna said, 'I thought the mouth of the Ganges was in Bangladesh?'

'Much of it is. But you must know that it is a very big delta, and the west side of it is in India. Part of Bengal. Many islands. The Sundarbans? You have not heard?'

Their pizzas arrived, and Drepung began talking between big bites. 'Lightly populated islands, the Sundarbans. Some of them anyway. Ours was uninhabited.'

'Did you say uninhabitable?'

'No no. Inhabitable, obviously.'

Another noise from Rudra Cakrin.

'People with lots of choices might say they were uninhabitable,' Drepung went on. 'And they may yet become so. They are best for tigers. But we have done well there. We have become like tigers. Over the years we have built a nice town. A little seaside potala for Gyatso Rudra and the other lamas. Schools, houses – hospital. All that. And sea walls. The whole island has been ringed by dykes. Lots of work. Hard labour.' He nodded as if personally acquainted with this work. 'Dutch advisors helped us. Very nice. Our home, you know? Khembalung has moved from age to age. But now . . .' He waggled a hand again, took another slice of pizza, bit into it.

'Global warming?' Anna ventured.

He nodded, swallowed. 'Our Dutch friends suggested that we establish an embassy here, to join their campaign to influence American policy in these matters.'

Anna quickly bit into her pizza, so that she would not reveal the thought that had struck her, that the Dutch must be desperate indeed if they had been reduced to help like this. She thought things over as she chewed. 'So here you are,' she said. 'Have you been to America before?'

Drepung shook his head. 'None of us have.'

'It must be pretty overwhelming.'

He frowned at this word. 'I have been to Calcutta.'

'Oh I see.'

'This is very different, of course.'

'Yes, I'm sure.'

She liked him: his musical Indian English, his round face and big liquid eyes, his ready smile. The two men made quite a contrast: Drepung young and tall, round-faced, with a kind of baby-fat look; Rudra Cakrin old, small and wizened, his face lined with a million wrinkles, his cheekbones and narrow jaw prominent in an angular, nearly fleshless face.

The wrinkles were laugh lines, however, combined with the lines of a wide-eyed expression of surprise that bunched up his forehead. Despite his noises and muttering under Drepung's account, he still seemed cheerful enough. He certainly attacked his pizza with the same enthusiasm as his young assistant. With their shaved heads they shared a certain family resemblance.

She said, 'I suppose going from Tibet to a tropical island must have been a bigger shock than coming from the island to here.'

'I suppose. I was born in Khembalung myself, so I don't know for sure. But the old ones like Rudra here, who made that very move, seem to have adjusted quite well. Just to have any kind of home is a blessing, I think you will find.'

Anna nodded. The two of them did project a certain calm. They sat in the booth as if there was no hurry to go anywhere else. Anna couldn't imagine any such state of mind. She was always in a tearing hurry. She tried to match their air of being at ease. At ease in Arlington, Virginia, after a lifetime on an island in the Ganges. Well, the climate would be familiar. But everything else had to have changed quite stupendously.

And, on closer examination, there was a certain guardedness to them. Drepung glanced surreptitiously at their waiter; he looked at the pedestrians passing by; he watched Anna herself, all with a slightly cautious look, reminding her of the pained expression she had seen earlier in the day.

'How is it that you came to rent a space in this particular building?'

Drepung paused and considered this question for a surprisingly long time. Rudra Cakrin asked him something and he replied, and Rudra said something more.

'We had some advice there also,' Drepung said. 'The Pew Center on Global Climate Change has been helping us, and their office is located on Wilson Boulevard, nearby.'

'I didn't know that. They've helped you to meet people?'

'Yes, with the Dutch, and with some island nations, like Fiji and Tuvalu.'

'Tuvalu?'

'A very small country in the Pacific. They have perhaps been less than helpful to the cause, telling people that sea level has risen in their area of the Pacific but not elsewhere, and asking for financial compensation for this from Australia and other countries.'

'In their area of the Pacific only?'

'Measurements have not confirmed the claim.' Drepung smiled. 'But I can assure you, if you are on a storm track and spring tides are upon you, it can seem like sea level has risen quite a great deal.'

'I'm sure.'

Anna thought it over while she ate. It was good to know that they hadn't just rented the first office they found vacant. Nevertheless, their effort in Washington looked to her to be underpowered at this point. 'You should meet my husband,' she said. 'He works for a senator, one who is up on all these things, a very helpful guy, the chair of the foreign relations committee.'

'Ah – Senator Chase?'

'Yes. You know about him?'

'He has visited Khembalung.'

'Has he? Well, I'm not surprised, he's been every – he's been a lot of places. Anyway, my husband Charlie works for him as an environmental policy advisor. It would be good for you to talk to Charlie and get his perspective on your situation. He'll be full of suggestions for things you could do.'

'That would be an honour.'

'I don't know if I'd go that far. But useful.'

'Useful, yes. Perhaps we could have you to dinner at our residence.'

'Thank you, that would be nice. But we have two small boys and we've lost all our baby-sitters, so to tell the truth it would be easier if you and some of your colleagues came to our place. In fact I've already talked to Charlie about this, and he's looking forward to meeting you. We live in Bethesda, just across the border from the District. It's not far.'

'Red line.'

'Yes, very good. Red line, Bethesda stop. I can give you directions from there.'

She got out her calendar, checked the coming weeks. Very full, as always. 'How about a week from Friday? On a Friday we'll be able to relax a little.'

'Thank you,' Drepung said, ducking his head. He and Rudra Cakrin had an exchange in Tibetan. 'That would be very kind. And on the full moon, too.'

'Is it? I'm afraid I don't keep track.'

'We do. The tides, you see.'

THREE

Intellectual Merit

Water flows through the oceans in steady recycling patterns, determined by the Coriolis force and the particular positions of the continents in our time. Surface currents can move in the opposite direction to bottom currents below them, and often do, forming systems like giant conveyor belts of water. The largest one is already famous, at least in part: the Gulf Stream is a segment of a warm surface current that flows north up the entire length of the Atlantic, all the way to Norway and Greenland. There the water cools and sinks, and begins a long journey south on the Atlantic ocean floor, to the Cape of Good Hope and then east towards Australia, and even into the Pacific, where the water upwells and rejoins the surface flow, west to the Atlantic for the long haul north again. The round trip for any given water molecule takes about a thousand years.

Cooling salty water sinks more easily than fresh water. Trade winds sweep clouds generated in the Gulf of Mexico west over Central America to dump their rain in the Pacific, leaving the remaining water in the Atlantic that much saltier. So the cooling water in the North Atlantic sinks well, aiding the power of the Gulf Stream. If the surface of the North Atlantic were to become rapidly fresher, it would not sink so well when it cooled, and that could stall the conveyor belt. The Gulf Stream would have nowhere to go, and would slow down, and sink farther south. Weather everywhere would change, becoming windier and drier in the northern hemisphere, and colder in places, especially in Europe.

The sudden desalination of the North Atlantic might seem an unlikely occurrence, but it has happened before. At the end of the last Ice Age, for instance, vast shallow lakes were created by the melting of the polar ice cap. Eventually these lakes broke through their ice dams and poured off into the oceans. The Canadian shield still sports the scars from three or four of these cataclysmic floods; one flowed down the Mississippi, one the Hudson, one the St Lawrence.

These flows apparently stalled the world ocean conveyor belt current, and the climate of the whole world changed as a result, sometimes in as little as three years.

Now, would the Arctic sea ice, breaking into bergs and flowing south past Greenland, dump enough fresh water into the North Atlantic to stall the Gulf Stream again?

Frank Vanderwal kept track of climate news as a sort of morbid hobby. His friend Kenzo Hayakawa, an old climbing partner and grad school housemate, had spent time at the National Oceanic and Atmospheric Administration before coming to NSF to work with the weather crowd on the ninth floor, and so Frank occasionally checked in with him, to say hi and find out the latest. Things were getting wild out there; extreme weather events were touching down all over the world, the violent, short-termed ones almost daily, the chronic problem situations piling one on the next, so that never were they entirely clear of one or another of them. The Hyperniño, severe drought in India and Peru, lightning fires perpetual in Malaysia; then on the daily scale, a typhoon destroying most of Mindanao, a snap freeze killing crops and breaking pipes all over Texas, and so on. Something every day.

Like a lot of climatologists and other weather people Frank had met, Kenzo presented all this news with a faintly proprietarial air, as if he were curating the weather. He liked the wild stuff, and enjoyed sharing news of it, especially if it seemed to support his contention that the heat added anthropogenically to the atmosphere had been enough to change the Indian Ocean monsoon patterns for good, triggering global repercussions; this meant, in practice, almost everything that happened. This week for instance it was tornadoes, previously confined almost entirely to North America, as a kind of freak of that continent's topography and latitude, but now

65

appearing in east Africa and in central Asia. Last week it had been the weakening of the Great World Ocean Current in the Indian Ocean rather than the Atlantic.

'Unbelievable,' Frank would say.

'I know. Isn't it great?'

Before leaving for home at the end of the day, Frank often passed by another source of news, the little room filled with file cabinets and copy machines informally called 'The Department of Unfortunate Statistics'. Someone had started to tape on the beige walls of this room extra copies of pages that held interesting statistics or other bits of recent quantitative information. No one knew who had started the tradition, but now it was clearly a communal thing.

The oldest ones were headlines, things like:

World Bank President Says Four Billion Live on Less Than Two Dollars a Day

or

America: Five Percent of World Population, Fifty Percent of Corporate Ownership

Later pages were charts, or tables of figures out of journal articles, or short articles of a quantitative nature out of the scientific literature.

When Frank went by on this day, Edgardo was in there at the coffee machine, as he so often was, looking at the latest. It was another headline:

352 Richest People Own As Much as the Poorest Two Billion, Says Canadian Food Project

'I don't think this can be right,' Edgardo declared.

'How so?' Frank said.

'Because the poorest two billion have nothing, whereas the richest three hundred and fifty-two have a big percentage of the world's total capital. I suspect it would take the poorest four billion at least to match the top three hundred and fifty.'

Anna came in as he was saying this, and wrinkled her nose as she went to the copying machine. She didn't like this kind

of conversation, Frank knew. It seemed to be a matter of dis-
taste for belabouring the obvious. Or distrust in the data.
Maybe she was the one who had taped up a brief quote,
'*72.8% of all statistics are made up on the spot.*'

Frank, wanting to bug her, said, 'What do you think, Anna?'

'About what?'

Edgardo pointed to the headline and explained his objec-
tion.

Anna said, 'I don't know. Maybe if you add two billion
small households up, it matches the richest three hundred.'

'Not this top three hundred. Have you seen the latest
Forbes 500 reports?'

Anna shook her head impatiently, as if to say, Of course
not, why would I waste my time? But Edgardo was an invet-
erate student of the stock market and the financial world
generally. He tapped another taped-up page. 'The average
surplus value created by American workers is thirty-three dollars an hour.'

Anna said, 'I wonder how they define surplus value.'

'Profit,' Frank said.

Edgardo shook his head. 'You can cook the books and get
rid of profit, but the surplus value, the value created beyond
the pay for the labour, is still there.'

Anna said, 'There was a page in here that said the average
American worker puts in 1950 hours a year. I thought that
was questionable too, that's forty hours a week for about
forty-nine weeks.'

'Three weeks of vacation a year,' Frank pointed out. 'Pretty
normal.'

'Yeah, but that's the average? What about all the part-time
workers?'

'There must be an equivalent number of people who work
overtime.'

'Can that be true? I thought overtime was a thing of the
past.'

'You work overtime.'

'Yeah but I don't get *paid* for it.'

The men laughed at her.

'They should have used the median,' she said. 'The average is a skewed measure of central tendency. Anyway, that's . . .' – Anna could do calculations in her head – 'sixty-four thousand three hundred and fifty dollars a year, generated by the average worker in surplus value. If you can believe these figures.'

'What's the average income?' Edgardo asked. 'Thirty thousand?'

'Maybe less,' Frank said.

'We don't have any idea,' Anna objected.

'Call it thirty, and what's the average taxes paid?'

'About ten? Or is it less?'

Edgardo said, 'Call it ten. So let's see. You work every day of the year, except for three lousy weeks. You make around a hundred thousand dollars. Your boss takes two thirds, and gives you one third, and you give a third of that to the government. Your government uses what it takes to build all the roads and schools and police and pensions, and your boss takes his share and buys a mansion on an island somewhere. So naturally you complain about your bloated inefficient Big Brother of a government, and you always vote for the pro-owner party.' He grinned at Frank and Anna. 'How stupid is that?'

Anna shook her head. 'People don't see it that way.'

'But here are the statistics!'

'People don't usually put them together like that. Besides, you made half of them up.'

'They're close enough for people to get the idea! But they are not taught to think! In fact they're taught *not* to think. And they are stupid to begin with.'

Even Frank was not willing to go this far. 'It's a matter of what you can see,' he suggested. 'You see your boss, you see your paycheck, it's given to you. You have it. Then you're forced to give some of it to the government. You never know about the surplus value you've created, because it was disappeared in the first place. Cooked in the books.'

'But the rich are all over the news! Everyone can see they have more than they have earned, because no one *earns* that much.'

'The only things people understand are sensory,' Frank insisted. 'We're hardwired to understand life on the savannah. Someone gives you meat, they're your friend. Someone takes your meat, they're your enemy. Abstract concepts like surplus value, or statistics on the value of a year's work, these just aren't as real as what you see and touch. People are only good at what they can think out in terms of their senses. That's just the way we evolved.'

'That's what I'm saying,' Edgardo said cheerfully. 'We are stupid!'

'I've got to get back to it,' Anna said, and left. It really wasn't her kind of conversation.

Frank followed her out, and finally headed home. He drove his little fuel-cell Honda out along Old Dominion Parkway, already jammed; over the Beltway, and then up to a condo complex called Swink's New Mill, where he had rented a condominium for his year at NSF.

He parked in the complex's cellar garage and took the elevator up to the fourteenth floor. His apartment looked out towards the Potomac – a long view and a nice apartment, rented out for the year from a young State Department guy who was doing a stint in Brasilia. It was furnished in a stripped-down style that suggested the man did not live there very often. But a nice kitchen, functional spaces, everything easy, and most of the time Frank was home he was asleep anyway, so he didn't care what it was like.

He had picked up one of the free papers back at work,

and now as he spooned down some cottage cheese he looked again at the *Personals* section, a regrettable habit he had had for years, fascinated as he was by the glimpse these pages gave of a subworld of radically efflorescing sexual diversity – a subculture that had understood the implications of the removal of biological constraints in the techno-urban land-scape, and were therefore able and willing to create a kind of polymorphous panmixia. Were these people really out there, or was this merely the collective fantasy life of a bunch of lonely souls like himself? He had never contacted any of the people putting in the ads to try to find out. He suspected the worst, and would rather be lonely. Although the sections devoted to people looking for LTRs, meaning 'long-term rela-tionships', went far beyond the sexual fantasies, and some-times struck him with force. *ISO LTR:* in search of long-term relationship. The species had long ago evolved towards monog-amous relationships, they were wired into the brain's struc-ture, every culture manifesting the same overwhelming tendency toward pair bonding. Not a cultural imposition but a biological instinct. They might as well be storks in that regard.

And so he read the ads, but never replied. He was only here for a year; San Diego was his home. It made no sense to take any action on this particular front, no matter what he felt or read.

The ads themselves also tended to stop him.

Husband hunting, SWF, licensed nurse, seeks a hard-working, handsome SWM for LTR. Must be a dedicated Jehovah's Witness.

SBM, 5′5″, shy, quiet, a little bit serious, seeking Woman, age open. Not good-looking or wealthy but Nice Guy. Enjoy foreign movies, opera, theater, music, books, quiet evenings.

These entries were not going to get a lot of responses. But they, like all the rest, were as clear as could be on the fun-damental primate needs they were asking for. Frank could

70

have written the urtext underneath them, and one time he had, and had even sent it in to a paper, as a joke of course, for all those reading these confessions with the same analytical slant he had – it would make them laugh. Although of course if any woman reading it liked the joke well enough to call, well, that would have been a sign.

Male homo sapiens desires company of female homo sapiens for mutual talk and grooming behavior, possibly mating and reproduction. Must be happy, run fast.

But no one had replied.

He went out onto the bas-relief balcony, into the sultry late afternoon. Another two months and he would be going home, back to resume his real life. He was looking forward to it. He wanted to float in the Pacific. He wanted to walk around beautiful UCSD in its cool warmth, eat lunch with old colleagues among the eucalyptus trees.

Thinking about that reminded him of the grant application from Yann Pierzinski. He went inside to his laptop and googled him to try to learn more about what he had been up to. Then he re-opened his application, and found the section on the part of the algorithm to be developed. Primitive recursion at the boundary limit . . . it was interesting.

After some more thought, he called up Derek Gaspar at Torrey Pines Generique.

'What's up?' Derek said after the preliminaries.

'Well, I just got a grant proposal from one of your people, and I'm wondering if you can tell me anything about it.'

'From one of mine, what do you mean?'

'A Yann Pierzinski, do you know him?'

'No, never heard of him. He works here you say?'

'He was there on a temporary contract, working with Simpson. He's a post-doc from Caltech.'

'Ah yeah, here we go. Mathematician, got a paper in *Biomathematics* on algorithms.'

'Yeah, that comes up first on my google too.'

71

'Well sure. I can't be expected to know everyone who ever worked with us here, that's hundreds of people, you know that.'

'Sure sure.'

'So what's his proposal about? Are you going to give him a grant?'

'Not up to me, you know that. We'll see what the panel says. But meanwhile, maybe you should check it out.'

'Oh you like it then?'

'I think it may be interesting, it's hard to tell at this stage. Just don't drop him.'

'Well, our records show him as already gone back up to Pasadena, to finish his work up there I presume. Like you said, his gig here was temporary.'

'Ah ha. Man, your research groups have been gutted.'

'Not gutted, Frank, we're down to the bare bones in some areas, but we've kept what we need to. There have been some hard choices to make. Kenton wanted his note repaid, and the timing couldn't have been worse, coming after that stage two in India. It's been tough, really tough. That's one of the reasons I'll be happy when you're back out here.'

'I don't work for Torrey Pines any more.'

'No I know, but maybe you could rejoin us when you move back here.'

'Maybe. If you get new financing.'

'I'm trying, believe me. That's why I'd like to have you back on board.'

'We'll see. Let's talk about it when I'm out there. Meanwhile, don't cut any more of your other research efforts. They might be what draws the new financing.'

'I hope so. I'm doing what I can, believe me. We're trying to hold on till something comes through.'

'Yeah. Hang in there then. I'll be out looking for a place to live in a couple of weeks, I'll come see you then.'

'Good, make an appointment with Susan.'

Frank clicked off his phone, sat back in his chair thinking it over. Derek was like a lot of first-generation CEOs of biotech start-ups. He had come out of the biology department at UCSD, and his business acumen had been gained on the job. Some people managed to do this successfully, others didn't, but all tended to fall behind on the actual science being done, and had to take on faith what was really possible in the labs. Certainly Derek could use some help in guiding policy at Torrey Pines Generique.

Frank went back to studying the grant proposal. There were elements of the algorithm missing, as was typical. That was what the grant was for, to pay for the work that would finish the project. And some people made a habit of describing crucial aspects of their work in general terms when at the pre-pub stage, a matter of being cautious. So he could not be sure about it, but he could see the potential for a very powerful method there. Earlier in the day he had thought he saw a way to plug one of the gaps that Pierzinski had left, and if that worked as he thought it might . . .

'Hmmmm,' he said to the empty room.

If the situation was still fluid when he went out to San Diego, he could perhaps set things up quite nicely. There were some potential problems, of course. NSF's guidelines stated explicitly that although any copyrights, patents or project income belonged to the grant-holder, NSF always kept a public-right use for all grant-subsidized work. That would keep any big gains from being made by any individual or company on a project like this, if it was awarded a grant. Purely private control could only be maintained if there had not been any public money granted.

Also, the PI on the proposal was Pierzinski's advisor at Caltech, battening off the work of his students in the usual way. Of course it was an exchange – the advisor gave the student credibility, and a licence to apply for a grant, by contributing his name and prestige to the project. The student provided the work, sometimes all of it, sometimes just a portion of it. In this case, it looked to Frank like all of it.

Anyway, the grant proposal came from Caltech. Caltech and the PI would hold the rights to anything the project made, along with NSF itself, even if Pierzinski moved afterwards. So, if for instance an effort was going to be made to bring Pierzinski to Torry Pines Generique, it would be best if this particular proposal were to be declined. And if the algorithm worked and became patentable, then again, keeping control of what it made would only be possible if the proposal were to be declined.

That line of thought made him feel jumpy. In fact he was on his feet, pacing out to the mini-balcony and back in again. Then he remembered he had been planning to go out to Great Falls anyway. He quickly finished his cottage cheese, pulled his climbing kit out of the closet, changed clothes, and went back down to his car.

The Great Falls of the Potomac was a complicated thing, a long tumble of whitewater falling down past a few islands. The complexity of the falls was its main visual appeal, as it was no very great thing in terms of total height, or even volume of water. Its roar was the biggest thing about it.

The spray it threw up seemed to consolidate and knock down the humidity, so that paradoxically it was less humid here than elsewhere, although wet and mossy underfoot. Frank walked downstream along the edge of the gorge. Below the falls the river recollected itself and ran through a defile called Mather Gorge, a ravine with a south wall so steep that climbers were drawn to it. One section called Carter Rock was Frank's favourite. It was a simple matter to tie a rope to a top belay, usually a stout tree trunk near the cliff's edge, and then abseil down the rope to the bottom and either free-climb up, or clip onto the rope with an ascender and go through the hassles of self-belay.

One could climb in teams too, of course, and many did, but there were about as many singletons like Frank here as there were duets. Some even free soloed the wall, dispensing with all protection. Frank liked to play it just a little safer than that, but he had climbed here so many times now that sometimes he abseiled down and free-climbed next to his rope, pretending to himself that he could grab it if he fell. The few routes available were all chalked and greasy from repeated use. He decided this time to clip onto the rope with the ascender.

The river and its gorge created a band of open sky that was unusually big for the metropolitan area. This as much as anything else gave Frank the feeling that he was in a good place: on a wall route, near water, and open to the sky. Out of the claustrophobia of the great hardwood forest, one of the things about the East Coast that Frank hated the most. There were times he would have given a finger for the sight of open land.

Now, as he abseiled down to the small tumble of big boulders at the foot of the cliff, chalked his hands, and began to climb the fine-grained old schist of the route, he cheered up. He focused on his immediate surroundings to a degree unimaginable when he was not climbing. It was like the maths work, only then he wasn't anywhere at all. Here, he was right on these very particular rocks.

This route he had climbed before many times. About a 5.8 or 5.9 at its crux, much easier elsewhere. Hard to find really difficult pitches here, but that didn't matter. Even climbing up out of a ravine, rather than up onto a peak, didn't matter. The constant roar, the spray, those didn't matter. Only the climbing itself mattered.

His legs did most of the work. Find the footholds, fit his rockclimbing shoes into cracks or onto knobs, then look for handholds; and up, and up again, using his hands only for balance, and a kind of tactile reassurance that he was seeing what he was seeing, that the footholds he was expecting to use would be enough. Climbing was the bliss of perfect attention, a kind of devotion, or prayer. Or simply a retreat into the supreme competencies of the primate cerebellum. A lot was conserved.

By now it was evening. A sultry summer evening, sunset near, the air itself going yellow. He topped out and sat on the rim, feeling the sweat on his face fail to evaporate.

There was a kayaker, below in the river. A woman, he thought, though she wore a helmet and was broad-shouldered and flat-chested – he would have been hard-pressed to say exactly how he knew, and yet he was sure. This was another savannah competency, and indeed some anthropologists postulated that this kind of rapid identification of reproductive possibility was what the enlarged neocortex had grown to do. The brain growing with such evolutionary speed, specifically to get along with the other sex. A depressing thought given the results so far.

This woman was paddling smoothly upstream, into the hissing water that only around her seemed to be recollecting itself as a liquid. Upstream it was a steep rapids, leading to the white smash at the bottom of the falls proper.

The kayaker pushed up into this wilder section, paddling harder upstream, then held her position against the flow while she studied the falls ahead. Then she took off hard, attacking a white smooth flow in the lowest section, a kind of ramp through the smash, up to a terrace in the whitewater. When she reached the little flat she could rest again, in another slightly more strenuous maintenance paddle, gathering her strength for the next salmonlike climb.

Abruptly leaving the strange refuge of that flat spot, she attacked another ramp that led up to a bigger plateau of flat black water, a pool that had an eddy in it, apparently, rolling backward and allowing her to rest in place. There was no room there to gain any speed for another leap up, so that

76

she appeared to be stuck; but maybe she was only studying her way, or waiting for a moment of reduced flow, because all of a sudden she attacked the water with a fierce flurry of paddle strokes, and seemingly willed her craft up the next pouring ramp. Five or seven desperate seconds later she levelled out again, on a tiny little bench of a refuge that did not have a pushback eddy, judging by the intensity of her maintenance paddling there. After only a few seconds she had to try a ramp to her right or get pushed back off her perch, and so she took off and fought upstream, fists moving fast as a boxer's, the kayak at an impossible angle, looking like a miracle – until all of sudden it was swept back down, and she had to make a quick turn and then take a wild ride, bouncing down the falls by a different and steeper route than the one she had ascended, losing in a few swift seconds the height that she had taken a minute or two's hard labour to gain.

'Wow,' Frank said, smitten.

She was already almost down to the hissing tapestry of flat river right below him, and he felt an urge to wave to her, or stand and applaud. He restrained himself, not wanting to impose upon another athlete obviously deep in her own space. But he did whip out his cell phone and try out a GPS-oriented directory search, figuring that if she had a cell phone with a transponder in the kayak, it had to be very close to his own phone's position. He checked his position, entered thirty metres north of that; got nothing. Same with the position twenty metres farther east.

'Ah well,' he said, and stood to go. It was sunset now, and the smooth stretches of the river had turned a pale orange. Time to go home and try to fall asleep.

'In search of kayaker gal, seen going upstream at Great Falls. Great ride, I love you, please respond.'

He would not send that in to the free papers, but only spoke it as a kind of prayer to the sunset. Down below the kayaker was turning to start upstream again.

It could be said that science is boring, or even that science wants to be boring, in that it wants to be beyond all dispute. It wants to understand the phenomena of the world in ways that everyone can agree on and share; it wants to make assertions from a position that is not any particular subject's position, assertions that if tested for accuracy by any sentient being would cause that being to agree with the assertions. Complete agreement; the world put under a description – stated that way, it begins to sound interesting.

And indeed it is. Nothing human is boring. Nevertheless, the minute details of the everyday grind involved in any particular bit of scientific practice can be tedious even to the practitioners. A lot of it, as with most work in this world, involves wasted time, false leads, dead ends, faulty equipment, dubious techniques, bad data, and a huge amount of detail work. Only when it is written up in a paper does it tell a tale of things going right, step by step, in meticulous and replicable detail, like a proof in Euclid. That stage is a highly artificial result of a long process of grinding.

In the case of Leo and his lab, and the matter of the new targeted non-viral delivery system from Maryland, several hundred hours of human labour, and many more of computer time, were devoted to an attempted repetition of an experiment described in the crucial paper, 'In Vivo Insertion of cDNA 1568rr Into CBA/H, BALB/c, and C57BL/6 Mice'.

At the end of this process, Leo had confirmed the theory

he had formulated the very moment he had read the paper describing the experiment.

'It's a goddamned artifact.'

Marta and Brian sat there staring at the print-outs. Marta had killed a couple hundred of the Jackson Lab's finest mice in the course of confirming this theory of Leo's, and now she was looking more murderous than ever. You didn't want to mess with Marta on the days when she had to sacrifice some mice, nor even talk to her.

Brian sighed.

Leo said, 'It only works if you pump the mice full of the stuff till they just about explode. I mean look at them. They look like hamsters. Or guinea pigs. Their little eyes are about to pop out of their heads.'

'No wonder,' Brian said. 'There's only two millilitres of blood in a mouse, and we're injecting them with one.'

Leo shook his head. 'How the hell did they get away with that?'

'The CBAs are kind of round and furry.'

'What are you saying, they're bred to hide artifacts?'

'No.'

'It's an artifact!'

'Well, it's useless, anyway.'

An artifact was what they called an experimental result that was specific to the methodology of the experiment, but not illustrating anything beyond that. A kind of accident or false result, and in a few celebrated cases, part of a deliberate hoax.

So Brian was trying to be careful using the word. It was possible that it was no worse than a real result that happened to be generated in a way that made it useless for their particular purposes. Trying to turn things that people have learned about biological processes into medicines led to that sort of thing. It happened all the time, and all those experimental results were not necessarily artifacts. They just weren't useful facts.

Not yet, anyway. That's why there were so many experiments, and so many stages to the human trials that had to be so carefully conducted; so many double-blind studies, held with as many patients as possible included, to get good statistical data. Hundreds of Swedish nurses, all with the same habits, studied for half a century – but these kinds of powerful long-term studies were very rarely possible. Never, when the substances being tested were brand-new – literally, in the sense that they were still under patent and had brand names different from their scientific appellations.

So all the little baby biotechs, and all the start-up pharmaceuticals, paid for the best stage-one studies they could afford. They scoured the literature, and ran experiments on computers and lab samples, and then on mice or other lab animals, hunting for data that could be put through a reliable analysis that would tell them something about how a potential new medicine worked in people. Then the human trials.

It was usually a matter of two to ten years of work, costing anywhere up to five hundred million dollars, though naturally cheaper was better. Longer and more expensive than that, and the new drug or method would almost certainly be abandoned; the money would run out, and the scientists involved would by necessity move on to something else.

In this case, however, where Leo was dealing with a method that Derek Gaspar had bought for fifty-one million dollars, there could be no stage-one human trials. They would be impossible. 'No one's gonna let themselves be blown up like a balloon! Blown up like a goddam bike tyre! Your kidneys would get swamped or some kind of oedema would kill you.'

'We're going to have to tell Derek the bad news.'

'Derek is not going to like it.'

'Not going to like it! Fifty-one million dollars? He's going to hate it!'

'Think about blowing that much money. What an idiot he is.'

80

'Is it worse to have a scientist who is a bad businessman as your CEO, or a businessman who is a bad scientist?'

'What about when they're both?'

They sat around the bench looking at the mice cages and the rolls of data sheets. A Dilbert cartoon mocked them as it peeled away from the end of the counter. It was a sign of something deep that this lab had Dilberts taped to the walls rather than Far Sides.

'An in-person meeting for this particular communication is contra-indicated,' said Brian.

'No shit,' Leo said.

Marta snorted. 'You can't get a meeting with him anyway.'

'Ha ha.' But Leo was far enough out on the periphery of Torrey Pine Generique's power structure that getting a meeting with Derek was indeed difficult.

'It's true,' Marta insisted. 'You might as well be trying to schedule a doctor's appointment.'

'Which is stupid,' Brian pointed out. 'The company is totally dependent on what happens in this lab.'

'Not totally,' Leo said.

'Yes it is! But that's not what the business schools teach these guys. The lab is just another place of production. Management tells production what to produce, and the place of production produces it. Input from the agency of production would be wrong.'

'Like the assembly line choosing what to make,' Marta said.

'Right. Thus the idiocy of business management theory in our time.'

'I'll send him an e-mail,' Leo decided.

So Leo sent Derek an e-mail concerning what Brian and Marta persisted in calling the exploding mice problem. Derek (according to reports they heard later) swelled up like one of their experimental subjects. It appeared he had been IVed with two quarts of genetically-engineered right-eous indignation.

'It's in the literature!' he was reported to have shouted at Dr Sam Houston, his vice president in charge of research and development. 'It was in *The Journal of Immunology*, there were two papers that were peer-reviewed, they *got a patent for it*, I went out there to Maryland and checked it all out myself! It worked there, damn it. So *make it work here.*'

'*Make* it work?' Marta said when she heard this story. 'You see what I mean?'

'Well, you know,' Leo said grimly. 'That's the tech in bio-tech, right?'

'Hmmm,' Brian said, interested despite himself.

After all, the manipulations of gene and cell that they made were hardly ever done 'just to find things out', though they did that too. They were done to accomplish certain things inside the cell, and hopefully, later, inside a living body. Biotechnology, *bio techno logos*; the word on how to put the tool into the living organism. Genetic engineering meant designing and building something new inside a body's DNA, to effect something in the metabolism.

They had done the genetics; now it was time for the engi-neering.

So Leo and Brian and Marta, and the rest of Leo's lab, and some people from labs elsewhere in the building, began to work on this problem. Sometimes at the end of a day, when the sun was breaking sideways through gaps in the clouds out to sea, shining weakly in the tinted windows and illuminating their faces as they sat around two desks cov-ered by reprints and offprints, they would talk over the issues involved, and compare their most recent results, and try to make sense of the problem. Sometimes one of them would stand up and use the whiteboard to sketch out some diagram illustrating his or her conception of what was going on, down there forever below the level of their physical senses. The rest would comment, and drink coffee, and think it over.

For a while they considered assumptions the original experimenters had made:

'Maybe the flushing dose doesn't have to be that high.'

'Maybe the solution could be stronger, they seem to have topped out kind of low.'

'But that's because of what happens to the . . .'

'See the group at UW found that out when they were working on . . .'

'Yeah that's right. Shit.'

'The thing is, it does work, when you do everything they did. I mean the transference will happen in vitro, and in mice.'

'What about drawing blood, treating it and then putting it back in?'

'Or hepatocytes?'

'Uptake is in blood.'

'What we need is to package the inserts with a ligand that is really specific for the target cells. If we could find that specificity, out of all the possible proteins, without going through all the rigmarole of trial and error . . .'

'Too bad we don't still have Pierzinski here. He could run the array of possibilities through his operation set.'

'Well, we could call him up and ask him to give it a try.'

'Sure, but who's got time for that kind of thing?'

'He's still working on a paper with Eleanor over on campus,' Marta said, meaning UCSD. 'I'll ask him when he comes down.'

Brian said, almost as if joking, 'Maybe you could try to make the insertion in a limb, away from the organs. Tourniquet a lower leg or a forearm, blow it up with the full dose, wait for it to permeate the endothelial cells lining the veins and arteries in the limb, then release the tourniquet. They'd pee off the extra water, and still have a certain number of altered cells. It wouldn't be any worse than chugging a few beers, would it?'

'Your hand would hurt.'

'Big fucking deal.'

'You might get phlebitis if it was your leg. Isn't that how it happens?'

'Well use the hand then.'

'Interesting,' Leo said. 'Heck, let's try it at least. The other options look worse to me. Although we should probably try the mice on the various limits on volume and dosage in the original experiment, just to be sure.'

So the meeting petered out, and they wandered off to go home, or back to their desks and benches, thinking over plans for more experiments. Getting the mice, getting the time on the machines, sequencing genes, sequencing schedules; when you were doing science the hours flew by, and the days, and the weeks. This was the main feeling: there was never enough time to do it all. Was this different from other kinds of work? Papers almost written were rewritten, checked, rewritten again – finally sent off. Papers with their problems papered over. Lots of times the lab was like some old-fashioned newspaper office with a deadline approaching, all the starving journalists churning out the next day's fishwrap. Except people would not wrap fish with these papers; they would save them, file them by category, test all their assertions, cite them – and report any errors to the authorities.

Leo's THINGS TO DO list grew and shrank, grew and shrank, grew and then refused to shrink. He spent much less time than he wanted to at home in Leucadia with Roxanne. Roxanne understood, but it bothered him, even if it didn't bother her.

He called the Jackson labs and ordered new and different strains of mice, each strain with its own number and bar code and genome. He got his lab's machines scheduled, and assigned the techs to use them, moving some things to the front burner, others to the back, all to accomodate this project's urgency.

On certain days, he went into the lab where the mouse cages were kept, and opened a cage door. He took out a mouse, small and white, wrigging and sniffing the way they did, checking things out with its whiskers. Quickly he shifted it so that he was holding it at the neck with the forefingers and thumbs of both hands. A quick hard twist and the neck broke. Very soon after that the mouse was dead.

This was not unusual. During this round of experiments, he and Brian and Marta and the rest of them tourniqueted and injected about three hundred mice, drew their blood, then killed and rendered and analysed them. That was an aspect of the process they didn't talk about, not even Brian. Marta in particular went black with disgust; it was worse than when she was pre-menstrual, as Brian joked (once). Her headphones stayed on her head all day long, the music turned up so loud that even the other people in the lab could hear it. Terrible ultra-profane hip-hop rap whatever. If she can't hear she can't feel, Brian joked right next to her, Marta oblivious and trembling with rage, or something like it.

But it was no joke, even though the mice existed to be killed, even though they were killed mercifully, and usually only some few months before they would have died naturally. There was no real reason to have qualms, and yet still there was no joking about it. Maybe Brian would joke about Marta (if she couldn't hear him), but he wouldn't joke about that. In fact he insisted on using the word *kill* rather than *sacrifice*, even in write-ups and papers, to keep it clear what they were doing. Usually they had to break their necks right behind the head; you couldn't inject them to 'put them to sleep', because their tissue samples had to be clear of all contaminants. So it was a matter of breaking necks, as if they were tigers pouncing on prey. Marta was as blank as a mask as she did it, and very deftly too. If done properly it paralysed them so that it was quick and painless – or at least quick. No feeling below the head, no breathing, immediate loss of mouse consciousness, one hoped. Leaving only the killers to think it over. The victims were dead, and their bodies had been donated to science for many generations on end. The lab had the pedigrees to prove it. The scientists involved went home and thought about other things, most of the time. Usually the mice deaths occurred in the mornings, so they could get to work on the samples. By the time the scientists got home the experience was somewhat forgotten, its effects muted. But people like Marta went home and dosed themselves with drugs on those days – she said she did – and played the most hostile music they could find, 110 decibels of forgetting. Or went out surfing. They didn't talk about it to anyone, at least most of them didn't – this was what made Marta so obvious, she would talk about it – but most of them didn't, because it would sound both silly and vaguely shameful at the same time. If it bothered them so much, why did they keep doing it? Why did they stay in that line of business?

But – that line of business was doing science. It was doing biology, it was studying life, improving life, increasing life! And in most labs the mouse-killing was done only by the lowliest of techs, so that it was only a temporary bad job that one had to get through on the way to the good jobs.

Someone's got to do it, they thought.

In the meantime, while they were working on this problem, their good results with the HDL 'factory cells' had been plugged into the paper they had written about the process, and sent upstairs to Torrey Pines' legal department, where it had been held up. Repeated queries from Leo got the same e-mailed response – still reviewing – do not publish yet.

'They want to find what they can patent in it,' Brian said.

86

'They won't let us publish until we have a delivery method and a patent,' Marta predicted.

'But that may never happen!' Leo cried. 'It's good work, it's interesting! It could help make a big breakthrough!'

'That's what they don't want,' Brian said.

'They don't want a big breakthrough unless it's our big breakthrough.'

'Shit.'

This had happened before, but Leo had never gotten used to it. Sitting on results, doing private science, secret science – it went against the grain. It wasn't science as he understood it, which was a matter of finding out things and publishing them for all to see and test, critique, put to use.

But it was getting to be standard operating procedure. Security in the building remained intense; even e-mails out had to be checked for approval, not to mention laptops, brief-cases, and boxes leaving the building. 'You have to check in your brain when you leave,' as Brian put it.

'Fine by me,' Marta said.

'I just want to publish,' Leo insisted grimly.

'You'd better find a targeted delivery method if you want to publish that particular paper, Leo.'

So they continued to work on the Urtech method. The new experiments slowly yielded their results. The volumes and dosages had sharp parameters on all sides. The 'tourniquet injection' method did not actually insert very many copy DNAs into the subject animals' endothelial cells, and a lot of what was inserted was damaged by the process, and later flushed out of the body.

In short, the Maryland method was still an artifact.

By now, however, enough time had passed that Derek could pretend that the whole thing had never happened. It was a new financial quarter; there were other fish to fry, and for now the pretence could be plausibly maintained that it was a work in progress rather than a total bust. It wasn't as if anyone else had solved the targeted non-viral delivery problem, after all. It was a hard problem. Or so Derek could say, in all truth, and did so whenever anyone was inconsiderate enough to bring the matter up. Whiners on the company's website chat room could be ignored as always.

Analysts on Wall Street, however, and in the big pharmaceuticals, and in relevant venture capital firms, could not be ignored. And while they weren't saying anything directly, investment money started to go elsewhere. Torrey Pines' stock fell, and because it was falling it fell some more, and then more again. Biotechs were fluky, and so far Torrey Pines had not generated any potential cash cows. They remained a start-up. Fifty-one million dollars was being swept under the rug, but the big lump in the rug gave it away to anyone who remembered what it was.

No. Torrey Pines Generique was in trouble.

In Leo's lab they had done what they could. Their job had been to get certain cell lines to become unnaturally prolific protein factories, and they had done that. Delivery wasn't their part of the deal, and they weren't physiologists, and now they didn't have the wherewithal to do that part of the job. Torrey Pines needed a whole different wing for that, a whole different field of science. It was not an expertise that could be bought for fifty-one million dollars. Or maybe it could have been, but Derek had bought defective expertise. And because of that, a multi-billion-dollar cash-cow method was stalled right on the brink; and the whole company might go under.

Nothing Leo could do about it. He couldn't even publish his results.

The Quiblers' small house was located at the end of a street of similar houses. All of them stood blankly, blinds drawn, no clues given as to who lived inside. They could have been empty for all an outsider could tell: no cars in the driveways, no kids in the yards, no yard or porch activity of any kind. They could have been walled compounds in Saudi Arabia, hiding their life from the desert outside.

Walking these streets with Joe on his back, Charlie assumed as he always did that these houses were mostly owned by people who worked in the District, people who were always either working or on vacation. Their homes were places to sleep. Charlie had been that way himself before the boys had arrived. That was how people lived in Bethesda, west of Wisconsin Avenue – west all the way to the Pacific, Charlie didn't know. But he didn't think so; he tended to put it on Bethesda specifically.

So he walked to the grocery store shaking his head as he always did. 'It's like a ghost town, Joe, it's like some *Twilight Zone* episode in which we're the only two people left on Earth.'

Then they rounded the corner, and all thought of ghost towns was rendered ridiculous. Shopping centre. They walked through the automatic glass doors into a giant Giant grocery store. Joe, excited by the place as always, stood up in his baby backpack, his knees on Charlie's shoulders, and whacked Charlie on the ears as if he were directing an elephant. Charlie reached up, lifted him around and stuffed him into the baby seat of the grocery cart, strapped him down with the cart's little red seat-belt. A very useful feature, that.

Okay. Buddhists coming to dinner, Asians from the mouth of the Ganges. He had no idea what to cook. He assumed they were vegetarians. It was not unusual for Anna to invite people from NSF over to dinner and then be somewhat at a loss in the matter of the meal itself. But Charlie liked that. He enjoyed cooking, though he was not good at it, and had become worse in the years since the boys had arrived. Time had grown short, and he and Anna had both cooked and recooked their repertoire of recipes until they were sick of them, and yet hadn't learned anything new. So now they often ordered take-out, or ate as plainly as Nick; or Charlie tried something new and botched it. Dinner guests were a chance to do that again.

Now he decided to resuscitate an old recipe from their student years, pasta with an olive and basil sauce that a friend had first cooked for them in Italy. He wandered the familiar aisles of the store, looking for the ingredients. He should have made a list. On a typical trip he would go home having forgotten something crucial, and today he wanted to avoid that, but he was also thinking of other things, and making comments aloud from time to time. Joe's presence disguised his tendency to talk to himself in public spaces. 'Okay, whole peeled tomatoes, pitted kalamatas, olive oil extra virgin first cold press, it's the first press that really matters,' slipping into their friend's Italian accent, 'now vat I am forgetting, hm, hm, oh, ze pasta! But you must never keel ze pasta, my God! Oh and bread. And wine, but not more than we can carry home, huh Joe.'

Groceries tucked into the backpack pocket under Joe's butt, and slung in plastic bags from both hands, Charlie walked Joe back along the empty street to their house, singing

'I Can't Give You Anything But Love', one of Joe's favourites. Then they were up the steps and home.

Their street dead-ended in a little triangle of trees next to Woodson Avenue, a feeder road that poured its load of cars onto Wisconsin south. It was a nice location, within sight of Wisconsin and yet peaceful. An old four-storey apartment block wrapped around their back yard like a huge brick sound barrier, its stacked windows like a hundred live webcasts streaming all at once, daily lives that were much too partial and mundane to be interesting. No *Rear Window* here, and thank God for that. The wall of apartments was like a dull screensaver, and might as well have been trees, though trees would have been nicer. The world outside was irrelevant. Each nuclear family in its domicile is inside its own pocket universe, and for the time it is together it exists inside a kind of event horizon: no one sees it and it sees no one. Millions of pocket universes, scattered across the surface of the planet like the dots of light in night-time satellite photos.

On this night, however, the bubble containing the Quiblers was breached. Visitors from afar, aliens! When the doorbell rang they almost didn't recognize the sound.

Anna was occupied with Joe and a diaper upstairs, so Charlie left the kitchen and hurried through the house to answer the door. Four men in off-white cotton pants and shirts stood on the stoop, like visitors from Calcutta; only their vests were the maroon colour Charlie associated with Tibetan monks. Joe had run to the top of the stairs, and he grabbed the banister to keep his balance, agog at the sight of them. In the living room Nick was struck shy, his nose quickly back into his book, but he was glancing over the top of it frequently as the strangers were ushered in and made comfortable around him. Charlie offered them drinks, and they accepted beers, and when he came back with those, Anna and Joe were downstairs and had joined the fun. Two of their visitors sat on the living-room floor, laughing off Anna's offer of the little couches, and they all put their beer bottles on the coffee table.

The oldest monk and the youngest one leaned back against the radiator, down at Joe's level, and soon they were engaged with his vast collection of blocks – a heaping mound of plain or painted cubes, rhomboids, cylinders and other polygons, which they quickly assembled into walls and towers, working with and around Joe's Godzillalike interventions.

The young one, Drepung, answered Anna's questions directly, and also translated for the oldest one, named Rudra Cakrin. He was the official ambassador of Khembalung, but while he was without English, apparently, his two middle-aged associates, Sucandra and Padma Sambhava, spoke it pretty well – not as well as Drepung, but adequately.

These two followed Charlie back out into the kitchen and stood there, beer bottles in hand, talking to him as he cooked. They stirred the unkilled pasta to keep the pot from boiling over, checked out the spices in the spice rack, and stuck their noses deep into the saucepot, sniffing with great interest and appreciation. Charlie found them surprisingly easy to talk to. They were about his age. Both had been born in Tibet, and both had spent years, they did not say how many, imprisoned by the Chinese, like so many other Tibetan Buddhist monks. They had met in prison, and after their release they had crossed the Himalayas and escaped Tibet together, afterwards making their way gradually to Khembalung.

'Amazing,' Charlie kept saying to their stories. He could not help but compare these to his own relatively straight-forward and serene passage through the years. 'And now, after all that, you're getting flooded?'

'Many times,' they said in unison. Padma, still sniffing Charlie's sauce as if it were the perfect ambrosia, elaborated. 'Used to happen only every eighteen years or about, moon tides, you know. We could plan it happening, and be prepared. But now, whenever the monsoon hits hard.'

'Also every month at moontide,' Sucandra added. 'Certainly three, four times a year. No one can live that way for long. If it gets worse, then the island will no longer be habitable. So we came here.'

Charlie shook his head, tried to joke: 'This place may be lower in elevation than your island.'

They laughed politely. Not the funniest joke. Charlie said, 'Listen, speaking of elevation, have you talked to the other low-lying countries?'

Padma said, 'Oh yes, we are part of the League of Drowning Nations, of course. Charter member.'

'Headquarters in the Hague, near the World Court.'

'Very appropriate,' Charlie said. 'And now you are establishing an embassy here . . .'

'To argue our case, yes.'

Sucandra said, 'We must speak to the hyperpower.'

The two men smiled cheerily.

'Well. That's very interesting.' Charlie tested the pasta to see if it was ready. 'I've been working on climate issues myself, for Senator Chase. I'll have to get you in there to talk to him. And you need to hire a good firm of lobbyists too.'

'Yes?' They regarded him with interest. Padma said, 'You think it best?'

'Yes. Definitely. You're here to lobby the US government, that's what it comes down to. And there are pros in town to help foreign governments do that. I used to do it myself, and I've still got a good friend working for one of the better firms. I'll put you in touch with him and you can see what he tells you.'

Charlie slipped on potholders and lifted the pasta pot over to the sink, tipped it into the colander until it was overflowing. Always a problem with their little colander, which he never thought to replace except at moments like this. 'I

93

think my friend's firm already represents the Dutch on these issues – oops – so it's a perfect match. They'll be knowledgeable about your suite of problems, you'll fit right in there.'

'Do they lobby for Tibet?'

'That I don't know. Separate issues, I should think. But they have a lot of client countries. You'll see how they fit your needs when you talk to them.'

They nodded. 'Thank you for that. We will enjoy that.'

They took the food into the little dining room, which was a kind of corner in the passageway between kitchen and living room, and with a great deal of to-and-froing all of them just managed to fit around the dining room table. Joe consented to a booster seat to get his head up to the level of the table, where he shovelled baby food industriously into his mouth or onto the floor as the case might be, narrating the process all the while in his own tongue. Sucandra and Rudra Cakrin had seated themselves on either side of him, and they watched his performance with pleasure. Both attended to him as if they thought he was speaking a real language. They ate in a style that was not that dissimilar to his, Charlie thought – absorbed, happy, shovelling it in. The sauce was a hit with everyone but Nick, who ate his pasta plain. Joe tossed a roll across the table at Nick, who batted it aside expertly, and all the Khembalis laughed.

Charlie got up and followed Anna out to the kitchen when she went to get the salad. He said to her under his breath, 'I bet the old man speaks English too.'

'What?'

'It's like in that Ang Lee movie, remember? The old man pretends not to understand English, but really he does? It's like that I bet.'

Anna shook her head. 'Why would he do that? It's a hassle, all that translating. It doesn't give him any advantage.'

'You don't know that! Watch his eyes, see how he's getting it all.'

'He's just paying attention. Don't be silly.'

'You'll see.' Charlie leaned into her conspiratorily: 'Maybe he learned English in an earlier incarnation. Just be aware of that when you're talking around him.'

'Quit it,' she said, laughing her low laugh. '*You* be aware. *You* learn to pay attention like that.'

'Oh and then you'll believe I understand English?'

'That's right, yeah.'

They returned to the dining room, laughing, and found Joe holding forth in a language anyone could understand, a language of imperious gesture and commanding eye, and the assumption of authority in the world. Which worked like a charm over them all, even though he was babbling.

After salad, and seconds on the pasta, they returned to the living room and settled around the coffee table again. Anna brought out tea and cookies. 'We'll have to have Tibetan tea next time,' she said.

The Khembalis nodded uncertainly.

'An acquired taste,' Drepung suggested. 'Not actually tea as you know it.'

'Bitter,' Padma said appreciatively.

'You can use as blood coagulant,' Sucandra said.

Drepung added, 'Also we add yak butter to it, aged until a bit rancid.'

'The butter has to be rancid?' Charlie said.

'Traditional.'

'Think fermentation,' Sucandra explained.

'Well, let's have that for sure. Nick will love it.'

A scrunch-faced pretend-scowl from Nick: Yeah right Dad.

Rudra Cakrin sat again with Joe on the floor. He stacked blocks into elaborate towers. Whenever they began to sway, Joe leaned in and chopped them to the floor. Tumbling clack of coloured wood, instant catastrophe: the two of them cast their heads back and laughed in exactly the same way. Kindred souls.

The others watched. From the couch Drepung observed the old man, smiling fondly, although Charlie thought he also saw traces of the look that Anna had tried to describe to him when explaining why she had invited them to lunch in the first place: a kind of concern that came perhaps from an intensity of love. Charlie knew that feeling. It had been a good idea to invite them over. He had groaned when Anna told him about it, life was simply Too Busy for more to be added. Or so it had seemed; though at the same time he was somewhat starved for adult company. Now he was enjoying himself, watching Rudra Cakrin and Joe play on the floor as if there were no tomorrow.

Anna was deep in conversation with Sucandra. Charlie heard Sucandra say to her, 'We give patients quantities, very small, keep records, of course, and judge results. There is a personal element to all medicine, as you know. People talking about how they feel. You can average numbers, I know you do that, but the subjective feeling remains.'

Anna nodded, but Charlie knew she thought this aspect of medicine was unscientific, and it annoyed her as such. She kept to the quantitative as much as she could in her work, as far as he could tell, precisely to avoid this kind of subjective residual in the facts.

Now she said, 'But you do support attempts to make objective studies of such matters?'

'Of course,' Sucandra replied. 'Buddhist science is much like Western science in that regard.'

Anna nodded, brow furrowed like a hawk. Her definition of science was extremely narrow. 'Reproducible studies?'

'Yes, that is Buddhism precisely.'

Now Anna's eyebrows met in a deep vertical furrow that split the horizontal ones higher on her brow. 'I thought Buddhism was a kind of feeling, you know – meditation, compassion?'

'This is to speak of the goal. What the investigation is for. Same for you, yes? Why do you pursue the sciences?'

'Well, to understand things better, I guess.'

This was not the kind of thing Anna thought about. It was like asking her why she breathed.

'And why?' Sucandra persisted, watching her.

'Well – just because.'

'A matter of curiosity.'

'Yes, I suppose so.'

'But what if curiosity is a luxury?'

'How so?'

'In that first you must have a full belly. Good health, a certain amount of leisure time, a certain amount of serenity. Absence of pain. Only then can one be curious.'

Anna nodded, thinking it over.

Sucandra saw this and continued. 'So, if curiosity is a value – a quality to be treasured – a form of contemplation, or prayer – then you must reduce suffering to reach that state. So, in Buddhism, understanding works to reduce suffering, and by reduction of suffering gains more knowledge. Just like science.'

Anna frowned. Charlie watched her, fascinated. This was a basic part of her self, this stuff, but largely unconsidered. Self-definition by function. She was a scientist. And science was science, unlike anything else.

Rudra Cakrin leaned forward to say something to Sucandra, who listened to him, then asked him a question in Tibetan. Rudra answered, gesturing at Anna.

Charlie shot a quick look at her – see, he was following things! Evidence!

Rudra Cakrin insisted on something to Sucandra, who then said to Anna, 'Rudra wants to say, What do you believe in?'

'Me?'

'Yes. "What do you believe in?" he says.'

'*I* don't know,' she said, surprised. 'I believe in the double-blind study.'

Charlie laughed, he couldn't help it. Anna blushed and beat on his arm, crying 'Stop it! It's *true*!'

'I *know* it is,' Charlie said, laughing harder, until she started laughing too, along with everyone else, the Khembalis looking delighted – everyone so amused that Joe got mad and stomped his foot to make them stop. But this only made them laugh more. In the end they had to stop so he would not throw a fit.

Rudra Cakrin restored his mood by diving back into the blocks. Soon he and Joe sat half-buried in them, absorbed in their play. Stack them up, knock them down. They certainly spoke the same language.

The others watched them, sipping tea and offering particular blocks to them at certain moments in the construction process. Sucandra and Padma and Anna and Charlie and Nick sat on the couches, talking about Khembalung and Washington DC and how much they were alike.

Then one tower of cubes and beams stood longer than the others had. Rudra Cakrin had constructed it with care, and the repetition of primary colours was pretty: blue, red, yellow, green, blue, yellow, red, green, blue, red, green, red. It was tall enough that ordinarily Joe would have already knocked it over, but he seemed to like this one. He stared at it, mouth hanging open in a less-than-brilliant expression. Rudra Cakrin looked over at Sucandra, said something. Sucandra replied quickly, sounding displeased, which surprised Charlie. Drepung and Padma were suddenly paying attention. Rudra Cakrin picked out a yellow cube, showed it to Sucandra and said something more. He put it on the top of the tower.

'Oooh,' Joe said. He tilted his head to one side, then the other, observing it.

'He likes that one,' Charlie noted.

At first no one answered. Then Drepung said, 'It's an old Tibetan pattern. You see it in mandalas.' He looked to Sucandra, who said something sharp in Tibetan. Rudra Cakrin replied easily, shifted so that his knee knocked a long blue cylinder into the tower, collapsing it. Joe shuddered as if startled by a noise on the street.

'Ah ga,' he declared.

The Tibetans resumed the conversation. Nick was now explaining to Padma the distinction between whales and dolphins. Sucandra went out and helped Charlie a bit with the clean-up in the kitchen; finally Charlie shooed him out, feeling embarrassed that their pots were going to end up substantially cleaner after this visit than they had been before. Sucandra had been expertly scrubbing their bottoms with a wire pad found under the sink.

Around nine-thirty they took their leave. Anna offered to call a cab, but they said the Metro was fine. They did not need guidance back to the station: 'Very easy. Interesting too. There are many fine carpets in the windows of this part of town.'

Charlie was about to explain that this was the work of Iranians who had come to Washington after the fall of the Shah, but then he thought better of it. Not a happy precedent.

Instead he said to Sucandra, 'I'll give my friend Sridar a call and ask him to agree to meet with you. He'll be very helpful to you, even if you don't end up hiring his firm.'

'I'm sure. Many thanks.' And they were off into the balmy night.

FOUR

Science in the Capital

What's New From the Department of Unfortunate Statistics?

Extinction Rate in Oceans Now Faster Than on Land. Coral Reef Collapses Leading to Mass Extinctions; Thirty Percent of Warm-water Species Estimated Gone. Fishing Stocks Depleted, UN Declares Scaleback Necessary or Commercial Species Will Crash.

Topsoil Loss Nears a Million Acres a Year. Deforestation now faster in temperate than tropical forests. Only thirty-five per cent of tropical forests left.

The average Indian consumes 200 kilograms of grain a year; the average American, 800 kilograms; the average Italian, 400 kilograms. The Italian diet was rated best in the world for heart disease.

Three hundred Tons of Weapons-grade Uranium and Plutonium Unaccounted For. High Mutation Rate of Micro-organisms Near Radioactive Waste Treatment Sites. Antibiotics in Animal Feed Reduce Medical Effectiveness of Antibiotics for Humans. Environmental oestrogens suspected in lowest-ever human sperm counts.

Two Billion Tons of Carbon Added to the Atmosphere This Year. One of the five hottest years on record. The Fed Hopes US Economy Will Grow by Four Percent in the Final Quarter.

Anna Quibler was in her office getting pumped. Her door was closed, the drapes (installed for her) were drawn. The pump was whirring in its triple sequence: low sigh, wheeze, clunk. The big suction cup made its vacuum pull during the wheeze, tugging her distended left breast outward and causing drips of white milk to fall off the end of her nipple. The milk then ran down a clear tube into the little transparent bag in a plastic protective tube, which she would fill to the ten-ounce mark.

It was an unconscious activity by now, and she was working on her computer while it happened. She only had to remember not to overfill the bottle, and to switch breasts. Her right breast produced more than the left even though they were the same size, a mystery that she had given up trying to solve. She had long since explored the biological and engineering details of this process, and had gotten not exactly bored, but as far as she could go with it, and used to the sameness of it all. There was nothing new to investigate, so she was on to other things. What Anna liked was to study new things. This was what kept her co-authoring papers with her some-time-collaborators at Duke, and kept her on the editorial board of *The Journal of Statistical Biology*, despite the fact that her job at NSF as director of the Bioinformatics Division might be said to be occupying her more than full-time already; but much of that job was administrative, and like the milk pumping, fully explored. It was in her other projects where she could still learn new things.

103

Right now her new thing was a little search investigating the NSF's ability to help Khembalung. She navigated her way through the online network of scientific institutions with an ease born of long practice, click by click.

Among the NSF's array of departments was an Office of International Science and Engineering, which Anna was impressed to find had managed to garner ten per cent of the total NSF budget. It ran an International Biological Programme, which sponsored a project called TOGA – Tropical Oceans, Global Atmosphere. TOGA funded study programmes, many including an infrastructure-dispersion element, in which the scientific infrastructure built for the work was given to the host institution at the end of the study period.

Anna had already been tracking NSF's infrastructure dispersion programmes for another project, so she added this one to that list too. Projects like these were why people joked about the mobile hanging in the atrium being meant to represent a hammer and sickle, deconstructed so that outsiders would not recognize the socialistic nature of NSF's tendency to give away capital and to act as if everyone owned the world equally. Anna liked these tendencies and the projects that resulted, though she did not think of them in political terms. She just liked the way NSF focused on work rather than theory or talk. That was her preference too. She liked quantitative solutions to quantified problems.

In this case, the problem was the Khembalis' little island (fifty-two square kilometres, their website said), which was clearly in all-too-good a location to contribute to ongoing studies of Gangean flooding and tidal storms in the Indian Ocean. Anna tapped at her keyboard, bookmarking for an e-mail to Drepung, cc-ing also the Khembalung Institute for Higher Studies, which he had told her about. This institute's website indicated it was devoted to medicinal and religious studies (whatever those were, she didn't want to know) but that would be all right – if the Khembalis could get a good proposal together, the need for a wider range of fields among their researchers could become part of its 'broader impacts' element, and thus an advantage.

She searched the web further. USGCRP, the US Global Change Research Programme, two billion dollars a year; the South Asian START Regional Research Centre (SAS-RRC), based at the National Physical Laboratory in New Dehli, stations in Bangladesh, Nepal, and Mauritius . . . China and Thailand, aerosol study . . . INDOEX, the Indian Ocean Experiment, also concerned with aerosols, as was its offspring, Project Asian Brown Cloud. These studied the ever-thickening haze covering South Asia and making the monsoon irregular, with disastrous results. Certainly Khembalung was well situated to join that study. Also ALGAS, the Asia Least Cost Greenhouse Gas Abatement Strategy; and LOICZ, Land Ocean Interaction In the Coastal Zones. That one had to be right on the money. Sri Lanka was the leader there, lots of estuarine modelling – Khembalung would make a perfect study site. Training, networking, bio-geo-chemical cycle budgeting, socio-economic modelling, impacts on the coastal systems of South Asia. Bookmark the site, add to the e-mail. A research facility in the mouth of the Ganges would be a very useful thing for all concerned.

'Ah shit.'

She had overflowed the milk bottle. Not the first time for that mistake. She turned off the pump, poured off some of the milk from the full bottle into a four-ounce sac. She always filled quite a few four-ouncers, for use as snacks or supplements when Joe was feeling extra hungry; she had never told Charlie that most of these were the result of her inattention. Since Joe often was extra hungry, Charlie said, they were useful.

As for herself, she was starving. It was always that way after pumping sessions. Each twenty ounces of milk she gave was the result of some thousand calories burned by her in the previous day, as far as she had been able to calculate; the analyses she had found had been pretty rough. In any case, she could with a clear conscience (and great pleasure) run down to the pizza place and eat till she was stuffed. Indeed she needed to eat or she would get light-headed.

But first she had to pump the other breast at least a little, because let-down happened in both when she pumped, and she would end up uncomfortable if she didn't. So she put the ten-ouncer in the little refrigerator, then got the other side going into the four-ouncer, while printing out a list of all the sites she had visited, so that over her lunch she could write notes on them before she forgot what she had learned.

She called Drepung, who answered his cell phone number.

'Drepung, can you meet for lunch? I've got some ideas for how you might get some science support there in Khembalung. Some of it's from NSF, some from elsewhere.'

'Yes, of course Anna, thanks very much. I'll meet you at the Food Factory in twenty minutes, if that's all right, I'm just trying to buy some shoes for Rudra down the street here.'

'Perfect. What kind are you getting him?'

'Running shoes. He'll love them.'

On her way out she ran into Frank, also headed for the elevator.

'What you got?' he asked, gesturing at her list.

'Some stuff for the Khembalis,' she said. 'Various programmes we run or take part in that might help them out.'

'So they can study how to adapt to higher sea levels?'

She frowned. 'No, it's more than that. We can get them a lot of infrastructural help if it's configured right.'

'Good. But, you know. In the end they're going to need

more than studies. And NSF doesn't do remediation. It just serves its clients. Pays for their studies.'

Frank's comment bugged Anna, and after a pleasant lunch with Drepung she went up to her office and called Sophie Harper, NSF's liaison to Congress.

'Sophie, does NSF ever do requests for proposals?'

'Not for a long time. In general it's been policy to make the programme proposal-driven.'

'So is there any way that NSF can, you know, set the agenda so to speak?'

'I don't know what you mean. We ask Congress for funding in very specific ways, and they earmark the money they give us for very specific purposes.'

'So we might be able to ask for funds for various things?'

'Yes, we do that. I think the way to think of it is that science sets its own agenda. To tell the truth, that's why the appropriations committees don't like us very much.'

'Why?'

'Because they hold the purse strings, honey. And they're very jealous of that power. I've had senators who believe the Earth is flat say to me, "Are you trying to tell me that *you* know what's good for science better than *I* do?" And of course that's exactly what I'm trying to tell them, because it's true, but what can you say? That's the kind of person we sometimes have to deal with. Even with the best of committees, there's a basic dislike for science's autonomy.'

'But we're only free to study things.'

'I don't know what you mean.'

Anna sighed. 'I don't either. Listen Sophie, thanks for that. I'll get back to you when I have a better idea what I'm trying to ask.'

'Always here. Check out NSF's history pages on the website, you'll learn some things you didn't know.'

*   *   *

Anna hung up, and then did that very thing.

She had never gone to the website's history pages before; she was not much for looking back. But she valued Sophie's advice, and as she read, she realized Sophie had been right; because she had worked there for so long, unconsciously she had felt that she knew the Foundation's story. But it wasn't true.

Basically it was a story of science struggling to extend its reach in the world, with mixed success. After World War Two, Vannevar Bush, head of the wartime Office of Science and Technology, advocated a permanent federal agency to support basic scientific research. He argued that it was basic scientific research that had won the war (radar, penicillin, the bomb), and Congress had been convinced, and had passed a bill bringing the NSF into being.

After that it was one battle after another, with both Congress and the President, contesting how much say scientists would have in setting national policy. President Truman forcing a presidentially-selected board of directors on the Foundation in the beginning. President Nixon abolishing the Office of Science and Technology, which NSF had in effect staffed, replacing it with a single 'scientific advisor'. The Gingrich Congress abolishing its Office of Technology Assessment. The Bush administration's zeroing out major science programmes in every single budget. On it went.

Only occasionally in this political battle did science rally and win a few. After Sputnik, scientists were begged to take over again; NSF's budget had ballooned. Then in the 1960s, when everyone was an activist, NSF had created a programme called 'Interdisciplinary Research Relevant to Problems of Our Society'. What a name from its time that was!

Although, come to think of it, the phrase described very well what Anna had had in mind when querying Sophie in the first place. Interdisciplinary research, relevant to problems of our society – was that really such a Sixties joke of an idea?

Back then, IRRPOS had morphed into RANN, 'Research Applied to National Needs'. RANN had then been killed for being too applied; President Nixon had not liked its objections to his anti-ballistic missile defence. At the same time he pre-emptively established the Environmental Protection Agency so that it would be under him rather than Congress.

The battle for control of science went on. Many administrations and Congresses hadn't wanted technology or the environment assessed at all, as far as Anna could see. It might get in the way of business. They didn't want to know.

For Anna there could be no greater intellectual crime. It was incomprehensible to her: *they didn't want to know.* And yet they did want to call the shots. To Anna this was clearly crazy. Even Joe's logic was stronger. How could such people exist, what could they be thinking? On what basis did they build such an incoherent mix of desires, to want to stay ignorant and to be powerful as well? Were these two parts of the same insanity?

She abandoned that train of thought, and read on to the end of the piece. 'No agency operates in a vacuum,' it said. That was one way to put it! The NSF had been buffeted, grown, stagnated, adapted – done the best it could. Throughout all, its core purposes and methods had held fast: to support basic research; to award grants rather than purchase contracts; to decide things by peer review rather than bureaucratic fiat; to hire skilled scientists for permanent staff; to hire temporary staff from the expert cutting edges in every field.

Anna believed in all these, and she believed they had done demonstrable good. Fifty thousand proposals a year, eighty thousand people peer-reviewing them, ten thousand new proposals funded, twenty thousand grants continuing to be supported. All functioning to expand scientific knowledge, and the influence of science in human affairs.

She sat back in her chair, thinking it over. All that basic research, all that good work; and yet – thinking over the state of the world – somehow it had not been enough. Possibly they would have to consider doing something more.

Primates in the driver's seat. It looked like they should all be dead. Multi-car accidents, bloody incidents of road rage. Cars should have been ramming each other in huge demolition derbies, a global auto-da-fé.

But they were primates, they were social creatures. The brain had ballooned to its current size precisely to enable it to make the calculations necessary to get along in groups. These were the parts of the brain engaged when people drove in crowded traffic. Thus along with all the jockeying and frustration came the almost subliminal satisfactions of winning a competition, or the grudging solidarities of cooperating to mutual advantage. Let that poor idiot merge before his onramp lane disappeared; it would pay off in the overall speed of traffic. Thus the little primate buzz.

When things went well. But so often what one saw were people playing badly. It was like a giant game of prisoner's dilemma, the classic game in which two prisoners are separated and asked to tell tales on the other one, with release offered to them if they do. The standard computer model scoring system had it that if the prisoners cooperate with each other by staying silent, they each get three points; if both defect against the other, they each get one point; and if one defects and the other doesn't, the defector gets five points and the sap gets zero points. Using this scoring system to play the game time after time, there is a first iteration which says, it is best always to defect. That's the strategy that will

gain the most points over the long haul, the computer simulations said – if you are only playing strangers once, and
never seeing them again. And of course traffic looked as if
it was that situation.

But the shadow of the future made all the difference. Day
in and day out, you drove into the same traffic jam, with the
same basic population of players. If you therefore played the
game as if playing with the same opponent every time, which
in a sense you were, with you learning them and them learning
you, then more elaborate strategies would gain more points
than 'always defect'. The first version of the more successful
strategy was called 'tit-for-tat', in which you did to your
opponent what they last did to you. This out-competed 'always
defect', which in a way was a rather encouraging finding.
But tit-for-tat was not the perfect strategy, because it could
spiral in either direction, good or bad, and the bad was an
endless feud. Thus further trials had found successful variously revised versions of tit-for-tat, like 'generous tit-for-tat',
in which you gave opponents one defection before turning
on them, or 'always-generous', which in certain limited conditions worked well. Or, the most powerful strategy Frank
knew of, an irregularly generous tit-for-tat where you for-
gave defecting opponents once before turning on them, but
only about a third of the time, and unpredictably, so you
were not regularly taken advantage of by one of the less coop-
erative strategies, but could still pull out of a death spiral of
tit-for-tat feuding if one should arise. Various versions of
these 'firm-but-fair' irregular strategies appeared to be best
if you were dealing with the same opponent over and over.

In traffic, at work, in relationships of every kind – social
life was nothing but a series of prisoner's dilemmas. Compete
or cooperate? Be selfish or generous? It would be best if you
could always trust other players to cooperate, and safely
practise always-generous; but in real life people did not turn
out to earn that trust. That was one of the great shocks of

adolescence, perhaps, that realization; which alas came to many at an even younger age. And after that you had to work things out case by case, your strategy a matter of your history, or your personality, who could say.

Traffic was not a good place to try to decide. Stop and go, stop and go, at a speed just faster than Frank could have walked. He wondered how it was that certain turn-signal indicators managed to express a great desperation to change lanes, while others seemed patient and dignified. The speed of blinking, perhaps, or how close the car hugged the lane line it wanted to cross. Although rapid blinking did look insistent and whiny, while slow blinking bespoke a determined inertia.

It had been a bad mistake to get on the Beltway in the first place. By and large Beltway drivers were defectors. In general, drivers on the East Coast were less generous than Californians, Frank found. On the West Coast they played tit-for-tat, or even firm-but-fair, because it moved things along faster. Maybe this only meant Californians had lived through that many more freeway traffic jams. People had learned the game from birth, sitting in their baby-seats, and so in California cars in two merging lanes would alternate like the halves of a zipper, at considerable speed, everyone trusting everyone else to know the game and play it right. Even young males cooperated. In that sense if none other, California was indeed the edge of history, the evolutionary edge of *homo automobilicus*.

Here on the Beltway, on the other hand, it was always defect. That was what all the SUVs were about, everyone girding up to get one point in a crash. Every SUV was a defection. Then there were the little cars that always gave way, the saps. A terrible combination. It was so slow, so unnecessarily, unobservantly slow. It made you want to scream.

And from time to time, Frank did. This was a different primate satisfaction of traffic: you could loudly curse people from ten feet away and they did not hear you. There was no way the primate brain could explain this, so it was like witnessing magic, the 'technological sublime' people spoke of, which was the emotion experienced when the primate mind could not find a natural explanation for what it saw.

And it was indeed sublime to lose all restraint and just *curse* someone ferociously, from a few feet away, and yet have no ramifications to such a grave social transgression. It was not much compared to the satisfactions of cooperation, but perhaps rarer. It was something, anyway.

He crept forward in his car, cursing. He should not have come onto the Beltway. It was often badly overloaded at this hour. Stop and go, inch along. Curse defectors and saps. Inch along.

It stayed so bad that Frank realized he was going to be late to work. And this was the morning when his bioinformatics panel was to begin! He needed to get there for the panel to start on time; there was no slack in the schedule. The panel members were all in town, having spent a boring night the night before, probably. And the Holiday Inn in the Ballston complex often did not have enough hot water to supply everyone showering at that hour of the morning, so some of the panellists would be grumpy about that. Some would be gathering at this very moment in their third-floor conference room, ready to go and feeling that there wasn't enough time to judge all the proposals on the docket. Frank had crowded it on purpose, and they had flights home late the next day that they could not miss. To arrive late in this situation would be bad form indeed, no matter how jammed the traffic on the Beltway. There would be looks, or perhaps a joke or two from Pritchard or Lee; he would have to explain himself, make excuses. It could interfere with his plan. He cursed the driver of a car cutting uselessly in front of him.

Then he was coming up to Route 66, and impulsively he decided to get on it going east, even though at this hour it was restricted to High Occupancy Vehicles only. Normally Frank obeyed this rule, but feeling a little desperate, he took the turn and curved onto 66, where traffic was indeed moving faster. Every vehicle was occupied by at least two people, of course, and Frank stayed in the right lane and drove as unobtrusively as possible, counting on the generally inward attention of multiply-occupied vehicles to keep too many people from noticing his transgression. Of course there were highway patrol cars on the look-out for lawbreakers like Frank, so he was taking a risk that he didn't like to take, but it seemed to him a lower risk than staying on the Beltway as far as arriving late was concerned.

He drove in great suspense, therefore, until finally he could signal to get off at Fairfax. Then as he approached he saw a police car parked beside the exit, its officers walking back towards their car after dealing with another miscreant. They might easily look up and see him.

A big old pick-up truck was slowing down to exit before him, and again without pausing to consider his actions, Frank floored the accelerator, swerved around the truck on its left side, using it to block the policemen's view, then cut back across in front of the truck, accelerating so as not to bother it. Room to spare and no one the wiser. He curved to the right down the exit lane, slowing for the light around the turn.

Suddenly there was loud honking from behind, and his rearview mirror had been entirely filled by the front grille of the pick-up truck, its headlights at about the same height as the roof of his car. Frank speeded up. Then, closing on the car in front of him, he had to slow down. Suddenly the truck was now passing him on the left, as he had passed it earlier, even though this took the truck up onto the exit lane's tilted shoulder. Frank looked and glimpsed the infuriated face of the driver, leaning over to shout down at him. Long stringy hair, moustache, red skin, furious anger.

Frank shrugged, making a face and gesture that said *What?*. He slowed down so that the truck could cut in front of him, a good thing as it slammed into the lane so hard it missed Frank's left headlight by an inch. He would have struck Frank for sure if Frank hadn't slowed down. What a jerk!

Then the guy hit his brakes so hard that Frank nearly rear-ended him, which could have been a disaster given how high the truck was jacked up. Frank would have hit windshield first.

'What the *fuck*!' Frank said, shocked. 'Fuck you! I didn't come anywhere near you!'

The truck came to a full stop, right there on the exit.

'Jesus, you fucking idiot!' Frank shouted.

Maybe Frank had cut closer to this guy than he thought he had. Or maybe the guy was hounding him for driving solo on 66, even though he had been doing the same thing himself. Now his door flew open and out he jumped, swaggering back towards Frank. He caught sight of Frank still shouting, stopped and pointed a quivering finger, reached into the bed of his truck and pulled out a crowbar.

Frank reversed gear, backed up and braked, shifted into drive and hauled on his steering wheel as he accelerated around the pick-up truck's right side. People behind them were honking, but they didn't know the half of it. Frank zoomed down the now empty exit lane, shouting triumphant abuse at the crazy guy.

Unfortunately the traffic light at the end of the exit ramp was red and there was a car stopped there, waiting for it to change. Frank had to stop. Instantly there was a *thunk* and he jerked forward. The pick-up truck had rear-ended him, tapping him hard from behind.

'YOU FUCKER!' Frank shouted, now frightened; he had tangled with a madman! The truck was backing up, presumably to ram him again, so he put his little Honda in reverse and shot back into the truck, like hitting a wall, then shifted again and shot off into the narrow gap to the right of the car waiting at the light, turning right and accelerating into a gap between the cars zipping by, which caused more angry honks. He checked his rearview mirror and saw that the light had changed and the pick-up truck was turning to follow him, and not far behind. 'Shit!'

Frank accelerated, saw an opening in traffic coming the other way, and took a sharp left across all lanes onto Glebe, even though it was the wrong direction for NSF. Then he floored it and began weaving desperately through cars he was rapidly overtaking, checking the rearview mirror when he could. The pick-up appeared in the distance, squealing onto Glebe after him. Frank cursed in dismay.

He decided to drive directly to a fire station he recalled seeing on Lee Highway. He took a left on Lee and accelerated as hard as the little fuel-cell car could to the fire station, squealing into its parking lot and then jumping out and hurrying toward the building, looking back down Lee towards Glebe.

But the madman never appeared. Gone. Lost the trail, or lost interest. Off to harass someone else.

Cursing still, Frank checked his car's rear. No visible damage, amazingly. He got back in and drove south to the NSF building, involuntarily reliving the experience. He had no clear idea why it had happened. He had driven around the guy but he had not really cut him off, and though it was true he had been poaching on 66, so had the guy. It was inexplicable; and it occurred to him that in the face of such behaviour, modeling devises like prisoner's dilemma were useless. People did not make rational judgements. Especially, perhaps, the people driving too-large pick-up trucks, this one of the dirty-and-dinged variety rather than the factory-fresh steroidal battleships that the area's carpenters drove. Possibly then it had been some kind of class thing, the resentment of an unemployed gas-guzzler against a white-collar type in a fuel-cell car. The past attacking the future, reactionary attacking progressive, poor attacking affluent. A beta male in an alpha machine, enraged that an alpha male thought he was so alpha he could zip around in a beta machine and get away with it.

Something like that. Some kind of asshole jerk-off loser, already drunk and disorderly at seven a.m.

Despite all that, Frank found himself driving into the NSF building's basement parking with just enough time to get to the elevators and up to the third floor at the last possible on-time moment. He hurried to that floor's men's room, splashed water on his face. He had to clear his mind of the ugly incident immediately, and it had been so strange and unpleasant that this was not particularly difficult. Incongruent awfulness without consequence is easily dismissed from the mind. So he pulled himself together, went out to do his job. Time to concentrate on the day's work. His plan for the panel was locked in by the people he had convened for it. The scare on the road only hardened his resolve, chilled his blood.

He entered the conference room assigned to their panel. Its big inner window gave everyone the standard view of the rest of NSF, and the panellists who hadn't been there before looked up into the beehive of offices making the usual comments about *Rear Window* and the like. 'A kind of ersatz collegiality,' one of them said, must have been Nigel Pritchard.

'Keeps people working.'

On the savannah a view like this would have come from an high outcrop, where the troop would be resting in relative safety, surveying everything important in their lives. In the realm of grooming, of chatter, of dominance conflicts. Perfect, in other words, for a grant proposal evaluation panel, which in essence was one of the most ancient of discussions: whom do we let in, whom do we kick out? A basic troop economy, of social credit, of access to food and mates – everything measured and exchanged in deeds good and bad – yes – it was another game of prisoner's dilemma. They never ended.

Frank liked this one. It was very nuanced compared to most of them, and one of the few still outside the world of money. Anonymous peer review – unpaid labor – a scandal!

But science didn't work like capitalism. That was the rub, that was one of the rubs in the general dysfunction of the world. Capitalism ruled, but money was too simplistic and inadequate a measure of the wealth that science generated. In science, one built up over the course of a career a fund of 'scientific credit', by giving work to the system in a way that could seem altruistic. People remembered what you gave, and later on there were various forms of return on the gift – jobs, labs. In that sense a good investment for the individual, but in the form of a gift to the group. It was the non-zero-sum game that prisoner's dilemma could become if everyone played by the strategies of always-generous, or, better, firm-but-fair. That was one of the things science was – a place that one entered by agreeing to hold to the strategies of cooperation, to maximize the total return of the game.

In theory that was true. It was also the usual troop of primates. There was a lot of tit-for-tat. Defections happened. Everyone was jockeying for a lab of their own, or any project of their own. As long as that was generating enough income for a comfortable physical existence for oneself and one's family, then one had reached the optimal human state. Having money beyond that was unnecessary, and usually involved a descent into the world of hassle and stupidity. That was what greed got you. So there was in science a sufficiency of means, and an achievable limit to one's goals, that kept it tightly aligned with the brain's deepest savannah values. A scientist wanted the same things out of life as an *Australopithecus*; and here they were.

Thus Frank surveyed the panellists milling about the room with a rare degree of happiness. 'Let's get started.'

They sat down, putting laptops and coffee cups beside the computer consoles built into the tabletop. These allowed the panellists to see a spreadsheet page for each proposal in turn, displaying their grades and comments. This particular group all knew the drill. Some of them had met before, more had read each other's work.

There were eight of them sitting around the long cluttered conference table.

Dr Frank Vanderwal, moderator, NSF (on leave from University of California, San Diego, Dept. of Bioinformatics)

Dr Nigel Pritchard, Georgia Institute of Technology, Computer Sciences

Dr Alice Freundlich, Harvard University, Dept. of Biochemistry

Dr Habib Ndina, University of Virginia Medical School

Dr Stuart Thornton, University of Maryland, College Park, Genomics Department

Dr Francesca Taolini, Massachusetts Institute of Technology, Center for Biocomputational Studies

Dr Jerome Frenkel, University of Pennsylvania, Department of Genomics

Dr Yao Lee, Cambridge University (visiting GWU's Dept. of Microbiology)

Frank made his usual introductory remarks and then said, 'We've got a lot of them to go through this time. I'm sorry it's so many, but that's what we've received. I'm sure we'll hack our way through them all if we keep on track. Let's start with the fifteen-minutes-per-jacket drill, and see if we can get twelve or even fourteen done before lunch. Sound good?'

Everyone nodded and tapped away, calling up the first one.

'Oh, and before we start, let's have everyone give me their conflict-of-interest forms, please. I have to remind you that

120

as referees here, you have a conflict if you're the applying principal investigator's thesis advisor or advisee, an employee of the same institution as the PI or a co-PI, a collaborator within the last four years of the PI or a co-PI, an applicant for employment in any department at the submitting institution, a recipient of an honorarium or other pay from the submitting institution within the last year, someone with a close personal relationship to the PI or a co-PI, a shareholder in a company participating in the proposal, or someone who would otherwise gain or lose financially if the proposal were awarded or declined.

'Everybody got that? Okay, hand those forms down to me, then. We'll have a couple of people step outside for some of the proposals today, but mostly we're clear as far as I know, is that right?'

'I'll be leaving for the Esterhaus proposal, as I told you,' Stuart Thornton said.

Then they started the group evaluations. This was the heart of their task for that day and the next – also the heart of NSF's method, indeed of science more generally. Peer review; a jury of fellow-experts. Frank clicked the first proposal's page onto his screen. 'Seven reviewers, forty-four jackets. Let's start with EIA-02 18599, "Electromagnetic and Informational Processes in Molecular Polymers". Habib, you're the lead on this?'

Habib Ndina nodded and opened with a description of the proposal. 'They want to immobilize cytoskeletal networks on biochips, and explore whether tubulin can be used as bits in protein logic gates. They intend to do this by measuring the electric dipole moment, and what the PI calls the predicted kink-solitonic electric dipole moment flip waves.'

'Predicted by whom?'

'By the PI.' Habib smiled. 'He also states that this will be a method to test out the theories of the so-called "quantum brain".'

121

'Hmm.' People read past the abstract.

'What are you thinking?' Frank said after a while. 'I see Habib has given it a good, Stuart a fair, and Alice a very good.'

This represented the middle range of their scale, which ran Poor, Fair, Good, Very Good and Excellent.

Habib replied first. 'I'm not so sure that you can get these biochips to array in neural nets. I saw Inouye try something like that at MIT, and they got stuck at the level of chip viability.'

'Hmm.'

The others chimed in with questions and opinions. At the end of fifteen minutes, Frank stopped the discussion and asked them to mark their final judgements in the two categories they used, *Intellectual Merit* and *Broader Impacts*.

Frank summed up. 'Four Goods, two Very Goods and a Fair. Okay, let's move on. But tell you what, I'm going to start the big board right now.'

He had a whiteboard in the corner next to him, and a pile of Post-it pads on the table. He drew three zones on the whiteboard with a marker, and wrote at the top *Fund*, *Fund If Possible*, and *Don't Fund*.

'I'll put this one in the *Fund If Possible* column for now, although naturally it may get bumped.' He stuck the proposal's Post-it in the middle zone. 'We'll move these around as the day progresses and we get a sense of the range.'

Then they began the next one. 'Okay. "Efficient Decoherence Control Algorithms for Computing Genome Construction."'

This jacket Frank had assigned to Stuart Thornton.

Thornton started by shaking his head. 'This one's gotten two Goods and two Fairs, and it wasn't very impressive to me either. It may be a candidate for limited discussion. It doesn't really exhibit a grasp of the difficulties involved with codon tampering, and I think it replicates the work being done in Seattle by Johnson's lab. The applicant seems to have been too busy with the broader impacts component to fully acquaint himself with the literature. Besides which, it won't work.'

People laughed shortly at this extra measure of disdain, which was palpable, and to those who didn't know Thornton, a little surprising. But Frank had seen Stuart Thornton on panels before. He was the kind of scientist who habitually displayed an ultra-pure devotion to the scientific method, in the form of a relentless scepticism about everything. No study was designed tightly enough, no data were clean enough. To Frank it seemed obvious that it was really a kind of insecurity, part of the gestural set of a beta male convincing the group he was tough enough to be an alpha male, and maybe already was.

The problem with these gestures was that in science one's intellectual power was like the muscle mass of an *Australopithecus*, there for all to see. You couldn't fake it. No matter how much you ruffed your fur or exposed your teeth, in the end your intellectual strength was discernible in what you said and how insightful it was. Mere scepticism was like baring teeth; anyone could do it. For that reason Thornton was a bad choice for a panel, because while people could see his attitude and try to discount it, he set a tone that was hard to shake off. If there was an always-defector in the group, one had to be less generous oneself in order not to become a sap.

That was why Frank had invited him.

Thornton went on, 'The basic problem is at the level of their understanding of an algorithm. An algorithm is not just a simple sequence of mathematical operations that can each be performed in turn. It's a matter of designing a grammar that will adjust the operations at each stage, depending on what the results are from the stage before. There's a very specific encoding math that makes that work. They don't have that here, as far as I can tell.'

The others nodded and tapped in notes at their consoles. Soon enough they were on to the next proposal, that one posted under *Don't Fund*.

Now Frank could predict with some confidence how the rest of the day would go. A depressed norm had been set, and even though the third reporter, Alice Freundlich from Harvard, subtly rebuked Thornton by talking about how well-designed her first jacket was, she did so in a less generous context, and was not over-enthusiastic. 'They think that the evolutionary processes of gene conservation can be mapped by cascade studies, and they want to model it with big computer array simulations. They claim they'll be able to identify genes prone to mutation.'

Habib Ndina shook his head. He too was a habitual sceptic, although from a much deeper well of intelligence than Thornton's; he wasn't just making a display, he was thinking. 'Isn't the genome's past pretty much mapped by now?' he complained. 'Do we really need more about evolutionary history?'

'Well, maybe not. Broader impacts might suffer there.'

And so the day proceeded, and, with some subliminal prompting from Frank ('Are you sure they have the lab space?' 'Do you think that's really true though?' 'How would that work?' 'How could that work?') the full Shooting Gallery Syndrome slowly emerged. The panellists very slightly lost contact with their sense of the proposals as human efforts performed under a deadline, and started to compare them to some perfect model of scientific practice. In that light, of course, all the candidates were wanting. They all had feet of clay and their proposals all became clay pigeons, cast into the air for the group to take potshots at. New jacket tossed up: bang! bang! bang!

'This one's toast,' someone said at one point.

Of course a few people in such a situation would stay anchored, and begin to shake their heads or wrinkle their

124

noses, or even protest the mood, humorously or otherwise. But Frank had avoided inviting any of the real stalwarts he knew, and Alice Freundlich did no more than keep things pleasant. The impulse in a group towards piling on was so strong that it often took on extraordinary momentum. On the savannah it would have meant an expulsion and a hungry night out. Or some poor guy torn limb from limb.

Frank didn't need to tip things that far. Nothing explicit, nothing heavy. He was only the facilitator. He did not express an obvious opinion on the substance of the proposals at any point. He watched the clock, ran down the list, asked if everybody had said what they wanted to say when there was three minutes left out of the fifteen; made sure everyone got their scores into the system at the end of the discussion period. 'That's an Excellent and five Very Goods, Alice do you have your scores on this one?'

Meanwhile the discussions got tougher and tougher.

'I don't know what she could have been thinking with this one, it's absurd!'

'Let me start by suggesting limited discussion.'

Frank began subtly to apply the brakes. He didn't want them to think he was a bad panel manager.

Nevertheless, the attack mood gained momentum. Baboons descending on wounded prey; it was almost Pavlovian, a food-rewarded joy in destruction that did not bode well for the species. The pleasure taken in wrecking anything meticulous. Frank had seen it many times: a carpenter doing demolition with a sledgehammer, a vet who went duck-hunting at weekends . . . It was unfortunate, given their current overextended moment in planetary history, but nevertheless real. As a species they were therefore probably doomed. And so the only real adaptive strategy, for the individual, was to do one's best to secure one's own position. And sometimes that meant a little strategic defection.

*　　　*　　　*

125

Near the end of the day it was Thornton's turn again. Finally they had come to the proposal from Yann Pierzinski. People were getting tired.

Frank said, 'Okay, almost done here. Let's finish them off, shall we? Two more to go. Stu, we're to you again, on "Mathematical and Algorithmic Analysis of Palindromic Codon Sequences as Predictors of Gene/Protein Expression". Mandel and Pierzinski, Caltech.'

Thornton shook his head wearily. 'I see it's got a couple of Very Goods from people, but I give it a fair. It's a nice thought, but it seems to be promising too much. I mean, predicting the proteome from the genome would be enough in itself, but then understanding how the genome evolved, building error-tolerant biocomputers – it's like a list of the big unsolved problems.'

Francesca Taolini asked him what he thought of the algorithm that the proposal hoped to develop.

'It's too sketchy to be sure! That's really what he's hoping to find, as far as I can tell. There would be a final tool box with a software environment and language, then a gene grammar to make sense of palindromes in particular, he seems to think those are important, but I think they're just redundancy and repair sequences, that's why the palindromic structure. They're like the reinforcement at the bottom of a zipper. To think that he could use this to predict all the proteins that a particular gene would produce!'

'But if you could, you would see what proteins you would get without needing to do microassays and use crystallography to see what came up,' Francesca pointed out. 'That would be very useful. I thought the line he was following had potential, myself. I know people working on something like this, and it would be good to have more people on it, it's a broad front. That's why I gave it a Very Good, and I'd still recommend we fund it.' She kept her eyes on her screen.

'Well yeah,' Thornton said crossly, 'but where would he get the biosensors that would tell him if he was right or not? There's no controls.'

'That would be someone else's problem. If the predictions were turning out good you wouldn't have to test all of them, that would be the point.'

Frank waited a beat. 'Anyone else?' he said in a neutral tone.

Pritchard and Yao Lee joined in. Lee obviously thought it was a good idea, in theory. He started describing it as a kind of cookbook with evolving recipes, and Frank ventured to say, 'How would that work?'

'Well, by successive iterations of the operation, you know. It would be to get you started, suggest directions to try.'

'Look,' Francesca interjected, 'eventually we're going to have to tackle this issue, because until we do, the mechanics of gene expression are just a black box. It's a very valid line of enquiry.'

'Habib?' Frank asked.

'It would be nice, I guess, if he could make it work. It's not so easy. It would be like a roll of the dice to support it.'

Before Francesca could collect herself and start again, Frank said, 'Well, we could go round and round on that, but we're out of time on this one, and it's late. Those of you who haven't done it yet, write down your scores, and let's finish with one more from Alice before we go to dinner.'

Hunger made them nod and tap away at their consoles, and then they were on to the last one for the day, 'Ribozymes as Molecular Logic Gates'. When they were done with that, Frank stuck its Post-it on the whiteboard with the rest. Each little square of paper had its proposal's averaged scores written on it. It was a tight scale; the difference between 4.63 and 4.70 could matter a great deal. They had already put three proposals in the *Fund* column, two in the *Fund If Possible*, and six in the *Don't Fund*. The rest were stuck to the bottom of the board, waiting to be sorted out the following day. Pierzinski's was among those.

That evening the group went out for dinner at Tara, a good nearby Thai restaurant with a wall-sized fish tank. The conversation was animated and wide-ranging, the mood getting better as the meal wore on. Afterwards a few of them went to the hotel bar; the rest retreated to their rooms. At eight the next morning they were back in the conference room doing everything over again, working their way through the proposals with an increasing efficiency. Thornton recused himself for a discussion of a proposal from someone at his university, and the mood in the room noticeably lightened; even when he returned they held to this. They were learning each other's predilections, and sometimes jetted off into discussions of theory that were very interesting even though they were only a few minutes long. Some of the proposals brought up interesting problems, and several strong ones in a row made them aware of just how amazing contemporary work in bioinformatics was, and what some of the potential benefits for human health might be, if all this were to come together and make a robust biotechnology. The shadow of a good future drove the group towards more generous strategies. The second day went better. The scores were, on average, higher.

'My Lord,' Alice said at one point, looking at the whiteboard. 'There are going to be some very good proposals that we're not going to be able to fund.'

Everyone nodded. It was a common feeling at the end of a panel.

'I sometimes wonder what would happen if we could fund about ninety per cent of all the applications. You know, only reject the limited-discussions. Fund everything else.'

'It might speed things up.'

'Might cause a revolution.'

'Now back to reality,' Frank suggested. 'Last jacket here.'

When they had all tapped in their grading of the forty-fourth jacket, Frank quickly crunched the numbers on his general spreadsheet, sorting the applicants into a hierarchy from one to forty-four, with a lot of ties.

He printed out the results, including the funding each proposal was asking for; then called the group back to order. They started moving the unsorted Post-its up into one or another of the three columns.

Pierzinski's proposal had ended up ranked fourteenth out of the forty-four. It wouldn't have been that high if it weren't for Francesca. Now she urged them to fund it; but because it was in fourteenth place, the group decided it should be put in *Fund If Possible*, with a bullet.

Frank moved its Post-it on the whiteboard up into the *Fund If Possible* column, keeping his face perfectly blank. There were eight in *Fund If Possible*, six in *Fund*, twelve in *Don't Fund*. Eighteen to go, therefore, but the arithmetic of the situation would doom most of these to the *Don't Fund* column, with a few stuck into the *Fund If Possible* as faint hopes.

Later it would be Frank's job to fill out a Form Seven for every proposal, summarizing the key aspects of the discussion, acknowledging outlier reviews that were more than one full place off the average, and explaining any 'Excellents' awarded to non-funded reviews; this was part of keeping the process transparent to the applicants, and making sure that nothing untoward happened. The panel was advisory only, NSF had the right to overrule it, but in the great majority of cases the panels' judgements would stand – that was the whole point – that was scientific objectivity, at least in this part of the process.

In a way it was funny. Solicit seven intensely subjective and sometimes contradictory opinions; quantify them; average them; and that was objectivity. A numerical grading that you could point to on a graph. Ridiculous, of course. But it was the best they could do. Indeed, what other choice did they have? No algorithm could make these kinds of decisions. The only computer powerful enough to do it was one made up of a networked array of human brains – that is to say, a panel. Beyond that they could not reach.

So they discussed the proposals one last time, their scientific potential and also their educational and benefit-to-society aspects, the 'broader impacts' rubric, usually spelled out rather vaguely in the proposals, and unpopular with research purists. But as Frank put it now, 'NSF isn't here just to *do* science but also to *promote* science, and that means all these other criteria. What it will add to society.' What Anna will do with it, he almost said.

And speak of the devil, Anna came in to thank the panellists for their efforts, slightly flushed and formal in her remarks. When she left, Frank said, 'Thanks from me too. It's been exhausting as usual, but good work was done. I hope to see all of you here again at some point, but I won't bother you too soon either. I know some of you have planes to catch, so let's quit now, and if any of you have anything else you want to add, tell me individually. Okay, we're done.'

Frank printed out a final copy of the spreadsheet. The money numbers suggested they would end up funding about ten of the forty-four proposals. There were seven in the *Fund* column already, and six of those in the *Fund If Possible* column had been ranked slightly higher than Yann Pierzinski's proposal. If Frank, as NSF's representative, did not exercise any of his discretionary power to find a way to fund it, Pierzinski's proposal would be declined.

Another day for Charlie and Joe. A late spring morning, temperatures already in the high nineties and rising, humidity likewise.

They stayed in the house for the balm of the air-conditioning, falling out of the ceiling vents like spills of clear syrup. They wrestled, they cleaned house, they ate breakfast and elevenses. Charlie read some of the *Post* while Joe devastated dinosaurs. Something in the *Post* about India's drought reminded Charlie of the Khembalis, and he put in his earphone and gave his friend Sridar a call.

'Hey Sridar, it's Charlie.'

'Charlie, good to hear from you! I got your message.'

'Oh good, I was hoping you had. How's the lobbying business going?'

'We're keeping at it. We've got some interesting clients, if you know what I mean.'

'Yes I do.'

Charlie and Sridar had worked together for a lobbying firm, several years before. Now Sridar worked for Branson and Ananda, a small but prestigious firm representing several foreign governments in their dealings with the American government. Some of these governments had customs at home that made representing them to Congress a challenge.

'So you said something about a new country? I'm glad you're keeping an eye out for new clients for me.'

'Well it was through Anna, like I said.' Charlie explained

how they had met. 'When I was talking to them I thought they could use your help.'

'Oh dear, how nice.'

'Yeah well, you need some challenges.'

'Right, like I have no challenges. What's this new country then?'

'Have you heard of Khembalung?'

'I think so. One of the League of Drowning Nations?'

'Yeah that's right.'

'You're asking me to take on a sinking island nation?'

'Actually they're not sinking, it's the ocean that's rising.'

'Even worse. I mean what are we going to be able to do about that, stop global warming?'

'Well, yeah. That's the idea. But you know. There'll be all sorts of other countries working on the same thing. You'd have lots of allies.'

'Uh huh.'

'Anyway they could use your help, and they're good guys. Interesting. I think you'd enjoy them. You should at least meet with them and see.'

'Yeah okay. My plate is kinda full right now, but I could do that. No harm in meeting.'

'Oh good. Thanks Sridar, I appreciate that.'

'No problem. Hey, can I have Krakatoa too?'

'Bye.'

'Bye.'

After that Charlie was in the mood to talk, but he had no real reason to call anybody. He and Joe played again. Bored, Charlie even resorted to turning on the TV. A pundit show came on and helplessly he watched. 'They are such *lapdogs*,' he complained to Joe. 'See, that whole studio is a kind of pet's bed, and these guys sit in their places like pets in the palm of a giant, speaking what the giant wants to hear. My God how can they stand it! They know *perfectly well* what they're up to, you can see the way they parade their little hobbies to try to distract us, see that one copies definitions out of the dictionary, and that one there has memorized all the rules of *pinochle* for Christ's sake, all to disguise the fact that they have not a single principle in their heads except to defend the rich. Disgusting.'

'BOOM!' Joe concurred, catching Charlie's mood and flinging a tyrannosaurus into the radiator with a clang.

'That's right,' Charlie said. 'Good job.'

He changed the channel to ESPN 5, which showed classic women's beach volleyball all day along. Retired guys at home must be a big demographic. And so tall muscular women in bathing suits jumped around and dived in the sand; they were amazingly skilful. Charlie particularly liked the exploits of the Brazilian Jackie Silva, who always won even though she was not the best hitter, server, passer, blocker, or looker. But she was always in the right place doing the best thing, making miraculous saves and accidental winners.

'I'm going to be the Jackie Silva of Senate staffers,' Charlie told Joe.

But Joe had had enough of being in the house. 'Go!' he said imperiously, hammering the front door with a diplodocus. 'Go! Go! Go!'

'All right all right.'

His point was undeniable. They couldn't stay in this house all day. 'Let's see. What shall we do? I'm tired of the park. Let's go down to the Mall, we haven't done that for a while. The Mall, Joe! But you have to get in your backpack.'

Joe nodded and tried to climb into his baby backpack immediately, a very precarious business. He was ready to party.

'Wait, let's change your diaper first.'

'NO!'

'Ah come on Joe. Yes.'

'NO!'

'But yes.'

They fought like maniacs through the change, each ruthless

and determined, each shouting, beating, pinching. Charlie followed Jackie Silva's lead and did the necessary things.

Red-faced and sweating, finally they were ready to emerge from the house into the steambath of the city. Out they went. Down to the Metro, down into that dim cool underground world.

It would have been good if the Metro pacified Joe as it once had Nick, but in fact it usually energized him. Charlie could not understand that, he himself found the dimness and coolness a powerful soporific. But Joe wanted to play around just above the drop to the power rail, he was naturally attracted to that enormous source of energy. The hundred-thousand-watt child. Charlie ran around keeping Joe from the edge like Jackie Silva keeping the ball off the sand.

Finally a train came. Joe liked the Metro cars. He stood on the seat next to Charlie and stared at the concrete walls sliding by outside the tinted windows, then at the bright orange or pink seats, the ads, the people in their car, the brief views of the underground stations they stopped in.

A young black man got on carrying a helium-filled birthday balloon. He sat down across the car from Charlie and Joe. Joe stared at the balloon, boggled by it. Clearly it was for him a kind of miraculous object. The youth pulled down on its string and let the balloon jump back up to its full extension. Joe jerked, then burst out laughing. His giggle was like his mom's, a low gorgeous burbling. People in the car grinned to hear it. The young man pulled the balloon down again, let it go again. Joe laughed so hard he had to sit down. People began to laugh with him, they couldn't help it. The young man was smiling shyly. He did the trick again and now the whole car followed Joe into paroxysms of laughter. They laughed all the way to Metro Center.

Charlie got out, grinning, and carried Joe to the Blue/Orange level. He marvelled at the infectiousness of moods in a group. Strangers who would never meet again, unified suddenly by

134

a youth and a toddler playing a game. By laughter. Maybe the real oddity was how much one's fellow-citizens were usually like furniture in one's life.

Joe bounced in Charlie's arms. He liked Metro Center's criss-crossing mysterious vastness. The incident of the balloon was already forgotten. It had been unremarkable to him; he was still in that stage of life where all the evidence supported the idea that he was the centre of the universe, and miracles happened. Kind of like a US Senator.

Luckily Phil Chase was not like that. Certainly Phil enjoyed his life and his public role, it reminded Charlie of what he had read about FDR's attitude towards the presidency. But that was mostly a matter of being the star of one's own movie; thus, just like everyone else. No, Phil was very good to work for, Charlie thought, which was one of the ultimate tests of a person.

Their next Metro car reached the Smithsonian station, and Charlie put Joe into the backpack and on his back, and rode the escalator up and out, into the kiln blaze of the Mall.

The sky was milky-white everywhere. It felt like the inside of a sauna. Charlie fought his way through the heat to an open patch of grass in the shade of the Washington Monument. He sat them down and got out some food. The big views up to the Capitol and down to the Lincoln Memorial pleased him. Out from under the great forest. It was like escaping Mirkwood. This in Charlie's opinion accounted for the great popularity of the Mall; the monuments and the big Smithsonian buildings were nice but supplementary, it was really a matter of getting out into the open. The ordinary reality of the American West was like a glimpse of heaven here in the green depths of the swamp.

Charlie knew and cherished the old story: how the first thirteen states had needed a capital, and so someone had to give up some land for it, or else one particular state would nab the honour; and Virginia and the other southern states

135

were particularly concerned it would go to Philadelphia or New York. And so they had bickered, you give up some land, no you give it. No bureaucracy ever wanted to give up sovereignty over anything whatsoever, be it the smallest patch of sand in the sea; and so finally Virginia had said to Maryland, look, where the Potomac meets the Anacostia there's a big nasty swamp. It's worthless, dreadful, pestilent land. You'll never be able to make anything out of a festering pit like that.

True, Maryland had said, you're right. Okay, we'll give that land to the nation for its capital. But not too much! Just a section of the worst part. And good luck draining it!

And so here they were. Charlie sat on the grass, drowsing. Joe gambolled about him like a bumblebee, investigating things. The diffuse midday light lay on them like asthma. Big white clouds mushroomed to the west, and the scene turned glossy, bulging with internal light, like a computer photo with more pixels than the human eye could process. The ductile world, everything bursting with light. He really had to try to remember to bring his sunglasses on these trips.

To get a good long nap from Joe, he needed to tank him up. Charlie fought his own sleep, got the food bag out of the backpack's under-carriage pocket, waved it so Joe could see it. Joe trundled over, eyelids at half-mast; there was no time to lose. He settled into Charlie's lap and Charlie popped a bottle of Anna's milk into his mouth just as his head was snapping to the side.

They were like zombies together: Joe sucked himself unconscious while Charlie slumped over him, chin on chest, comatose. Snuggling an infant in mind-numbing heat, what could be cosier.

Clouds over the White House were billowing up like the spirit of the building's feisty inhabitant, round, dense, shiny white. In the other direction, over the Supreme Court's neighbourhood, stood a black nine-lobed cloud, dangerously laden

136

with incipient lightning. Yes, the powers of Washington were casting up thermals and forming clouds over themselves, clouds that filled out precisely the shapes and colours of their spirits. Charlie saw that each cumulobureaucracy transcended the individuals who temporarily performed its functions in the world. These transhuman spirits all had inborn characters, and biographies, and abilities and desires and habits all their own; and in the sky over the city they contested their fates with each other. Humans were like cells in their bodies. Probably one's cells also thought their lives were important and under their individual control. But the great bodies knew better.

Thus Charlie now saw that the White House was a great white thunderhead of a spirit, like an old emperor or a small-town sheriff, dominating the landscape and the other players. The Supreme Court on the other hand was dangerously dark and low, like a multi-headed minotaur, brooding and powerful. Over the white dome of the Capitol, the air shimmered; Congress was a roaring thermal so hot that no cloud could form in it.

Oh yes – there were big spirits above this low city, hammering each other like Zeus and his crowd, or Odin, or Krishna, or all of them at once. To make one's way in a world like that one had to blow like the North Wind.

He had fallen into a slumber as deep as Joe's when his phone rang. He answered it before waking, his head snapping dangerously on his neck.

'Wha.'

'Charlie? Charlie, where are you? We need you down here right now.'

'I'm already down here.'

'Really? That's great. Charlie?'

'Yes, Roy?'

'Look, Charlie, sorry to bother you, but Phil is out of town and I've got to meet with Senator Ellington in twenty minutes, and we just got a call from the White House saying that Doctor Strangelove wants to meet with us to talk about Phil's climate bill. It sounds like they're ready to listen, maybe ready to talk too, or even to deal. We need someone to get over there.'

'Now?'

'Now. You've got to get over there.'

'I'm already over there, but look, I can't. I've got Joe here with me. Where is Phil again?'

'San Francisco.'

'Wasn't Wade supposed to get back?'

'No, he's still in Antarctica. Listen Charlie, there's no one here who can do this right but you.'

'What about Andrea?' Andrea Palmer was Phil's legislative director, the person in charge of all his bills.

'She's in New York today. Besides you're the point man on this, it's your bill more than anyone else's and you know it inside and out.'

'But I've got Joe!'

'Maybe you can take Joe along.'

'Yeah right.'

'Hey, why not? Won't he be taking a nap soon?'

'He is right now.'

Charlie could see the trees backing the White House, there on the other side of the Ellipse. He could walk over there in ten minutes. Theoretically Joe would stay asleep a couple of hours. And certainly they should seize the moment on this, because so far the President and his people had shown no interest whatsoever in dealing on this issue.

'Listen,' Roy cajoled, 'I've had entire lunches with you where Joe is asleep on your back, and believe me, no one can tell the difference. I mean you hold yourself upright like you've got the weight of the world on your shoulders, but you did that *before* you had Joe, so now he just fills up that space and makes you look more normal, I swear to God. You've voted with him on your back, you've shopped, you've *showered*, hey once you even *made love with your wife* while Joe was on your back, didn't you tell me that?'

'What!'

'You told me that, Charlie.'

'I must have been drunk to tell you that, and it wasn't really sex anyway. I couldn't even move.'

Roy laughed his raucous laugh. 'Since when does that make it not sex? You had sex with Joe in a backpack asleep on your back, so you sure as hell can talk to the President's science advisor that way. Doctor Strangelove isn't going to care.'

'He's a jerk.'

'So? They're all jerks over there but the President, and he is too but he's a nice guy. And he's the *family* President, right? He would approve on principle, you can tell Strengloft that. You can say that if the President were there he would love it. He would autograph Joe's head like a baseball.'

'Yeah right.'

'Charlie, this is your bill!'

'Okay okay okay!' It was true. 'I'll go give it a try.'

So, by the time Charlie got Joe back on his back (the child was twice as heavy when asleep) and walked across the Mall and the Ellipse, Roy had made the calls and they were expecting him at the west entry to the White House. Joe was passed through security with a light-fingered shakedown that was especially squeamish around his diaper. Then they were through, and quickly escorted into a conference room.

The room was brightly lit, and empty. Charlie had never been in it before, though he had visited the White House several times. Joe weighed on his shoulders.

Dr Zacharius Strengloft, the President's science advisor, entered the room. He and Charlie had sparred by proxy several times before, Charlie whispering killer questions into Phil's ear while Strengloft testified before Phil's committee, but the two of them had never spoken one-on-one. Now they shook hands, Strengloft peering curiously over Charlie's shoulder. Charlie explained Joe's presence as briefly as he could, and Strengloft received the explanation with precisely the kind of frosty faux benevolence that Charlie had been expecting. Strengloft in Charlie's opinion was a pompous ex-academic of the worst kind, hauled out the depths of a second-rate conservative think tank when the administration's first science advisor had been sent packing for saying that global warming might be real and not only that, amenable to human mitigations. That went too far for this administration. Their line was that no one knew for sure and it would be much too expensive to do anything about even if they were certain it was coming – everything would have to change, the power generation system, cars, a shift from hydrocarbons to helium or something, they didn't know, and they didn't own patents or already existing infrastructure for that kind of new thing, so they were going to dodge the issue and let the next generation solve their own problems in their own time. In other words, the hell with them. Easier to destroy the world than to change capitalism even one little bit.

All this had become quite blatant since Strengloft's appointment. He had taken over the candidate lists for most of the federal government's science-advisory panels, and very quickly candidates were being routinely asked who they had voted for in the last election, and what they thought of stem-cell research, and abortion, and evolution. This had recently culminated in a lead industry defence witness being appointed to the panel for setting safety standards for lead in children's blood, and immediately declaring that seventy micrograms per decilitre would be harmless to children, though the EPA's maximum was ten. When his views were publicized and criticized, Strengloft had commented, 'You need a diversity of opinions to get good advice.' Mentioning his name was enough to make Anna hiss.

Be that as it may, here he was standing before Charlie; he had to be dealt with, and in the flesh he seemed friendly.

They had just got through their introductory pleasantries when the President himself entered the room.

Strengloft nodded complacently, as if he were often joined in his crucial work by the happy man.

'Oh, hello Mr President,' Charlie said helplessly.

'Hello, Charles,' the President said, and came over and shook his hand.

This was bad. Not unprecedented, or even terribly surprising; the President had become known for wandering into meetings like this, apparently by accident but perhaps not. It had become part of his legendary informal style.

Now he saw Joe asleep on Charlie's back, and stepped around Charlie to get a better view. 'What's this, Charles, you got your kid with you?'

'Yes sir, I was called in on short notice when Dr Strengloft asked for a meeting with Phil and Wade, they're both out of town.'

The President found this amusing. 'Ha! Well, good for you. That's sweet. Find me a marker pen and I'll sign his little head.' This was another signature move, so to speak. 'Is he a boy or a girl?'

'A boy. Joe Quibler.'

'Well that's great. Saving the world before bedtime, that's your story, eh Charles?' He smiled to himself and moved restlessly over to the chair at the window end of the table. One of his people was standing in the door, watching them without expression.

The President's face was smaller than it appeared on TV, Charlie found. The size of an ordinary human face, no doubt, looking small precisely because of all the TV images. On the other hand it had a tremendous solidity and three-dimensionality to it. It gleamed with reality.

His eyes were slightly close-set, as was often remarked, but apart from that he looked like an ageing movie star or catalogue model. A successful businessman who had retired to get into public service. His features, as many observers had observed, mixed qualities of several recent presidents into one blandly familiar and reassuring face, with a little dash of Ross Perot to give him a piquant antiquity and edgy charm.

Now his amused look was like that of everyone's favourite uncle. 'So they reeled you in for this on the fly.' Then, holding a hand up to stop all of them, he nearly-whispered: 'Sorry – should I whisper?'

'No sir, no need for that,' Charlie assured him in his ordinary speaking voice. 'He's out for the duration. Pay no attention to that man behind the shoulder.'

The President smiled. 'Got a wizard on your back, eh?'

Charlie nodded, smiling quickly to conceal his surprise. It was a pastime in some circles to judge just how much of a dimwit the President was, how much of a performing puppet for the people manipulating him; but facing him in person Charlie felt instantly confirmed in his minority position that the man had such a huge amount of low cunning that it amounted to a kind of genius. The President was no fool. And hip to at least the most obvious of movie trivia. Charlie couldn't help feeling a bit reassured.

Now the President said, 'That's nice, Charles, let's get to it then, shall we? I heard from Dr S. here about the meeting this morning, and I wanted to check in on it in person, because I like Phil Chase. And I understand that Phil now wants us to join in with the actions of the Intergovernmental Panel on Climate Change, to the point of introducing a bill mandating our participation in whatever action they recommend, no matter what it is. And this is a UN panel.'

'Well,' Charlie said, shifting gears into ultra-diplomatic

mode, not just for the President but for the absent Phil, who was going to be upset with him no matter what he said, since only Phil should actually be talking to the President about this stuff. 'That isn't exactly how I would put it, Mr President. You know the Senate Foreign Relations Committee held a number of hearings this year, and Phil's conclusion after all that testimony was that the global climate situation is quite real. And serious to the point of being already almost too late.'

The President shot a glance at Strengloft. 'Would you agree with that, Dr S?'

'We've agreed that there is general agreement that the observed warming is real.'

The President looked to Charlie, who said, 'That's good as far as it goes, certainly. It's what follows from that that matters – you know, in the sense of us trying to do something about it.'

Charlie swiftly rehearsed the situation, known to all: average temperatures up by six degrees Fahrenheit already, CO_2 levels in the atmosphere topping six hundred parts per million, from a start before the industrial revolution of 280, and predicted to hit a thousand ppm within a decade, which would be higher than it had been at any time in the past seventy million years. Two and a half billion metric tons of CO_2 added to the atmosphere by American industry every year, some 150 per cent more than the Kyoto agreement would have allowed if they had signed it, and rising fast. Also long-term persistence of greenhouse gases, on the order of thousands of years.

Charlie also spoke briefly of the death of all coral reefs, which would lead to even more severe consequences for oceanic ecosystems. 'The thing is, Mr President, the world's climate can shift very rapidly. There are scenarios in which the general warming causes parts of the northern hemispere to get quite cold, especially in Europe. If that were to

143

happen, Europe could become something like the Yukon of Asia.'

'Really!' the President said. 'Are we sure that would be a bad thing? Just kidding of course.'

'Of course sir, ha ha.'

The President fixed him with a look of mock displeasure. 'Well, Charles, all that may be true, but we don't know for sure if any of that is the result of human activity. Isn't that a fact?'

'Depends on what you mean by "know for sure",' Charlie said doggedly. 'Two and a half billion tons of carbon per year, that's got to make a difference, it's just plain physics. You could say it isn't for sure that the sun will come up tomorrow morning, and in a limited sense you'd be right, but I'll bet you the sun will come up.'

'Don't be tempting me to gamble now.'

'And besides, Mr President, there's also what they call the precautionary principle, meaning you don't delay acting on crucial matters when you have a disaster that might happen, just because you can't be one hundred per cent sure that it will happen. Because you can never be one hundred per cent sure of anything, and some of these matters are too important to wait on.'

The President frowned at this, and Strengloft interjected, 'Charlie, you know the precautionary principle is an imitation of actuarial insurance that has no real resemblance to it, because the risk and the premium paid can't be calculated. That's why we refused to hear any precautionary principle language in the discussions we attended at the UN. We said we wouldn't even attend if they talked about precautionary principles or ecological footprints, and we had very good reasons for those exclusions, because those concepts are not good science.'

The President nodded his 'So That Is That' nod, familiar to Charlie from many a press conference. He added, 'I always thought a footprint was kind of a simplistic measurement for something this complex anyway.'

Charlie countered, 'It's just a name for a good economic index, Mr President, calculating use of resources in terms of how much land it would take to provide them. It's pretty educational, really,' and he launched into a quick description of the way it worked. 'It's a good thing to know, like balancing your chequebook, and what it shows is that America is consuming the resources of ten times the acreage it actually occupies. So that if everyone on Earth tried to live as we do, given the greater population densities in much of the world, it would take fourteen Earths to support us all.'

'Come on, Charlie,' Dr Strengloft objected. 'Next you'll be wanting us to use Bhutan's Gross Domestic Happiness, for goodness' sake. But we can't use little countries' indices, they don't do the job. We're the hyperpower. And really, the anti-carbon dioxide crowd is a special interest lobby in itself. You've fallen prey to their arguments, but it's not like CO_2 is some toxic pollutant. It's a gas that is natural in our air, and it's essential for plants, even good for them. The last time there was a significant rise in atmospheric carbon dioxide, human agricultural productivity boomed. The Norse settled Greenland during that period, and there were generally rising lifespans.'

'The end of the Black Death might account for that,' Charlie pointed out.

'Well, maybe rising CO_2 levels ended the Black Death.'

Charlie felt his jaw gape.

'It's the bubbly in my club soda,' the President told him gently.

'Yes.' Charlie rallied. 'But a greenhouse gas nevertheless. It holds in heat that would otherwise escape back into space. And we're putting more than two billion tons of it into the atmosphere every year. It's like putting a plug in your exhaust pipe, sir. The car is bound to warm up. There's general agreement from the scientific community that it causes *really significant warming*. Has already caused it.'

'Our models show the recent temperature changes to be within the range of natural fluctuation,' Dr Strengloft replied. 'In fact, temperatures in the stratosphere have gone down. It's complex, and we're studying it, and we're going to make the best and most cost-effective response to it, because we're taking the time to do that. Meanwhile, we're already taking effective precautions. The President has asked American businesses to keep to a new national goal of limiting the growth of carbon dioxide emissions to one-third of the economy's rate of growth.'

'But that's the same ratio of emissions to growth that we have already.'

'Yes, but the President has gone further, by asking American businesses to try to reduce that ratio over the next decade by eighteen per cent. It's a growth-based approach that will accelerate new technologies, and the partnerships that we'll need with the developing world on climate change.'

As the President looked to Charlie to see what he would reply to this arrant nonsense, Charlie felt Joe stir on his back. This was unfortunate, as things were already complicated enough. The President and his science advisor were not only ignoring the specifics of Phil's bill, they were actively attacking its underlying concepts. Any hope Charlie had had that the President had come to throw his weight behind some real dickering was gone.

And Joe was definitely stirring. His face was burrowed sideways into the back of Charlie's neck, as usual, and now he began doing something that he sometimes did when napping: he latched onto the right tendon at the back of Charlie's neck and began sucking it rhythmically, like a pacifier. Always before Charlie had found this a sweet thing, one of the most momlike moments of his Mr Momhood. Now he had to steel himself against it and forge on.

The President said, 'I think we have to be very careful what kind of science we use in matters like these.'

Joe sucked a ticklish spot and Charlie smiled reflexively and then grimaced, not wanting to appear amused by this double-edged pronouncement.

'Naturally that's true, Mr President. But the arguments for taking vigorous action are coming from a broad range of scientific organizations, also governments, the UN, NGOs, universities, about ninety-seven per cent of all the scientists who have ever declared on the issue,' everyone but the very far right end of the think tank and pundit pool, he wanted to add, everyone but hack pseudo-scientists who would say anything for money, like Dr Strengloft here – but he bit his tongue and tried to shift track. 'Think of the world as a balloon, Mr President. And the atmosphere as the skin of the balloon. Now, if you wanted the thickness of the skin of a balloon to correctly represent the thickness of our atmosphere in relation to Earth, the balloon would have to be about as big as a basketball.'

This barely made sense even to Charlie, although it was a good analogy if you could enunciate it clearly. 'What I mean is that the atmosphere is really, really thin, sir. It's well within our power to alter it greatly.'

'No one contests that, Charles. But look, didn't you say the amount of CO_2 in the atmosphere was six hundred parts per million? So if that CO_2 were to be the skin of your balloon, and the rest of the atmosphere was the air inside it, then that balloon would have to be a lot bigger than a basketball, right? About the size of the moon or something?'

Strengloft snorted happily at this thought, and went to a computer console on a desk in the corner, no doubt to compute the exact size of the balloon in the President's analogy. Charlie suddenly understood that Strengloft would never have thought of this argument, and realized further – instantly thereby understanding several people in his past who had mystified him at the time – that sometimes people known for intelligence were actually quite dim, while people who seemed simple could be very sharp.

'Granted, sir, very good,' Charlie conceded. 'But think of that CO_2 skin as being a kind of glass that lets in light but traps all the heat inside. It's that kind of barrier. So the thickness isn't as important as the glassiness.'

'Then maybe more of it won't make all that much of a difference,' the President said kindly. 'Look, Charles. Fanciful comparisons are all very well, but the truth is we have to slow these emissions' growth before we can try to stop them, much less reverse them.'

This was exactly what the President had said at a recent press conference, and over at the computer Strengloft beamed and nodded to hear it, perhaps because he had authored the line. The absurdity of taking pride in writing stupid lines for a quick president suddenly struck Charlie as horribly funny. He was glad Anna wasn't there beside him, because in moments like these they could with the slightest shared glance set each other off. Even the thought of her in such a situation almost made him laugh.

So now he banished his wife and her glorious hilarity from his mind, not without a final bizarre tactile image of the back of his neck as one of her breasts, being suckled more and more hungrily by Joe. Very soon it would be time for a bottle.

Charlie persevered nevertheless. 'Sir, it's getting kind of urgent now. And there's no downside to taking the lead on this issue. The economic advantages of being in the forefront of climate rectification and bioinfrastructure mitigation are *huge*. It's a growth industry with uncharted potential. It's the future no matter which way you look at it.'

Joe clamped down hard on his neck. Charlie shivered. Hungry, no doubt about it. Would be ravenous on waking. Only a bottle of milk or formula would keep him from going ballistic at that point. He could not be roused now without

148

disaster striking. But he was beginning to inflict serious pain. Charlie lost his train of thought. He twitched. A little snort of agony combined with a giggle. He choked it back, disguised it as a smothered cough.

'What's the matter, Charles, is he waking up on you?'

'Oh no sir, still out. Maybe stirring a little ah! The thing is, if we don't address these issues now, nothing else we're doing will matter. None of it will go well.'

'That sounds like alarmist talk to me,' the President said, an avuncular twinkle in his eye. 'Let's calm down about this. You've got to stick to the commonsense idea that sustainable economic growth is the key to environmental progress.'

'Sustainable, ah!'

'What's that?'

He clamped down on a giggle. 'Sustainable's the point! Sir.'

'We need to harness the power of markets,' Strengloft said, and nattered on in his usual vein, apparently oblivious to Charlie's problem. The President however eyed him closely. Huge chomp. Charlie's spine went electric. He suppressed the urge to swat his son like a mosquito. His right fingers tingled. Very slowly he lifted a shoulder, trying to dislodge him. Like trying to budge a limpet. Sometimes Anna had to squeeze his nostrils shut to get him to come off. Don't think about that.

The President said, 'Charles, we'd be sucking the life out of the economy if we were to go too far with this. You chew on that a while. As it is, we're taking *bites* out of this problem every day. Why, I'm like a dog with a bone on this thing! Those enviro special interests are like pigs at a trough. We're weaning them from all that now, and they don't like it, but they're going to have to learn that if you can't *lick* them, you –'

And Charlie dissolved into gales of helpless laughter.

FIVE

Athena on the Pacific

California is a place apart.

Gold-chasers went west until the ocean stopped them, and there in that remote and beautiful land, separated from the rest of the world by desert and mountain, prairie and ocean, they saw there could be no more moving on. They would have to stop and make a life there.

Civil society, post-Civil War. A motley of argonauts, infused with manifest destiny and gold fever, also with Emerson and Thoreau, Lincoln and Twain, their own John Muir. They said to each other, Here at the end of the road it had better be different, or else world history has all come to naught.

So they did many things, good and bad. In the end it turned out the same as everywhere else, maybe a little more so.

But among the good things, encouraged by Lincoln, was the founding of a public university. 1867 in Berkeley, the farm at Davis in 1905, the other campuses after that; in the 1960s new ones sprang up like flowers in a field. The University of California. A power in this world.

An oceanographic institute near La Jolla wanted one of the new campuses of the sixties to be located nearby. Next door was a US Marine Corps rifle-training facility. The oceanographers asked the Marines for the land, and the

Marines said yes. Donated land, just like Washington DC, but in this case a eucalyptus grove on a sea cliff, high over the Pacific.

The University of California, San Diego.

By then California had become a crossroads, east and west all met together, San Francisco the great city, Hollywood the dream machine. UCSD was the lucky child of all that, Athena leaping out of the tall forehead of the state. Prominent scientists came from everywhere to start it, caught by the siren song of a new beginning on a Mediterranean edge to the world.

They founded a school and helped to invent a technology: biotech, Athena's gift to humankind. University as teacher and doctor too, owned by the people, no profit skimmed off. A public project in an ever-more-privatized world, tough and determined, benign in intent but very intent. What does it mean to give?

Frank considered adding a postscript to Yann Pierzinski's Form Seven, suggesting that he pursue internal support at Torrey Pines Generique. Then he decided it would be better to work through Derek Gaspar. He could do it in person during the trip he was making to San Diego to prepare for his move back.

A week later he was off. On the first flight west he fell asleep watching a DVD. Transfer at Dallas, a good people-watching airport, then up into the air again, and back to sleep.

He woke when he felt the plane tilt down. They were still over Arizona, its huge baked landforms flowing by underneath. A part of Frank that had been asleep for much longer than the nap began to wake up too: he was returning to home ground. It was amazing the way things changed when you crossed to the dry side of the ten-inches-of-rain-a-year isobar. Frank put his forehead against the inner window of the plane, looked ahead to the next burnt range coming into view. Thought to himself, I'll go surfing.

The pale umber of the Mojave gave way to southern California's big scrubby coastal mountains. West of those suburbia hove into view, spilling eastward on filled valleys and shaved hilltops: greater San Diego, bigger all the time. He could see bulldozers busy scraping platforms of flat soil for the newest neighbourhood. Freeways glittering with their arterial flow.

Frank's plane slowed and drifted down, past the last peaks and over the city proper. Downtown's cluster of glassy skyscrapers came into view immediately to the left of the plane, seemingly at about the same height. Those buildings had been Frank's workplace for a time when he was young, and he watched them as he would any old home. He knew exactly which buildings he had climbed; they were etched on his mind. That had been a good year. Disgusted with his advisor, he had taken a leave of absence from graduate school, and after a season of climbing in Yosemite and living at Camp Four, he had run out of money and decided to do something for a living that would require his physical skills and not his intellectual ones. A young person's mistake, although at least he had not thought he could make his living as a professional climber. But the same skills were needed for the work of skyscraper window maintenance; not just window cleaning, which he had also done, but repair and replacement. It had been an odd but wonderful thing, going off the roofs of those buildings and descending their sides to clean windows, repair leaking caulk and flashing, replace cracked panes, and so on. The climbing was straightforward, usually involving platforms for convenience; the belays and T-bars and dashboards and other gear had been bombproof. His fellow workers had been a mixed bag, as was always true with climbers – everything from nearly illiterate cowboys to eccentric scholars of Nietzsche or Adam Smith. And the window work itself had been a funny thing, what the Nietzsche scholar had called the apotheosis of kindergarten skills, very satisfying to perform – slicing out old caulk, applying heated caulk, unscrewing and screwing screws and bolts, sticking giant suckers to panes, levering them out and winching them up to the roofs or onto the platforms – and all under the cool onrush of the marine layer, just under clouds all mixed together with bright sun, so that it was warm when it was sunny, cool when it was cloudy, and the whole spread of downtown San Diego there below to entertain him when he wasn't working. Often he had felt surges of happiness, filling him in moments when he stopped to look around: a rare thing in his life.

Eventually the repetition got boring, as it will, and he had moved on, first to go travelling, until the money he had saved was gone; then back into academia again, as a sort of test, in a different lab, with a different advisor, at a different university. Things had gone better there. Eventually he had ended up back at UCSD, back in San Diego – his childhood home, and still the place where he felt most comfortable on this earth.

He actually noticed that feeling as he left the airport terminal's glassed-in walkway over the street, and hopped down the outdoor escalator to the rental car shuttles. The comfort of a primate on home ground, no doubt – a familiarity in the slant of the light and the shape of the hills, but above all in the air itself, the way it felt on his skin, that combination of temperature, humidity and salinity that together marked it as particularly San Diegan. It was like putting on familiar old clothes after spending a year in a tux. He was home, and his cells knew it.

He got in his rental car (always the same one, it seemed) and drove out of the lot. North on the freeway, crowded but not impossibly so, people zipping along like starlings, following the flocking rules *keep as far apart from the rest as possible* and *change speeds as little as possible*. The best drivers in the world. Past Mission Bay and Mount Soledad on the left, into the region where every offramp had been a major feature of his life at one time or another. Off at Gilman, up the tight canyon of apartments hanging over the freeway, past the one where he had once spent a night with a girl, ah, back in the days when such things had happened to him. Down a hill and onto campus.

UCSD. Home base. The school in the eucalyptus grove. Quick-witted, sophisticated, scarily powerful – even from

155

inside it, Frank remained impressed by the place. Among other things it was a very effective troop of primates, collaborating to further the welfare of its members.

Even after a year in the east coast's great hardwood forest, there was something appealing about the campus's eucalyptus grove – something charming, even soothing. The trees had been planted as a railway-sleeper farm, before it was discovered that the wood was unsuitable. Now they formed a kind of mathematically gridded space, within which the architectural melange of UCSD's colleges lay scattered, connected by two broad promenades that ran north and south.

Frank had arranged an afternoon of appointments. The department had given him the use of an empty office facing the Revelle Plaza; his own was still occupied by a visiting researcher from Berlin. After getting the key from Rosaria, the department secretary, he sat at a dusty desk by a functioning phone, and discussed dissertation progress with his four remaining graduate students. Forty-five minutes each, and aware the whole time that he really wasn't doing them justice, that it had been their bad luck to get him as their advisor, because of his decision to go to NSF for a year. Well, he would try to make up for it on his return – but not all at once, and certainly not today. The truth was that none of their projects looked that interesting. Sometimes it happened that way.

After that there was an hour and a half to go before his meeting with Derek. Parking at UCSD was a nightmare, but he had gotten a pass to a department slot from Rosaria, and Torrey Pines was only a few hundred yards up the road, so he decided to walk. Then, feeling restless, and even a bit jumpy, it occurred to him to take the climbers' route that he and some friends had devised for a kind of run/climb workout, when they were all living at Revelle; that would nicely occupy about the amount of time he had to kill.

It involved walking down La Jolla Shores and turning onto

La Jolla Farms Road and heading out onto the bluff of land owned by the university – a squarish plateau between two canyons running down to the beach, ending in a steep 350-foot cliff over the sea. This land had been left in its natural state, more or less – there were some old World War Two bunkers melting away on it – and as they had found seven thousand-year-old graves on it, likely to stay forever protected in the University of California Natural Reserve System. A superb prospect and one of Frank's favourites places on Earth. He had lived on it, sleeping out there every night and using the old gym as his bathroom; he had had romantic encounters out there; and he had often dropped down the steep surfer's trail that descended to the beach right at Blacks Canyon.

When he got to the cliff's edge he found a sign announcing that the route down was closed due to erosion of the cliff, and it was hard to argue, as the old trail was now a kind of gully down the edge of a sandstone buttress. But he still wanted to do it, and he strolled south along the cliff's edge, looking out at the Pacific and feeling the onshore wind blow through him. The view was just as mind-boggling as ever, despite the grey cloud layer; as often happened, the clouds seemed to accentuate the great distances to the horizon, the two plates of ocean and sky converging at such a very slight angle towards each other. California, the edge of history – it was a stupid idea, and totally untrue in all senses of the word, except for this physical one, and the reach beyond to a metaphorical landscape: it did appear to be the edge of something.

An awesome spot. And the tighter, steeper canyon on the south side of the empty bluff had an alternative trail down that Frank was willing to break the rules and take. No one but a few cronies of his had ever used this one, because the initial drop was a scarily exposed knife-edge of a buttress, the gritty sandstone eroding in the wind to steep gullies on

157

both sides. The drop into the gully to the left was similarly hairy. The trick was to descend fast and boldly and so Frank did that, skidding out as he turned into the gully, and sliding onto his side and down; but against the other wall of the gully he stopped, and was able to hop down after that very quickly and uneventfully.

Down to the salt roar of the beach, the surf louder here because of the tall cliff leaping up from the back of the beach. He walked north down the strand, enjoying yet another familiar place. Blacks Beach, the UCSD surfers' home away from home.

The ascent to Torrey Pines Generique reversed the problems of the descent, in that here all the problems were right down on the beach. A hanging gully dripped over a hard sill some forty feet up, and he had to freeclimb the grit to the right of the green algal spill; then merely scramble up that gully, to the clifftop near the hang-glider port. At the top he discovered a sign that declared this climb too had been illegal.

Oh well. He had loved it. He felt refreshed, awake for the first time in weeks somehow. This was what it meant to be home. He could brush his hands through his slightly sweaty and seaspray-dampened hair, and walk in and see what happened.

Onto the parklike grounds of Torrey Pines Generique, through the newly-beefed-up security gates. The place was looking empty, he thought as he entered the main building and walked down its halls to Derek's office. They had definitely let a lot of people go; several labs he passed stood empty and unused.

Frank entered the reception room and greeted Derek's secretary, Roxie, who buzzed him in. Derek got up from his broad desk to shake hands.

'Good to see you again, how are you?'

'Fine, and you?'

'Oh, getting by, getting by.'

His office looked the same as the last time Frank had visited: window view of the Pacific; framed copy of Derek's cover portrait on a *US News and World Report*; skiing photos.

'So, what's new with the great bureaucrats of science?'

'They call themselves technocrats, actually.'

'Oh I'm sure it's a big difference.' Derek shook his head. 'I never understood why you went out there. I suppose you made good use of your time.'

'Yes.'

'And now you're almost back.'

'Yes. I'm almost done.' Frank paused. 'But look, like I said to you on the phone, I did see something interesting come in from someone who has worked here.'

'Right, I looked into it. We could still hire him full-time, I'm pretty sure. He's on soft money up at Caltech.'

'Good. Because I thought it was a very interesting idea.'

'So NSF funded it?'

'No, the panel wasn't as impressed as I was. And they might have been right – it was a bit undercooked. But the thing is, if it did work, you could test genes by computer simulation, and identify proteins you wanted, even down to specific ligands, so you could get better attachments to cells in vivo. It would really speed the process. Sharpen it.'

Derek regarded him closely. 'You know we don't really have any funds for new people.'

'Yeah I know. But this guy is a post-doc, right? And a mathematician. He was only asking NSF for some computer time really. You could hire him full-time for a starter salary, and put him on the case, and it would hardly cost you a thing. I mean, if you can't afford that . . . Anyway, it could be interesting.'

'What do you mean, interesting?'

'I just told you. Hire him full-time, and get him to sign the usual contract concerning intellectual property rights and all. Really secure those.'

'I get that, but interesting how?'

Frank sighed. 'In the sense that it might be the way to solve your targeted delivery problem. If his methods work and you get a patent, then the potential for licensing income might be really considerable. Really.'

Derek was silent. He knew that Frank knew the company was nearly on life support. That being the case, Frank would not bother him with trifles, or even with big deals that needed capital and time to get going. He had to be offering a fix of some kind.

'Why did he send this grant proposal to NSF?'

'Beats me. Maybe he was turned down by one of your guys when he was here. Maybe his advisor at Caltech told him to do it. It doesn't matter. But have your people working on the delivery problem take a look at it. After you get this guy hired.'

'Why don't you talk to them? Go talk to Leo Mulhouse about this.'

'Well . . .' Frank thought it over. 'Okay. I'll go talk to them and see how things are going. You get this Pierzinski back on board. Call him today. We'll see what happens from there.'

Derek nodded, still not happy. 'You know, Frank, what we really need here is you. Like I said before. Things haven't been the same in the labs since you left. Maybe when you get back here we could rehire you at whatever level UCSD will allow.'

'I thought you just said you didn't have any money for hires.'

'Well that's true, but for you we could try to work something out, right?'

'Maybe. But let's not talk about that now. I need to get out of NSF first, and see what the blind trust has done with my stock. I used to have some options here.'

'You sure did. Hell, we could bury you in those, Frank, I'd love to do that.'

Giving people options to buy stock cost a company nothing. They were feel-good gestures, unless everything went right with the company and the market; and with Nasdaq having been in the tank for so long, they were not often seen as real compensation anymore. More a kind of speculation. And in fact Frank expressing interest in them had cheered Derek up, as it was a sign of confidence in the future of Torrey Pines Generique. Also a sign of Frank's interest in taking part in it, on his return.

'Do what you can to get some funding to tide you over a bit longer,' Frank suggested as he got up to leave.

'Oh I will. I always am.'

Outside, Frank sighed. Torrey Pines was looking like a thin reed. But it was his reed, and anything might happen. Derek was good at keeping things afloat. But Sam Houston was a loss. Derek needed Frank there as scientific advisor. Or consultant, given his UCSD position. And if they had Pierzinski under contract, things might work out. By the end of the year the whole Torrey Pines situation might be turned around. And if it all worked out, the potential was there for it to do very well indeed.

Frank wandered down to Leo's lab. It was noticeably lively compared to the rest of the building – people bustling about, the smell of solvents in the air, machines whirring away. Where there's life there's hope. Or perhaps they were only like the musicians on the *Titanic*, playing on while the ship went down.

This, however, represented an attempt to bail the ship out. Frank felt encouraged. He went in and exchanged pleasantries with Leo and his people, feeling that it was easy to be friendly and encouraging. This was the guts of the machine, after all. He mentioned that Derek had sent him down to talk about their current situation, and Leo nodded noncommittally and gave him a run-down, truncated but functional.

Frank regarded him as he spoke, thinking: Here is a scientist at work in a lab. He is in the optimal scientific space. He has a lab, he has a problem, he's fully absorbed and going full tilt. He should be happy. But he isn't happy. He has a tough problem he's trying to solve, but that's not it; people always have tough problems in the lab.

It was something else. Probably, that he was aware of the company's situation – of course, he had to be. Probably this was the source of his unease. The musicians feeling the tilt in the deck. In which case there really was a kind of heroism in the way they played on, focused to the end.

But for some reason Frank was also faintly annoyed by this. People plugging away in the same old ways, trying to do things according to the plan, even a flawed plan: normal science, in Kuhnian terms, as well as in the more ordinary sense. All so normal, so trusting that the system worked, when obviously the system was both rigged and broken. How could they persevere? How could they be so blinkered, so determined, so dense?

Frank slipped his content in. 'Maybe if you had a way to test the genes in computer simulations, find your proteins in advance.'

Leo looked puzzled. 'You'd have to have a, what? A theory of how DNA codes its gene expression functions. At the least.'

'Yes.'

'That would be nice, but I'm not aware anyone has that.'

'No, but if you did . . . Wasn't George working on something like that, or one of his temporary guys? Pierzinski?'

'Yeah that's right, Yann was trying some really interesting things. But he left.'

'I think Derek is trying to bring him back.'

'Good idea.'

Then Marta walked into the lab. When she saw Frank she stopped, startled.

'Oh, hi Marta.'

'Hi Frank. I didn't know you were going to be coming by.'

'Neither did I.'

'Oh no? Well –' She hesitated, turned. The situation called for her to say something, he felt, something like *Good to see you*, if she was going to leave so quickly. But she said only, 'I'm late, I've got to get to work.'

And then she was out the door.

Only later, when reviewing his actions, did Frank see that he had cut short the talk with Leo, and pretty obviously at that, in order to follow Marta. In the moment itself he simply found himself walking down the hall, catching up to her before he even realized what he was doing.

She turned and saw him. 'What,' she said sharply, looking at him as if to stop him in his tracks.

'Oh hi I was just wondering how you're doing, I haven't seen you for a while, I wondered. Are you up for, how about going out and having dinner somewhere and catching up?'

She surveyed him. 'I don't think so. I don't think that would be a good idea. We might as well not even go there. What would be the point?'

'I don't know, I'm interested to know how you're doing I guess is all.'

'Yeah I know, I know what you mean. But sometimes there are things you're interested in that you can't really ever get to know any more, you know?'

'Ah yeah.'

He pursed his lips, looked at her. She looked good. She was both the strongest and the wildest woman he had ever met. Somehow things between them had gone wrong anyway.

Now he looked at her and understood what she was saying. He was never going to be able to know what her life was like these days. He was biased, she was biased; the scanty data would be inescapably flawed. Talking for a couple of hours would not make any difference. So it was pointless to

163

try. Would only bring up bad things from the past. Maybe in another ten years. Maybe never.

Marta must have seen something of this train of thought in his face, because with an impatient nod she turned and was gone.

A few days after Frank dropped by, Leo turned on his computer when he came in to the lab and saw there was an e-mail from Derek. He opened and read it, then the attachment that had come with it. When he was done he printed it all out, and forwarded it to Brian and Marta. When Marta came in about an hour later she had already done some work on it.

'Hey Brian,' she called from Leo's door, 'come check this out. Derek has sent us a new paper from that Yann Pierzinski who was here. He was funny. It's a new version of the stuff he was working on when he was here. That was interesting I thought. If we could get it to find us better matching ligands, you might not need the hydrodynamic pressures to get them to stick in the body.'

Brian had come in while she was telling him this, and she pointed to parts of the diagram on Leo's screen as he caught up. 'See what I mean?' Liver cells, endothelial cells – all the cells in the body had receptor ligands that were extremely specific for the ligands on the particular proteins that they needed to obtain from the blood; together they formed something like lock-and-key arrangements, coded by the genes and embodied in the proteins. In effect they were locksmithing at the microscopic level, working with living cells as their material . . .

'Well, yeah. It would be great. If it worked . . . Maybe crunch them through this programme over and over, until you see repeats, if you did . . . then test the ones with the ligands that fit best, and look strongest chemically.'

'And Pierzinski is back to work on it with us!'

'Is he?'

'Yeah, he's coming back. Derek says in his e-mail that we'll have him at our disposal.'

'Cool.'

Leo checked this in the company's directory. 'Yep, here he is. Rehired just this week. Frank Vanderwal came by and mentioned this guy, he must have told Derek about it I bet. He was asking me about it too. Well, Vanderwal should know, this is his field.'

'It's my field too,' Marta said sharply.

'Right, of course, I'm just saying Frank might have, you know. Well, let's ask Yann to look at what we've got. If it works . . .'

Brian said, 'Sure. It's worth trying anyway. Pretty interesting.' He googled Yann, and Leo leaned over his shoulder to look at the list.

'Derek obviously wants us to talk to him right away.'

'He must have rehired him for us.'

'I see that. So let's get him before he gets busy with something else. A lot of labs could use another biomathematician.'

'True, but there aren't a lot of labs. I think we'll get him. Look, what do you think Derek means here, "write up the possibilities right away"?'

'I suppose he wants to get started using the idea to try to secure more funding.'

'Shit. Yeah, that's probably right. Unbelievable. Okay, let's pass on that for now, and give Yann a call.'

Their talk with Yann Pierzinski was indeed interesting. He breezed into the lab just a few days later, as friendly as ever, and happy to be back at Torrey Pines with a permanent job. He was going to be based in George's maths group, he told

166

them, but had already been told by Derek to expect to work a lot with Leo's lab; so he arrived curious, and ready to go.

Leo enjoyed seeing him again. Yann still had a tendency to become a speedtalker when excited, and he still canted his head to the side when thinking, as if to flood that half of his brain with blood, in just the kind of 'rapid hydrodynamic forcing' that they were trying to get away from in their work (and he tilted it to the right, so was giving the boost to the so-called intuitive side, Leo noted). His algorithm sets were still works in progress, he said, and under-developed precisely in the gene grammars that Leo and Marta and Brian needed from him for their work; but all that was okay, because they could help him, and he was there to help them. They could collaborate, and when it came right down to it, Yann was a powerful thinker, and good to have on the case. Leo felt secure in his own lab abilities, devising and running experiments and the like, but when it came to the curious mixture of maths, symbolic logic, and computer programming that these biomathematicians dived into – mathematicizing human logic, among other things, and reducing it to mechanical steps that could be scripted into the computers – he was way out of his depth. So Leo was happy to watch Yann sit down and plug his laptop into their desktop.

In the days that followed, they tried his algorithms out on the genes of their 'HDL factory' cells, Yann substituting different procedures in the last steps of his operations, then checking what they got in the computer simulations, and selecting some for their dish trials. Pretty soon they found one version of the operation that was consistently good at predicting proteins that matched well with their target cells – making keys for their locks, in effect. 'That's what I've been focusing on for the past *year*,' Yann said happily after one such success.

As they worked, Pierzinski told them some of how he had gotten to that point in his work, following aspects of his advisor's work at Cal Tech and the like. Marta and Brian asked him where he had hoped to take it all, in terms of applications. Yann shrugged; not much of anywhere, he told them. He thought the main interest of the operation was what it revealed about the mathematics of codon function. Just finding out more about the mathematics of how genes became organisms. He had not thought much about the implications for clinical or therapeutic applications, though he freely acknowledged they might be there. 'It stands to reason the more you know about this, the more you'll be able to see what's going on.' The rest of it was not his field of interest. It was a classic mathematician thing.

'But Yann, don't you see what the applications of this could be?'

'I guess. I'm not really interested in pharmacology.'

Leo and Brian and Marta stood there staring at him. Despite his earlier stint there, they didn't know him very well. He seemed normal enough in most ways, aware of the outside world and so on. To an extent.

Leo said, 'Look, let's go get some lunch, let us take you out to lunch. I want to tell you more about what all this could help us with.'

The lobbying firm of Branson and Ananda occupied offices off Pennsylvania Avenue, near the intersection of Indiana and C Streets, about halfway between the White House and the Capitol, and overlooking the Marketplace. It was a very nice office.

Charlie's friend Sridar met them at the front door. First he took them in to meet old Branson himself, then led them into a meeting room dominated by a long table under a window that gave a view of early summer leaves on gnarly branches. Sridar got the Khembalis seated, then offered them coffee or tea; they all took tea. Charlie stood near the door, flexing his knees and bobbing mildly about, keeping Joe asleep on his back, ready to make a quick escape if he had to.

Drepung spoke for the Khembalis, although Sucandra and Padma also pitched in with questions from time to time. They all consulted with Rudra Cakrin, who asked them a lot of questions in Tibetan. Charlie began to think he had been wrong about the old man understanding English; it was too cumbersome to be a trick, just as Anna had said.

All the Khembalis stared intently at Sridar or Charlie whenever they spoke. They made for a very attentive audience. They definitely had a presence. It had come to the point where Charlie felt that their Calcutta cottons, maroon vests and sandals were normal, and that it was the room itself that was rather strange, so smooth and spotlessly grey. Suddenly it looked to him like the inside of a Gymboree crawl-space.

'So you've been a sovereign country since 1960?' Sridar was saying.

'The relationship with India is a little more . . . complicated than that. We have had sovereignty in the sense you suggest since about 1993.' Drepung rehearsed the history of Khembalung, while Sridar asked questions and took notes.

'So – fifteen feet above sea level at high tide,' Sridar said at the end of this recital. 'Listen, one thing I have to say at the start – we are not going to be able to promise you anything much in the way of results on this global warming thing. That's been given up on by Congress –' He glanced at Charlie: 'Sorry, Charlie. Maybe not so much given up on as swept under the rug.'

Charlie glowered despite himself. 'Not by Senator Chase or anyone else who's really paying attention to the world. And we're still working on it, we've got a big bill coming up and –'

'Yes, yes, of course,' Sridar said, holding up a hand to stop him before he got into rant mode. 'You're doing what you can. But let's put it this way – there are quite a few members of Congress who think of it as being too late to do anything.'

'Better late than never!' Charlie insisted, almost waking Joe.

'We understand,' Drepung said to Sridar, after a glance at the old man. 'We won't have any unrealistic expectations of you. We only hope to engage help that is experienced in the procedures used, the usual protocols you see. We ourselves will be responsible for the content of our appeals to the reluctant bodies, trusting you to arrange the meetings with them.'

Sridar kept his face blank, but Charlie knew what he was thinking. Sridar said, 'We do our best to give our clients all the benefits of our expertise. I'm just reminding you that we are not miracle-workers.'

The Khembalis nodded.

'The miracles will be our department,' Drepung said, face as blank as Sridar's.

Charlie thought, these two jokers might get along fine.

Slowly they worked out what they would expect from each other, and Sridar wrote down the details of an agreement. The Khembalis were happy to have him write up what in essence was their request for proposal. 'That sure makes it easier,' Sridar remarked. 'A clever way to make me write you a fair deal.' During this part of the negotiation (for such it was) Joe finished waking up, so Charlie left them to it.

Later that day Sridar gave Charlie a call. Charlie was sitting on a bench in Dupont Circle, feeding Joe a bottle and watching two of the local chess hustlers practise on each other. They played too fast for Charlie to follow the game.

'Look, Charlie, this is a bit ingrown, since you put me in touch with these guys, but really it's your man that the lamas ought to be meeting first, or at least early on. The Foreign Relations Committee is one of the main ones we'll have to work on, so it all begins with Chase. Can you set us up with a good chunk of the Senator's quality time?'

'I can with some lead time,' Charlie said, glancing at Phil's master calendar on his wrist screen. 'How about next Thursday, he's had a cancellation?'

'Is that late morning, so he's at his best?'

'He's always at his best.'

'Yeah right.'

'No I'm serious. You don't know Phil.'

'I'll take your word for it. Thursday at?'

'Ten to ten-twenty.'

'Perfect.'

Charlie could have made a good case for the energy of Senator Phil Chase being more or less invariant, and always very high. Here in the latter part of his third term he had fully settled into Washington, and his seniority was such that he had

171

become very powerful, and very busy. He was constantly on the go, with every hour from six a.m. to midnight scheduled in twenty-minute units. It was hard to understand how he could keep his easy demeanour and relaxed ways.

Almost too relaxed. He did not sweat the details on most topics. He was a delegating senator, a hands-off senator. As many of the best of them were. Some senators tried to learn everything, and burned out; others knew almost nothing, and were in effect living campaign posters. Phil was somewhere in the middle. He used his staff well – as an exterior memory bank, if nothing else, but often for much more – for advice, for policy, even occasionally for their accumulated wisdom.

His longevity in office, and the strict code of succession that both parties obeyed, had now landed him the chair of the Foreign Relations Committee, and a seat on Environment and Public Works. These were A-list committees, and the stakes were high. The Democrats had come out of the recent election with a one-vote advantage in the Senate, a two-vote disadvantage in the House, and the President was still a Republican. This was in the ongoing American tradition of electing as close to a perfect gridlock of power in Washington as possible, presumably in the hope that nothing further would happen and history would freeze for good. An impossible quest, like building a card house in a gale, but it made for tight politics and good theatre. Inside the Beltway it was considered to be an invigorating thing.

In any case, Phil was now very busy with important matters, and heading towards re-election time himself. His old chief of staff Wade Norton was on the road now, and though Phil valued Wade's advice and kept him on staff as a telecommuting general advisor, Andrea had taken over the executive staff duties, and Charlie the environmental research, though he too was a part-timer, and telecommuting much of the time.

When he did make it in, he found operations in the office

172

fully professional, but with a chaotic edge which he had long ago concluded was mostly engendered by Phil himself. Phil would seize the minutes he had between appointments and wander from room to room, looking to needle people. At first this appeared to be wasting time, but Charlie had come to believe it was a kind of quick polling method, Phil squeezing in impressions and reactions in the little time he had that was not scheduled. 'We're surfing the big picture today!' he would exclaim as he wandered the offices, or stood by the refrigerator drinking another ginger ale. Those were the moments when he would start arguments for the hell of it. His staff loved it. Congressional staffers were by definition policy nerds; many had joined their high school debate clubs of their own free will. Talking shop with Phil was right up their alley. And his enthusiasm was infectious, his grin like a double-shot of espresso. He had one of those smiles that invariably looked as if he was genuinely delighted. If it was directed at you, you felt a glow inside. In fact Charlie was convinced that it was Phil's smile that had got him elected the first time, and maybe every time since. What made it so beautiful was that it wasn't faked. He didn't smile if he didn't feel like it. But he often felt like it. That was very revealing, and so Phil had his effect.

With Wade gone, Charlie was now his chief advisor on global climate issues. Actually Charlie and Wade functioned as a sort of tag-team telecommuting advisor, both of them part-time, Charlie calling in every day, dropping by every week; Wade calling in every week, and dropping by every month. It worked because Phil didn't always need them for help when environmental issues came up. 'You guys have educated me,' he would tell them. 'I can take this on my own. Naturally I'll be doing what you told me to do anyway. So don't worry, stay at the South Pole, stay in Bethesda. I'll let you know how it went.'

That would have been fine with Charlie, if only Phil had

in fact always done what Charlie and Wade advised. But Phil had other advisors as well, and pressures from many directions; and he had his own opinions. So there were divergences.

He would grin his infectious grin whenever he crossed Charlie. It seemed to give him special pleasure. 'There are more things in heaven and earth,' he would murmur, only half-listening to Charlie's remonstrances. Like most Congresspeople, he thought he knew better than his staff how best to get things done; and because he got to vote and his staff didn't, in effect he was right.

On the following Thursday at ten a.m., when the Khembalis had their twenty minutes head-to-head with Phil, Charlie was very interested to see how it would go, but that morning he had to attend a Washington Press Club appearance by a scientist from the Heritage Foundation who was claiming rapidly rising temperatures would be good for agriculture. Marking such people and assisting in the immediate destruction of their pseudo-arguments was important work, which Charlie undertook with a fierce indignation; at some point the manipulation of facts became a kind of vast lie, and this was what Charlie felt when he had to confront people like Strengloft: he was combating liars, people who lied about science for money, thus obscuring the clear signs of the destruction of their present world. So that they would end up passing on to all the children a degraded planet, devoid of animals and forests and coral reefs and all the other aspects of a biological support system and home. Liars, cheating their own children, and the many generations to come: this is what Charlie wanted to shout at them, as vehemently as any street-corner nutcase preacher. So that when he went at them, with his tightly polite questions and pointed remarks, there was a certain edge to him. Opponents tried to deflect it by labelling it as self-righteousness, or affluent hypocrisy or whatnot; but the edge could still cut if he hit the right spots.

In any case it was perhaps best that Charlie not be there at Phil's meeting with the Khembalis, so that Phil would not be distracted, or feel that Charlie was somehow coaching the visitors. Phil could form his own impressions, and Sridar would be there to do any shepherding necessary. By now Charlie had seen enough of the Khembalis to trust that Rudra Cakrin and his gang would be up to the task of representing themselves. Phil would experience their weird persuasiveness, and he knew enough of the world not to discount them just because they were not Beltway operators dressed in suit and tie.

So Charlie hustled back from the predictably irritating hearing, and arrived right at 10:20. He hurried up the stairs to Phil's offices on the third floor. These offices had a great view down the Mall – the best any senator had, obtained in a typical Phil coup. The Senate, excessively cramped in the old Russell, Dirksen and Hart buildings, had finally bitten the bullet and taken by eminent domain the head-quarters of the United Brothers of Carpenters and Joiners of America, who had owned a fine building in a spectacular location on the Mall, between the National Gallery and the Capitol itself. The carpenters' union had howled at the take-over, of course – only a Republican House and Senate would have dared to do it, happy as they were to smack a union whenever possible – but it had left a political stink such that very few senators were actually willing to brave the negative PR of moving into the new acquisition once all the legal wrangling was over and the building was theirs. Phil, however, had been quite happy to move in, claiming he would represent the carpenters' and all the other unions so faithfully that it would be as if they had never left the building. 'Where better to defend the working people of America?' he had asked, smiling his famous smile. 'I'll keep

175

a hammer on the windowsill to remind myself who I'm representing.'

At 10:23 a.m., Phil ushered the Khembalis out of his corner office, chatting with them cheerfully. 'Yes, thanks, of course, I'd love to – talk to Evelyn about setting up a time.'

The Khembalis looked pleased. Sridar looked impassive but faintly amused, as he often did.

Just as he was leaving, Phil spotted Charlie and stopped. 'Charlie! Good to see you at last!'

Grinning hugely, he came back and shook his blushing staffer's hand. 'So you laughed in the President's face!' He turned to the Khembalis: 'This man burst out laughing in the President's face! I've always wanted to do that!'

The Khembalis nodded neutrally.

'So what did it feel like?' Phil asked Charlie. 'And how did it go over?'

Charlie, still blushing, said, 'Well, it felt involuntary, to tell the truth. Like a sneeze. Joe was really tickling me. And as far as I could tell, it went over okay. The President looked pleased. He was trying to make me laugh, so when I did, he laughed too.'

'Yeah I bet, because he had you.'

'Well, yes. Anyway he laughed, and then Joe woke up and we had to get a bottle in him before the Secret Service guys did something rash.'

Phil laughed, then shook his head, growing more serious. 'Well, it's too bad, I guess. But what could you do. You were ambushed. He loves to do that. Hopefully it won't cost us. It might even help. But look, I'm late, I've got to go. You hang in there.' And he put a hand to Charlie's arm, said goodbye again to the Khembalis, and hustled out the door.

The Khembalis gathered around Charlie, looking cheerful. 'Where is Joe? How is it he is not with you?'

'I really couldn't bring him to this thing I was at, so my friend Asta from Gymboree is looking after him. Actually I have to get back to him soon,' checking his watch. 'But come on, tell me how it went.'

They all followed Charlie into his cubicle by the stairwell, stuffing it with their maroon robes (they had dressed formally for Phil, Charlie noted) and their strong brown faces. They still looked pleased.

'Well?' Charlie said.

'It went very well,' Drepung said, and nodded happily. 'He asked us many questions about Khembalung. He visited Khembalung seven years ago, and met Padma and others at that time. He was very interested, very . . . sympathetic. He reminded me of Mr Clinton in that sense.'

Apparently the ex-president had also visited Khembalung a few years previously, and had made a big impression.

'And, best of all, he told us he would help us.'

'He did? That's great! What did he say, exactly?'

Drepung squinted, remembering: 'He said – "I'll see what I can do."'

Sucandra and Padma nodded, confirming this.

'Those were his exact words?' Charlie asked.

'Yes. "I'll see what I can do."'

Charlie and Sridar exchanged a glance. Which one was going to tell them?

Sridar said carefully, 'Those were indeed his exact words,' thus passing the ball to Charlie.

Charlie sighed.

'What's wrong?' Drepung asked.

'Well . . .' Charlie glanced at Sridar again.

'Tell them,' Sridar said.

Charlie said, 'What you have to understand is that no Congressperson likes to say no.'

'No?'

'No. They don't.'

'They never say no,' Sridar amplified.

'Never?'

'Never.'

'They like to say yes,' Charlie explained. 'People come to them, asking for things – favours, votes – consideration of one thing or another. When they say yes, people go away happy. Everyone is happy.'

'Constituents,' Sridar expanded. 'Which mean votes, which means their job. They say yes and it means votes. Sometimes one yes can mean fifty thousand votes. So they just keep saying yes.'

'That's true,' Charlie admitted. 'Some say yes no matter what they really mean. Others, like our Senator Chase, are more honest.'

'Without, however, ever actually saying no,' Sridar added.

'In effect they only answer the questions they can say yes to. The others they avoid in one way or another.'

'Right,' Drepung said. 'But he said . . .'

'He said, I'll see what I can do.'

Drepung frowned. 'So that means no?'

'Well, you know, in circumstances where they can't get out of answering the question in some other way –'

'Yes!' Sridar interrupted. 'It means no.'

'Well . . .' Charlie tried to temporize.

'Come on, Charlie.' Sridar shook his head. 'You know it's true. It's true for all of them. Yes means maybe; I'll see what I can do means no. It means, not a chance. It means, I can't believe you're asking me this question, but since you are, this is how I will say no.'

'He will not help us?' Drepung asked.

'He will if he sees a way that will work,' Charlie declared. 'I'll keep on him about it.'

Drepung said, 'You'll see what you can do.'

'Yes – but I mean that, really.'

Sridar smiled sardonically at Charlie's discomfiture. 'And

Phil's the most environmentally aware senator of all, isn't that right Charlie?'

'Well, yeah. That's definitely true.'

The Khembalis pondered this.

SIX

The Capital in Science

Robot submarines cruise the depths, doing oceanography. Slocum gliders and other AUVs (autonomous underwater vehicles) like torpedos with wings, dock in underwater obser-vatories to recharge their batteries and download their data. Finally oceanographers have almost as much data as the meteorologists. Among other things they monitor a deep layer of relatively warm water that flows from the Atlantic into the Arctic (ALTEX, the Atlantic Layer Tracking Experiment).

But they are not as good at it as the whales. White beluga whales, living their lives in the open ocean, have been fitted with sensors for recording temperature, salinity and nitrate content, matched with a GPS record and a depth metre. Up and down in the blue world they sport, diving deep into the black realm below, coming back up for air, recording data all the while. Casper the Friendly Ghost, Whitey Ford, The Woman in White, Moby Dick, all the rest: they swim to their own desires, up and down endlessly within their immense territories, fast and supple, continuous and thorough, capable of great depths, pale flickers in the blackest blue, the bluest black. Then back up for air. Our cousins. White whales help us to know this world. The warm layer is attenuating.

The rest of Frank's stay in San Diego was a troubled time. The encounter with Marta had put him in a black mood that he could not shake.

He tried to look for a place to live when he returned in the fall, and checked out some real estate pages in the paper, but it was discouraging. He saw that he should rent an apartment first, and take the time to look around before trying to buy something. It was going to be hard, maybe impossible, to find a house he both liked and could afford. He had some financial problems. And it took a very considerable income to buy a house in north San Diego these days. He and Marta had bought a perfect couple's bungalow in Cardiff, but they had sold it when they split, adding greatly to the acrimony. Now the region was more expensive than a mere professor could afford. Extra income would be essential.

So he looked at some rentals in North County, and then in the afternoons he went to the empty office on campus, meeting with two post-docs who were still working for him in his absence. He also talked with the department chair about what classes he would teach in the fall. It was all very tiresome.

And worse than that, a letter appeared in his department mailbox from the UCSD Technology Transfer Office, Independent Review Committee. Pulse quickening, he ripped it open and scanned it, then got on the phone to the tech transfer office.

183

'Hi Delphina, it's Frank Vanderwal here. I've just gotten a letter from the review committee, can you please tell me what this is about?'

'Oh hello, Dr Vanderwal. Let me see . . . the oversight committee on faculty outside income wanted to ask you about some income you received from stock in Torrey Pines Generique. Anything over two thousand dollars a year has to be reported, and they didn't hear anything from you.'

'I'm at NSF this year, all my stocks are in a blind trust. I don't know anything about it.'

'Oh, that's right, isn't it. Maybe . . . just a second. Here it is. Maybe they knew that. I'm not sure. I'm looking at their memo here . . . ah. They've been informed you're going to be rejoining Torrey Pines when you get back, and –'

'Wait, what? How the hell could they hear that?'

'I don't know –'

'Because it isn't true! I've been talking to colleagues at Torrey Pines, but all that is private. What could they *possibly* have heard?'

'*I* don't know.' Delphina was getting tired of his indignation. No doubt her job put her at the wrong end of a lot of indignation, but that was too bad, because this time he had good cause.

He said, 'Come on, Delphina. We went over all this when I helped to start Torrey Pines, and I haven't forgotten. Faculty are allowed to spend up to twenty per cent of work time on outside consulting. Whatever I make doing that is mine, it only has to be reported. So even if I did go back to Torrey Pines, what's wrong with that? I wouldn't be joining their board, and I wouldn't use more than twenty per cent of my time!'

'That's good –'

'And most of it happens in my head anyway, so even if I *did* spend more time on it, how are you going to know? Are you going to read my mind?'

Delphina sighed. 'Of course we can't read your mind. In the end it's an honour system. Obviously. We ask people what's going on when we see things in the financial reports, to remind them what the rules are.'

'I don't appreciate the implications of that. Tell the oversight committee what the situation is on my stocks, and ask them to do their research properly before they bother people.'

'All right. Sorry about that.' She did not seem perturbed.

Frank went out for a walk around the campus. Usually this soothed him, but now he was too upset. Who had told the oversight committee that he was planning to rejoin Torrey Pines? And why? Would somebody at Torrey Pines have made a call? Only Derek knew for sure, and he wouldn't do it.

But others must have heard about it. Or could have deduced his intention after his visit. That had been only a few days before, but enough time had passed for someone to make a call. Sam Houston, maybe, wanting to stay head science advisor?

Or Marta?

Disturbed at the thought, at all these machinations, he found himself wishing he were back in DC. That was shocking, because when he was in DC he was always dying to return to San Diego, biding his time until his return, at which point his real life would recommence. But it was undeniable; here he was in San Diego, and he wanted to be in DC. Something was wrong.

Part of it must have been the fact that he was not really back in his San Diego life, but only previewing it. He didn't have a home, he was still on leave, his days were not quite full. That left him wandering a bit, as he was now. And that was unlike him.

Okay – what would he do with free time if he lived here?

He would go surfing.

Good idea. His possessions were stowed in a storage unit in the commercial maze behind Encinitas, so he drove there

and got his surfing gear, then returned to the parking lot at
Cardiff reef, at the south end of Cardiff-by-the-Sea. A few
minutes' observation while he pulled on his longjohn wetsuit
(getting too small for him) revealed that an ebb tide and a
south swell were combining for some good waves, breaking
at the outermost reef. There was a little crowd of surfers and
body-boarders out there.

Happy at the sight, Frank walked into the water, which
was very cool for midsummer, just as they all said. It never
got as warm as it used to. But it felt so good now that he
ran out and dived through a broken wave, whooping as he
emerged. He sat in the water and floated, pulled on his booties,
velcroed the ankle strap of the board cord to him, then took
off paddling. The ocean tasted like home.

The whole morning was good. Cardiff reef was a very
familiar break to him, and nothing had changed in all the
years he had come here. He had often surfed here with Marta,
but that had little to do with it. Although if he did run into
her out here, it would be another chance to talk. Anyway
the waves were eternal, and Cardiff reef with its simple point
break was like an old friend who always said the same things.
He was home. This was what made San Diego his home –
not the people or the jobs or the unaffordable houses, but
this experience of being in the ocean, which for so many
years of his youth had been the central experience of his life,
everything else colourless by comparison, all the way up until
he had discovered climbing.

As he paddled, caught waves and rode the lefts in long
ecstatic seconds, and then worked to get back outside, he
wondered again about this strangely powerful feeling of salt-
water as home. There must be an evolutionary reason for
such joy at being cast forward by a wave. Perhaps there was
a part of the brain that predated the split with the aquatic
mammals, some deep and fundamental part of mentation that
craved the experience. Certainly the cerebellum conserved

very ancient brain workings. On the other hand perhaps the moments of weightlessness, and the way one floated, mimicked the uterine months of life, which were then called back to mind when one swam. Or maybe it was a very sophisticated aesthetic response, an encounter with the sublime, as one was constantly falling and yet not dying or even getting hurt, so that the discrepancy in information between the danger signals and the comfort signals was experienced as a kind of triumph over reality.

Whatever; it was a lot of fun. And made him feel vastly better.

Then it was time to go. He took one last ride, and rather than kicking out when the fast part was over, rode the broken wave straight in towards the shore.

He lay in the shallows and let the hissing whitewater shove him around. Back and forth, ebb and flow. For a long time he lolled there. In his childhood and youth he had spent a fair bit of time at the end of every ocean session doing this, *grunioning* he called it; and he had often thought that no matter how much people worked to make more complicated sports in the ocean, grunioning was all you really needed. Now he splayed out and letting the water wash him back and forth, feeling the sandy surges lift and push him. Grooming by ocean. As it ran back out to sea the water sifted the fine black flakes in the sand, mixing them into the rounded tan and white grains until they made networks of overlapping black Vs. Coursing patterns of nature –

'Are you okay?'

He jerked his head up. It was Marta, on her way out.

'Oh, hi. Yeah I'm okay.'

'What's this, stalking me now?'

'No,' then realizing it might be a little bit true: '*No!*'

He stared at her, getting angry. She stared back.

'I'm just catching some waves,' he said, mouth tight. 'You've got no reason to say such a thing to me.'

'No? Then why did you ask me out yesterday?'

'A mistake, obviously. I thought it might do some good to talk.'

'Last year, maybe. But you didn't want to then. You didn't want to so much that you ran off to NSF instead. Now it's too late. So just leave me alone, Frank.'

'I am!'

'*Leave me alone.*'

She turned and ran into the surf, diving onto her board and paddling hard. When she got out far enough she sat up on her board and balanced, looking outward.

Women in wetsuits looked funny, Frank thought as he watched her. Not just the obvious, but also the subtler differences in body morphology were accentuated: the callipygosity, the shorter torso-to-leg ratio, the 0.7 waist-to-hip ratio – whatever it was, it was different, and it drew his eye like a magnet. He could tell the difference from as far away as he could see people at all. Every surfer could.

What did that mean? That he was in thrall to a woman who despised him? That he had messed up the main relationship of his life and his best chance so far for reproductive success? That sexual dimorphism was a powerful driver in the urge to reproduction? That he was a slave to his sperm, and an idiot?

All of the above.

His good mood shattered, he hauled himself to his feet. He stripped off the booties and longjohn, towelled off at his rental car, drove back up to his storage unit and dropped off his gear. Returned to his hotel room, showered, checked out, and drove down the coast highway to the airport, feeling like an exile even while he was still here on his own home ground.

Something was deeply wrong.

He checked in the car, roboted through the routines to get him on his plane to Dallas. Sat in a window seat looking down at the view as the plane roared off. Point Loma, the ocean blue from up here, the waves breaking on the coast, perpetually renewing their white tapestry. Bank, turn, Mount Soledad, up through the cloud layer, fly up and east.

He fell asleep. By the time he woke up again they were descending into Dallas. It was strange to watch the process of falling towards the Earth, the buildings and cars like toys at first, quickly growing to real things that sped by. Then standing, out, into the big curves of the Dallas airport, onto its rail shuttle, over to another arc, to sit and wait for the plane to DC.

Grimly he watched America walk by. Who were these people who could live so placidly while the world fell into an acute global environmental crisis? Experts at denial. Experts at filtering their information to hear only what made it seem sensible to behave as they behaved. Many of those walking by went to church on Sundays, believed in God, voted Republican, spent their time shopping and watching TV. Obviously nice people. The world was doomed.

He was settled in his next plane seat (on the aisle this time, because the view didn't matter), feeling more and more disgusted and angry. NSF was part of it; they weren't doing a thing to help. He got out his laptop, turned it on and called up a new word-processing file. He started to write.

Critique of NSF, first draft. Private to Diane Chang.

NSF was established to support basic scientific research, and it is generally given high marks for that. But its budget has never surpassed ten billion dollars a year, in an overall economy of some ten trillion. It is to be feared that as things stand, NSF is simply too small to have any real impact.

Meanwhile humanity is exceeding the planet's carrying capacity for our species, badly damaging the biosphere. Neoclassical economics cannot cope with this situation, and indeed, with its falsely exteriorized costs, was designed

189

in part to disguise it. If the Earth were to suffer a cata-strophic anthropogenic extinction event over the next ten years, which it will, American business would continue to focus on its quarterly profit and loss. There is no economic mechanism for dealing with catastrophe. And yet govern-ment and the scientific community are not tackling this sit-uation either, indeed both have consented to be run by neoclassical economics, an obvious pseudo-science. We might as well agree to be governed by astrologers. Everyone at NSF knows this is the situation, and yet no one does anything about it. They don't try to instigate the saving of the biosphere, they don't even call for certain kinds of mit-igation projects. They just wait and see what comes in. It is a ridiculously passive position.

Why such passivity, you ask? Because NSF is chicken! It's a chicken with its smart little head stuck in the sand like an ostrich! It's a chicken ostrich (fix). It's afraid to take on Congress, it's afraid to take on business, it's afraid to take on the American people. Free market fundamentalists are dragging us back to some dismal feudal eternity and destroying everything in the process, and yet we have the technological means to feed everyone, house everyone, clothe everyone, doctor everyone, educate everyone – the ability to end suf-fering and want as well as ecological collapse is right here at hand, and yet NSF continues to dole out its little grants, fid-dling while Rome burns!!!

Well whatever nothing to be done about it, I'm sure you're thinking poor Frank Vanderwal has spent a year in the swamp and has gone crazy as a result, and that is true but what I'm saying is still right, the world is in big trouble and NSF is one of the few organizations on Earth that could actually help get it out of trouble, and yet it's not. It should be charting worldwide scientific policy and forcing certain kinds of climate mitigation and biosphere management, insisting on them as emergency necessities, it should be working

Congress like the fucking NRA to get the budget it deserves, which is a much bigger budget, as big as the Pentagon's, really those two budgets should be reversed to get them to their proper level of funding, but none of it is happening or will happen, and that is why I'm not coming back and no one in his right mind would come back either.

The plane had started to descend.

Well, it would need a little revision. Mixed metaphors; something was either a chicken or an ostrich, even if in fact it was both. But he could work on it. He had a draft in hand, and he would revise it and then give it to Diane Chang, head of NSF, in the slim hope that it would wake her up.

He hit the save button for the first time in about an hour. The plane turned for its final descent into Ronald Reagan Airport. Soon he would be back in the wasteland of his current life. Back in the swamp.

Back in Leo's lab, they got busy running trials of Pierzinski's algorithm, while continuing the ongoing experiments in 'rapid hydrodynamic insertion', as it was now called in the emerging literature. Many labs were working on the delivery problem and, crazy as it seemed, this was one of the more promising methods being investigated. A bad sign.

Thus they were so busy on both fronts that they didn't notice at first the results that one of Marta's collaborators was getting with Pierzinski's method. Marta had done her PhD studying the microbiology of certain algae, and she was still co-authoring papers with a post-doc named Eleanor Dufours. Leo had met Eleanor, and then read her papers, and been impressed. Now Marta had introduced Eleanor to a version of Pierzinski's algorithm, and things were going well, Marta said. Leo thought his group might be able to learn some things from their work, so he set up a little brown-bag lunch for Eleanor to give a talk.

'What we've been looking into,' Eleanor said that day in her quiet steady voice, very unlike Marta's, 'is the algae in certain lichens. DNA histories are making it clear that some lichens are really ancient partnerships of algae and fungus, and we've been genetically altering the algae in one of the oldest, *Cornicularia cornuta*. It grows on trees, and works its way into the trees to a quite suprising degree. We think the lichen is helping the trees it colonizes by taking over the tree's hormone regulation and increasing

192

the tree's ability to absorb lignins through the growing season.'

She talked about the possibility of changing their metabolic rates. 'Lately we've been trying these algorithms Marta brought over, trying to find symbiotes that speed the lichen's ability to add lignin to the trees.'

Evolutionary engineering, Leo thought, shaking his head. His lab was trying to do similar things, of course, but he seldom thought of it that way. He needed to get this outside view to defamiliarize what he did, to see better what was going on.

'Why speed up lignin banking?' Brian wanted to know. 'I mean, what use would it be?'

'We've been thinking it might work as a carbon sink.'

'How so?'

'Well, you know, people are talking about capturing and sequestering some of the carbon we've put into the atmosphere, in carbon sinks of one kind or other. But no method has looked really good yet. Stimulating plant growth has been one suggestion, but the problem is that most of the plants discussed have been very short-lived, and rotting plant life quickly releases its captured CO_2 back into the atmosphere. So unless you can arrange lots of very deep peat bogs, capturing CO_2 in small plants hasn't looked very effective.'

Her listeners nodded.

'So, the thing is, living trees have had hundreds of millions of years of practice in not being eaten and outgassed by bugs. So one possibility would be to grow bigger trees. That turns out not to be so easy,' and she sketched a ground and a tree growing out of it on the whiteboard with a red marker, so that it looked like something a five-year-old would draw. 'Sorry. See, most trees are already as tall as they can get, because of physical constraints like soil qualities and wind speeds. So, you can make them thicker, or –' drawing more roots under the ground line – 'you can make the roots thicker.

But trying to do that directly involves genetic changes that harm the trees in other ways, and anyway is usually very slow.'

'So it won't work,' Brian said.

'Right,' she said patiently, 'but many trees host these lichen, and the lichen regulate lignin production in a way that might be bumped, so the tree would quite quickly capture carbon that would remain sequestered for as long as the tree lived.

'So, given all this, what we've been working on is basically a kind of altered tree lichen. The lichen's photosynthesis is accomplished by the algae in it, and we've been using this algorithm of Yann's to find genes that can be altered to accelerate that. And now we're getting the lichen to export the excess sugar into its host tree, down in the roots. It seems like we might be able to really accelerate the root growth and girth of the trees that these lichens grow on.'

'Capturing like how much carbon?'

'Well, we've calculated different scenarios, with the altered lichen being introduced into forests of different sizes, all the way up to the whole world's temperate forest belt. That one has the amount of CO_2 drawn down in the billions of tons.'

'Wow.'

'Yes. And pretty quickly, too.'

'Watch out,' Brian joked, 'you don't want to be causing an ice age here.'

'True. But that would be a problem that came later. And we know how to warm things up, after all. But at this point any carbon capture would be good. There are some really bad effects coming down the pike these days, as you know.'

'True.'

They all sat and stared at the mess of letters and lines and little tree drawings she had scribbled on the whiteboard.

Leo broke the silence. 'Wow, Eleanor. That's very interesting.'

'I know it doesn't help you with your delivery problem.'

194

'No, but that's okay, that isn't what you do. This is still very interesting. It's a different problem is all, but that happens. This is great stuff. Have you shown this to the chancellor yet?'

'No.' She looked surprised.

'You should. He loves stuff like this, and, you know, he's a working scientist himself. He still keeps his lab going even while he's doing all the chancellor stuff.' This gave him credit to burn all over the town's scientific community.

Now Eleanor was nodding. 'I'll do that, thanks. He has been very supportive.'

'Right. And look, I hope you and Marta keep collaborating. Maybe we can get you here to Torrey Pines. Maybe there's some aspect of hormone regulation you'll spot that we're not seeing.'

'Oh I doubt that, but thanks.'

Soon after that, Leo got an e-mail from Derek, asking him to attend an appointment with a representative of a venture capital group, to explain the scientific issues. This had happened a few times back when Torrey Pines was a hot new start-up, so Leo knew the drill, and was therefore extremely uncomfortable with the idea of doing it again – especially if it came to a discussion of 'rapid hydrodynamic insertion'. No way did Leo want to be supporting Derek's unfounded assertions to an outsider.

Derek assured him that he would handle any of this guy's 'speculative questions' – exactly the sort of questions a venture capitalist would have to ask.

'And so I'll be there to . . .'

'You'll be there to answer any technical questions about the method as we're using it now.'

Great.

Before the meeting Leo was shown a copy of the executive summary and offering memorandum Derek had sent to

Biocal, a venture capital firm that Derek had acquired an investment from in the company's early years. This document was very upbeat about the possibilities of the hydrodynamic delivery method. On finishing it Leo's stomach had contracted to the size of a walnut.

Later that week, on the day of the meeting, Leo drove down from work to Biocal's offices, located in an upscale building in downtown La Jolla, just off Prospect near the point. Their meeting room windows had a great view up the coast. Leo could almost spot their own building, on the cliff across La Jolla Cove.

Their host, Henry Bannet, was a trim man in his forties, relaxed and athletic-looking, friendly in the usual San Diego manner. His firm was a private partnership, doing strategic investing in biotechnologies. A billion-dollar fund, Derek had said. And they didn't expect any return on their investments for four to six years, sometimes longer. They could afford to work, or had decided to work, at the pace of medical progress itself. Their game was high-risk, high-return, long-range investment. This was not a kind of investment that banks would make, nor anyone else in the loaning world. The risks were too great, the returns too distant. Only venture capitalists would do it.

So naturally these guys' help was much in demand from small biotech companies. There were something like three hundred biotechs in the San Diego area alone, and many of them were hanging on by the skin of their teeth, hoping for that first successful cash cow to keep them going or get them bought. Venture capitalists could therefore pick and choose what they wanted to invest in; and many of them were pursuing particular interests, or even passions. Naturally in these areas they were very well-informed, expert in combining scientific and financial analysis into what they called 'doing due diligence'. They spoke of being 'value-added investors', of bringing much more than money to the table – expertise, networking, advice.

196

Bannet looked to Leo to be one of the passionate ones. He was friendly, but intent. A man at work. There was very little chance Derek was going to be able to impress him with smoke and mirrors.

'Thanks for seeing us,' Derek said.

Bannet waved a hand. 'Always interested to talk to you guys. I've been reading some of your papers, and I went to that symposium in LA last year. You're doing some great stuff.'

'It's true, and now we're on to something really good, with real potential to revolutionize genetic engineering by getting tailored DNA into people who need it. It could be a method useful to a whole bunch of different therapies, which is one of the reasons we're so excited about it – and trying to ramp up our efforts to speed the process along. So I remembered how much you helped us during the start-up, and how well that's paid off for you, so I thought I'd bring by the current situation and see if you would be interested in doing a PIPE with us.'

This sounded weird to Leo, like Indians offering a peace pipe, or college students passing around a bong, but Bannet didn't blink; a PIPE was one of their mechanisms for investment, as Leo quickly learned. 'Private Investment in Public Equity'. And for once it was a pretty good acronym, because it meant creating a pipeline for money to run directly from their cash-flush fund to Derek's penniless company.

But Bannet was a veteran of all this, alert to all the little strategic opacities that were built into Derek's typical talk to stock-holders or potential investors. Something like sixty per cent of biotech start-ups failed, so the danger of losing some or all of an investment to bankruptcy was very real. No way could Derek finesse him. They would have to come clean and hope he liked what he saw.

Leo gazed out of the window at the foggy Pacific, listening to Derek go on. Unbroken waves wrapped around La Jolla

Point and pulsed into the cove. The huge apartment block at the end of La Jolla Point blocked his view west, reminding him that big money could accomplish some unlikely things.

Derek finished leading Bannet through a series of financial spreadsheets on his laptop, unable to disguise their tale of woe. Bad profit and loss; lay-offs; sale of some subsidiary contracts, even some patents, their crown jewels; empty coffers.

'We've had to focus on the things that we think are really the most important,' Derek admitted. 'It's made us more efficient, that's for sure. But it means there really isn't any fat anywhere, no resources we can put to the task, even though it's got such incredible potential. So, it seemed like it was time to ask for some outside funding help, with the idea that the financing now would be so crucial that the returns to the investor could and should be really significant.'

'Uh huh,' Bannet said, though it wasn't clear what he was agreeing with. He made thoughtful clucking sounds as he scanned the spreadsheets, murmuring 'Um hmmm, um hmmm,' in a sociable way, but now that he was thinking about the information in the spreadsheets, his face betrayed an almost burning intensity. This guy was one of the passionate ones, Leo saw.

'Tell me about this algorithm,' he said finally.

Derek looked to Leo, who said, 'Well, the mathematician developing it is a recent hire at Torrey Pines, and he's been collaborating with our lab to test a set of operations he's developed, to see how well they can predict the proteins associated with any given gene, and as you can see,' clicking his own laptop screen to the first of the project report slides, 'it's been really good at predicting them in certain situations,' pointing to them on the screen's first slide.

'And how would this affect the targeted delivery system you're working on?'

'Well, right now it's helping us to find proteins with ligands that bind better to their receptor ligands in target organ cells. It's also helping us test for proteins that we can more successfully shove across cell walls, using the hydrodynamic methods we've been investigating for the past few months.' He clicked ahead to the slide that displayed this work's results, trying to banish Brian and Marta's names from his mind, he definitely did not want to be calling it the Popping Eyeball Method, the Exploding Mouse Method. 'As you can see,' pointing to the relevant results, 'saturation has been good in certain conditions.' This seemed a little weak, and so he added, 'The algorithm is also proving to be very successful in guiding work we've been doing with botanists on campus, on algal designs.'

'How does that connect with this?'

'Well, it's for plant engineering.'

Bannet looked at Derek.

Derek said, 'We plan to use it to pursue the improvement of targeted delivery. Clearly the method is robust, and people can use it in a wide variety of applications.'

But there was no hiding it, really. Their best results so far were in an area that would not necessarily ever become useful to human medicine. And yet human medicine was what Torrey Pines Generique was organized to do.

'It looks really promising, eh?' Derek said. 'It could be that it's an algorithm that is more than just a mathematical exercise, but more like a law of nature. The grammar of how genes express themselves. It could mean a whole suite of patents when the applications are all worked out.'

'Mm hmmm,' Bannet said, looking down again at Derek's laptop, which was still at the financial page. Almost pathetic, really; except it must have been a fairly common story, so that Bannet would not necessarily be shocked or put off. He would simply be considering the investment on a risk-adjusted basis, which would take the present situation into account.

Finally he said, 'It looks very interesting. Of course it's

always a bit sketchy feeling, when you've gotten to the point of having all your eggs in one basket like this. But sometimes one is all you need. The truth is, I don't really know yet.'

Derek nodded in reluctant agreement. 'Well, you know. We believe very strongly in the importance of therapies for the most serious diseases, and so we concentrated on that, and now we kind of have to, you know, go on from there with our best ideas. That's why we've focused on the HDL upgrade. With this targeted delivery, it could be worth billions.'

'And the HDL upgrade . . .'

'We haven't published yet. We're still looking into the patent situation there.'

Leo's stomach tightened, but he kept his face blank.

Bannet was even blanker; still friendly and sympathetic enough, but with that piercing eye. 'Send me the rest of your business plan, and all the scientific publications that relate to this. All the data. I'll discuss it with some of my partners here. It seems like the kind of thing that I'd like to get my partners' inputs on. That's not unusual, it's just that it's bigger than what I usually do on my own. And some of my colleagues are into agro-pharmacy stuff.'

'Sure,' Derek said, handing over a glossy folder of material he had already prepared. 'I understand. We can come back and talk to them too if you like, answer any questions.'

'That's good, thanks.' Bannet put the folder on the table. With a few more pleasantries and a round of hand-shaking, Derek and Leo were ushered out.

Leo found he had no idea whether the meeting had gone well or poorly. And would that be a good sign or a bad one?

SEVEN

Tit for Tat

The Earth's atmosphere now contains a percentage of carbon dioxide and other greenhouse gases higher than it has been since the end of the Cretaceous. This means more heat from the sun is being trapped in our air, and the high-pressure cells we saw this year are bigger, warmer, and loft higher in the tropical atmosphere. Many common jet-stream patterns have been disrupted, and the storms spiralling out of the tropics have gained in both frequency and intensity. The hurricane season in the Atlantic ran from April to November, and there were eight hurricanes and six tropical storms. Typhoons in the east Pacific happened all year, twenty-two all told. Mass flooding resulted, but it should be noted that in other regions droughts have been breaking records.

So the effects have been various, but the changes are general and pervasive, and the damage for the year was recently estimated at six hundred billion dollars, with deaths in the thousands. So far the United States has escaped major catastrophe, and attention to the problem has not been one of the administration's central concerns. 'In a healthy economy the weather isn't important,' the President remarked. But the possibility is there that the added energy in the atmosphere could trigger what climatologists call abrupt climate change. How that might begin, no one can be sure.

Anna flew through the blur of a midweek day. Up and off, Metro to the office; pound the keys, wrestling with some faulty data from an NSF educational outreach programme, the spreadsheet work eating up hours like minutes. Stop to pump, then to eat at her desk (it felt a little too weird to eat and pump at the same time), all the while data-wrangling. Then a look at an e-mail from Drepung and Sucandra about their grant proposals.

Anna had helped them to write a small raft of proposals, and it had indeed been a pleasure, as they did all the real work – and very well too – while she just added her expertise in grant-writing, honed through some tens of thousands of grant evaluations. She definitely knew that world, how to sequence the information, what to emphasize, what language to use, what supporting documents, what arguments – all of it. Every word and punctuation mark of a grant proposal she had a feel for, one way or the other. It had been a pleasure to apply that expertise to the Khembalis' attempts.

Now she was pleased again to find that they had heard back from three of them, two positively. NSF had awarded them a quick temporary starter grant in the 'Tropical Oceans, Global Atmosphere' effort; and the INDOEX countries had agreed informally to expand their Project Asian Brown Cloud (ABC) to include a big new monitoring facility on Khembalung, including researchers. This would cement a partnership with the START units already scattered all over south Asia.

Altogether it meant funding streams for several years to come – tens of millions of dollars all told, with infrastructure built, and relationships with neighbouring countries established. Allies in the struggle.

'Oh that's *very* nice,' Anna said, and hit the print button. She cc'd the news to Charlie, sent congratulations to Drepung, and then got back to work on the spreadsheet.

After a while she remembered about the print-outs, and went around the corner to the Department of Unfortunate Statistics to get the hard copies.

She found Frank inside, shaking his head over the latest.

'Have you seen this one?' he said, gesturing with his nose at a taped-up print-out of yet another spreadsheet.

'No, I don't think so.'

'It's the latest Gini figures, do you know those?'

'No?'

'They're a measurement of income distribution in a population, so an index of the gap between rich and poor. Most industrialized democracies rate at between 2.5 and 3.5, that's where we were in the 1950s, see, but our numbers started to shoot up in the 1980s, and now we're worse than the worst third-world countries. 4.0 or greater is considered to be very inequitable, and we're at 5.2 and rising.'

Anna looked briefly at the graph, interested in the statistical method. A Lorenz curve, plotting the distance away from perfect equality's straight line tilted at forty-five degrees.

'Interesting . . . So this is for annual incomes?'

'That's right.'

'So if it were for capital holdings –'

'It would be worse, I should think. Sure.' Frank shook his head, disgusted. He had come back from San Diego in a permanently foul mood. No doubt anxious to finish and go home.

'Well,' Anna said, looking at her print-out, 'maybe the Khembalis aren't so bad off after all.'

'How's that?'

Anna showed him the pages. 'They've gotten a couple grants. It'll make them some good contacts.'

'Very nice, did you do this?' Frank took the pages.

'I just pointed them at things. They're turning out to be good at following through. And I helped Drepung rewrite the grant proposals. You know how it is, after doing this job for a few years, you do know how to write a grant proposal.'

'No lie. Nice job.' He handed the pages back to her. 'Good to see someone doing *something*.'

Anna returned to her desk, glancing after him. He was definitely edgy these days. He had always been that way, of course, ever since the day he arrived. Dissatified, cynical, sharp-tongued; it was hard not to contrast him to the Khembalis. Here he was, about to go home to one of the best departments in one of the best universities in one of the nicest cities in the world's richest country, and he was unhappy. Meanwhile the Khembalis were essentially multi-generational exiles, occupying a tidal sandbar in near poverty, and they were happy.

Or at least cheerful. She did not mean to downplay their situation, but these days she never saw that unhappy look that had so struck her the first time she had seen Drepung. No, they were cheerful, which was different from happy; a policy perhaps, rather than a feeling. But that only made it more admirable.

Well, everyone was different. She got back to the tedious grind of changing data. Then Drepung called, and they shared the pleasure of the good news about the grant proposals. They discussed the details, and then Drepung said, 'We have you to thank for this, Anna. So thank you.'

'You're welcome, but it wasn't really me, it's the Foundation and all the other organizations.'

'But you are the one who piloted us through the maze. We owe you big-time.'

Anna laughed despite herself.

'What?'

'Nothing, it's just that you sound like Charlie. You sound like you've been watching sports on TV.'

'I do like watching basketball, I must admit.'

'That's fine. Just don't start listening to that rap music okay? I don't think I could handle that.'

'I won't. You know me, I like Bollywood. Anyway, you must let us thank you somehow for this. We will have you to dinner.'

'That would be nice.'

'And maybe you can join us at the zoo when our tigers arrive. Recently a pair of Bengal tigers were rescued off Khembalung after a flood, the papers in India call them the Swimming Tigers, and they are coming for a stay at the National Zoo here, and we will have a small ceremony when they arrive.'

'That would be great. The boys would love that. And also –' An idea had occurred to her.

'Yes?'

'Maybe also you could come upstairs and visit us here, and give one of our lunchtime lectures. That would be a great way to return a favour. We could learn more about your situation, and, you know, your approach to science, or to life or whatever. Something like that. Do you think Rudra would be interested?'

'I'm sure he would. It would be a great opportunity.'

'Well not exactly, it's just a lunchtime series of talks that Aleesha runs, but I do think it would be interesting. We could use some of your attitude here, I think, and you could talk about these programmes too, if you wanted.'

'I'll talk to the rimpoche about it.'

'Okay good. I'll put Aleesha in touch.'

After that Anna worked on the stats again, until she saw the time and realized it was her day to visit Nick's class and help them with maths hour. 'Ah shit.' Throw together a bag of work stuff, shut down, heft the shoulder bag of chilled milk bottles, and off she went. Down into the Metro, working as she sat, then standing on the crowded *Red Line Shady Grove* train; out and up and into a taxi, of all things, to get to Nick's school on time.

She arrived just a little late, dumped her stuff, and settled down to work with the kids. Nick was in third grade now, but had been put in an advanced maths group. In general the class did things in math that Anna found surprising for their age. She liked working with them; there were twenty-eight kids in the class, and Mrs Wilkins, their teacher, was grateful for the help.

Anna wandered from group to group, helping with multipart problems that involved multiplication, division and rounding off. When she came to Nick's group she sat down on one of the tiny chairs next to him, and they elbowed each other playfully for room at the round low table. He loved it when she came to his class, which she had tried to do on a semi-regular basis every year since he had started school.

'All right Nick quit that, show the gang here how you're going to solve this problem.'

'Okay.' He furrowed his brow in a way she recognized inside the muscles of her own forehead. 'Thirty-nine divided by two, that's . . . nineteen and a half . . . round that up to twenty –'

'No, don't round off in the middle of the process.'

'Mom, come on.'

'Hey, you shouldn't.'

'Mom, you're quibbling again!' Nick exclaimed.

The group cackled at this old joke.

'It's not quibbling,' Anna insisted, 'it's a very important distinction.'

'What, the difference between nineteen and a half and twenty?'

207

'Yes,' over their squeals of laughter, '*because* you should never round off in the middle of an operation, because then the things you do later will exaggerate the inaccuracy! It's an *important principle!*'

'Mrs Quibler is a quibbler, Mrs Quibler is a quibbler!'

Anna gave in and gave them The Eye, a squinting, one-eyed glare that she had worked up long ago when playing Lady Bracknell in high school. It never failed to crack them up. She growled, 'That's Quibler *with one b*,' melting them with laughter, as always, until Mrs Wilkins came over to join the party and quiet it down.

After school Anna and Nick walked home together. It took about half an hour, and was one of the treasured rituals of their week – the only time they got to spend together, just the two of them. Past the big public pool where they would go swimming in the summers, past the grocery store, then down their quiet street. It was hot, of course, but bearable in the shade. They talked about whatever came into their heads.

Then they entered the coolness of their house, and returned to the wilder world of Joe and Charlie. Charlie was bellowing as he cooked in the kitchen, an off-key, wordless aria. Joe was killing dinosaurs in the living room. As they entered he froze, considering how he was going to signify his displeasure at Anna's treasonous absence for the day. When younger this had been a genuine emotion, and sometimes when he saw her come in the door he had simply burst into tears. Now it was calculated, and she was immune.

He smacked himself in the forehead with a *Compsognathus*, then collapsed to the rug face-first.

'Oh come on,' Anna said. 'Give me a break Joe.' She started to unbutton her blouse. 'You better be nice if you want to nurse.'

Joe popped right up and ran over to give her a hug.

'Right,' Anna said. 'Blackmail will get you everywhere. Hi hon!' she yelled in at Charlie.

'Hi babe.' Charlie came out to give her a kiss. For a second all her boys hung on her. Then Joe was latched on, and Charlie and Nick went into the kitchen. From there Charlie shouted out from time to time, but Anna couldn't yell back without making Joe mad enough to bite her, so she waited until he was done and then walked around the corner into the kitchen.

'How was your day?' Charlie said.

'I fixed a data error all day long.'

'That's good dear.'

She gave him a look. 'I swore I wasn't going to do it,' she said darkly, 'but I just couldn't bring myself to ignore it.'

'No, I'm sure you couldn't.'

He kept a straight face, but she punched him on the arm anyway. 'Smartass. Is there any beer in the fridge?'

'I think so.'

She hunted for one. 'There was some good news that came in, did you see that? I forwarded it. The Khembalis got a couple of grants.'

'Really! That is good news.' He was sniffing at a yellow curry bubbling in the frying pan.

'Something new?'

'Yeah, I'm trying something out of the paper.'

'You're being careful?'

He grinned. 'Yeah, no blackened redfish.'

'Blackened redfish?' Nick repeated, alarmed.

'Don't worry, even I wouldn't try it on you.'

'He wouldn't want you to catch fire.'

'Hey, it was in the recipe. It was right out of the recipe!'

'So? A tablespoon each of black pepper, white pepper, cayenne *and* chili powder?'

'How was I supposed to know?'

'What do you mean, you use pepper. You should have

209

known what a tablespoon of pepper would taste like, and that was the least hot of them.'

'I guess I didn't know it would all stick to the fish.'

Nick was looking appalled. 'I wouldn't eat that.'

'You aren't kidding,' Anna laughed. 'One touch with your tongue and you would spontaneously combust.'

'It was in a cookbook.'

'Even going in the kitchen next day was enough to burn your eyes out.'

Charlie was giggling at his folly, holding the stirring spoon down to Nick to gross him out, although now he had a very light touch with the spices. The curry would be fine. Anna left him to it and went out to play with Joe.

She sat down on the couch, relaxed. Joe began to pummel her knees with blocks, babbling energetically. At the same time Nick was telling her something about something. She had to interrupt him, almost, to tell him about the coming of the Swimming Tigers. He nodded and took off again with his account. She heaved a great sigh of relief, took a sip of the beer. Another day flown past like a dream.

Another heat wave struck, the worst so far. People had thought it was hot before, but now it was July, and one day the temperature in the metropolitan area climbed to 105 degrees, with the humidity over 90 per cent. The combination had all the Indians in town waxing nostalgic about Uttar Pradesh just before the monsoon broke. 'Oh very much yes, just like this in Dehli, actually it would be a blessing if it were to be like this in Dehli, that would be an improvement over what they have now, third year of drought you see, they are needing the monsoon to be coming very badly.'

The morning *Post* included an article informing Charlie that a chunk of the Ross Ice Shelf had broken off, a chunk more than half the size of France. The news was buried in the last pages of the international section. So many pieces of Antarctica had fallen off that it wasn't big news anymore.

It wasn't big news, but it was a big iceberg. Researchers joked about moving onto it and declaring it a new nation. It contained more fresh water than all the Great Lakes combined. It had come off near Roosevelt Island, a low black rock that had been buried under the ice and known only to radar probes, and so was exposed to the air for the first time in either two or fifteen million years, depending on which research team you believed. Although it might not be exposed for long; pouring down towards it, researchers said, was the rapid ice of the West Antarctic Ice Sheet, unimpeded now that the Ross Shelf in that region had embarked, and therefore moving faster than ever.

This accelerated flow of ice towards the sea had big ramifications. The West Antarctic Ice Sheet was much bigger than the Ross Ice Shelf, and had been resting on ground that was below sea level but that held the ice much higher than it would have been if it had been floating freely in the ocean. So when it broke up and sailed away, it would displace more ocean water than it had before.

Charlie read on, feeling somewhat amazed that he was learning this in the back pages of the *Post*. How fast could this happen? The researchers didn't appear to know. As the sheet broke away, they said, sea water was lifting the edges of the ice still resting on the bottom, deeper and deeper at every tide, tugging with every current, and thus beginning to tear the sheet apart in big vertical cracks, and to launch it out to sea.

Charlie checked this on the web, and watched one trio of researchers explain on camera that it could become an accelerating process, their words likewise accelerating a bit as if to illustrate how it would go. Modelling inconclusive because the sea bottom under the grounded ice is irregular, they said, and has active volcanoes in it, so who knows? But it very well might happen fast.

Charlie heard in their voices the kind of repressed delirium of scientific excitement that he had heard once or twice when listening to Anna talk about some extraordinary thing in statistics that he had not even been able to understand. This, however, he understood; they were saying that the possibility was very real that the whole mass of the West Antarctic Ice Sheet would break apart and float away, each giant piece of it then sinking more deeply into the water, thus displacing more water than it had when grounded in place – so much more that sea level worldwide could rise by an eventual total of about – seven metres. This could happen fast, one glaciol-

212

ogist emphasized, 'and I'm not talking geology fast here, I'm talking tide fast. A matter of several years in some simulations.' The hard thing to pinpoint was whether it would start to accelerate or not. It depended on variables programmed into the models – on they went, the usual kind of scientist talk.

And yet the *Post* had it at the back of the international section! People were talking about it the same way they did any other disaster. There did not seem to be any way to register a distinction in response between one coming catastrophe and another. They were all bad. If it happened it happened. That seemed to be the way people were processing it. Of course the Khembalis would have to be extremely concerned. The whole League of Drowning Nations, for that matter. Meaning everyone. Charlie had done enough research on the tidal power stuff, and other coastal issues, to give him a sharpened sense that this was serious, and perhaps the tipping point into something worse. All of a sudden it coalesced into a clear vision standing before him, and what he saw frightened him. Twenty per cent of humanity lived on the coast. He felt like he had one time driving in winter when he had taken a turn too fast and hit an icy patch he hadn't seen, and the car had detached and he found himself flying forward, free of friction or even gravity, as if sideslipping in reality itself . . .

But it was time to go downtown. He was going to take Joe with him to the office. He pulled himself together, got out the buggy so they would spare each other their body heat. Life had to go on; what else could he do?

Out they ventured into the steambath of the capital. It really didn't feel that much different from an ordinary summer day. As if the sensation of heat hit an upper limit where it just blurred out. Joe was seatbelted in like a racing driver, so that he would not launch himself out at inopportune moments. Naturally he did not like this and he objected to the buggy

213

because of it, but Charlie had decorated its front bar as an airplane cockpit dashboard, which placated Joe enough that he did not persist in his howls or attempts to escape. 'Resistance is futile!'

They took the elevators in the Metro stations, and came up on the Mall to stroll over to Phil's office in the old carpenters' union. A bad idea, as crossing the Mall was like being blanched in boiling air. Charlie, as always, experienced the climate deviation with a kind of grim 'I Told You So' satisfaction. But once again he resolved to quit eating boiled lobsters.

At Phil's they rolled around the rooms trying to find the best spots in the falls of chilled air pouring from the air-conditioning vents. Everyone was doing this, drifting around to find the coolest draughts, like a science museum exercise investigating the Coriolis force.

Charlie parked Joe out with Evelyn, who loved him, and went to work on Phil's revisions to the climate bill. It certainly seemed like a good time to introduce it. More money for CO_2 remediation, new fuel-efficiency standards and the money to get Detroit through the transition to hydrogen, new fuels and power sources, carbon-capture methods, carbon sink identification and formation, hydrocarbon-to-carbohydrate-to-hydrogen conversion funds and exchange credit programmes, deep geothermal, tide power, wave power, money for basic research in climatology, money for the Extreme Global Research in Emergency Salvation Strategies project (EGRESS), money for the Global Disaster Information Network (GDIN) – and so on and so forth. It was a grab-bag of programs, many designed to look like pork to help the bill get the votes, but Charlie had done his best to give the whole thing organization, and a kind of coherent shape, as a narrative of the near future.

There were many in Phil's office who thought it was a mistake to try to pass an omnibus or comprehensive bill like this, rather than get the programmes funded one by one, or in smaller related groupings. But the comprehensive had been Phil's chosen strategy, and Charlie felt that at this late point it was better to stick to that plan. He added language to make the revisions Phil wanted, pushing the envelope in each case, as it seemed now, if ever, was the time to strike.

Joe was beginning to get rowdy with Evelyn, he could hear the unmistakable sound of dinosaurs hitting walls. All this language would get chopped up anyway; still, all the more reason to get it precise and smooth, armoured against attack, low-keyed and unobjectionable, invisibly effective. Bill language as low-post moves to the basket, subtle, quick, unstoppable.

He rushed to a finish and took the revised bill in to Phil, with Joe leading the way in his buggy. They found the senator sitting with his back directly against an air-conditioning duct.

'Jeez Phil, don't you get *too* cold sitting there?'

'The trick is to set up before you're all sweaty, and then don't get the evaporative cooling. And I keep my head above it,' banging the wall with the back of his noggin, 'so I don't catch as many A/C colds. I learned that a long time ago, when I was stationed on Okinawa.'

He glanced over Charlie's new revision, and they argued over some of the changes. At one point Phil looked at him: 'Something bugging you today?' He glanced over at Joe. 'Joe here seems to be grooving. The President's favourite toddler.'

'It's not Joe that's getting to me, it's you. You and the rest of the Senate. This is it, Phil – the current situation *requires* a response that is more than business as usual. And that's worrying me, because you guys are only geared to do business as usual.'

'Well . . .' Phil smiled. 'We call that democracy, youth. It's a blessing when you think of it. Some give and take, and then some agreement on how to proceed. How can we do without

215

that? There's a certain accountability to it. So if you have a better way of doing it you tell me. But please, meanwhile, no more "If I Were King" fantasies. There's no king and it's up to us. So help me get this final draft as tight as we can.'

'Okay.'

They worked together with the speed and efficiency of old teammates. Sometimes collaboration could be a pleasure, sometimes it really was a matter of only having to do half of it, and the two halves adding up to more than the sum of their parts.

Then Joe got restive, and nothing would keep him in his buggy but a quick departure and a tour of the street scene. 'I'll finish,' Phil said.

So, back out into the stupendous heat. Charlie was knocked out by it faster than Joe. The world melted around them. Charlie gumbied along, leaning on the stroller for support. Down an elevator into the Metro. Air-conditioning again, thank God. Crash into pink seat cushions. As they rode north, slumped and rocking slightly with their train, Charlie drowsily entertained Joe with some of the toys in the buggy, picking them up and fingering them one by one. 'See, this turtle is NIH. Your Frankenstein monster is the FDA, look how poorly he's put together. This little mole, that's mom's NSF. These two guys, they're like the guy on the Monopoly game, they must be the two parts of Congress, yeah, very Tammany Hall. Where the hell did you get those? Your Iron Giant is of course the Pentagon, and this yellow bulldozer is the US Army Corp of Engineers. The magnifying glass is the General Accountancy Office, and this, what is it, like Barbie? That must be the Office of Management and Budgets, those bimbos, or maybe this Pinocchio here. And your cowboy on a horse is the President of course, he's your friend, he's your friend, he's your friend.'

They were both falling asleep. Joe batted the toy figures into a pile.

216

'Careful Joe. Ooh, there's your tiger. That's the press corps, that's a circus tiger, see its collar? Nobody's scared of it. Although sometimes it does get to eat somebody.'

In the days that followed, Phil took the climate bill back to the foreign relations committee, and the process of marking it up began in earnest. *To mark up* was a very inadequate verb to express the process: 'carving', 'rendering', 'hacking', 'hatcheting', 'stomping', any of these would have been more accurate, Charlie thought as he tracked the gradual deconstruction of the language of the bill, the result turning slowly into a kind of sausage of thought.

The bill lost parts as they fought it out. Winston opposed every phrase of it, and he had to be given some things or nothing would proceed. No precisely spelled-out fuel efficiencies, no acknowledgement of any measurements like the ecological footprint. Phil gave on these because Winston was promising that he would get the House to agree to this version in conference, and the White House would back him too. And so entire methodologies of analysis were being declared off-limits, something that would drive Anna crazy. Another example of science and capital clashing, Charlie thought. Science was like Beeker from the Muppets, haplessly struggling with the round top-hatted guy from the Monopoly game. Right now Beeker was getting his butt kicked.

Two mornings later Charlie learned about it in the *Post* (and how irritating was that?):
CLIMATE SUPER-BILL SPLIT UP IN COMMITTEE
'Say *what*!' Charlie cried. He hadn't even heard of the possibility of such a manoeuvre.

He read paragraphs per eye-twitch while he got on the phone and told it to call Roy:
    ... proponents of the new bills claimed compromises would not damage effectiveness ... President made it clear he would

217

veto the comprehensive bill . . . promised to sign specific bills on a case-by-case if and when they came to his desk

'Ah shit. *Shit.* God damn it!'

'Charlie, that must be you.'

'Roy what is this shit, when did this happen?'

'Last night. Didn't you hear?'

'No I didn't! How could Phil do this!'

'We counted votes, and the biggie wasn't going to get out of committee. And if it did, the House wasn't going to go for it. Winston couldn't deliver, or wouldn't. So Phil decided to support Ellington on Ellington's alternative fuels bill, and he made sure they put more of Ellington's stuff in the first several shorter bills.'

'And Ellington agreed to vote for it on that basis?'

'That's right.'

'So Phil traded horses.'

'The comprehensive was going to lose.'

'You don't know that for sure! They had Speck with them and so they could have carried it on party lines! Who cares what kind of fuel we're burning if the world has melted! This was *important*, Roy!'

'It wasn't going to win,' Roy said, enunciating each word. 'We counted the votes and it lost by one. After that we went for what we could. You know Phil. He likes to get things done.'

'As long as they're easy.'

'You're still pissed off about this. You should go talk to Phil yourself, maybe it will impact what he does next time. I've got to get to a meeting uptown.'

'Okay maybe I'll do that.'

And as it was another morning of Joe and Dad on the town, he was free to do so. He sat on the Metro, absorbing Joe's punches and thinking things over, and when he got the buggy out of the elevator on the third floor of the office he drove it straight for Phil, who today was sitting on a desk

218

in the outer conference room, holding court as blithe and bald-faced as a monkey.

Charlie aimed the wadded *Post* like a stick at Phil, who saw him and winced theatrically. 'Okay!' he said, palm held out to stop the assault. 'Okay kick my ass! Kick my ass right here! But I'll tell you right now that they made me do it.'

He was turning it into another office debate, so Charlie went for it full bore. 'What do you mean *they made you do it*? You caved, Phil. You gave away the store!'

Phil shook his head vehemently. 'I got more than I gave. They're going to have to reduce carbon emissions anyway, we were never going to get much more from them on that –'

'What do you mean!' Charlie shouted.

Andrea and some of the others came out of their rooms, and even Evelyn looked in, though mostly to say hi to Joe. It was a regular schtick: Charlie hammering Phil for his compromises, Phil admitting to all and baiting Charlie to ever greater outrage. Charlie, recognizing this, was still determined to make his point, even if it meant he had to play his usual part. Even if he didn't convince Phil himself, if Phil's group here around him would bear down on him a little harder . . .

Charlie whacked Phil with the *Post*. 'If you would have stuck to your guns we could have sequestered *billions of tons* of carbon. The whole world's with us on this!'

Phil made a face. 'I would have stuck to my guns, Charlie, but then the rest of our wonderful party would have shot me in the foot with those guns. The House wasn't there either. This way we got what was possible. We got it out of committee, damn it, and that's not peanuts. We got out with the full roadless forest requirement and the Arctic refuge and the offshore drilling ban, all of those, and the President has promised to sign them already.'

'They were always gonna give you those! You would have

had to have *died* not to get those. Meanwhile you gave up on the really crucial stuff! They played you like a fish.'

'Did not.'

'Did too.'

'Did not.'

'Did too!'

Yes, this was the level of debate in the offices of one of the greatest senators in the land. It always came down to that between them.

But this time Charlie wasn't enjoying it like he usually did. 'What *didn't* you give up,' he said bitterly.

'Just the forests, streams and oil of North America!'

Their little audience laughed. It was still a debating society to them. Phil licked his finger and chalked one up, then smiled at Charlie, a shot of the pure Chase grin, fetching and mischievous.

Charlie was unassuaged. 'You'd better fund a bunch of submarines to enjoy all those things.'

That too got a laugh. And Phil chalked one up for Charlie, still smiling.

Charlie pushed Joe's buggy out of the building, cursing bitterly. Joe heard his tone of voice and absorbed himself in the passing scene and his dinosaurs. Charlie pushed him along, sweating, feeling more and more discouraged. He knew he was taking it too seriously, he knew that Phil's house style was to treat it as a game, to keep taking shots and not worry too much. But still, given the situation, he couldn't help it. He felt as if he had been kicked in the stomach.

This didn't happen very often. He usually managed to find some way to compensate in his mind for the various reversals of any political day. Bright side, silver lining, eventual revenge, whatever. Some fantasy in which it all came right. So when discouragement did hit him, it struck home with unaccustomed force. It became a global thing for which he had no defence; he couldn't see the forest for the trees, he couldn't see the good in anything. The black clouds had black linings. All bad! Bad bad bad bad bad bad bad.

He pushed into a Metro elevator, descended with Joe into the depths. They got on a car, came to the Bethesda stop. Charlie zombied them out. Bad, bad, bad. Sartrean nausea, induced by a sudden glimpse of reality; horrible that it should be so. That the true nature of reality should be so awful. The blanched air in the elevator was unbreathable. Gravity was too heavy.

Out of the elevator, onto Wisconsin. Bethesda was too dismal. A spew of office and apartment blocks, obviously organized (if that was the word) for the convenience of the cars roaring by. A ridiculous, inhuman autopia. It might as well have been Orange County.

He dragged down the sidewalk home. Walked in the front door. The screen door slapped to behind him with its characteristic *whack*.

From the kitchen: 'Hi hon!'

'Hi Dad!'

It was Anna and Nick's day to come home together after school.

'Momma Momma Momma!'

'Hi Joe!'

Refuge. 'Hi guys,' Charlie said. 'We need a rowboat. We'll keep it in the garage.'

'Cool!'

Anna heard his tone of voice and came out of the kitchen with a whisk in hand, gave him a hug and a peck on the cheek.

'Hmm,' he said, a kind of purr.

'What's wrong babe.'

'Oh, everything.'

'Poor hon.'

He began to feel better. He released Joe from the buggy

and they followed Anna into the kitchen. As Anna picked up Joe and held him on her hip while she continued to cook, Charlie began to shape the story of the day in his mind, to be able to tell her about it with all its drama intact.

After he had told the story, and fulminated for a bit, and opened and drunk a beer, Anna said, 'What you need is some way to bypass the political process.'

'Whoa babe. I'm not sure I want to know what you mean there.'

'I don't know anyway.'

'Revolution, right?'

'No way.'

'A completely non-violent and successful positive revolution?'

'Good idea.'

Nick appeared in the doorway. 'Hey Dad, want to play some baseball?'

'Sure. Good idea.'

Nick seldom proposed this, it was usually Charlie's idea, and so when Nick did it he was trying to make Charlie feel better, which just by itself worked pretty well. So they left the coolness of the house and played in the steamy backyard, under the blind eyes of the banked apartment windows. Nick stood against the brick back of the house while Charlie pitched wiffle balls at him, and he smacked them with a long plastic bat. Charlie tried to catch them if he could. They had about a dozen balls, and when they were scattered over the down-sloping lawn, they re-collected them on Charlie's mound and did it over again, or let Charlie take a turn at bat. The wiffle balls were great; they shot off the bat with a very satisfying plastic *whirr*, and yet it was painless to get hit by one, as Charlie often did. Back and forth in the livid dusk, sweating and laughing, trying to get a wiffle ball to go straight.

Charlie took off his shirt and sweated into the sticky air.

'Okay here comes the pitch. Sandy Koufax winds up, rainbow curve! Hey why didn't you swing?'

'That was a ball, Dad. It bounced before it got to me.'

'Okay here I'll try again. Oh Jesus. Never mind.'

'Why do you say Jesus, Dad?'

'It's a long story. Okay here's another one. Hey, why didn't you swing?'

'It was a ball!'

'Not by much. Walks won't get you off de island mon.'

'The strike zone is taped here to the house, Dad. Just throw one that would hit inside it and I'll swing.'

'That was a bad idea. Okay, here you go. Ooh, very nice. Okay, here you go. Hey come on swing at those!'

'That one was *behind me*.'

'Switch-hitting is a valuable skill.'

'Just throw strikes!'

'I'm trying. Okay here it comes, boom! Very nice! Home run, wow. Uh oh, it got stuck in the tree, see that?'

'We've got enough anyway.'

'True, but look, I can get a foot into this branch . . . here, give me the bat for a second. Might as well get it while we remember where it is.'

Charlie climbed a short distance up the tree, steadied himself, brushed leaves aside, reached in and embraced the trunk for balance, knocked the wiffle ball down with Nick's bat.

'There you go!'

'Hey Dad, what's that vine growing up into the tree? Isn't that poison ivy?'

EIGHT

A Paradigm Shift

Let's rehearse what we know about who we are.

We are primates, very closely related to chimps and other great apes. Our ancestors speciated from the other apes about five million years ago, and evolved in parallel lines and overlapping subspecies, emerging most clearly as hominids about two million years ago.

East Africa in this period was getting drier and drier. The forest was giving away to grassland savannahs dotted with scattered groves of trees. We evolved to adapt to that landscape: the hairlessness, the upright posture, the sweat glands and other physical features. They all made us capable of running long distances in the open sun near the equator. We ran for a living and covered broad areas. We used to run game down by following it until it tired out, sometimes days later.

In that basically stable mode of living the generations passed, and during the many millennia that followed, the size of hominid brains evolved from about 300 cubic millimetres to about 900 cubic millimetres. This is a strange fact, because everything else remained relatively stable. The implication is that the way we lived then was tremendously stimulating to the growth of the brain. Almost every aspect of hominid life has been proposed as the main driver of this growth, everything from the calculation of accurate rock-throwing to the ability to dream, but certainly among the most important must have been language and social life. We talked, we got along; it's a difficult process, requiring lots of thought. Because reproduction is crucial to any definition of evolutionary success, getting along with the group and with the opposite sex is fundamentally adaptive, and so it must be a big driver of increasing brain size. We grew so fast we can hardly fit through the birth canal these days. All that growth from trying to understand other people, the other sex, and look where we are.

Anna was pleased to see Frank back in the office, brusque and grouchy though he was. He made things more interesting. A rant against oversized pick-up trucks would morph into an explanation of everything in terms of yes or no, or a discussion of the social intelligence of gibbons, or an algebra of the most efficient division of labour in the lab. It was impossible to predict what he would say next. Sentences would start reasonably and then go strange, or vice versa. Anna liked that.

He did, however, seem overly impressed by game theory. 'What if the numbers don't correspond to real life?' she asked him. 'What if you don't get five points for defecting when the other person doesn't, what if all those numbers are off, or even backwards? Then it's just another computer game, right?'

'Well –' Frank was taken aback. A rare sight. Immediately he was thinking it over. That was another thing Anna liked about him; he would really think about what she said.

Then Anna's phone rang and she picked up.

'Charlie! Oh dovelie, how are you?'

'Screaming agony.'

'Oh babe. Did you take your pills?'

'I took them. They're not doing a thing. I'm starting to see things in the corners of my eyes, crawlies you know? I think the itches have gotten into my brain. I'm going nuts.'

'Just hold on. It'll take a couple of days for the steroids

to have an effect. Keep taking them. Is Joe giving you a break?'

'No. He wants to wrestle.'

'Oh God don't let him! I know the doctor said it wasn't transmissible, but still –'

'Don't worry. Not a fucking chance of wrestling.'

'You're not touching him?'

'And he's not touching me, that's right. He's getting pretty pissed off about it.'

'You're putting on the plastic gloves to change him?'

'Yes yes yes yes, tortures of the damned, when I take them off the skin comes too, blood and yuck, and then I get *so itchy*.'

'Poor babe. Just try not to do anything.'

Then he had to chase Joe out of the kitchen. Anna hung up.

Frank looked at her. 'Poison ivy?'

'Yep. He climbed into a tree that had it growing up its trunk. He didn't have his shirt on.'

'Oh no.'

'It got him pretty good. Nick recognized it, and so I took him to urgent care and the doctor put some stuff on him and put him on steroids even before the blistering began, but he's still pretty wiped out.'

'Sorry to hear.'

'Yeah, well, at least it's something superficial.'

Then Frank's phone rang, and he went into his cubicle to answer. Anna couldn't help but hear his end of it, as they had already been talking – and then also, as the call went on, his voice got louder several times. At one point he said 'You're kidding' four times in a row, each time sounding more incredulous. After that he only listened for a while, his fingers drumming on the tabletop next to his terminal.

Finally he said, 'I don't know what happened, Derek. You're the one who's in the best position to know that . . . Yeah that's right. They must have had their reasons . . . Well you'll be okay whatever happens, you were vested right? . . . Everyone has options they don't exercise, don't think about that, think about the stock you did have . . . Hey, that's one of the winning endgames. Go under, go public, or get bought. Congratulations . . . Yeah it'll be fascinating to see, sure. Sure. Yeah, that is too bad. Okay yeah. Call me back with the whole story when I'm not at work here. Yeah bye.'

He hung up. There was a long silence from his cubicle.

Finally he got up from his chair, *squeak-squeak*. Anna swivelled to look, and there he was, standing in her doorway, expecting her to turn.

He made a funny face. 'That was Derek Gaspar, out in San Diego. His company Torrey Pines Generique has been bought.'

'Oh really! That's the one you helped start?'

'Yeah.'

'Well, congratulations then. Who bought it?'

'A bigger biotech, called Small Delivery Systems, have you ever heard of it?'

'No.'

'I hadn't either. It's not one of the big pharmaceuticals by any means, mid-sized from what Derek says. Mostly into agropharmacy, he says, but they approached him and made the offer. He doesn't know why.'

'They must have said?'

'Well, no. At least he doesn't seem to be clear on why they did it.'

'Interesting. So, well – it's still good, right? I mean, I thought this was what start-ups hoped for.'

'True . . .'

'But you're not looking like someone who has just become a millionaire or whatever.'

He quickly waved that away, 'It's not that, I'm not involved like that. I was only ever a consultant, UCSD only lets you

229

have a small involvement in outside firms, and I had to stop even that when I came here. Can't be working for the Feds and someone else too, you know.'

'Uh huh.'

'My investments are in a blind trust, so who knows. I didn't have much in Torrey Pines, and the trust may have gotten rid of it. I heard something that made me think they did. I would have if I were them.'

'Oh well, that's too bad then.'

'Yeah yeah,' frowning at her, 'but that isn't the problem.'

He stared out of the window, across the atrium into all the other windows. There was a look on his face she had never seen before – chagrined – she couldn't quite read it. Distressed.

'What is then?'

Quietly he said, 'I don't know.' Then: 'The system is messed up.'

She said, 'You should come to the lunchtime lecture tomorrow. Rudra Cakrin, the Khembali ambassador, is going to be talking about the Buddhist view of science. No, you should. You sound more like them than anyone else, at least sometimes.'

He frowned as if this were a criticism.

'No, come on. I want you to.'

'Okay. Maybe. If I finish a letter I'm working on.'

He went back to his cubicle, sat down heavily. 'God damn it,' Anna heard him say.

Then he started to type. It was like the sound of thought itself, a rapid-fire plastic tipping and tapping, interrupted by hard whaps of his thumb against the space bar. His keyboard really took a pounding sometimes.

He was still typing like a madman when Anna saw her clock and rushed out the door to try to get home on time.

The next morning Frank drove in with his farewell letter in a manila envelope. He had decided to elaborate on it, make it into a fully substantiated, crushing indictment of NSF, which, if taken seriously, might do some good. He was going to give it directly to Diane Chang, head of NSF. Private letter, one hard copy. That way she could read it, consider it in private, and decide whether she wanted to do something about it. Meanwhile, whatever she did, he would have taken his shot at trying to improve the place, and could go back to real science with a clean conscience. Leave in peace. Leave behind some of the anger in him. Hopefully.

He had heavily revised the draft he had written on the flight back from San Diego. Bulked up the arguments, made the criticisms more specific, made some concrete suggestions for improvements. It was still a pretty devastating indictment when he had finished, but this time it was all in the tone of a scientific paper. No getting mad or getting eloquent. Five pages single-spaced, even after he had cut it to the bone. Well, they needed a kick in the pants. This would certainly do that.

He read it through one more time, then sat there in his office chair, tapping the manila envelope against his leg, looking sightlessly out into the atrium. Wondering, among other things, what had happened to Torrey Pines Generique. Wondering if the hiring of Yann Pierzinski had anything to do with it.

Suddenly he heaved out of his chair, walked to the elevators

231

with the manila envelope and its contents, took an elevator up to the twelfth floor. Walked around to Diane's office and nodded at Laveta, Diane's secretary. He put the envelope in Diane's in-box.

'She's gone for today,' Laveta told him.

'That's all right. Let her know when she comes in tomorrow that it's there, will you? It's personal.'

'All right.'

Back to the sixth floor. He went to his chair and sat down. It was done.

He heard Anna in her office, typing away. Her door was closed, so presumably she was using her electric breast pump to milk herself while she was working. Frank would have liked to have seen that, not just for prurient reasons, though there were those too, but more for the pleasure of seeing her multi-tasking like that. She typed with forefingers and thumbs only, like a reporter in a 1930s movie; whether this was an unconscious rejection of all secretarial skills or simply happenstance, he couldn't say. But he bet it made for an attractive sight.

He recalled that this was the day she wanted him to join her at the lunchtime lecture. She had apparently helped to arrange for the Khembali ambassador to give the talk. Frank had seen it listed on a sheet announcing the series, posted next to the elevators:

Purpose of Science From the Buddhist Perspective

It didn't sound promising to him. Esoteric at best, and perhaps much worse. That would not be atypical for these lunch talks, they were a very mixed bag. People were burnt out on regular lectures, the last thing they wanted to do at lunch was listen to more of the same, and so this series was deliberately geared towards entertainment. Frank remembered seeing titles like 'Antarctica as Utopia', or 'The Art of Body Imaging', or 'Ways Global Warming Can Help Us'. Apparently it was a case of the wackier the topic, the bigger the crowd.

232

This one would no doubt be well-attended.

Anna's door opened and Frank's head jerked up, reflexively seeking the sight of a bare-chested science goddess, something like the French figure of Liberty; but of course not. She was just leaving for the lecture.

'Are you going to come?' she asked.

'Yeah, sure.'

That pleased her. He accompanied her to the elevators, shaking his head at her, and at himself. Up to the tenth floor, past the spectacular Antarctic underwater photo gallery, into the big conference room. It held about two hundred people. By the time the Khembalis arrived, every seat was occupied.

Frank sat down near the back, pretending to work on his hand pad. Air-conditioned air fell on him like a blessing. People who knew each other were finding each other, sitting down in groups, talking about this and that. The Khembalis stood by the lectern, discussing mike arrangements with Anna and Laveta. The old ambassador, Rudra Cakrin, wore his maroon robes, while the rest of the Khembali contingent were in off-white cotton pants and shirts, as if in India. Rudra Cakrin needed his mike lowered. His young assistant helped him, then adjusted his own. Translation; what a pain. Frank groaned soundlessly.

They tested the mikes, and the noise of talk dampened. The room was impressively full, Frank had to admit, wacky factor or not. These were people still interested enough in ideas to spend a lunch hour listening to a lecture on the philosophy of science. It would be like that in some departments at UCSD, perhaps even on most university campuses, despite the insane pace of life. Surplus time and energy, given over to curiosity: a fundamental hominid behavioural trait. The basic trait that got people into science, that made science in the first place, surviving despite the mind-numbing regimes of its modern-day expression. Here he was himself, after all,

233

and no one could be more burnt-out and disenchanted than he was. But still following a tropism helplessly, like a sunflower turning to look at the sun.

The old monk cut quite a figure up at the lectern. Incongruous at best. This might be an admirably curious audience, but it was also a sceptical gang of hardened old technocrats. A tough sell, one would think, for a wizened man in robes, now peering out at them as if from a distant century, looking in fact quite like an early hominid.

And yet there he stood, and here they sat. Something had brought them together, and it wasn't just the air-conditioning. They sat in their chairs, attentive, courteous, open to suggestion. Frank felt a small glimmer of pride. This is how it had all begun, back in those Royal Society meetings in London in the 1660s: polite listening to a lecture by some odd person who was necessarily an autodidact; polite questions; the matter considered reasonably by all in attendance. An agreement to look at things reasonably. This was the start of it.

The old man stared out with a benign gaze. He seemed to mirror their attention, to study them.

'Good morning!' he said, then made a gesture with his hand to indicate that he had exhausted his store of English, except for what followed: 'Thank you.'

His young assistant then said, 'Rimpoche Rudra Cakrin, Khembalung's ambassador to the United States, thanks you for coming to listen to him.'

A bit redundant that, but then the old man began to speak in his own language – Tibetan, Anna had said – a low, guttural sequence of sounds. Then he stopped, and the young man, Anna's friend Drepung, began to translate.

'The rimpoche says, Buddhism begins in personal experience. Observation of one's surroundings and one's reactions, and one's thoughts. There is a scientific . . . foundation to the process. – He adds, if I truly understand what you mean in the West when you say science. – He says, I hope you will

234

tell me if I am wrong about it. But science seems to me to be about what happens that we can all agree on.'

Now Rudra Cakrin interrupted to ask a question of Drepung, who nodded, then added: 'What can be asserted. That if you were to look into it, you would come to agree with the assertion. And everyone else would as well.'

A few people in the audience were nodding.

The old man spoke again.

Drepung said, 'The things we can agree on are few, and general. And the closer to the time of the Buddha, the more general they are. Now, two thousand and five hundred years have passed, more or less, and we are in the age of the microscope, the telescope, and . . . the mathematical description of reality. These are realms we cannot experience directly with our senses. And yet we can still agree in what we say about these realms. Because they are linked in long chains of mathematical cause and effect, from what we can see.'

Rudra Cakrin smiled briefly, spoke. It began to seem to Frank that Drepung's translated pronouncements were much longer than the old man's utterances. Could Tibetan be so compact?

'This network is a very great accomplishment,' Drepung added.

Rudra Cakrin then sang in a low gravelly voice, like Louis Armstrong's, only an octave lower.

Drepung chanted in English:

'He who would understand the meaning of Buddha nature,
Must watch for the season and the causal relations.
Real life is the life of causes.'

Rudra Cakrin followed this with some animated speech.

Drepung translated, 'This brings up the concept of Buddha nature, rather than nature in itself. What is that difference? Buddha-nature is the appropriate . . . *response* to nature. The reply of the observing mind. Buddhist philosophy ultimately points to seeing reality as it is. And then . . .'

235

Rudra Cakrin spoke urgently.

'Then the response, the reply – the human moment – the things we say, and do, and think – that moment arrives. We come back to the realm of the expressible. The nature of reality – as we go deeper, language is left further behind. Even mathematics is no longer germane. But . . .'

The old man went on for quite some time, until Frank thought he saw Drepung make a gesture or expression with his eyelids, and instantly Rudra Cakrin stopped.

'But, when we come to what we should do, it returns to the simplest of words. Compassion. Right action. Helping others. It always stays that simple. Reduce suffering. There is something – reassuring in this. Greatest complexity of what is, greatest simplicity in what we should do. Much preferable to the reverse situation.'

Rudra Cakrin spoke in a much calmer voice now.

'Here again,' Drepung went on, 'the two approaches overlap and are one. Science began as the hunt for food, comfort, health. We learned how things work in order to control them better. In order to reduce our suffering. The methods involved, observation and trial, in our tradition were refined in medical work. That went on for many ages. In the West, your doctors too did this, and in the process, became scientists. In Asia the Buddhist monks were the doctors, and they too worked on refining methods of observation and trial, to see if they could . . . reproduce their successes, when they had them.'

Rudra Cakrin nodded, put a hand to Drepung's arm. He spoke briefly. Drepung said, 'The two are now parallel studies. On the one hand, science has specialized, through mathematics and technology, on natural observations, finding out what is, and making new tools. On the other, Buddhism has specialized in human observations, to find out – how to become. Behave. What to do. How to go forward. Now, I say, they are like the two eyes in the head. Both necessary to

236

create whole sight. Or rather . . . there is an old saying. Eyes that see, feet that walk. We could say that science is the eyes, Buddhism the feet.'

Frank listened to all this with ever more irritation. Here was a man arguing for a system of thought that had not contributed a single new bit of knowledge to the world for the last 2500 years, and he had the nerve to put it on an equal basis with science, which was now adding millions of new facts to its accumulated store of knowledge every day. What a farce!

And yet his irritation was filled with uneasiness as well. The young translator kept saying things that weirdly echoed things Frank had thought before, or answered things Frank was wondering at that very moment. Frank thought, for instance, Well, how would all this compute if we were remembering that we are all primates recently off the savannah, foragers with brains that grew to adapt to that particular surrounding, would any of this make sense? And at that very moment, answering a question from the audience (they seem to have shifted into that mode without a formal announcement of it), Drepung said, still translating the old man,

'We are animals. Animals whose wisdom has extended so far as to tell us we are mortal creatures. We die. For fifty thousand years we have known this. Much of our mental energy is spent avoiding this knowledge. We do not like to think of it. Then again, we know now that even the cosmos is mortal. Reality is mortal. All things change ceaselessly. Nothing remains the same in time. Nothing can be held onto. The question then becomes, what do we *do* with this knowledge? How do we live with it? How do we make sense of it?'

Well – indeed. Frank leaned forward, piqued, wondering what Drepung would tell them the old man had said next. That gravelly low voice, growling through its incomprehensible sounds – it was strange to think it was expressing such meanings. Frank suddenly wanted to know what he was saying.

'One of the scientific terms for compassion,' Drepung said, looking around the ceiling as if for the word, '. . . you say, *altruism*. This is a question in your animal studies. Does true altruism exist, and is it a good adaptation? Does compassion work, in other words? You have done studies that suggest altruism is the best adaptive strategy, if seen from the group context. This then becomes a kind of . . . admonishment. To practice compassion to successfully evolve – this, coming from your science, which claims to be descriptive only! Only describing what has worked to make us what we are. But in Buddhism we have always said, if you want to help others, practice compassion; if you want to help yourself, practice compassion. Now science adds, if you want to help your species, practice compassion.'

This got a laugh, and Frank also chuckled. He started to think about it in terms of prisoner's dilemma strategies; it was an invocation for all to make the 'always generous' move, for maximum group return, indeed maximum individual return . . . Thus he missed what Drepung said next, absorbed in something more like a feeling than a thought: *If only I could believe in something, no doubt it would be a relief.* All his rationality, all his acid scepticism; suddenly it was hard not to feel that it was really just some kind of disorder.

And at that very moment Rudra Cakrin looked right at him, him alone in all the audience, and Drepung said, 'An excess of reason is itself a form of madness.'

Frank sat back in his seat. What had the question been? Re-running his short-term memory, he could not find it.

Now he was lost to the conversation again. His flesh was tingling, as if he were a bell that had been struck.

'The experience of enlightenment can be sudden.'

He didn't hear that, not consciously.

'The scattered parts of consciousness occasionally assemble at once into a whole pattern.'

He didn't hear that either, as he was lost in thought. All his certainties were trembling. He thought, an excess of reason itself a form of madness – it's the story of my life. And the old man *knew*.

He found himself standing. Everyone else was too. The thing must be over. People were filing out. They were massed in a group at the elevators. Someone said to Frank, 'Well, what did you think?' clearly expecting some sharp put-down, something characteristically Frankish, and indeed his mouth was forming the words 'Not much for twenty-five hundred years of concentrated study.' But he said 'Not' and stopped, shuddering at his own habits. He could be such an asshole.

The elevator doors opened and rescued him. He flowed in, rubbed his forearms as if to warm them from the conference room's awesome a/c. He said to the enquiring eyes watching him, 'Interesting.'

There were nods, little smiles. Even that one word, often the highest expression of praise in the scientific tongue, was against type for him. He was making a fool of himself. His group expected him to conform to his persona. That was how group dynamics worked. Surprising people was an unusual thing, faintly unwelcome. Except was it? People certainly paid to be surprised; that was comedy; that was art. It could be proved by analysis. Right now he wasn't sure of anything.

'. . . paying attention to the real world,' someone was saying.

'A weak empiricism.'

'How do you mean?'

The elevator door opened; Frank saw it was his floor. He got out and went to his office. He stood there in the doorway looking at all his stuff, scattered about for disposal or for packing to be mailed back west. Piles of books, periodicals, offprints, xeroxed sheets of stapled or loose paper; folded or rolled graphs and charts and tables and spreadsheets. His exteriorized memory, the paper trail of his life. An excess of reason.

He sat there thinking.

Anna came in. 'Hi Frank. How did you like the talk?'

'It was interesting.'

She regarded him. 'I thought so too. Listen, Charlie and I are having a party for the Khembalis tonight at our place, a little celebration. You should come if you want.'

'Thanks,' he said. 'Maybe I will.'

'Good. That would be nice. I've gotta go get ready for it.'

'Okay. See you there maybe.'

'Okay.' With a last curious look, she left.

Sometimes certain images or phrases, ideas or sentences, tunes or snatches of tunes, stick in the head and repeat over and over. For some people this can be a problem, as they get stuck in such loops too often and too long. Most people skip into new ideas or new loops fairly frequently – others at an almost frightening rate of speed, the reverse of the stuck-in-a-loop problem.

Frank had always considered himself to be unstable in this regard, veering strongly either one way or the other. The shift from something like obsessive-compulsive to something like attention-deficit sometimes occurred so quickly that it seemed he might be exhibiting an entirely new kind of bipolarity.

No excess of reason there!

Or maybe that was the base cause of it all. An attempt to gain control. The old monk had looked him right in the eye. An excess of reason is itself a form of madness. Maybe in trying to be reasonable, he had been trying to stay on an even keel. Who could say?

He could see how this might be what Buddhists called a

koan, a riddle without an answer, which if pondered long enough might cause the thinking mind to balk, and give up thinking. Give up thinking! That was crazy. And yet in that moment, perhaps the sensory world would come pouring in. Experience of the present, unmediated by language. Unspeakable by definition. Just *felt*. Experienced in mentation of a different sort, languageless, or language-transcendent. Something *other*.

Frank hated that sort of mysticism. Or maybe he loved it; the experience of it, that is. Like anyone who has ever entered a moment of non-lingustic absorption, he recalled it as a kind of blessing. Like in the old days, hanging there cleaning windows, singing What's my line, I'm happy cleaning windows. Climbing, surfing . . . you could think far faster than you could verbalize in your mind. No doubt one knew the world by way of a flurry of impressions and thoughts that were far faster than consciousness could track. Consciousness was just a small part of it.

He left the building, went out into the humid afternoon. The sight of the street somehow repelled him. He couldn't drive right now. Instead he walked through the car-dominated, slightly junky commercial district surrounding Ballston, spinning with thoughts and with something more. It seemed to him that he was learning things as he walked that he couldn't have said out loud at that moment, and yet they were real, they were felt; they were quite real.

An excess of reason. Well, but he had always tried to be reasonable. He had tried very hard. That attempt was his mode of being. It had seemed to help him. Dispassionate; sensible; calm; reasonable. A thinking machine. He had loved those stories when he was a boy. That was what a scientist was, and that was why he was such a good scientist. That was the thing that had bothered him about Anna, that she was undeniably a good scientist but she was a passionate scientist too, she threw herself into her work

241

and her ideas, had preferences and took positions and was completely engaged emotionally in her work. She cared which theory was true. That was all wrong, but she was so smart that it worked, for her anyway. If it did. But it wasn't science. To care that much was to introduce biases into the study. It wasn't a matter of emotions. You did science simply because it was the best adaptation strategy in the environment into which they had been born. Science was the gene trying to pass itself along more successfully. Also it was the best way to pass the hours, or to make a living. Everything else was so trivial and grasping. Social primates, trapped in a technocosmos of their own devise; science was definitely the only way to see the terrain well enough to know which way to strike forward, to make something new for all the rest. No passion need be added to that reasoned way forward.

And yet, it occurred to him, why did things live? What got them through it, really? What made them make all these efforts, when death lay in wait at the end for every one of them? This was what these Buddhists had dared to ask.

He was walking towards the Potomac now, along Fairfax Drive, a huge commercial street rumbling with traffic, just a few cars away from gridlock. Long lines of vehicles, with most of the occupants in them talking on phones, talking to some other person somewhere else on the planet. A strange sight when you looked at it!

Reason had never explained the existence of life in this universe. Life was a mystery; reason had tried and failed to explain it, and science could not start it from scratch in a lab. Little localized eddies of anti-entropy, briefly popping into being and then spinning out, with bits of them carried elsewhere in long invisible chains of code that spun up yet more eddies. A succession of pattern dust devils. A mystery, a kind of miracle – a miracle struggling in harsh inimical conditions, succeeding only where it found water, which gathered in droplets in the universe just as it did on a window-pane, and gave life sustenance. Water of life. A miracle.

He felt the sweat breaking out all over his skin. When hominids went bipedal they lost hair and gained sweat glands, so they could convey away the extra heat caused by all that walking. But it didn't really work in a jungle. Tall trees, many species of trees and bushes; it could have been a botanical garden with a city laid into it, the plants a hundred shades of green. People walking by in small groups. Only runners were alone, and even they usually ran in pairs or larger groups. A social species, like bees or ants, with social rules that were invariant to the point of invisibility, people did not notice them. A species operating on pheromones, lucky in its adaptability, unstable in the environment. Knowledge of the existence of the future, awareness of the future as part of the calculations made in daily life, for daily living. Live for the future. A cosmic history read out of signs so subtle and mathematical that only the effort of a huge transtemporal group of powerful minds could ever have teased it out; but then those who came later could be given the whole story, with its unexplored edges there to take off into. *This* was the human project, *this* was science, this was what science was. This was what life was.

He stood there, thrumming with thought, queasy, anxious, frightened. He was a confused man. Free-floating anxiety, he thought anxiously; except it had clear causes. People said that paradigm shifts only occurred when the old scientists died, that people individually did not have them, they were too stubborn, too set in their ways, it was a more social process, a diachronic matter of successive generations.

Occasionally, however, it must be otherwise. Individual scientists, more open-minded or less certain than most, must have lived through one. Frank almost ran into a woman walking in the other direction, almost said, 'Sorry ma'am, I'm in the midst of a paradigm shift.' He was disoriented.

He saw that moving from one paradigm to the next was not like moving from one skyscraper to another, as in the diagrams he had once seen in a philosophy of science book. It was more like being inside a kaleidoscope, where he had become used to the pattern, and now the tube was twisting and he was falling and every aspect of what he saw was clicking to something different, click after click; colours, patterns, everything awash. Like dying and being reborn. Altruism, compassion, simple goddamned foolishness, loyalty to people who were not loyal to you, playing the sap for the defectors to take advantage of, competition, adaptation, displaced self-interest – or else something real, a real force in the world, a kind of physical constant, like gravity, or a basic attribute of life, like the drive to propagate one's DNA to subsequent generations. A reason for being. Something beyond DNA. A rage to live, an urge to goodness. Love. A green force, *élan vital*, that was metaphysics, that was bad, but how else were you going to explain the data?

An excess of reason wasn't going to do it.

Genes, however, were very reasonable. They followed their directive, they reproduced. They were a living algorithm, creatures of four elements. Strings of binaries, codes of enormous length, codes that spoke bodies. It was a kind of reason that did that. Even a kind of monomania –an excess of reason, as the koan suggested. So that perhaps they were all mad, not just socially and individually, but genomically too. Molecular obsessive-compulsives. And then up from there, in stacked emergent insanities. Unless it was infused with some other quality that was not rational, some late emergent property like altruism, or compassion, or love – something that was not a code – then it was all for naught.

He felt sick. It could have just been the heat and humidity, the speed of his walking, something he ate, a bug that he had caught or that had bit him. It felt like all those, even though

244

he suspected it was all starting in his mind, a kind of idea infection or moral fever. He needed to talk to someone.

But it had to be someone he trusted. That made for a very short list. A very, very, very short list. In fact, my God, who exactly would be on that list, now he came to think of it?

Anna. Anna Quibler, his colleague. The passionate scientist. A rock, in fact. A rock in the tide. Who *could* you trust after all? A good scientist. A scientist willing to take that best scientific attitude towards all of reality. Maybe that's what the old lama had been talking about. If too much reason was a form of madness, then perhaps *passionate reason* was what was called for. Passionate scientist, compassionate scientist, could analysis alone parse out which was which there? It could be a religion, some kind of humanism or biocentrism, philabios, philocosmos. Or simply Buddhism, if he had understood the old man correctly.

Suddenly he remembered that Anna and Charlie were hosting a party, and Anna had invited him. To help celebrate the day's lecture, ironically enough. The Khembalis would be there.

He walked, sweating, looking at street signs, figuring out where he was. Ah. Almost to Washington Boulevard. He could continue to the Clarendon Metro station. He did that, descended the Metro escalator into the ground. A weird action for a hominid to take – a religious experience. Following the shaman into the cave. We've never lost any of that.

He sat zoned in one of the train cars until the change of lines at Metro Center. The interior there looked weirder than ever, like a shopping mall in hell. A *Red Line Shady Grove* train pulled in, and he got on and stood with the multitude. It was late in the day, he had wandered a long time. It was near the end of the rush hour.

The travellers at this hour were almost all professionally dressed. They were headed home, out to the prosperous parts of Northwest and Chevy Chase and Bethesda and Rockville and Gaithersburg. At each stop the train got emptier, until he could sit down on one of the garish orange seats.

Sitting there, he began to feel calmer. The coolness of the air, the sassy but soothing orange and pink, the people's faces, all contributed to this feeling. Even the driver of the train contributed, with a stop in each station that was as smooth as any Frank had ever felt, a beautiful touch on the big brakes that most drivers could not help but jerk to one degree or another. This guy eased smoothly in, over and over, station after station. It was like a musical performance. The concrete caves changed their nameplates, otherwise each cave was almost the same.

Across from him sat a woman wearing a black skirt and white blouse. Hair short and curly, glasses, almost invisible touch of make-up. Bra strap showing at her collarbone. A professional of some sort, going home. Face intelligent and friendly-seeming, not pretty but attractive. Legs crossed, one running-shoed foot sticking into the aisle. Her skirt had ridden up her leg and Frank could see the side of one thigh, made slightly convex from her position and the mass of solid quadriceps muscles. No stockings, skin smooth, a few freckles. She looked strong.

Like Frank, she stood to get out at the Bethesda stop. Frank followed her out of the train. It was interesting the way dresses and skirts all were different, and framed or featured the bodies they covered uniquely. Height of bottom, width of hips, length and shape of legs, of back and shoulders, proportions of the whole, movement: the compounded variations were infinite, so that no two women looked the same to Frank. And he looked all the time.

This one was businesslike and moved fast. Her legs were just a touch longer than the usual proportion, which discrepancy drew the eye, as always. It was discrepancy from the norm that drew the eye. She looked like she was wearing high heels even though she wasn't. That was attractive; indeed, women wore high heels to look like her. Another savannah judgement, no doubt – the ability to outrun predators as part of the potential reproductive success. Whatever. She looked good. It was like a kind of balm, after what he had gone through. Back to basics.

Frank stood below her as they rose up the first escalator from trackside to the turnstiles, enjoying that view, which exaggerated the length of her legs and the size of her bottom. At that point he was hooked, and would therefore, as was his custom, follow her until their paths diverged, just to prolong the pleasure of watching her walk. This happened to him all the time, it was one of the habits one fell into, living in a city of such beautiful women.

Through the turnstiles, then, and along the tunnel towards the big escalator up and out. Then to his surprise she turned left, into the nook that held the station's elevators.

He followed her without thinking. He never took the Metro system's elevators, they were extremely slow. And yet there he was, standing beside her waiting for this one to arrive, feeling conspicuous but unable to do anything about it now that he was there, except look up at the display lights over the elevator doors. Although he could just walk away.

The light lit. The doors opened on an empty car. Frank followed the woman in and turned and stared at the closing doors, feeling red-faced.

She pushed the street-level button, and with a slight lift they were off. The elevator hummed and vibrated as they rose. It was hot and humid, and the little room smelled faintly of machine oil, sweat, plastics, perfume and electricity.

Frank studiously observed the display over the doors. The woman did the same. She had the strap of her armbag hooked under her thumb. Her elbow was pressed into her blouse just over the waistline of her skirt. Her hair was so curly that it was almost frizzy, but not quite; brown, and cut short, so that it curled tight as a cap on her head. A little longer in a fringe at the back of her neck, where two lines of fine blonde hairs curved down towards her deltoid muscles. Wide shoulders. A very impressive animal. Even in his peripheral vision he could see all this.

The elevator whined, then shuddered and stopped. Startled, Frank re-focused on the control panel, which still showed them as going up.

'Shit,' the woman muttered, and looked at her watch. She glanced at Frank.

'Looks like we're stuck,' Frank said, pushing the UP button.

'Yeah. Damn it.'

'Unbelievable,' Frank agreed.

She grimaced. 'What a day.'

A moment or two passed. Frank hit the DOWN button: nothing. He gestured at the little black phone console set in the panel above the UP and DOWN buttons.

'I guess we're at the point this is here for.'

'I think so.'

Frank picked up the receiver, put it to his ear. The phone was ringing already, which was good, as it had no numberpad. What would it have been like to pick up a phone and hear nothing?

But the ringing went on long enough to concern him.

Then it stopped, and a woman's voice said, 'Hello?'

'Hi? Hey listen, we're in the elevator at the Bethesda Metro stop, and it's stuck.'

'Okay. Bethesda did you say? Did you try pushing the close door button then the up button?'

'No.' Frank pushed these buttons. 'I am now, but ... nothing. It feels pretty stuck.'

'Try the down button too, after the close door.'

'Okay.' He tried it.

'Do you know how far up you are?'

'We must be near the top.' He glanced at the woman, and she nodded.

'Any smoke?'

'No!'

'Okay. There's people on the way. Just sit tight and stay cool. Are you crowded in there?'

'No, there's just two of us.'

'That's okay then. They said they'll be about half an hour to an hour, depending on traffic and the problem with the elevator. They'll call you on your phone there when they get there.'

'Okay. Thanks.'

'No problem. Pick up again if something changes. I'll be watching.'

'I will. Thanks again.'

The woman had already hung up. Frank did also.

They stood there.

'Well,' Frank said, gesturing at the phone.

'I could hear,' the woman said. She looked around at the floor. 'I guess I'll sit down while we wait. My feet are tired.'

'Good idea.'

They sat down next to each other, leaning against the back wall of the elevator.

'Tired feet?'

'Yeah. I went running today at lunch, and it was mostly on sidewalks.'

'You're a runner?'

'No, not really. That's why my feet hurt. I ride with a cycling club, and we're doing a triathlon, so I'm trying to add some running and swimming. I could just do the cycling leg of a team, but I'm seeing if I can get ready to do the whole thing.'

'What are the distances?'

'A mile swim, twenty-mile bike, ten-k run.'

'Ouch.'

'It's not so bad.'

They sat in silence.

'So are you going to be late for something here?'

'No,' Frank said. 'Well, it depends, but it's just a kind of party.'

'Too bad to miss that.'

'Maybe. It's a work thing. There was a lunchtime lecture today, and now the organizer is having a thing for the speakers.'

'What did they talk about?'

He smiled. 'A Buddhist approach to science, actually. They were the Buddhists.'

'And you were the scientists.'

'Yes.'

'That must have been interesting.'

'Well, yes. It was. It's given me a lot to think about. More than I thought it would. I don't exactly know what to say to them tonight though.'

'Hmm.' She appeared to consider it. 'Sometimes I think about cycling as a kind of meditation. Lots of times I kind of blank out, and when I come to a lot of miles have passed.'

'That must be a nice.'

'Your science isn't psychology, is it?'

'Microbiology.'

'Good. Sorry. Anyway, I like it, yeah. I don't think I could do it by trying for it, though. It just happens, usually late in a ride. Maybe it's low blood sugar. Not enough energy to think.'

'Could be,' Frank said. 'Thinking does burn some sugars.'

'There you go.'

They sat there burning sugars.

'So what about you, are you going to be late for something?'

'I was going to go for a ride, actually. My legs would be less sore tomorrow if I did. But after this, who knows what I'll feel like . . . maybe I still will. If we get out of here pretty soon.'

'We'll see about that.'

'Yeah.'

The trapped air was stifling. They sat there sweating. There was some quality to it, some combination of comfort and tension, their bodies simply breathing together, resting, almost touching, ever so slightly incandescent to each other . . . it was nice. Two animals resting side by side, one male one female. A lot of talk goes on below the radar. And indeed somehow it had come to pass that as they relaxed their legs had drifted outward, and met each other, so that now they were just very slightly touching, at the outsides of the knees, kind of resting against each other in a carefully natural way, her leg bare (her skirt had fallen down into her lap) and his covered by light cotton pants. Touching. Now the talk under the radar was filling Frank's whole bandwidth, and though he continued his part of the conversation, he could not have immediately said what they were talking about.

'So you must ride quite a lot?'

'Yeah, pretty much.'

She was in a cycling club, she told him. 'It's like any other club.' Except this one went out on long bike rides. Weekends, smaller groups more often than that. She too was making talk. 'Like a social club really. Like the Elks Club or something, only with bikes.'

'Good for you.'

'Yes, it's fun. A good workout.'

'It makes you strong.'

'Well, the legs anyway. It's good for legs.'

'Yes,' Frank agreed, and took the invitation to glance down at hers. She did as well, tucking her chin and looking as if inspecting something outside of herself. Her skirt had fallen so that the whole side of her left leg was exposed.

She said, 'It bulks up the quads.'

Frank intended to agree by saying 'Uh huh,' but somehow the sound got interrupted, as if he had been tapped lightly on the solar plexus while making it, so that it came out 'nnnnn,' like a short hum or purr. A little moan of longing, in fact, at the sight of such long strong legs, all that smooth skin, the sweet curve of the under-thigh. Her knees stood distinctly higher than his.

He looked up to find her grinning at him. He hunched his shoulders and looked away just a touch, yes, guilty as charged, feeling the corners of his mouth tug up in the helpless smile of someone caught in the act. What could he say, she had great legs.

Now she was watching him with an interrogatory gaze, searching his face for something specific, it seemed, her eyes alight with mischief, amused. It was a look that had a whole person in it.

And she must have liked something about what she saw, because she leaned his way, into his shoulder, and then pressed further in and stretched her head towards his and kissed him.

'Mmm,' he purred, kissing back. He shifted around the better to face her, his body moving without volition. She was shifting too. She pulled back briefly to look again in his eyes, then she smiled broadly and shifted into his arms. Their kiss grew more and more passionate, they were like teenagers making out. They flew off into that pocket universe of bliss. Time passed, Frank's thoughts scattered, he was absorbed in the feel of her mouth, her lips on his, her tongue, the awkwardness of their embrace. It was very hot. They were both literally dripping with sweat; their kisses tasted salty. Frank slid a hand under her skirt. She hummed and then shifted onto one knee and over onto him, straddling him. They kissed harder than ever.

The elevator phone rang.

She sat up. 'Oops,' she said, catching her breath. Her face was flushed and she looked gorgeous. She reached up and behind her and grabbed the receiver, staying solidly on him.

'Hello?' she said into the phone. Frank flexed under her and she put a hand to his chest to stop him.

'Oh yeah, we're here,' she said. 'You guys got here fast.' She listened and quickly laughed, 'No, I don't suppose you do hear that very often.' She glanced down at Frank to share a complicit smile, and it was in that moment that Frank felt the strongest bond of all with her. They were a pair in the world, and no one else knew it but them.

'Yeah sure – we'll be here!'

She rolled off him as she hung up. 'They say they've got it fixed and we're on our way up.'

'Damn it.'

'I know.'

They stood. She brushed down her skirt. They felt a few jerks as the elevator started up again.

'Wow, look at us. We are just *dripping.*'

'We would have been no matter what. It's hot in here.'

'True.' She reached up to straighten his hair and then they were kissing again, banging against the wall in a sudden blaze of passion, stronger than ever. Then she pushed him away, saying breathlessly, 'Okay, no more, we're almost there. The door must be about to open.'

'True.'

Confirming the thought, the elevator began its characteristic slow-motion deceleration. Frank took a deep breath, blew it out, tried to pull himself together. He felt flushed, his skin was tingling. He looked at her. She was almost as tall as he was.

She laughed. 'They're gonna bust us for sure.'

The elevator stopped. The doors jerked open. They were still a foot below street level, but it was an easy step up and out.

Before them stood three men, two in workers' overalls, one in a Metro uniform.

The one in the uniform held a clipboard. 'Y'all okay?' he said to them.

'Yeah' 'We're fine' they said together.

Everyone stood there for a second.

'Must have been hot in there,' the uniformed one remarked.

The three black men stared at them curiously.

'It was,' Frank said.

'But not much different than out here,' his companion quickly added, and they all laughed. It was true; getting out had not made any marked change. It was like stepping from one sauna to another. Their rescuers were also sweating profusely. Yes – the open air of a Washington DC evening was indistinguishable from the inside of an elevator stuck deep underground. This was their world: and so they laughed.

They were on the sidewalk flanking Wisconsin Avenue, next to the elevator box and the old post office. Passersby glanced at them. The foreman gave the woman his clipboard. 'If you'd fill out and sign the report, please. Thanks. Looks like it was about half an hour from your call to when we pulled you.'

'Pretty fast,' the woman said, reading the text on her form before filling in some blanks and signing. 'It didn't even seem that long.' She looked at her watch. 'All right, well – thanks very much.' She faced Frank, extended a hand. 'It was nice to meet you.'

'Yes it was,' Frank said, shaking her hand, struggling for words, struggling to think. In front of these witnesses nothing came to him, and she turned and walked south on Wisconsin. Frank felt constrained by the gazes of the three men; all would be revealed if he were to run after her and ask for her name, her phone number, and besides now the foreman was holding the clipboard out to him, and it occurred to him that he could read what she had written down there.

But it was a fresh form, and he looked up to see that down the street she was turning right, onto one of the smaller streets west of Wisconsin.

The foreman watched him impassively while the technicians went back to the elevator.

Frank gestured at the clipboard. 'Can I get that woman's name, please?'

The man frowned, surprised, and shook his head. 'Not allowed to,' he said. 'It's a law.'

Frank felt his stomach sink. There had to be a physiological basis for that feeling, some loosening of the gut as fear or shock prepared the body for fight-or-flight. Flight in this case. 'But I need to get in touch with her again,' he said.

The man stared at him, stone-faced. He had to have worked on that look in a mirror, it was like something out of the movies. Samuel L. Jackson perhaps.

'Should have thought of that when you was stuck with her,' he said, sensibly enough. He gestured in the direction she had gone. 'You could probably still catch her.'

Released by these words Frank took off, first walking fast, then, after he turned right on the street she had taken, running. He looked forward down the street for her black skirt, white blouse, short brown hair; there was no sign of her. He began sweating hard again, a kind of panic response. How far could she have gone? What had she said she was late for? He couldn't remember – horribly, his mind seemed to have blurred on much that she had said before they started kissing. He needed to know all that now! It was like some memory experiment foisted on undergraduates, how much could you remember of the incidents right before a shock? Not much! The experiment had worked like a charm.

But then he found the memory, and realized that it was not blurred at all, that on the contrary it was intensely detailed, at least up until the point when their legs had touched, at which point he could still remember perfectly, but only the feel on the outside of his knee, not their words. He went back before that, rehearsed it, relived it – cyclist, triathlon, one mile twenty-mile ten-k. Good for the legs, oh my God was it. He had to find her!

There was no sign of her at all. By now he was on Woodson,

running left and right, looking down all the little side streets and into shop windows, feeling more and more desperate. She wasn't anywhere to be seen. He had lost her.

It started to rain.

The doorbell rang. Anna went to the door and opened it.

'Frank! Wow, you're soaked.'

He must have been caught in the downpour that had begun about half an hour before, and was already mostly finished. It was odd he hadn't taken shelter during the worst of it. He looked like he had dived into a swimming pool with all his clothes on.

'Don't worry,' she said as he hesitated on the porch, dripping like a statue in a fountain. 'Here, you need a towel for your face.' She provided one from the vestibule's coat closet. 'The rain really got you.'

'Yeah.'

She was somewhat surprised to see him. She had thought he was uninterested in the Khembalis, even slightly dismissive of them. And he had sat through the afternoon's lecture wearing one of his signature looks – he had the kind of face that was able to express fifty minute gradations of displeasure, and the one at the lecture had been the one that said 'I'm keeping my eyes from rolling in my head only by the greatest of efforts.' Not the most pleasant of expressions on anyone's face, and it had only worsened as the lecture went on, until eventually he had looked stunned and off in his own world.

On the other hand, he had gone to it. He had left in silence, obviously thinking something over. And now here he was.

So Anna was pleased. If the Khembalis could capture Frank's

interest, they should be able to do it with any scientist. Frank was the hardest case she knew.

Now he seemed slightly disoriented by his drenching. He was shaking his head ruefully.

Anna said, 'Do you want to change into one of Charlie's shirts?'

'No, I'll be all right. I'll steam dry.' Then he lifted his arms and looked down. 'Well – maybe a shirt I guess. Will his fit me?'

'Sure, you're only just a bit bigger than he is.'

She went upstairs to get one, calling down, 'The others should be here any minute. There was flooding on Wisconsin, apparently, and some problems with the Metro.'

'I know about those, I got caught in one!'

'You're kidding! What happened?' She came down with one of Charlie's bigger T-shirts.

'The elevator I was in got stuck halfway up.'

'Oh no! For how long?'

'About half an hour I guess.'

'Jesus. That must have been spooky. Were you by your-self?'

'No, there was someone else, a woman. We got to talking, and so the time passed fast. It was interesting.'

'That's nice.'

'Yes. It was. Only I didn't get her name, and then when we got out they had forms for us to fill out and, and she took off while I was doing mine, so I never caught what hers was. And then the guy from the Metro wouldn't give it to me from her form, so now I'm kicking myself, because – well. I'd like to talk to her again.'

Anna inspected him, startled by this story. He was looking past her abstractedly, perhaps remembering the incident. He noticed her gaze and grinned, and this startled her once again, because it was a real smile. Always before Frank's smile had been a sceptical thing, so ironic and knowing that only one side of his mouth tugged back. Now he was like a stroke victim who had recovered the use of the damaged side of his face.

It was a nice sight, and it had to have been because of this woman he had met. Anna felt a sudden surge of affection for him. They had worked together for quite some time, and that kind of collaboration can take two people into a realm of shared experience that is not like family or marriage but rather some other kind of bond that can be quite deep. A friendship formed in the world of thought. Maybe they were always that way. Anyway he looked happy, and she was happy to see it.

'This woman filled out a form, you say?'

'Yeah.'

'So you can find out.'

'They wouldn't let me look at it.'

'No, but you'll be able to get to it somehow.'

'You think so?'

Now she had his complete attention. 'Sure. Get a reporter from the *Post* to help you, or an archival detective, or someone from the Metro. Or from Homeland Security for that matter. The fact you were in there with her, that might be the way to get it, I don't know. But as long as it's written down, something will work. That's informatics, right?'

'True.' He smiled again, looking quite happy. Then he took Charlie's shirt from her and walked around towards the kitchen while changing into it. He took a towel from her and towelled off his head. 'Thanks. Here, can I put this in your dryer? Down in the basement, right?' He stepped over the baby gate, went downstairs. 'Thanks Anna,' he called back up to her. 'I feel better now.' When he came back up, the sound of the dryer on behind him, he smiled again. 'A lot better.'

'You must have liked this woman!'

'I did. It's true, I did. I can't believe I didn't get her name!'

259

'You will. Want a beer?'

'You bet I do.'

'In the door of the fridge. Oops, there's the door again, here come the rest.'

Soon the Khembalis and many other friends and acquaintances from NSF filled the Quiblers' little living room, and the dining room flanking it, and the kitchen beyond the dining room. Anna rushed back and forth from the yellow kitchen through the dining room to the living room, carrying drinks and trays of food. She enjoyed this, and was doing it more than usual to keep Charlie from doing too much and inflaming his poison ivy. As she hurried around she enjoyed seeing Joe playing with Drepung, and Nick discussing Antarctic dinosaurs with Curt from the office right above hers; he was one of the US Antarctic Programme managers. That NSF also ran one of the continents of the world was something she tended to forget, but Curt had come to the talk, and liked it. 'These Buddhist guys would go over big in McMurdo,' he told Nick. Meanwhile Charlie, skin devastated to a brown crust across wide regions of his neck and face, eyes brilliantly bloodshot with sleep deprivation and steroids, was absorbed in conversation with Sucandra. Then he noticed her running around and joined her in the kitchen to help. 'I gave Frank one of your shirts,' she told him.

'I saw. He said he got soaked.'

'Yes. I think he was chasing around after a woman he met on the Metro.'

'*What?*'

She laughed. 'I think it's great. Go sit down, babe, don't move your poor torso, you'll make yourself itchy.'

'I've transcended itchiness. I'm only itchy for you.'

'Come on don't. Go sit down.'

Only later in the evening did she see Frank again. He was sitting in the corner of the room, on the floor between the

260

couch and the fireplace, quizzing Drepung about something or other. Drepung looked as if he was struggling to understand him. Anna was curious, and when she got a chance she sat down on the couch just above the two of them.

Frank nodded to her and then continued pressing a point, using one of his catchphrases: 'But how does that work?'

'Well,' Drepung said, 'I know what Rudra Cakrin says in Tibetan, obviously. His import is clear to me. Then I have to think what I know of English. The two languages are different, but so much is the same for all of us.'

'Deep grammar,' Frank suggested.

'Yes, but also just nouns. Names for things, names for actions, even for meanings. Equivalencies of one degree or another. So, I try to express my understanding of what Rudra said, but in English.'

'But how good is the correspondence?'

Drepung raised his eyebrows. 'How can I know? I do the best I can.'

'You would need some kind of exterior test.'

Drepung nodded. 'Have other Tibetan translators listen to the rimpoche, and then compare their English versions to mine. That would be very interesting.'

'Yes it would. Good idea.'

Drepung smiled at him. 'Double-blind study, right?'

'Yes, I guess so.'

'Elementary, my dear Watson,' Drepung intoned, reaching out for a cracker with which to dip hummus. 'But I expect you would get a certain, what, range. Maybe you would not uncover many surprises with your study. Maybe just that I personally am a bad translator. Although I must say, I have a tough job. When I don't understand the rimpoche, translating him gets harder.'

'So you make it up!' Frank laughed. His spirits were still high, Anna saw. 'That's what I've been saying all along.' He settled back against the side of the couch next to her.

But Drepung shook his head. 'Not making things up. Re-creation, maybe.'

'Like DNA and phenotypes.'

'I don't know.'

'A kind of code.'

'Well, but language is never just a code.'

'No. More like gene expression.'

'You must tell me.'

'From an instruction sequence, like a gene, to what the instruction creates. Language to thought. Or to meaning, or comprehension. Whatever! To some kind of living thought.'

Drepung grinned. 'There are about fifty words in Tibetan that I would have to translate to the word thinking.'

'Like Eskimos with snow.'

'Yes. Like Eskimos have snow, we Tibetans have thoughts.'

He laughed at the idea and Frank laughed too, shaken by that low giggle which was all he ever gave to laughter, but now emphatic and helpless with it, bubbling over with it. Anna could scarcely believe her eyes. He was as ebullient as if he were drunk, but he was still holding the same beer she had given him on his arrival. And she knew what he was high on anyway.

He pulled himself together, grew intent. 'So today, when you said, "An excess of reason is itself a form of madness," what did your lama really say?'

'Just that. That's easy, that's an old proverb.' He said the sentence in Tibetan. 'One word means "excess" or "too much", you know, like that, and *rig-gnas* is reason, or sci-ence. Then *zugs* is "form", and *zhe sdang* is "madness", a version of hatred, from an older word that was like angry. One of the *dug gsum*, the Three Poisons of the Mind.'

'And the old man said that?'

'Yes. An old saying. Milarepa, I should think.'

'Was he talking about science, though?'

'The whole lecture was on science.'

'Yeah yeah. But I found that idea in particular pretty striking.'

'A good thought is one you can act on.'

'That's what mathematicians say.'

'I'm sure.'

'So, was the lama saying that NSF is crazy? Or that western science is crazy? Because it is pretty damned reasonable. I mean, that's the point. That's the method in a nutshell.'

'Well, I guess so. To that extent. We are all crazy in some way or other, right? He did not mean to be critical. Nothing alive is ever quite in balance. It might be he was suggesting that science is out of balance. Feet without eyes.'

'I thought it was eyes without feet.'

Drepung waggled his hand: either way. 'You should ask him.'

'But you'd be translating, so I might as well just ask you and cut out the middleman!'

'No,' laughing, '*I* am the middleman, I assure you.'

'But you can tell me what he *would* say,' teasing him now. 'Cut right to the chase!'

'But he surprises me a lot.'

'Like when, give me an example.'

'Well. One time last week, he was saying to me . . .'

But at that point Anna was called away to the front door, and she did not get to hear Drepung's example, but only Frank's distinctive laughter, burbling under the clatter of conversation.

By the time she ran into Frank again he was out in the kitchen with Charlie and Sucandra, washing glasses and cleaning up. Charlie could only stand there and talk. He and Frank were discussing Great Falls, both recommending it very highly to Sucandra. 'It's more like Tibet than any other place in town,' Charlie said, and Frank giggled again, more so when Anna exclaimed, 'Oh come on love, they aren't the slightest bit the same!'

'No, yes! I mean they're more alike than anywhere else around here is like Tibet.'

'What does that mean?' she demanded.

'Water! Nature!' Then: '*Sky*,' Frank and Charlie both said at the same time.

Sucandra nodded. 'I could use some sky. Maybe even a horizon.' And all the men were chuckling.

Anna went back out to the living room to see if anyone needed anything. She paused to watch Rudra Cakrin and Joe playing with blocks on the floor again. Joe was filled with happiness to have such company, stacking blocks and babbling. Rudra nodded and handed him more. They had been doing that off and on for much of the evening. It occurred to Anna that they were the only two people at the party who did not speak English.

She went back to the kitchen and took over Frank's spot at the sink, and sent Frank down to the basement to get his shirt out of the dryer. He came back up wearing it, and leaned against a counter talking.

Charlie saw Anna rest against the counter and got her a beer from the fridge. 'Here snooks have a drink.'

'Thanks dove.'

Sucandra asked about the kitchen's wallpaper, which was an uncomfortably brilliant yellow, overlaid with large white birds caught in various moments of flight. When you actually looked at it it was rather bizarre. 'I like it,' Charlie said. 'It wakes me up. A bit itchy, but basically fine.'

Frank said he was going to go home. Anna walked him around the ground floor to the front door.

'You'll be able catch one of the last trains,' she said.

'Yeah, I'll be okay.'

'Thanks for coming, that was fun.'

'Yes it was.'

Again Anna saw that whole smile brighten his face.

'So what's she like?'

'Well – I don't know!'

They both laughed.

Anna said, 'I guess you'll find out when you find her.'

'Yeah,' Frank said, and touched her arm briefly, as if to thank her for the thought. Then as he was walking down the sidewalk he looked over his shoulder and called, 'I hope she's like you!'

Frank left Anna and Charlie's and walked through a warm drizzle back toward the Metro, thinking hard. When he came to the fateful elevator's box he stood before it, trying to order his thoughts. It was impossible – especially there. He moved on reluctantly, as if leaving the place would put the experience irrevocably in the past. But it already was. Onward, past the hotel, to the stairs, down to the Metro entry level. He stepped onto the long down escalator and descended into the earth, thinking.

He recalled Anna and Charlie, in their house with all those people. The way they stood by each other, leaned into each other. The way Anna put a hand on Charlie when she was near him – on this night, avoiding his poisoned patches. The way they shuffled their kids back and forth between them, without actually seeming to notice each other. Their endlessly varying nicknames for each other, a habit Frank had noticed before, even though he would rather have not: not just the usual endearments like hon, honey, dear, sweetheart, or babe, but also more exotic ones that were saccharine or suggestive beyond belief – snooks, snookybear, honeypie, lover, lovey, lovedove, sweetie-pie, angel man, goddessgirl, kitten, it was unbelievable the inwardness of the monogamous bond, the unconscious twin-world narcissism of it – disgusting! And yet Frank craved that very thing, that easy, deep intimacy that one could take for granted, could lose oneself in. *ISO LTR. Primate seeks partner for life.* An urge seen in every human culture, and across many species too. It was not crazy of him to want it.

Therefore he was now in a quandary. He wanted to find the woman from the elevator. And Anna had given him hope that it could be done. It might take some time, but as Anna had pointed out, everyone was in the data banks somewhere. In the Department of Homeland Security records, if nowhere else; but of course elsewhere too. Beg or break your way into Metro maintenance records, how hard could that be? There were people breaking into the genome!

But he wasn't going to be able to do it from San Diego. Or rather, maybe he could make the hunt from there – you could google someone from anywhere – but if he then succeeded in finding her, it wouldn't do him any good. It was a big continent. If he found her, if he wanted that to matter, he would need to be in the DC area.

And what would he do if he found her?

He couldn't think about that now. About anything that might happen past the moment of locating her. That would be enough. After that, who knew what she might be like. After all, she had jumped him (he shivered at the memory, still there in his flesh), jumped a total stranger in a stuck elevator after twenty minutes of conversation. There was no doubt in his mind that she had initiated the encounter; it simply wouldn't have occurred to him. Maybe that made him an innocent or a dimwit, but there it was. Maybe on the other hand she was some kind of sexual adventuress, the free papers might be right after all, and certainly everyone talked all the time about women being all Buffied and sexually assertive, though he had seen little personally to confirm it. Though it had been true of Marta too, come to think of it.

Howsoever that might be, he had been there in the elevator, had shared all responsibility for what happened. And happily so – he was pleased at himself, amazed but glowing. He wanted to find her.

But after that – if he could do it – whatever might happen, if anything were to happen – he needed to be in DC.

Fine. Here he was.

But he had just put his parting shot in Diane's in-box that very day, and tomorrow morning she would come in and read it. A letter that was, now that he thought of it, virulently critical, possibly even contemptuous – and how stupid was *that*, how impolitic, self-indulgent, irrational, maladaptive – what could he have been *thinking*? Well, somehow he had been angry. Something had made him bitter. He had done it to burn his bridges, so that when Diane had read it he would be toast at NSF.

Whereas without that letter, it would have been a relatively simple matter to sign up for another year. Anna had asked him to, and she had been speaking for Diane, Frank was sure. A year more, and after that he would know where things stood, at least.

A Metro train finally came rumbling windily into the station. Sitting in it as it jerked and rolled into the darkness towards the city, he mulled over in jagged quick images of memory and consideration all that had occurred recently, all crushed and scattered into a kind of kaleidoscope or mandala: Pierzinski's algorithm, the panel, Marta, Derek, the Khembalis' lecture; seeing Anna and Charlie, leaning side by side against a kitchen counter. He could make no sense of it really. The parts made sense, but he could not pull a theory out of it. Just part of a more general sense that the world was going smash.

And, in the context of that sort of world, did he want to go back to a single lab anyway? Could he bear to work on a single tiny chip of the giant mosaic of global problems? It was the way he had always worked before, and it might be the only way one could, really; but might he not be better off deploying his efforts in a way that magnified them by using them in this small but potentially strong arm of the government, the National Science Foundation? Was that what his letter's furious critique of NSF had been all about – his frustration that it was doing so little of what it could? If I can't find a lever I won't be able to move the world, isn't that what Archimedes had declared?

In any case his letter was there in Diane's in-box. He had torched his bridge already. It was very stupid to forestall a possible course of action in such a manner. He was a fool. It was hard to admit, but he had to admit it. The evidence was clear.

But he could go to NSF now and take the letter back.

Security would be there, as always. But people went to work late or early, he could explain himself that way. Still, Diane's offices would be locked. Security might let him in to his own office, but the twelfth floor? No.

Perhaps he could get there as the first person arrived on the twelfth floor next morning, and slip in and take it.

But on most mornings the first person to the twelfth floor, famously, was Diane Chang herself. People said she often got there at four a.m. So, well . . . He could be there when she arrived. Just tell her he needed to take back a letter he had put in her box. She might with reason ask to read it first, or she might hand it back, he couldn't say. But either way, she would know something was wrong with him. And something in him recoiled from that. He didn't want anyone to know any of this, he didn't want to look emotionally overwrought or indecisive, or as if he had something to hide. His few encounters with Diane had given him reason to believe she was not one to suffer fools gladly, and he hated to be thought of as one. It was bad enough having to admit it to himself.

And if he were going to continue at NSF, he wanted to be able to do things there. He needed Diane's respect. It would be so much better if he could take the letter back without her ever knowing he had left it.

Unbidden an old thought leapt to mind. He had often sat

in his office cubicle, looking through the window into the central atrium, thinking about climbing the mobile hanging in there. There was a crux in the middle, shifting from one piece of it to another, a stretch of chain that looked to be hard if you were free-climbing it. And a fall would be fatal. But he could make an abseil down to it from the skylight topping the atrium. He wouldn't even have to descend as far as the mobile. Diane's offices were on the twelfth floor, so it would be a short drop. A matter of using his climbing craft and gear, and his old skyscraper window skills. Come down through the skylight, do a pendulum traverse from above the mobile over to her windows, tip one out, slip in, snatch his letter out of the in-box, and climb back out, sealing the windows as he left. No security cameras pointed upward in the atrium, he had noticed during one of his climbing fantasies; there were no alarms on window framing; all would be well. And the top of the building was accessible by a maintenance ladder bolted permanently to the south wall. He had noticed that once while walking by, and had already worked it into various day-dreams of the past year. Occupying his mind with images of physical action, perhaps to model the kind of dexterity needed to solve some abstract problem, biomathematics as a kind of climbing up the walls of reality – or perhaps just to compensate for the boredom of sitting in a chair all day.

Now it was a plan, fully formed and ready to execute. He did not try to pretend to himself that it was the most rational plan he had ever made, but he urgently needed to do something physical, right then and there. He was quivering with the tension of contained action. The operation's set of physical manoeuvres were all things he could do, and that being the case, all the other factors of his situation inclined him to do it. In fact he had to, if he was really going to take responsibility for his life at last, and cast it in the direction of his desire. Make a sea change, start anew – make possible whatever follow-up with the woman in the elevator he might later be able accomplish.

It had to be done.

He got out at the Ballston station, still thinking hard. He walked to the NSF parking garage door by way of the south side of the building to confirm the exterior ladder's lower height. Bring a box to step on, that's all it would need. He walked to his car and drove west to his apartment over wet empty streets, not seeing a thing.

At the apartment he went to the closet and pawed through his climbing gear. Below it, as in an archeological dig, were the old tools of a window man's trade.

When it was all spread on the floor it looked like he had spent his whole life preparing to do this. For a moment, hefting his caulking gun, he hesitated at the sheer weirdness of what he was contemplating. For one thing the caulking gun was useless without caulk, and he had none. He would have to leave cut seals, and eventually someone would see them.

Then he remembered again the woman in elevator. He felt her kisses still. Only a few hours had passed, though since then his mind had spun through what seemed like years. If he were to have any chance of seeing her again, he had to act. Cut seals didn't matter. He stuffed all the rest of the gear into his faded red nylon climber's backpack, which was shredded down one side from a rockfall when he was a student, long ago. He had done crazy things often back then.

He went to his car, threw the bag in, hummed over the dark streets back to Arlington, past the Ballston stop. He parked on a wet street well away from the NSF building. No one was about. There were eight million people in the immediate vicinity, but it was two a.m. and so there was not a person to be seen. Who could deny sociobiology at a moment like that! What a sign of their animal natures, completely

271

diurnal in the technosurround of postmodern society, fast asleep in so many ways, and most certainly at night. Unavoidably fallen into a brain state that was still very poorly understood. Frank felt a little exalted to witness such overwhelming evidence of their animal nature. A whole city of sleeping primates. Somehow it confirmed his feeling that he was doing the right thing. That he himself had woken up for the first time in many years.

On the south side of the NSF building it was the work of a moment to stand a plastic crate on its side and hop up to the lowest rung of the service ladder bolted to the concrete wall, and then quickly to pull himself up and ascend the twelve stories to the roof, using his leg muscles for all the propulsion. As he neared the top of the ladder it felt very high and exposed, and it occurred to him that if it was really true that an excess of reason was a form of madness, he seemed to be cured. Unless of course this truly was the most reasonable thing to do – as he felt it was.

Over the coping, onto the roof, land in a shallow rain puddle against the coping. In the centre of a flat roof, the atrium skylight.

It was a muggy night, the low clouds orange with the city's glow. He pulled out his tools. The big central skylight was a low four-sided pyramid of triangular glass windowpanes. He went to the one nearest the ladder and cleaned the plate of glass, then affixed a big sucker to it.

Using his old Exacto knife he cut the sun-damaged polyurethane caulking on the window's three sides. He pulled it away and found the window screws, and zipped them out with his old Grinder screwdriver. When the window was unscrewed he grabbed the handle on the sucker and yanked to free the window, then pulled back gently; out it came, balanced in the bottom frame stripping. He pulled it back until the glass was almost upright, then tied the sling-rope from the handle of the sucker to the lowest rung of the ladder. The open gap near the top of the atrium was more than big enough for him to fit through. Cool air wafted up from some very slight internal pressure.

He laid a towel over the frame, stepped into his climbing harness, and buckled it around his waist. He tied his ropes off on the top rung of the service ladder; that would be bombproof. Now it was just a matter of slipping through the gap and abseiling down the rope to the point where he would begin his pendulum.

He sat carefully on the angled edge of the frame. He could feel the beer from Anna's reception still sloshing in him, impeding his coordination very slightly, but this was climbing, he would be all right. He had done it in worse condition in his youth, fool that he had been. Although it was perhaps the wrong time to be critical of that version of himself.

Turning around and leaning back into the atrium, he tested the Figure 8 device constricting the line – good friction – so he leaned farther back into the atrium, and immediately plummeted down into it. Desperately he twisted the abseiling device and felt the rope slow; it caught fast and he was bungeeing down on it when he crashed into something – a horrible surprise because it didn't seem that he had had time to fall to the ground, so he was confused for a split second – then he saw that he had struck the top piece of the mobile, and was now hanging over it, head downward, grasping it and the rope both with a desperate prehensile clinging.

And very happy to be there. The brief fall seemed to have effected him like a kind of electrocution. His skin burned everywhere. He tugged experimentally on his rope; it seemed fine, solidly tied to the roof ladder. Perhaps after putting the Figure 8 on the rope he had forgotten to take all the slack out of the system, he couldn't remember doing it. That would be forgetting a well-nigh instinctual action for any climber, but he couldn't honestly put it past himself on this night. His mind was full or perhaps overfull.

Carefully he reached into his waistbag. He got out two ascenders and carabinered their long loops to his harness, then connected them to the rope above him. Next he whipped the rope below him around his thigh, and had a look around. He would have to use the ascenders to pull himself back up to the proper pendulum point for Diane's window.

The whole mobile was twisting slightly. Frank grabbed it and tried to torque it until it stilled, afraid some security person would walk through the atrium and notice the motion. Suddenly the big space seemed much too well-lit for comfort, even though it was only a dim greenish glow created by a few nightlights in the offices around him.

The mobile's top piece was a bar bent into a big circle, hanging by a chain from a point on its circumference, with two shorter bars extending out from it – one about thirty degrees off from the top, bending to make a staircase shape, the other across the circle and below, its two bends making a single stair down. The crescent bar hung about fifteen feet below the circle. In the dark they appeared to be different shades of grey, though Frank knew they were primary colours. For a second that made it all seem unreal.

Finally the whole contraption came still. Frank ran one ascender up his rope, put his weight on it. Every move had to be delicate, and for a time he was lost to everything else, deep in that climber's space of purely focused concentration.

He placed the other ascender even higher, and carefully shifted his weight to it, and off the first ascender. A very mechanical and straightforward process. He wanted to leave the mobile with no push on it at all.

But the second ascender slipped when he put his weight on it, and instinctively he grabbed the rope with his hand and burned his palm before the other ascender caught him. A totally unnecessary burn.

Now he really began to sweat. A bad ascender was bad news. This one was slipping very slightly and then catching.

Looking at it he thought that maybe it had been smacked in the fall onto the top of the mobile, breaking its housing. Ascender housings were often cast, and sometimes bubbles left in the casting caused weaknesses that broke when struck. It had happened to him before, and it was major adrenalin time. No one could climb a rope unaided for long.

But this one kept holding after its little slips, and fiddling with his fingertips he could see that shoving the cam back into place in the housing after he released it helped it to catch sooner. So with a kind of teeth-clenching patience, a holding-the-breath anti-gravitational effort, he could use the other one for the big pulls of the ascent, and then set the bad one by hand, to hold him (hopefully) while he moved the good one up above it again.

Eventually he got back up to the height he had wanted to descend to in the first place, finally ready to go. He was drenched in sweat and his right hand was burning. He tried to estimate how much time he had wasted, but could not. Somewhere between ten minutes and half an hour, he supposed. Ridiculous.

Swinging side to side was easy, and soon he was swaying back and forth, until he could reach out and place a medium sucker against Laveta's office window. He depressed it slightly as he swung in close, and it stuck first try.

Held thus against her window, he could pull a T-bar from his waist bag and reach over, just barely, and fit it into the window washer's channel next to the window. After that he was set, and could reach up and place a dashboard into the slot over the window, and rig a short rope he had brought to tie the sucker handle up to the dashboard, holding open Laveta's window.

All set. Deploy the Exacto, unscrew the frame, haul up the window towards the dashboard, almost to horizontal, keeping its top edge in the framing. Tie it off. Gap biggest at the bottom corner; slip under there and pull into the office, twisting as agilely as the gibbons at the National Zoo, then kneeling on the carpeted floor, huffing and puffing as quietly as possible.

Clip the line to a chair leg, just to be sure it didn't swing back out into the atrium and leave him stuck. Tip-toe across Laveta's office, over to Diane's in-box where he had left his letter.

Not there.

A quick search of the desk top turned up nothing there either.

He couldn't think of any other high-probability places to look for it. The halls had surveillance cameras, and besides, where would he look? It was supposed to be here, Diane had been gone when he had left it in her in-box. Laveta had nodded, acknowledging receipt of same. Laveta?

Helplessly he searched the other surfaces and drawers in the office, but the letter was not there. There was nothing else he could do. He went back to the window, unclipped his line. He clipped his ascenders back onto it, making sure the good one was high, and that he had taken all the slack out before putting his weight on it. Faced with the tilted window and the open air, he banished all further consideration of the mystery of the absent letter, with one last thought of Laveta and the look he sometimes thought he saw in her eye; perhaps it was a purloined letter. On the other hand, Diane could have come back. But enough of that for now; it was time to focus. He needed to focus. The dreamlike quality of the descent had vanished, and now it was only a sweaty and poorly-illuminated job, awkward, difficult, somewhat dangerous. Getting out, letting down the window, rescrewing the frame, leaving the cut seal to surprise some future window washer. . . . Luckily, despite feeling stunned by the setback, the automatic pilot skills from hundreds of work hours came through. In the end it was an old expertise, a kid skill, something he could do no matter what.

Which was a good thing, because he wasn't actually focusing very well. On various levels his mind was racing. What could have happened? Who had his letter? Would he be able to find the woman from the elevator?

Thus only the next morning, when he came into the building in the ordinary way, did he look up self-consciously and notice that the mobile now hung at a ninety-degree angle to the position it had always held before. But no one seemed to notice.

NINE

Trigger Event

Department of Homeland Security CONFIDENTIAL

Transcript NSF 3957396584
  Phones 645d/922a
  922a: Frank are you ready for this?
  645d: I don't know Kenzo, you tell me.
  922a: Casper the Friendly Ghost spent last week swimming over the sill between Iceland and Scotland, and she never got a salinity figure over 34.
  645d: Wow. How deep did she go?
  922a: Surface water, central water, the top of the deep water. And never over 34. 33.8 on the surface once she got into the Norwegian Sea.
  645d: Wow. What about temperatures?
  922a: 0.9 on the surface, 0.75 at three hundred metres. Warmer to the east, but not by much.
  645d: Oh my God. It's not going to sink.
  922a: That's right.
  645d: What's going to happen?
  922a: I don't know. It could be the stall.
  645d: Someone's got to do something about this.

922a: Good luck my friend! I personally think we're in for some fun. A thousand years of fun.

Anna was working with her door open, and once again she heard Frank's end of a phone conversation. Having eavesdropped once, it seemed to have become easier; and as before, there was a strain in Frank's voice that caught her attention. Not to mention louder sentences like:

'*What?* Why would they do *that?*'

Then silence, except for a squeak of his chair and a brief drumming of fingers.

'Uh huh, yeah. Well, what can I say. It's too bad. It sucks, sure . . . Yeah. But, you know. You'll be fine either way. It's your workforce that will be in trouble. – No no, I understand. You did your best. Nothing you can do after you sell. It wasn't your call, Derek . . . Yeah I know. They'll find work somewhere else. It's not like there aren't other biotechs out there, it's the biotech capital of the world, right? . . . Yeah, sure. Let me know when you know . . . Okay, I do too. Bye.'

He hung up hard, cursed under his breath.

Anna looked out of her door. 'Something wrong?'

'Yeah.'

She got up and went to her doorway. He was looking down at the floor, shaking his head disgustedly.

He raised his head and met her gaze. 'Small Delivery Systems closed down Torrey Pines Generique and let almost everyone go.'

'Really! Didn't they just buy them?'

'Yes. But they didn't want the people.' He grimaced. 'It

was for something Torrey Pines had, like a patent. Or one of the people they kept. There were a few they invited to join the Small Delivery lab in Atlanta. Like that mathematician I told you about. The one who sent us a proposal, did I tell you about him?'

'One of the jackets that got turned down?'

'That's right.'

'Your panel wasn't that impressed, as I recall.'

'Yeah, that's right. But I'm not so sure they were right.' He shrugged. 'We'll never know now. They'll get him to sign a contract that gives them the rights to his work, and then they'll have it to patent, or keep as a trade secret, or even bury if it interferes with some other product of theirs. Whatever their legal department thinks will make the most.'

Anna watched him brood. Finally she said, 'Oh well.'

He gave her a look. 'A guy like him belongs at NSF.'

Anna lifted an eyebrow. She was well aware of Frank's ambivalent or even negative attitude towards NSF, which he had let slip often enough.

Frank understood her look and said, 'The thing is, if you had him here then you could, you know, sic him on things. Sic him like a dog.'

'I don't think we have a programme that does that.'

'Well you should, that's what I'm saying.'

'You can add that to your talk to the Board this afternoon,' Anna said. She considered it herself. A kind of human search engine, hunting maths-based solutions . . . .

Frank did not look amused. 'I'll already be out there far enough as it is,' he muttered. 'I wish I knew why Diane asked me to give this talk anyway.'

'To get your parting wisdom, right?'

'Yeah right.' He looked at a pad of yellow legal-sized paper, scribbled over with notes.

Anna surveyed him, feeling again the slightly irritated fondness for him she had felt on the night of the party for the

Khembalis. She would miss him when he was gone. 'Want to go down and get a coffee?'

'Sure.' He got up slowly, lost in thought, and reached out to close the program on his computer.

'Wow, what did you do to your hand?'

'Oh. Burned it in a little climbing fall. Grabbed the rope.'

'My God, Frank.'

'I was belayed at the time, it was just a reflex thing.'

'It looks painful.'

'It is when I flex it.' They left the offices and went to the elevators. 'How is Charlie getting along with his poison ivy?'

'Still moaning and groaning. Most of the blisters are healing, but some of them keep breaking open. I think the worst part now is that it keeps waking him up at night. He hasn't slept much since it happened. Between that and Joe he's kind of going crazy.'

In the Starbuck's she said, 'So are you ready for this talk to the Board?'

'No. Or as much as I can be. Like I said, I don't really know why Diane wants me to do it.'

'It must be because you're leaving. She wants to get your parting wisdom. She does that with some of the visiting people. It's a sign she's interested in your take on things.'

'But how would she know what that is?'

'I don't know. Not from me. I would only say good things, of course, but she hasn't asked me.'

He rubbed a finger gently up and down the burn on his palm.

'Tell me,' he said, 'have you ever heard of someone getting a report and, you know, just filing it away? Taking no action on it?'

'Happens all the time.'

'Really.'

'Sure. With some things it's the best way to deal with them.'

'Hmm.'

283

They had made their way to the front of the line, and so paused for orders, and the rapid production of their coffees. Frank continued to look thoughtful. It reminded Anna of his manner when he had arrived at her party, soaking wet from rain, and she said, 'Say, did you ever find that woman you were stuck in the elevator with?'

'No. I was going to tell you about it. I did what you suggested and contacted the Metro offices, and asked service and repair to get her name from the report. I said I needed to contact her for my insurance report.'

'Oh really! And?'

'And the Metro person read it right off to me, no problem. Read me everything she wrote. But it turns out she wrote down the wrong stuff.'

'What do you mean?'

They walked out of the Starbuck's back into the building.

'It was a wrong address she put down. There's no residence there. And she wrote down her name as Jane Smith. I think she made everything up.'

'That's strange! I guess they didn't check your IDs.'

'No.'

'I'd have thought they would.'

'People just freed from stuck elevators are not in the mood to be handing over their IDs.'

'No, I suppose not.' An up elevator opened and they got in. They had it to themselves. 'Like your friend, apparently.'

'Yeah.'

'I wonder why she would write down the wrong stuff though.'

'Me too.'

'What about what she told you – something about being in a cycling club, was it?'

'I've tried that. None of the cycling clubs in the area will give out membership lists. I cracked into one in Bethesda, but there wasn't any Jane Smith.'

'Wow. You've really been looking into it.'

'Yes.'

'Maybe she's a spook. Hmm. Maybe you could go to all the cycling club meetings, just once. Or join one and ride with it, and look for her at meets, and show her picture around.'

'What picture?'

'Get a portrait program to generate one.'

'Good idea, although,' sigh, 'it wouldn't look like her.'

'No, they never do.'

'I'd have to get better at riding a bike.'

'At least she wasn't into skydiving.'

'Ha. True. Well, I'll have to think about it. But thanks, Anna.'

Later that afternoon they met again, on the way up to one of Diane's meetings with the NSF Board of Directors. They got out on the twelfth floor and walked around the hallways. The outer windows at the turns in the halls revealed that the day had darkened, low black clouds now tearing over themselves in their hurry to reach the Atlantic, sheeting down rain as they went.

In the big conference room Laveta and some others were repositioning a whiteboard and powerpoint screen according to Diane's instructions. Frank and Anna were the first ones there.

'Come on in,' Diane said. She busied herself with the screen and kept her back to Frank.

The rest of the crowd trickled in. NSF's Board of Directors was composed of twenty-four people, although usually there were a couple of vacant positions in the process of being filled. The directors were all powers in their parts of the scientific world, appointed by the President from lists provided by NSF and the National Academy of Science, and serving six-year terms.

Now they were looking wet and windblown, straggling into the room in ones and twos. Some of Anna's fellow division directors came in as well. Eventually fifteen or sixteen people were seated around the big table, including Sophie Harper, their Congressional liaison. The light in the room flickered faintly as lightning made itself visible diffusely through the coursing rain on the room's exterior window. The grey world outside pulsed as if it were an aquarium.

Diane welcomed them and moved quickly through the agenda's introductory matter. After that she ran down a list of large projects that had been proposed or discussed in the previous year, getting the briefest of reports from Board members assigned to study the projects. They included climate mitigation proposals, many highly speculative, all extremely expensive. A carbon sink plan included reforestations that would also be useful for flood control; Anna made a note to tell the Khembalis about that one.

But nothing they discussed was going to work on the global situation, given the massive nature of the problem, and NSF's highly constricted budget and mission. Ten billion dollars; and even the fifty-billion dollar items on their list of projects only addressed small parts of the global problem.

At moments like these Anna could not help thinking of Charlie playing with Joe's dinosaurs, holding up a little pink mouselike thing, a first mammal, and exclaiming, 'Hey it's NSF!'

He had meant it as a compliment to their skill at surviving in a big world, or to the way they represented the coming thing, but unfortunately the comparison was also true in terms of size. Scurrying about trying to survive in a world of dying dinosaurs – worse yet, trying to save the dinosaurs too – where was the mechanism? As Frank would say, How could that work?

She banished these thoughts and made her own quick report, about the infrastructure distribution programmes that she had been studying. These had been in place for some years, and she could therefore provide some quantitative data, tallying increased scientific output in the participating countries. A lot of infrastructure had been dispersed in the last decade. Anna's concluding suggestion that the programmes were a success and should be expanded was received with nods all around, as an obvious thing to do. But also expensive.

There was a pause as people thought this over.

Finally Diane looked at Frank. 'Frank, are you ready?'

Frank stood to answer. He did not exhibit his usual ease. He walked over to the whiteboard, took up a red marker, fiddled with it. His face was flushed.

'All the programmes described so far focus on gathering data, and the truth is we have enough data already. The world's climate has already changed. The Arctic Ocean ice pack break-up has flooded the surface of the North Atlantic with fresh water, and the most recent data indicate that that has stopped the surface water from sinking, and stalled the circulation of the big Atlantic current. That's been pretty conclusively identified as a major trigger event in Earth's climactic history, as most of you no doubt know. Abrupt climate change has almost certainly already begun.'

Frank stared at the whiteboard, lips pursed. 'So. The question becomes, what do we do? Business as usual won't work. For you here, the effort should be toward finding ways that NSF can make a much broader impact than it has up until now.'

'Excuse me,' one of the Board members said, sounding a bit peeved. He was a man in his sixties, with a grey Lincoln beard; Anna did not recognize him. 'How is this any different from what we are always trying to do? I mean, we've talked about trying to do this at every Board meeting I've ever been to. We always ask ourselves, how can NSF get more bang for its buck?'

'Maybe so,' said Frank. 'But it hasn't worked.'

Diane said, 'What are you saying, Frank? What should we be doing that we haven't already tried?'

Frank cleared his throat. He and Diane stared at each other for a long moment, locked in some kind of undefined conflict.

Frank shrugged, went to the whiteboard, uncapped his red marker. 'Let me make a list.'

He wrote a *1* and circled it.

'One. We have to knit it all together.' He wrote, *Synergies at NSF*.

'I mean by this that you should be stimulating synergistic efforts that range across the disciplines to work on this problem. Then,' he wrote and circled a *2*, 'you should be looking for immediately relevant applications coming out of the basic research funded by the foundation. These applications should be hunted for by people brought in specifically to do that. You should have a permanent in-house innovation and policy team.'

Anna thought, That would be that mathematician he just lost.

She had never seen Frank so serious. His usual manner was gone, and with it the mask of cynicism and self-assurance that he habitually wore, the attitude that it was all a game he condescended to play even though everyone had already lost. Now he was serious, even angry it seemed. Angry at Diane somehow. He wouldn't look at her, or anywhere else but at his scrawled red words on the whiteboard.

'Third, you should commission work that you think needs to be done, rather than waiting for proposals and funding choices given to you by others. You can't afford to be so passive any more. Fourth, you should assign up to fifty per cent of NSF's budget every year to the biggest outstanding problem you can identify, in this case catastrophic climate change, and direct the scientific community to attack and solve it. Both public and private science, the whole culture. The effort could

288

be organized through something like Germany's Max Planck Institutes, which are funded by the government to go after particular problems. There's about a dozen of them, and they exist while they're needed and get disbanded when they're not. It's a good model.

'Fifth, you should make more efforts to increase the power of science in policy decisions everywhere. Organize all the scientific bodies on Earth into one larger body, a kind of UN of scientific organizations, which then would work together on the important issues, and would collectively *insist* they be funded, for the sake of all the future generations of humanity.'

He stopped, stared at the whiteboard. He shook his head. 'All this may sound, what. Large-scaled. Or interfering. Anti-democratic, or elitist or something – something beyond what science is supposed to be.'

The man who had objected before said, 'We're in no position to stage a coup.'

Frank shook him off. 'Think of it in terms of Kuhnian paradigms. The paradigm model Kuhn outlined in *The Structure of Scientific Revolutions*.'

The bearded man nodded, granting this.

'Kuhn postulated that in the usual state of affairs there is general agreement to a group of core beliefs that structure people's theories, that's a paradigm, and the work done within it he called "normal science". He was referring to a theoretical understanding of nature, but let's apply the model to science's social behaviour. We do normal science. But as Kuhn pointed out, anomalies crop up. Undeniable events occur that we can't cope with inside the old paradigm. At first scientists just fit the anomalies in as best they can. Then when there are enough of them, the paradigm begins to fall apart. In trying to reconcile the irreconcilable, it becomes as weird as Ptolemy's astronomical system.

'That's where we are now. We have our universities, and the foundation and all the rest, but the system is too

289

complicated, and flying off in all directions. Not capable of coming to grips with the aberrant data.'

Frank looked briefly at the man who had objected. 'Eventually, a new paradigm is proposed that accounts for the anomalies. It comes to grips with them better. After a period of confusion and debate, people start using it to structure a new normal science.'

The old man nodded. 'You're suggesting we need a paradigm shift in how science interacts with society.'

'Yes I am.'

'But what is it? We're still in the period of confusion, as far as I can see.'

'Yes. But if we don't have a clear sense of what the next paradigm should be, and I agree we don't, then it's our job now as scientists to force the issue and make it happen, by employing all our resources in an organized way. To get to the other side faster. The money and the institutional power that NSF has assembled ever since it began has to be used like a tool to build this. No more treating our grantees like clients whom we have to satisfy if we want to keep their business. No more going to Congress with hat in hand, begging for change and letting them call the shots as to where the money is spent.'

'Whoa now,' objected Sophie Harper. 'They have the right to allocate federal funds, and they're very jealous of that right, believe you me.'

'Sure they are. That's the source of their power. And they're the elected government, I'm not disputing any of that. But we can go to them and say, look, the party's over. We need this list of projects funded or civilization will be hammered for decades to come. Tell them they can't give half a trillion dollars a year to the military and leave the rescue and rebuilding of the world to chance and some kind of free market religion. It isn't working, and science is the only way out of the mess.'

'You mean the scientific deployment of human effort in these causes,' Diane said.

'Whatever,' Frank snapped, then paused, as if recognizing what Diane had said. His face went even redder.

'I don't know,' another Board member said, 'we've been trying more outreach, more lobbying of Congress, all that. I'm not sure more of that will get the big change you're talking about.'

Frank nodded. 'I'm not sure they will either. They were the best I could think of, and more needs to be done there.'

'In the end, NSF is a small agency,' someone else said.

'That's true too. But think of it as an information cascade. If the whole of NSF was focused for a time on this project, then our impact would hopefully be multiplied. It would cascade from there. The math of cascades is fairly probabilistic. You push enough elements at once, and if they're the right elements and the situation is at the angle of repose or past it, boom. Cascade. Paradigm shift. New focus on the big problems we're facing.'

The people around the table were thinking it over.

Diane never took her eye off Frank. 'I'm wondering if we are at such an obvious edge-of-the-cliff moment that people will listen to us if we try to start such a cascade.'

'I don't know,' Frank said. 'I think we're past the angle of repose. The Atlantic current has stalled. We're headed for a period of rapid climate change. That means problems that will make normal science impossible to pursue.'

Diane smiled tautly. 'You're suggesting we have to save the world so science can proceed?'

'Yes, if you want to put it that way. If you're lacking a better reason to do it.'

Diane stared at him, offended. He met her gaze unapologetically.

Anna watched this stand-off, on the edge of her seat. Something was going on between those two, and she had no idea what it was. To ease the suspense she wrote down on her handpad, *saving the world so science can proceed*. The Frank Principle, as Charlie later dubbed it.

'Well,' Diane said, breaking the frozen moment, 'what do people think?'

A discussion followed. People threw out ideas: creating a kind of shadow replacement for Congress's Office of Technology Assessment; campaigning to make the President's scientific advisor a cabinet post; even drafting a new amendment to the Constitution that would elevate a body like the National Academy of Science to the level of a branch of government. Then also going international, funding a world body of scientific organizations to push everything that would create a sustainable civilization. These ideas and more were mooted, hesitantly at first, and then with more enthusiasm as people began to realize that they all had harboured various ideas of this kind, visions that were usually too big or strange to broach to other scientists. 'Pretty wild notions,' as one of them noted.

Frank had been listing them on the whiteboard. 'The thing is,' he said, 'the way we have things organized now, scientists keep themselves out of political policy decisions in the same way that the military keeps itself out of civilian affairs. That comes out of World War II, when science *was* part of the military. Scientists recused themselves from policy decisions, and a structure was formed that created civilian control of science, so to speak.

'But I say to hell with that! Science isn't like the military. It's the solution, not the problem. And so it has to *insist on itself*. That's what looks wild about these ideas, that scientists should take a stand and become a part of the political decision-making process. If it were the folks in the Pentagon saying that, I would agree there would be reason to worry, although they do it all the time. What I'm saying is that it's a *perfectly legitimate move for us to make*, even a necessary move, because we are not the military, we are already civilians, and we have the only methods there are to deal with these global environmental problems.'

The group sat for a moment in silence, thinking that over. Monsoonlike rain coursed down the room's window, in an infinity of shifting delta patterns. Darker clouds rolled over, making the room dimmer still, submerging it until it was a cube of lit neon, hanging in aqueous greyness.

Anna's notepad was covered by squiggles and isolated words. So many problems were tangled together into the one big problem. So many of the suggested solutions were either partial or impractical, or both. No one could pretend they were finding any great strategies to pursue at this point. It looked as if Sophie Harper was about to throw her hands in the air, perhaps taking Frank's talk as a critique of her efforts to date, which Anna supposed was one way of looking at it, although not really Frank's point.

Now Diane made a motion as if to cut the discussion short. 'Frank,' she said, drawing his name out; 'Fraannnnnk – you're the one who's brought this up, as if there is something we could do about it. So maybe you should be the one who heads up a committee tasked with figuring out what these things are. Sharpening up the list of things to try, in effect, and reporting back to this Board. You could proceed with the idea that your committee was building the way to the next paradigm.'

Frank stood there, looking at all the red words he had scribbled so violently on the whiteboard. For a long moment he continued to look at it, his expression grim. Many in the room knew that he was due to go back to San Diego. Many did not. Either way Diane's offer probably struck them as another example of her managerial style, which was direct, public, and often had an element of confrontation or challenge in it. When people felt strongly about taking an action she often said, You do it, then. Take the lead if you feel so strongly.

At last Frank turned and met her eye. 'Yeah, sure,' he said. 'I'd be happy to do that. I'll give it my best shot.'

Diane revealed only a momentary gleam of triumph. Once when Anna was young she had seen a chess master play an entire room of opponents, and there had been only one player among them he was having trouble with; when he had check-mated that person, he had moved on to the next board with that very same quick satisfied look.

Now, in this room, Diane was already on to the next item on her agenda.

Afterwards, the bioinformatics group sat in Anna and Frank's rooms on the sixth floor, sipping cold coffee and looking into the atrium.

Edgardo came in. 'So,' he said cheerily, 'I take it the meeting was a total waste of time.'

'No,' Anna snapped.

Edgardo laughed. 'Diane changed NSF top to bottom?'

'No.'

They sat there. Edgardo went and poured himself some coffee.

Anna said to Frank, 'It sounded like you were telling Diane you would stay another year.'

'Yep.'

Edgardo came back in, amazed. 'Will wonders never cease! I hope you didn't give up your apartment yet!'

'I did.'

'Oh no! Too bad!'

Frank flicked that away with his burned hand. 'The guy is coming back anyway.'

Anna regarded him. 'So you really are changing your mind.'

'Well . . .'

The lights went out, computers too. Power failure.

'Ah shit.'

A blackout. No doubt a result of the storm.

Now the atrium was truly dark, all the offices lit only by the dim green glow of the emergency exit signs. EXIT. The shadow of the future.

Then the emergency generator came on, making an audible hum through the building. With a buzz and several computer pings, electricity returned.

Anna went down the hall to look north out of the corner window. Arlington was dark to the rain-fuzzed horizon. Many emergency generators had already kicked in, and more did so as she watched, powering glows that in the rain looked like little campfires. The cloud over the Pentagon caught the light from below and gleamed blackly.

Frank came out and looked over her shoulder. 'This is what it's going to be like all the time,' he predicted gloomily. 'We might as well get used to it. '

Anna said, 'How would that work?'

He smiled briefly. But it was a real smile, a tiny version of the one Anna had seen at her house. 'Don't ask me.' He stared out the window at the darkened city. The low thrum of rain was cut by the muffled sound of a siren below.

The Hyperniño that was now into its forty-second month had spun up another tropical system in the east Pacific, north of the equator, and now this big wet storm was barrelling northeast towards California. It was the fourth in a series of pineapple express storms that had tracked along this course of the jet stream, which was holding in an exceptionally fast run directly at the north coast of San Diego County. Ten miles above the surface, winds flew at a hundred and seventy miles an hour, so the air underneath was yanked over the ground at around sixty miles an hour, all roiled, torn, downdraughted and compressed, its rain squeezed out of it the moment it slammed into land. The sea-cliffs of La Jolla, Blacks, Torrey Pines, Del Mar, Solana Beach, Cardiff-by-the-Sea, Encinitas and Leucadia were all taking a beating, and in many places the sandstone, eaten by waves from below and saturated with rain from above, began to fall into the sea.

Leo and Roxanne Mulhouse had a front seat on all this, of course, because of their house's location on the cliff edge in Leucadia. Leo had spent many an hour since being let go sitting before their west window, or even standing out on the porch in the elements, watching the storms come onshore. It was an astonishing thing to see that much weather crashing into a coastline. The clouds and sky appeared to pour up over the southwest horizon together. They flew overhead and yet the cliffs and the houses held, making the wind howl at the impediment, compressed and intensified in this first assault on the land.

This particular morning was the worst yet. Tree branches tossed violently; three eucalyptus trees had been knocked over on Neptune Avenue alone. And Leo had never seen the sea look like this before. All the way out to where rapidly approaching black squalls blocked the view of the horizon, the ocean was a giant sheet of raging surf. Millions of white-caps rolled towards the land under flying spume and spray, the waves toppling again and again over infinitely wind-rippled grey water. The squalls flew by rapidly, or came straight on in black bursts of rain against the house's west side. Brief patches and shards of sunlight lanced between these squalls, but failed to light the sea surface in their usual way; the water was too shredded. The grey shafts of light appeared to be eaten by spray.

Up and down Neptune Avenue, their cliff was wearing away. It happened irregularly, in sudden slumps of various sizes, some at the cliff top, some at the base, some in the middle.

The erosion was not a new thing. The cliffs of San Diego had been breaking off throughout the period of modern set-tlement, and presumably for all the centuries before that. But along this level stretch of seaside cliff north and south of Moonlight Beach, the houses had been built close to the edge. Surveyors studying photos had seen little movement in the cliff's edge between 1928 and 1965, when the construction began. They had not known about the storm of October 12, 1889, when 7.58 inches of rain had fallen on Encinitas in eight hours, triggering a flood and bluff collapse so severe that A, B and C Streets of the new town had disappeared into the sea. They also did not understand that grading the bluffs and adding drainage pipes that led out of the cliff face destroyed natural drainage patterns that led inland. So the homes and apartment blocks had been built with their fine views, and then years of efforts had been made to stabilize the cliffs.

Now, among other problems, the cliffs were often unnaturally vertical as a result of all the shoring up they had been given. Concrete and steel barriers, iceplant berms, wooden walls and log beams, plastic sheets and moulding, crib walls, boulder walls, wire mesh, concrete abutments – all these efforts had been made in the same period when the beaches were no longer being replenished by sand washing out of the lagoons to the north, because all these had had their watersheds developed and their rivers made much less prone to flooding sand out to sea. So over time the beaches had disappeared, and these days waves struck directly at the bases of ever-steepening cliffs. The angle of repose was very far exceeded.

Now the ferocity of the Hyperniño was calling all that to account, overwhelming a century's work all at once. The day before, just south of the Mulhouses's property, a section of the cliff a hundred feet long and fifteen feet deep went, burying a concrete berm lying at the bottom of the cliff. Two hours later a hemispheric arc forty feet deep had fallen into the surf just north of them, leaving a raw new gap between two apartment blocks – a gap that quickly turned into a gritty mudslide that slid down into the tormented water, staining it brown for hundreds of yards offshore. The usual current was southerly, but the storm was shoving the ocean as well as the air northward, so that the water offshore was chaotic with drifts, with discharge from suddenly raging rivermouths, with backwash from the strikes of the big swells, and with the everpresent wind, slinging spray over all. It was so bad no one was even surfing.

As the dark morning wore on, many of the residents of Neptune Avenue went out to look at their stretch of the bluff. Various authorities were there as well, and interested spectators were filling the little cross streets that ran east to the Coast Highway, and gathering at public places along the cliff's edge. Many residents had gone the previous evening to hear a team from the US Army Corps of Engineers give a presentation at the town library, explaining their plan to stabilize the cliff at its most vulnerable points with impromptu rip-rap seawalls made of boulders dumped from above. In some places getting the boulders over the side would damage the iceplant covering. Routes out to some of the clifftop dumping points might also be trashed. Given the situation it was felt the damage was justified for the greater good. Repairs when the crisis had passed were promised. Of course some things could not be fixed; in many places the already narrow beach would be buried, becoming a wall of boulders even at low tide – like the side of a jetty, or a stretch of some very rocky coastline. Some people at the meeting lamented this loss of the area's signature landscape feature, a beach that had been four hundred yards wide in the 1920s, and even in its present narrowed state, the thing that made San Diego what it was. There were people there who felt that was worth more than houses built too close to the edge. Let them go!

But the cliff-edge homeowners had argued that it was not necessarily true that the cliffside line of houses would be the end of the losses. Everyone now knew the story behind the westernmost street in Encinitas being named D Street. The whole town was on the edge of a sandstone cliff, when you got right down to it, a cliff badly fractured and faulted. If massive rapid erosion had happened before, it could happen again. One look at the raging surface of the Pacific roaring in at them was enough to convince people it was possible.

So, later that morning, Leo found himself standing near the edge of the cliff at the south end of Leucadia, his rain jacket and pants plastered to his windward side as he shoved a wheelbarrow over a wide plank path. Roxanne was inland, helping at her sister's, and so he was free to pitch in, and happy to have something to do. A county dumptruck working with the Army Corps of Engineers was parked on Europa, and men running a small hoist were lifting granite boulders from the truck bed down into wheelbarrows. A lot of amateur help milled about, looking like a volunteer fire company that had never met before. The county and Army people supervised the operations, lining up plankways and directing rocks to the various points on the cliff's edge where they were dumping them over.

Meanwhile scores or even hundreds of people had come out in the storm, to stand on the Coast Highway or in the viewpoint parking lots, and watch the wheelbarrowed boulders bound down the cliff and crash into the sea. It was already the latest spectator event, like a new extreme sport. Some of the bounding rocks caught really good air, or spun, or held still like knuckleballs, or splashed hugely. The surfers who were not helping (and there were only so many volunteers who could be accommodated at any one time) cheered lustily at the most dramatic falls. Every surfer in the county was there, drawn like moths to flame, entranced, and on some level itching to go out; but it was not possible. The water was crazy everywhere, and when the big broken waves smashed into the bottom of the cliffs, they had nowhere to go. Big surges shoved up, disintegrated into a white smash of foam and spray, hung suspended for a moment – balked masses of water, regathering themselves high against the cliff face – then they fell and muscled back out to sea, bulling into the incoming waves and creating thick tumultuous backwash collisions, until all in the brown shallows was chaos and disorder, and another surge managed to crash in only slightly impeded.

And all the while the wind howled over them, through them, against them. It was basically a warm wind, perhaps sixty or even sixty-five degrees. Leo found it impossible to judge its speed. Even though the cliffs in this area were low compared to those at Torrey Pines, about eighty feet tall

301

rather than three hundred and fifty, that was still enough and more to block the terrific onshore flow and cause the wind to shoot up the cliffs and over them, so that a bit back from the edge it could be almost still, while right at the edge a blasting updraught was spiked by frequent gusts, like uppercuts from an invisible fist. Leo felt as if he could have leaned out over the edge and put out his arms and be held there at an angle – even jump and float down. Young windsurfers would probably be trying it soon, or surfers with their wetsuits altered to make them something like flying squirrels. Not that they would want to be in the water now. The sheer height of the whitewater surges against the cliffside was hard to believe, truly startling; bursts of spray regularly shot up into the wind and were whirled inland onto the already-drenched houses and people.

Leo got his wheelbarrow to the end of the plank road, and let a gang of people grasp his handles with him and help him tilt the stone out at the right place. After that he got out of the way and stood for a moment, watching people work. Restricted access to some of the weakest parts of the cliff meant that this was going to take days. Right now the rocks simply disappeared into the waves. No visible result whatsoever. 'It's like dropping rocks in the ocean,' he said to no one. The noise of the wind was terrific, a constant howl, like jets warming up for takeoff, interrupted by frequent invisible whacks on the ear. He could talk to himself without fear of being overheard, and did: a running narration of his day. His eyes watered in the wind, but that same wind tore the tears away and cleared his vision again and again.

This was purely a physical reaction to the gale; he was basically very happy to be there. Happy to have the distraction of the storm. A public disaster, a natural world event; it put everyone in the same boat, somehow. In a way it was even inspiring – not just the human response, but the storm itself. Wind as spirit. It felt uplifting. As if the wind had carried him off and out of his life.

Certainly it put things in a very different perspective. Losing a job, so what? How did that signify, really? The world was so vast and powerful. They were tiny things in it, like fleas, their problems the tiniest of flea perturbations.

So he returned to the dump truck and took another rock, and then focused on balancing the broken-edged thing at the front end of the wheelbarrow: turning it, keeping it on the flexing line of planks, shouldering into the blasts. Tipping a rock into the sea. Wonderful, really.

He was running the empty wheelbarrow back to the street when he saw Marta and Brian, getting out of Marta's truck parked down at the end of the street. 'Hey!' This was a nice surprise – they were not a couple, or even friends outside the lab, as far as Leo knew, and he had feared that with the lab shut down he would never see either of them again.

'Marta!' he bellowed happily. 'Bri-man!'

'LEO!'

They were glad to see him. Marta ran up and gave him a hug. Brian did the same.

'How's it going?' 'How's it going?'

They were jacked up by the storm and the chance to do something. No doubt it had been a long couple of weeks for them too, no work to go to, nothing to do. Well, they would have been out in the surf, or otherwise active. But here they were now, and Leo was glad.

Quickly they all got into the flow of the work, trundling rocks out to the cliff. Once Leo found himself following Marta down the plank line, and he watched her broad bunched shoulders and soaking black curls with a sudden blaze of friendship and admiration. She was a surfer gal, slim hips, broad shoulders, raising her head at a blast of the wind to howl back at it. Hooting with glee. He was going to miss her. Brian too. It had been good of them to come by like this;

303

but the nature of things was such that they would surely find other work, and then they would drift apart. It never lasted with old work colleagues, the bond just wasn't strong enough. Work was always a matter of showing up and then enjoying the people who had been hired to work there too. Not only their banter, but also the way they did the work, the experiments they made together. They had been a good lab.

The Army guys were waving them back from the edge of the cliff. It had been a lawn and now it was all torn up, and there was a guy there crouching over a big metal box, USGS on his soaking windbreaker. Brian shouted in their ears: they had found a fracture in the sandstone parallel to the cliff's edge here, and apparently someone had felt the ground slump a little, and the USGS guy's instrumentation was indicating movement. It was going to go. Everyone dumped their rocks where they were and hustled the empty wheelbarrows back to Neptune.

Just in time. With a short dull roar and *whump* that almost could have been the sound of more wind and surf – the impact of a really big wave – the cliff edge slumped. Then where it had been, they were looking through space at the grey sea hundreds of yards offshore. The clifftop was fifteen feet closer to them.

Very spooky. The crowd let out a collective shout that was audible above the wind. Leo and Brian and Marta drifted forward with the rest, to catch a glimpse of the dirty rage of water below. The break extended about a hundred yards to the south, maybe fifty to the north. A modest loss in the overall scheme of things, but this was the way it was happening, one little break at a time, all up and down this stretch of coast. The USGS guy had told them that there was a whole series of faults in the sandstone here, all parallel to the cliff, so that it was likely to flake off piece by piece as the waves gouged away support from below. That was how A to C street had gone in a single night. It could happen all the way inland to the Coast Highway, he said.

Amazing. Leo could only hope that Roxanne's mother's house had been built on one of the more solid sections of the bluff. It had always seemed that way when he descended the nearby staircase and checked it out; it stood over a kind of buttress of stone. But as he watched the ocean flail, and felt the wind strike them, there was no reason to be sure any section would hold. A whole neighbourhood could go. And all up and down the coast they had built close to the edge, so it would be much the same in many other places.

No house had gone over in the slump they had just witnessed, but one at the southern end of it had lost parts of its west wall − been torn open to the wind. Everyone stood around staring, pointing, shouting unheard in the roar of wind. Milling about, running hither and thither, trying to get a view.

There was nothing else to be done at this point. The end of their plank road was gone along with everything else. The Army and county guys were getting out sawhorses and rolls of orange plastic stripping; they were going to cordon off this section of the street, evacuate it, and shift the work efforts to safer platforms.

'Wow,' Leo said to the storm, feeling the word ripped out of his mouth and flung to the east. 'My Lord, what a wind.' He shouted to Marta: 'We were standing right out there!'

'Gone!' Marta howled. 'That baby is gone! It's as gone as Torrey Pines Generique!'

Brian and Leo shouted their agreement. Into the sea with the damned place!

They retreated to the lee of Marta's little Toyota pick-up, sat on the kerb behind its slight protection and drank some espressos she had in the cab, already cold in paper cups with plastic tops.

'There'll be more work,' Leo told them.

'That's for sure.' But they meant boulder work. 'I heard the Coast Highway is cut just south of Cardiff,' Brian said.

'San Elijo Lagoon is completely full, and now the surf is coming up the river mouth. Restaurant Row is totally gone. The overpass fell in and then the water started ripping both ways at the roadbed.'

'Wow!'

'It's going to be a mess. I bet that will happen at the Torrey Pines rivermouth too.'

'*All* the big lagoons.'

'Maybe, yeah.'

They sipped their espressos.

'It's good to see you guys!' Leo said. 'Thanks for coming by.'

'Yeah.'

'That's the worst part of this whole thing,' Leo said.

'Yeah.'

'Too bad they didn't hang on to us – they're putting all their eggs in one basket now.'

Marta and Brian regarded Leo. He wondered which part of what he had just said they disagreed with. Now that they weren't working for him, he had no right to grill them about it, or about anything else. On the other hand there was no reason to hold back either.

'What?'

'I just got hired by Small Delivery Systems,' Marta said, almost shouting to be heard over the noise. She glanced at Leo uncomfortably. 'Eleanor Dufours is working for them now, and she hired me. They want us to work on that algae stuff we've been doing.'

'Oh I see! Well good! Good for you.'

'Yeah, well. Atlanta.'

There was a whistle from the Army guys. A whole gang of Leucadians were trooping behind them down Neptune, south to another dump truck that had just arrived. There was more to be done.

Leo and Marta and Brian followed, went back to work.

Some people left, others arrived. Lots of people were documenting events on video cameras and digital cameras. As the day wore on, the volunteers were glad to take heavy-duty work gloves from the Army guys to protect their palms from further blistering.

About two that afternoon the three of them decided to call it quits. Their palms were trashed. Leo's thighs and lower back were getting shaky, and he was hungry. The cliff work would go on, and there would be no shortage of volunteers while the storm lasted. The need was evident, and besides it was fun to be out in the blast, doing something. Working made it seem like a practical contribution to be out there, although many would have been out to watch in any case.

The three of them stood on a point just north of Swami's, leaning into the storm and marvelling at the spectacle. Marta was bouncing a little in place, stuffed with energy still, totally fired up; she seemed both exhilarated and furious, and shouted at the biggest waves when they struck the stubborn little cliff at Pipes. 'Wow! Look at that. Outside, outside!' She was soaking wet, as they all were, the rain plastering her curls to her head, the wind plastering her shirt to her torso; she looked like the winner of some kind of extreme-sport wet T-shirt contest, her breasts and belly-button and ribs and collarbones and abs all perfectly delineated under the thin wet cloth. She was a power, a San Diego surf goddess, and good for her that she had been taken on by Small Delivery Systems. Again Leo felt a glow for this wild young colleague of his.

'This is so great,' he shouted. 'I'd rather do this than work in the lab!'

Brian laughed. 'They don't pay you for this, Leo.'

'Ah hey. Fuck that. This is still better.' And he howled at the storm.

Then Brian and Marta gave him hugs; they were taking off.

'Let's try to stay in touch you guys,' Leo said sentimentally.

'Let's really do it. Who knows, we may all end up working together again some day anyway.'

'Good idea.'

'I'll probably be available,' Brian said.

Marta shrugged, looking away. 'We either will be or we won't.'

Then they were off. Leo waved at Marta's receding truck. A sudden pang – would he ever see them again? The reflection of the truck's tail lights smeared in two red lines over the street's wet asphalt. Blinking right turn signal – then they were gone.

TEN

Broader Impacts

It takes no great skill to decode the world system today. A tiny percentage of the population is immensely wealthy, some are well off, a lot are just getting by, a lot more are suffering. We call it capitalism, but within it lies buried residual patterns of feudalism and older hierarchies, basic injustices framing the way we organize ourselves. Everybody lives in an imaginary relationship to this real situation; and that is our world. We walk with scales on our eyes, and only see what we think.

And all the while on a sidewalk over the abyss. There are islands of time when things seem stable. Nothing much happens but the rounds of the week. Later the islands break apart. When enough time has passed, no one now alive will still be here; everyone will be different. Then it will be the stories that will link the generations, history and DNA, long chains of the simplest bits – guanine, adenine, cytosine, thymine – love, hope, fear, selfishness – all recombining again and again, until a miracle happens

and the organism springs forth!

Charlie, awakened by the sound of a loud alarm, leapt to his feet and stood next to his bed, hands thrown out like a nineteenth-century boxer.

'What?' he shouted at the loud noise.

It was not an alarm. It was Joe in the room, wailing. He stared at his father amazed. 'Ba.'

'Jesus, Joe.' The itchiness began to burn across Charlie's chest and arms. He had tossed and turned in misery most of the night, as he had every night since encountering the poison ivy. He had probably fallen asleep only an hour or two before. 'What time is it? Joe, it's not even seven! Don't *yell* like that. All you have to do is tap me on the shoulder if I'm still asleep, and say, "Good morning Dad, can you warm up a bottle for me?"'

Joe approached and tapped his leg, staring peacefully at him. 'Mo da. Wa ba.'

'Wow Joe. Really good! Say, I'll get you your bottle warmed up right away! Very good! Hey listen, have you pooped in your diaper yet? You might want to pull it down and sit on *your own toilet* in the bathroom like a big boy, poop like Nick and then come on down to the kitchen and your bottle will be ready. Doesn't that sound good?'

'Ga da.' Joe trundled off towards the bathroom.

Charlie, amazed, padded after Joe and descended the stairs as gently as he could, hoping not to stimulate his itches. In the kitchen the air was delightfully cool and silky. Nick was there reading a book. Without looking up he said, 'I want to go down to the park and play.'

'I thought you had homework to do.'

'Well, sort of. But I want to play.'

'Why don't you do your homework first and then play, that way when you play you'll be able to really enjoy it.'

Nick cocked his head. 'That's true. Okay, I'll go do my homework first.' He slipped out, book under his arm.

'Oh, and take your shoes up to your room while you're on your way.'

'Sure Dad.'

Charlie stared at his reflection in the side of the cooker hood. His eyes were round.

'Hmm,' he said. He got Joe's bottle in its pot, stuck an earphone in his left ear. 'Phone, give me Phil. . . . Hello, Phil, look I wanted to catch you while the thought was fresh, I was thinking that if only we tried to introduce the Chinese aerosols bill again, then we could catch the whole air problem at a kind of fulcrum point and either start a process that would finish with the coal plants here on the East Coast, or else it would serve as a stalking horse, see what I mean?'

'So you're saying we go after the Chinese again?'

'Well yeah, but as part of your whole package of efforts.'

'And then it either works or it doesn't work, but gives us some leverage we can use elsewhere? Hmm, good idea Charlie, I'd forgotten that bill, but it was a good one. I'll give that a try. Call Roy and tell him to get it ready.'

'Sure Phil, consider it done.'

Charlie took the bottle out of the pot and dried it. Joe appeared in the door, naked, holding up his diaper for Charlie's inspection.

'Wow Joe, very good! You pooped in your toilet? Very, very good, here's your bottle all ready, what a perfect kind of Pavlovian reward.'

Joe snatched the bottle from Charlie's hand and waddled

off, a length of toilet paper trailing behind him, one end stuck between the halves of his butt.

Holy shit, Charlie thought. So to speak.

He called up Roy and told him Phil had authorized the re-introduction of the Chinese bill. Roy was incredulous. 'What do you mean, we went down big time on that, it was a joke then and it would be worse now!'

'No, not so, it lost bad but that was good, we got lots of credit for it that we deployed elsewhere, and it'll happen the same way when we do it again because it's *right*, Roy, we have right on our side on this.'

'Yes of course obviously that's not the point –'

'Not the point? Have we gotten so jaded that being right is no longer relevant?'

'No of course not, but that's not the point either, it's like playing a chess game, each move is just a move in the larger game, you know?'

'Yes I do know because that's my analogy, but that's my point, this is a good move, this checks them, they have to give up a queen to stop from being checkmated.'

'You really think it's that much leverage? Why?'

'Because Winston has such ties to Chinese industry, and he can't defend that very well to his hardcore constituency, Christian *realpolitik* isn't really a super-coherent philosophy and so it's a *vulnerability* he has don't you see?'

'Well yeah, of course. You said Phil okayed it already?'

'Yes he did.'

'Okay, that's good enough for me.'

Charlie got off and did a little dance in the kitchen, circling out into the living room, where Joe was sitting on the floor trying to get back into his diaper. Both adhesive tags had torn loose. 'Good try Joe, here let me help you.'

'Okay da.' Joe held out the diaper.

'Hmm,' Charlie said, suddenly suspicious.

He called up Anna and got her. 'Hey snooks, how are you,

yeah I'm just calling to say I love you and to suggest that we get tickets to fly to Jamaica, we'll find some kind of kid care and go down there just by ourselves, we'll rent a whole beach to ourselves and spend a week down there or maybe two, it would be good for us.'

'True.'

'It's really inexpensive down there now because of the unrest and all, so we'll have it all to ourselves almost.'

'True.'

'So I'll just call up the travel agent and have them put it all on my business expenses card.'

'Okay, go for it.'

Then there was a kind of cracking sound and Charlie woke up for real.

'Ah shit.'

He knew just what had happened, because it had happened before. His dreaming mind had grown sceptical at something in a dream that was going too well or badly – in this case his implausibly powerful persuasiveness – and so he had dreamed up ever-more unlikely scenarios, in a kind of test-to-destruction, until the dream had popped and he had awakened.

It was almost funny, this relationship to dreams. Except sometimes they crashed at the most inopportune moments. It was perverse to probe the limits of believability rather than just go with the flow, but that was the way Charlie's mind worked, apparently. Nothing he could do about it but groan and laugh, and try to train his sleeping mind into a more wish fulfilment-tolerant response.

It turned out that in the real world it was a work-at-home day for Anna, scheduled to give Charlie a kind of poison ivy vacation from Joe. Charlie was planning to take advantage of that to go down to the office by himself for once, and

314

have a talk with Phil about what to do next. It was crucial to get Phil on line for a set of small bills that would save the best of the comprehensive.

He padded downstairs to find Anna cooking pancakes for the boys. Joe liked to use them as little frisbees. 'Morning babe.'

'Hi hon.' He kissed her on the ear, inhaling the smell of her hair. 'I just had the most amazing dream. I could talk anybody into anything.'

'How exactly was that a dream?'

'Yeah right! Don't tease me about that, obviously I can't talk anybody into anything. No, this was definitely a dream. In fact I pushed it too far and killed it. I tried to talk you into going off with me to Jamaica, and you said yes.'

She laughed merrily at the thought, and he laughed to see her laugh, and at the memory of the dream. And then it seemed like a gift instead of a mockery.

He scanned the kitchen computer screen for the news. *Stormy Monday*, it proclaimed. Big storms were swirling up out of the subtropics, and the freshly-minted blue of the Arctic Ocean was dotted by a daisy chain of white patches, all falling south. The highest satellite photos, covering most of the northern hemisphere, reminded Charlie of how his skin had looked right after his outbreak of poison ivy. A huge white blister had covered southern California the day before; another was headed their way from Canada, this one a real bruiser – big, wet, slightly warmer than usual, pouring down on them from Saskatchewan.

The media meteorologists were already in a lather of anticipation and analysis, not only over the arctic blast but also in response to a tropical storm now leaving the Bahamas, even though it had wreaked less damage than had been predicted.

'Unimpressive, this guy calls it. My God! Everybody's a critic. Now people are *reviewing the weather*.'

315

'Tasteful little cirrus clouds,' Anna quoted from somewhere.

'Yeah. And I heard someone talking about an ostentatious thunderhead.'

'It's the melodrama,' Anna guessed. 'Climate as bad art, as soap opera. Or some kind of unstaged reality TV.'

'Or staged.'

'Do you think you should stay home?'

'No it'll be okay. I'll just be at work.'

'Okay.' This made sense to Anna; it took a lot to keep her from going to work. 'But be careful.'

'I will. I'll be indoors.'

Charlie went back upstairs to get ready. A trip out without Joe! It was like a little adventure.

Although once he was actually walking up Wisconsin, he found he kind of missed his little puppetmaster. He stood at a corner, waiting for the light to change, and when a tall semi rumbled by he said aloud, 'Oooh, big truck!' which caused the others waiting for the light to give him a look. Embarrassing; but it was truly hard to remember he was alone. His shoulders kept flexing at the unaccustomed lack of weight. The back of his neck felt the wind on it. It was somehow an awful realization: he would rather have had Joe along. 'Jesus, Quibler, what are you coming to.'

It was good, however, not to have the straps of the baby backpack cutting across his chest. Even without them the poison ivy damage was prickling at the touch of his shirt and the first sheen of sweat. Since the encounter with the tree he had slept so poorly, spending so much of every night awake in an agony of unscratchable itching, that he felt thoroughly and completely deranged. His doctor had prescribed powerful oral steroids, and given him a shot of them too, so maybe that was part of it. That or simply the itching itself. Putting on clothes was like a kind of skin-deep electrocution.

It had only taken a few days of that to reduce him to a

316

gibbering semi-hallucinatory state. Now, over a week later, it was worse. His eyes were sandy; things had auras around them; noises made him jump. It was like the dregs of a crystal meth jag, he imagined, or the last hours of an acid trip. A sand-papered brain, spacy and raw, everything leaping in through the senses.

He took the Metro to Dupont Circle, got off there just to take a walk without Joe. He stopped at Kramer's and got an espresso to go, then started around the circle to check the Dupont Second Story, but stopped when he realized he was doing exactly the things he would have done if he had had Joe with him.

He carried on southeastwards instead, strolling down Connecticut towards the Mall. As he walked he admired a great spectacle of clouds overhead, vast towers of pearly white lobes blooming upward into a high pale sky.

He stopped at the wonderful map store on Eye Street, and for a while lost himself in the cloud-shapes of other countries. Back outside the clouds were growing in place rather than heaving in from the west or the southeast. Brilliant anvil heads were blossoming sixty thousand feet overhead, forming a hyperhimalaya that looked as solid as marble.

He pulled out his phone and put it in his left ear. 'Phone, call Roy.'

After a second: 'Roy Anastophoulos.'

'Roy, it's Charlie. I'm coming on in.'

'I'm not there.'

'Ah come on!'

'I know. When was the last time I actually saw you?'

'I don't know.'

'You have two kids, right?'

'Oh, didn't you hear?'

'Ha ha ha. I'd like to see that.'

'Jesus no.'

'What are you going in for?'

317

'I need to talk to Phil. I had a dream this morning that I could convince anybody of anything, even Joe. I convinced Phil to reintroduce the Chinese aerosols bill, and then I got you to approve it.'

'That poison ivy has driven you barking mad.'

'Very true. It must be the steroids. I mean, the clouds today are like *pulsing*. They don't know which way to go.'

'That's probably right, there's two low-pressure systems colliding here today, didn't you hear?'

'How could I not.'

'They say it's going to rain really hard.'

'Looks like I'll beat it to the office, though.'

'Good. Hey listen, when Phil gets in, don't be too hard on him. He already feels bad enough.'

'He does?'

'Well, no. Not really. I mean, when have you ever seen Phil feel bad about anything?'

'Never.'

'Right. But, you know. He would feel bad about this if he were to go in for that kind of thing. And you have to remember, he's pretty canny at getting the most he can get from these bills. He sees the limits and then does what he can. It's not a zero-sum game to him. He really doesn't think of it as us-and-them.'

'But sometimes it *is* us-and-them.'

'True. But he takes the long view. Later some of them will be part of us. And meanwhile, he finds some pretty good tricks. Breaking the superbill into parts might have been the right way to go. We'll get back to a lot of this stuff later.'

'Maybe. We never tried the Chinese aerosols again.'

'Not yet.'

Charlie stopped listening to check the street he was crossing. When he started listening again Roy was saying, 'So you dreamed you were Xenophon, eh?'

'How's that?'

318

'Xenophon. He wrote the *Anabasis*, which tells the story of how he and a bunch of Greek mercenaries got stuck and had to fight all the way across Turkey to get home to Greece. They argue the whole time about what to do, and Xenophon wins every argument, and all his plans always work perfectly. I think of it as the first great political fantasy novel. So who else did you convince?'

'Well, I got Joe to potty-train himself, and then I convinced Anna to leave the kids at home and go with me on a vacation to Jamaica.'

Roy laughed heartily. 'Dreams are so funny.'

'Yeah, but bold. So bold. Sometimes I wake up and wonder why I'm not as bold as that all the time. I mean, what have we got to lose?'

'Jamaica, baby. Hey, did you know that some of those hotels on the north shore there are catering to couples who like to have a lot of semi-public sex, out around the pools and the beaches?'

'Talk about fantasy novels.'

'Yeah, but don't you think it'd be interesting?'

'You are sounding kind of, I don't want to say desperate here, but deprived maybe?'

'It's true, I am. It's been *weeks*.'

'Oh poor guy. It's been weeks since I left my house.'

Actually, for Roy a few weeks was quite a long time between amorous encounters. One of the not-so-hidden secrets of Washington DC was that among the ambitious young single people gathered there to run the world, there was a whole lot of collegial sex going on. Now Roy said dolefully, 'I guess I'll have to go dancing tonight.'

'Oh poor you! I'll be at home not scratching myself.'

'You'll be fine. You've already got yours. Hey listen, my food has come.'

'So where are you anyway?'

'Bombay Club.'

'Ah geez.' This was a restaurant run by a pair of Indian-Americans, its decor Raj, its food excellent. A favourite of staffers, lobbyists and other political types. Charlie loved it.

'Tandoori salmon?' he said.

'That's right. It looks and smells fantastic.'

'Yesterday my lunch was Gerber's baby spinach.'

'No. You don't really eat that stuff.'

'Yeah sure. It's not so bad. It could use a little salt.'

'Yuck!'

'Yeah, see what I do is I mix a little spinach and a little banana together?'

'Oh come on, quit it!'

'Bye.'

'Bye.'

The light under the thunderheads had gone dim. Rain was soon to arrive. The cloud bottoms were black. Splotches like dropped water balloons starred the sidewalk pavement. Charlie started hurrying, and got to Phil's office just ahead of a downpour.

He looked back out through the glass doors and watched the rain grow in strength, hammering down the length of the Mall. The skies had really opened. The raindrops remained large in the air; it looked like hail the size of baseballs had coalesced in the thunderheads, and then somehow been melted back to rain again before reaching the ground.

Charlie watched the spectacle for a while, then went upstairs. There he found out from Evelyn that Phil's flight in had been delayed, and that he might be driving back from Richmond instead.

Charlie sighed. No conferring with Phil today.

He read reports instead, and made notes for when Phil did arrive. Went down to get his mailbox cleared. Evelyn's office window had a southerly view, with the Capitol looming to the left, and across the Mall the Air and Space Museum. In the rainy light the big buildings took on an eerie cast. They looked like the cottages of giants.

Then it was past noon, and Charlie was hungry. The rain seemed to have eased a bit since its first impact, so he went out to get a sandwich at the Iranian deli on C Street, grabbing an umbrella at the door.

Outside it was raining steadily but lightly. The streets were deserted. Many intersections had flooded to the kerbs, and in a few places well over the kerbs, onto the sidewalks.

Inside the deli the grill was sizzling, but the place was almost as empty as the streets. Two cooks and the cashier were standing under a TV that hung from a ceiling corner, watching the news. When they recognized Charlie they went back to looking at the TV. The characteristic smell of basmati rice and hummus enfolded him.

'Big storm coming,' the cashier said. 'Ready to order?'

'Yeah, thanks. I'll have the usual, pastrami sandwich on rye and potato chips.'

'Flood too,' one of the cooks said.

'Oh yeah?' Charlie replied. 'What, more than usual?'

The cashier nodded, still looking at the TV. 'Two storms and high tide. Upstream, downstream and middle.'

'Oh my.'

Charlie wondered what it would mean. Then he stood watching the TV with the rest of them. Satellite weather photos showed a huge sheet of white pouring across New York and Pennsylvania. Meanwhile that tropical storm was spinning past Bermuda. It looked like another perfect storm might be brewing, like the eponymous one of 1993. Not that it took a perfect storm these days to make the Mid-Atlantic States seem like a literal designation. A far less than perfect storm could do it. The TV spoke of eleven-year tide cycles, of the longest and strongest El Niño ever recorded. 'It's a fourteen thousand square mile watershed,' the TV said.

'It's gonna get wet,' Charlie observed.

The Iranians nodded silently. Five years earlier they would probably have been closing the deli, but this was the fourth 'perfect storm' synergistic combination in the last three years, and they, like everyone else, were getting jaded. It was Peter crying wolf at this point, even though the previous three storms had all been major disasters at the time, at least in some places. But never in DC. Now people just made sure their supplies and equipment were okay and then went about their business, umbrella and phone in hand. Charlie was no different, he realized, even though he had been performing the role of Peter for all he was worth when it came to the global situation. But here he was, getting a pastrami sandwich with the intention of going back to work. It seemed like the best way to deal with it.

The Iranians finally finished his order, all the while watching the TV images: flooding fields, apparently in the upper Potomac watershed, near Harper's Ferry.

'Three metres,' the cashier said as she gave him his change, but Charlie wasn't sure what she meant. The cook chopped Charlie's wrapped sandwich in half, put it in a bag. 'First one is worst one.'

Charlie took it and hurried back through the darkening streets. He passed an occasional lit window, occupied by people working at computer terminals, looking like figures in an Edward Hopper painting.

Now it began to rain hard again, and the wind was roaring in the trees and hooting around the corners of buildings. The curiously low-angle nature of the city made big patches of lowering sky visible through the rain.

Charlie stopped at a street corner and looked around. His skin was on fire. Things looked too wet and underlit to be real; it looked liked stage lighting for some moment of ominous portent. Once again he felt that he had crossed over into a space where the real world had taken on all the qualities of a dream, becoming as glossy and surreal, as unlikely and beautiful, as stuffed to a dark sheen with ungraspable meaning. Sometimes just being outdoors in bad weather was all it took.

Back in the office he settled at his desk, and ate while looking over his list of things to do. The sandwich was good. The coffee from the office's coffee machine was bad. He wrote an update report to Phil, urging him to follow up on the elements of the bill that seemed to be dropping into the cracks. *We have to do these things.*

The sound of the rain outside made him think of the Khembalis and their low-lying island. What could they possibly do to help their watery home? Thinking about it he googled *Khembalung*, and when he saw there were over eight thousand references, googled *Khembalung + history*. That got him only dozens, and he called up the first one that looked interesting, a site called *Shambhala Studies* from an .edu site.

The first paragraph left his mouth hanging open: *Khembalung, a shifting kingdom. Previously Shambhala . . .* he skimmed down the screen, scrolling slowly:

when the warriors of Han invade central Tibet, Khembalung's turn will have arrived. A person named Drepung will come from the east, a person named Sonam will come from the north, a person named Padma will come from the west

'Holy shit –'

the first incarnation of Rudra was born as King of Olmolungring, in 16,017 BC.

then dishonesty and greed will prevail, an ideology of brutal materialism will spread all over the earth. The tyrant will come to believe there is no place left to conquer, but the mists will lift and reveal Shambhala. Outraged to find he does not rule all, the tyrant will attack, but at that point Rudra Cakrin will rise and lead a mighty host against the invaders. After a big battle the evil will be destroyed (see Plate 4)

'Holy moly.'

Charlie read on, face just inches from the screen, which was now also the dim room's lamp. *Reappearance of the kingdom . . . reincarnation of its lamas . . .* This began a section describing the methods used for locating reincarnated lamas when they reappeared in a new life. The hairs on Charlie's forearms suddenly prickled, and a wave of itching rolled over his body. Toddlers speaking in tongues, recognizing personal items from the previous incarnation's belongings –

His phone rang and he jumped a foot.

'Hello!'

'Charlie! Are you all right?'

'Hi babe, yeah, you just startled me.'

'Sorry, oh good. I was worried, I heard on the news that downtown is flooding, the Mall is flooding.'

'The what?'

'Are you at the office?'

'Yeah.'

'Is anyone else there with you?'

'Sure.'

'Are they just sitting there working?'

Charlie peered out of his carrel door to look. In fact his floor sounded empty. It sounded as if everyone was gathered down in Evelyn's office.

'I'll go check and call you back,' he said to Anna.

'Okay call me when you find out what's happening!'

'I will. Thanks for tipping me. Hey before I go, did you know that Khembalung is a kind of reincarnation of Shambhala?'

'What do you mean?'

'Just what I said. Shambhala, the hidden magical city –'

'Yes I know –'

324

'– well it's a kind of movable feast, apparently. Whenever it's discovered, or the time is right, it moves on to a new spot. They recently found the ruins of the original one in Kashgar, did you know that?'

'No.'

'Apparently they did. It was like finding Troy, or the Atlantis place on Santorini. But Shambhala didn't end in Kashgar, it moved. First to Tibet, then to a valley in east Nepal or west Bhutan, a valley called Khembalung. I suppose when the Chinese conquered Tibet they had to move it down to that island.'

'How do you know this?'

'I just read it online.'

'Charlie that's very nice, but right now go find out what's going on down there in your office! I think you're in the area that may get flooded!'

'Okay, I will. But look,' walking down the hall now, 'did Drepung ever talk to you about how they figure out who their reincarnated lamas have been reborn as?'

'No. Go check on your office!'

'Okay I am, but look honey, I want you to talk to him about that. I'm remembering that first dinner when the old man was playing games with Joe and his blocks, and Sucandra didn't like it.'

'So?'

'So I just want to be sure that nothing's going on there! This is serious, honey, I'm serious. Those folks looking for the new Panchen Lama got some poor little kid in terrible trouble a few years ago, and I don't want any part of anything like that.'

'What? I don't know what you're talking about Charlie, but let's talk about it later. Just find out what's going on there.'

'Okay okay, but remember.'

'I will!'

'Okay. Call you back in a second.'

He went into Evelyn's office and saw people jammed around the south window, with another group around a TV set on a desk.

'Look at this,' Andrea said to him, gesturing at the TV screen.

'Is that our door camera?' Charlie exclaimed, recognizing the view down Constitution. 'That's our door camera!'

'That's right.'

'My God!'

Charlie went to the window and stood on his tiptoes to see past people. The Mall was covered by water. The streets beyond were flooded. Constitution was under water that looked to be at least two feet deep, maybe deeper.

'Incredible isn't it.'

'Shit!'

'Look at that.'

'Will you look at that!'

'Why didn't you guys call me?' Charlie cried, shocked by the view.

'Forgot you were here,' someone said. 'You're never here.'

Andrea added, 'It just came up in the last half-hour, or even less. It happened all at once, it seemed like. I was watching.' Her voice quivered. 'It was like a hard downburst, and the raindrops didn't have anywhere to go, they were splashing into a big puddle everywhere, and then it was there, what you see.'

'A big puddle everywhere.'

Constitution Avenue looked like the Grand Canal in Venice. Beyond it the Mall was like a rainbeaten lake. Water sheeted equally over streets, sidewalks and lawns. Charlie recalled the shock he had felt many years before, leaving the Venice train station and seeing the canal right there outside the door. A city floored with water. Here it was quite shallow, of course. But the front steps of all the buildings came down into an expanse of brown water, and the water was all at one level, as with any other lake or sea. Brown-blue, blue-brown, brown-grey, brown, grey, dirty white – drab urban tints all. The rain pocked it into an infinity of rings and bounding droplets, and gusts of wind tore cat's-paws across it.

Charlie manoeuvred closer to the window as people left it. It seemed to him then that the water in the distance was flowing gently towards them; for a moment it looked (and even felt) as if their building had weighed anchor and was steaming westward. Charlie felt a lurch in his stomach, put his hand to the windowsill to keep his balance.

'Shit, I should get home,' he said.

'How are you going to do that?'

'We've been advised to stay put,' Evelyn said.

'You're kidding.'

'No. I mean, take a look. It could be dangerous out there right now. That's nothing to mess with – look at that!' A little electric car floated or rather was dragged down the street, already tipped on its side. 'You could get knocked off your feet.'

'Jesus.'

'Yeah.'

Charlie wasn't quite convinced, but he didn't want to argue. The water was definitely a couple of feet deep, and the rain was shattering its surface. If nothing else, it was too weird to go out.

'How extensive is it?' he asked.

Evelyn switched to a local news channel, where a very cheerful woman was saying that a big tidal surge had been predicted, because the tides were at the height of an eleven-year cycle. She went on to say that this tide was cresting higher than it would have normally because Tropical Storm Sandy's surge was now pushing up Chesapeake Bay. The combined tidal and storm surges were moving up the Potomac towards Washington, losing height and momentum all the

327

while, but impeding the outflow of the river, which had a watershed of 'fourteen thousand square miles' as Charlie had heard in the Iranian deli – a watershed which had that morning experienced record-shattering rainfall. In the last four hours ten inches of rain had fallen in several widely separated parts of the watershed, and now all that was pouring downstream and encountering the tidal bore, right in the metropolitan area. The four inches of rain that had fallen on Washington during its midday squall, while spectacular in itself, had only added to the larger problem; for the moment, there was nowhere for any of the water to go. All this the reporter explained with a happy smile.

Outside, the rain was falling no more violently than during many a summer evening's shower. But it was coming down steadily, and striking water when it hit.

'Amazing,' Andrea said.

'I hope this washes the International Monetary Fund away.'

This remark opened the floodgates, so to speak, on a loud listing of all the buildings and agencies the people in the room most wanted to see wiped off the face of the earth. Someone shouted 'the Capitol', but of course it was located on its eponymous hill to the east of them, high ground that stayed high for a good distance to the east before dipping down to the Anacostia. The people up there probably wouldn't even get stranded, as there should be a strip of high ground running to the east and north.

But as for them, below the Capitol by about forty vertical feet:

'We're here for a while.'

'The trains will be stopped for sure.'

'What about the Metro? Oh my God.'

'I've gotta call home.'

Several people said this at once, Charlie among them. People scattered to their desks and their phones. Charlie said, 'Phone, get me Anna.'

He got a quick reply: 'All circuits are busy. Please try again.' This was a recording he hadn't heard in many years, and it gave him a bad start. Of course it would happen now if at any time, everyone would be trying to call someone, and lines would be down. But what if it stayed like that for hours – or days? Or even longer? It was a sickening thought; he felt hot, and the itchiness blazed anew across his broken skin. He was almost overcome by something like dizziness, as if some invisible limb were being threatened with immediate amputation – his sixth sense, in effect, which was his link to Anna. All of a sudden he understood how completely he took his state of permanent communication with her for granted. They talked a dozen times a day, and he relied on those talks to know what he was doing, sometimes literally.

Now he was cut off from her. Judging by the voices in the offices, no one's connection was working. They regathered; had anyone found an open line? No. Was there an emergency phone system they could tap into? No.

There was, however, e-mail. Everyone sat down at their keyboards to type out messages home, and for a while it was like an office of secretaries or telegraph operators.

After that there was nothing to do but watch screens, or look out of windows. They did that, milling about restlessly, saying the same things over and over, trying the phones, typing, looking out the windows or checking out the channels and sites. The usual news channels' helicopter shots and all other overhead views lower than satellite level were impossible in the violence of the storm, but almost every channel had cobbled together or transferred direct images from various cameras around town, and one of the weather stations was flying drone camera balloons and blimps into the storm and showing whatever it was they got, mostly swirling grey clouds, but also astonishing shots of the surrounding countryside as vast tree- or roof-studded lakes. One camera on top of the Washington Monument gave a splendid view of the extent of the flooding around the Mall, truly breathtaking. The Potomac had almost overrun Roosevelt Island, and spilled over its banks until it disappeared into the huge lake it was forming, thus onto the Mall and all the way across it, up to the steps of the White House and the Capitol, both on little knolls, the Capitol's much higher. The entirety of the little Southwest district was floored by water, though its big buildings stood clear; the broad valley of the Anacostia looked like a reservoir. The city south of Pennsylvania Avenue was a building-studded lake.

And not just there. The flood had filled Rock Creek to the top of its deep but narrow ravine, and now water was pouring over at the sharp bends the gorge took while dropping through the city to the Potomac. Cameras on the bridges at M Street caught the awesome sight of the creek roaring around its final turn west, upstream from M Street, and pouring over Francis Junior High School and straight south on 23rd Street into Foggy Bottom, joining the lake covering the Mall.

Then on to a different channel, a different camera. The Watergate Building was indeed a curving water gate, like a remnant portion of a dam. The wave-tossed spate of the Potomac poured around its big bend looking as if it could knock the building down. Likewise the Kennedy Centre just south of it. The Lincoln Memorial, despite its pedestal mound, appeared to be flooded up to about Lincoln's feet. Across the Potomac the water was going to inundate the lower levels of Arlington National Cemetery. Reagan Airport was completely gone.

'Unbelievable.'

Charlie went back to the view out of their window. The water was still there. A voice on the TV was saying something about a million acre-feet of water converging in the metropolitan area, partially blocked in its flow downstream by the high tide. With more rain predicted.

Through the window Charlie saw that people were already

330

taking to the streets around them in small water craft, despite the wind and drizzle. Inflatables, kayaks, a waterski boat, canoes, rowboats; he saw examples of them all. Then as the evening wore on, and the dim light left the air below the black clouds, the rain returned with its earlier intensity. It poured down in a way that surely made it dangerous to be on the water. Most of the small craft had appeared to be occupied by men whom it did not seem had any good reason to be out there. Out for a lark – thrill-seekers, already!

'It looks like Venice,' Andrea said, echoing Charlie's earlier thought. 'I wonder what it would be like if it were like this all the time.'

'Maybe we'll get to find out.'

'How high above sea level are we here?'

No one knew, but Evelyn quickly found and clicked a topographical map to her screen. They jammed around her to look at it, or to get the address to bring it up on their own screens.

'Look at that.'

'Ten feet above sea level? Can that be true?'

'That's why they call it the Tidal Basin.'

'But isn't the ocean like what, fifty miles away? A hundred?'

'Ninety miles downstream to Chesapeake Bay,' Evelyn said.

'I wonder if the Metro has flooded.'

'How could it not?'

'True. I suppose it must have in some places.'

'And if in some places, wouldn't it spread?'

'Well, there are higher and lower sections. Seems like the lower ones would for sure. And anywhere the entries are flooded.'

'Well, yes.'

'Wow. What a mess.'

'Shit, I got here by Metro.'

Charlie said, 'Me too.'

They thought about that for a while. Taxis weren't going to be running either.

'I wonder how long it takes to walk home.'

But then again, Rock Creek ran between the Mall and Bethesda.

Hours passed. Charlie checked his e-mail frequently, and finally there was a note from Anna: *we're fine here glad to hear you're set in the office, be sure to stay there until it's safe, let's talk as soon as the phones will get through, love A and boys.*

Charlie took a deep breath, feeling greatly reassured. When the topo map had come up he had checked Bethesda first, and found that the border of the District and Maryland at Wisconsin Avenue was some two hundred and fifty feet above sea level. And Rock Creek was well to the east of it. Little Falls Creek was closer, but far enough to the west not to be a concern, he hoped. Of course Wisconsin Avenue itself was probably a shallow stream of sorts now, running down into Georgetown – and wouldn't it be great if snobbish little Georgetown got some of this, but wouldn't you know it, it was on a rise overlooking the river, in the usual correlation of money and elevation. Higher than the Capitol by a good deal. It was always that way; the poor people lived down in the flats, as witness the part of Southeast in the valley of the Anacostia River, now flooded from one side to the other.

It continued to rain. The phone connections stayed busy and no calls got through. People in Phil's office watched the TV, stretched out on couches, or even lay down to catch some sleep on chair cushions lined up on the floor. Outside the wind abated, rose again, dropped. Rain fell all the while. All the TV stations chattered on caffeinistically, talking to the emptied darkened rooms. It was strange to see how they were directly involved in an obviously historical moment, right in

332

the middle of it in fact, and yet they too were watching it on TV.

Charlie could not sleep, but wandered the halls of the big building. He visited the security team at the front doors, who had been using rolls of Department of Homeland Security gas-attack tape to try to waterproof the bottom halves of all the doors. Nevertheless the ground floor was getting soggy, and the basement even worse, though clearly the seal was fairly good, as the basement was by no means filled to the ceiling. Apparently over in the Smithsonian buildings there were hundreds of people moving stuff upstairs from variously flooding situations. People in their building mostly worked at screens or on laptops, though now some reported that they were having trouble getting online. If the internet went down they would be completely out of touch.

Finally Charlie got itchy enough from his walking, and tired enough from his already acute lack of sleep, to go back to Phil's office and lie down on a couch and try to sleep.

Gingerly he rested his fiery side on some couch cushions. 'Owwwwww.' The pain made him want to weep, and all of a sudden he wanted to be home so badly that he couldn't think about it. He moaned to think of Anna and the boys. He needed to be with them; he was not himself here, cut off from them. This was what it felt like to be in an emergency of this particular kind – scarcely able to believe it, but aware nevertheless that bad things could happen. The itching tortured him. He thought it would keep him from getting to sleep; but he was so tired that after a period of weird hypnagogic tossing and turning, during which the memory of the flood kept recurring to him like a bad dream that he was relieved to find was not true, he drifted off.

Across the great river it was different. Frank was at NSF when the storm got bad. He had received authorization from Diane to convene a new committee to report to the Board of Directors; his acceptance of the assignment had triggered a whole wave of communications to formalize his return to NSF for another year. His department at UCSD would be fine with it; it was good for them to have people working at NSF.

Now he was sitting at his screen, googling around, and for some reason he had brought up the website for Small Delivery Systems, just to look. While tapping through its pages he had come upon a list of publications by the company's scientists; this was often the best way to tell what a company was up to. And almost instantly his eye picked out one co-authored by Dr P. L. Emory, CEO of the company, and Dr F. Taolini.

Quickly he typed *consultants* into the search engine, and up came the company's page listing them. And there she was: Dr Francesca Taolini, Massachusetts Institute of Technology, Centre for Biocomputational Studies.

'Well I'll be damned.'

He sat back, thinking it over. Taolini had liked Pierzinski's proposal; she had rated it very good, and argued in favour of funding it, persuasively enough that at the time it had given him a little scare. She had seen its potential . . .

Then Kenzo called up, raving about the storm and the flood, and Frank joined everyone else in the building in

334

watching the TV news and the NOAA website, trying to get a sense of how serious things were. It became clear that things were serious indeed when one channel showed Rock Creek overflowing its banks and running deep down the streets towards Foggy Bottom; then the screen shifted the image to Foggy Bottom, waist-deep everywhere, and then came images from the inundated-to-the-rooftops Southwest district, including the classically pillared War College Building at the confluence of the Potomac and the Anacostia, sticking out of the water like a temple of Atlantis.

The Jefferson Memorial was much the same. Rainlashed rooftop cameras all over the city transmitted more images of the flood, and Frank stared, fascinated; the city was a lake.

The climate guys on the ninth floor were already posting topographical map projections with the flood peaking at various heights. If the surge got to twenty feet above sea level at the confluence of the Potomac and the Anacostia, which Kenzo thought was a reasonable projection given the the tidal bore and all, the new shore along this contour line would run roughly from the Capitol up Pennsylvania Avenue to where it crossed Rock Creek. That meant the Capitol on its hill, and the White House on its lower rise, would probably both be spared; but everything to the south and west of them was under water already, as the videos confirmed.

Upstream monitoring stations showed that the peak of the flood had not yet arrived.

'Everything has combined!' Kenzo exclaimed over the phone. 'It's all coming together!' His usual curatorial tone had shifted to that of an impresario – the Master of Disaster – or even to an almost parental pride. He was as excited as Frank had ever heard him.

'Could this be from the Atlantic stall?' Frank asked.

'Oh no, very doubtful. This is separate I think, a collisionary storm. Although the stall might bring more storms like this. Windier and colder. This is what that will be like!'

'Jesus . . . Can you tell me what's happening on the Virginia side?' There would be no way to cross the Potomac until the storm was over. 'Are people working anywhere around here?'

'They're sandbagging down at Arlington Cemetery,' Kenzo said. 'There's video on channel 44. It's got a call out for volunteers.'

'Really!'

Frank was off. He took the stairs to the basement, to be sure he didn't get caught in an elevator, and drove his car up onto the street. It was awash in places, but only to a depth of a few inches. Possibly this would soon get worse; run-off wouldn't work with the river flowing back up the drainpipes. But for now he was okay to get to the river.

As he turned right and stopped for the light, he saw the Starbuck's people out on the sidewalk, passing out bags of food and cups of coffee to the cars in front of him. Frank opened his window as one of them approached, and the employee passed in a bag of pastries, then handed him a paper cup of coffee.

'Thanks!' Frank shouted. 'You guys should take over emergency services.'

'We already did. You go and get yourself out of here.' She waved him on.

Frank drove east towards the river, laughing as he downed the pastry. Like everyone else still on the road, he ploughed through the water at about five miles an hour. Fire trucks passed through at a faster clip, leaving big wakes.

As he crossed one intersection Frank spotted a trio of men ducking behind a building carrying something. Could there be looters? Would anyone really do it? How sad to think that there were people so stuck in always-defect mode that they couldn't get out of it, even when a chance came for everything to change. What a waste of an opportunity!

Eventually he came to a roadblock and parked, following the directions of a man in an orange vest. It was a moment of hard rain. In the distance he could see people passing sand-bags down a line, just to the east of the US Marines' Memorial. He hustled over to join them.

From where he worked he could often see the Potomac, pouring down the Boundary Channel between the mainland and Columbia Island, tearing away the bridges and the marinas and threatening the low-lying parts of Arlington National Cemetery. Hundreds or perhaps even thousands of people were working around him, carrying small sandbags that looked like fifty-pound cement bags, and no doubt were about that heavy. Some big guys were lifting them off truck beds and passing them to people who passed them down lines, or carried them over shoulders, to near or far sections of a sandbag wall under the Virginia end of Memorial Bridge, where firemen were directing construction.

The noise of the river and the rain together made it hard to hear. People shouted to each other, sharing instructions and news. The airport was drowned, old Alexandria flooded, the Anacostia valley filled for miles. The Mall a lake, of course.

Frank nodded at anything said his way, not bothering to understand, and worked like a dervish. It was very satisfying. He felt deeply happy, and looking around he could see that everyone else was happy too. That's what happens, he thought, watching people carry limp sandbags like coolies in an old Chinese painting. It takes something like this to free people to be always-generous.

Late in the day he stood on their sandbag wall. It gave him a good view over the flood. The wind had died down, but the rain was falling almost as hard as ever. In some moments it seemed there was more water in the air than air.

His team had been given a break by a sudden end to the supply of sandbags. His back was stiff, and he stretched himself in circles, like the trunks of the trees had been doing all day. The wind had shifted frequently, and had included short hard blasts from the west or north, vicious slaps like microbursting downdraughts. But now there was some kind of aerial truce.

Then the rain too relented. It became a very light drizzle. Over the foamy water in the Boundary Channel he could now see far across the Potomac proper, a swirling brown plate sheeting as far as he could see to the east. The Washington Monument was a dim obelisk on a watery horizon. The Lincoln Memorial and Kennedy Center were both islands in the stream. Black clouds formed a low ceiling above them, and between the two, water and cloud, he could feel the air being smashed this way and that. Despite the disorderly gusts he was still warm from his exertions, wet but warm, with only his hands and ears slightly nipped by the wind. He stood there flexing his spine, feeling the tired muscles of his lower back.

A powerboat growled slowly up the Boundary Channel below them. Frank watched it pass, wondering how shallow its draught was; it was twenty-five or maybe even thirty feet long, a rescue boat like a sleek cabin cruiser, hull painted a shade of green that made it almost invisible. The illuminated cockpit shed its light on a person standing upright at the stern, looking like one of the weird sisters in the movie *Don't Look Now*.

This person looked over at the sandbag levee, and Frank saw that it was the woman from the elevator in Bethesda. Shocked, he put his hands to his mouth and shouted 'HEY' as loud as he could, emptying his lungs all at once.

No sign in the roar of flood and rain that she had heard him. Nor did she appear to see him waving. As the boat began to disappear around a bend in the channel, Frank spotted white lettering on its stern – GCX88A – then it was gone. Its wake had already splashed the side of the levee and roiled away.

Frank pulled his phone out of his windbreaker pocket,

shoved it in his ear, then tapped the button for NSF's climate office. Luckily it was Kenzo who picked up.

'Kenzo, it's Frank – listen, write down this sequence, it's very important, please? GCX88A, have you got that? Read it back. GCX88A. Great. Great. Wow. Okay, listen Kenzo, that's a boat's number, it was on the stern of a powerboat about twenty-six feet long. I couldn't tell if it was public or private, I suspect public, but I need to know whose it is. Can you find that out for me? I'm out in the rain and can't see my phonepad well enough to google it.'

'I can try,' Kenzo said. 'Here, let me . . . well, it looks like the boat belongs to the marina on Roosevelt Island.'

'That would make sense. Is there a phone number for it?'

'Let's see – that should be in the Coast Guard records. Wait, they're not open files. Hold a minute, please.'

Kenzo loved these little problems. Frank waited, trying not to hold his breath. Another instinctive act. As he waited he tried to etch the woman's face again on his mind, thinking he might be able to get a portrait program to draw something like what he was remembering. She had looked serious and remote, like one of the Fates.

'Yeah, Frank, here it is. Do you want me to call it and pass you along?'

'Yes please, but write it down for me too.'

'Okay, I'll pass you over and get off. I have to get back to it here.'

'Thanks Kenzo, thanks a lot.'

Frank listened, sticking a finger in his other ear. There was a pause, a ring. The ring had a rapid pulse and an insistent edge, as if it were designed to compete with the sounds of an inboard engine on a boat. Three rings, four, five; if an answering machine message came on, what would he say?

'Hello?'

It was her voice.

'Hello?' she said again.

He had to say something or she would hang up.

'Hi,' he said. 'Hi, this is me.'

There was a static-filled silence.

'We were stuck in that elevator together in Bethesda.'

'Oh my God.'

Another silence. Frank let her assimilate it. He had no idea what to say. It seemed like the ball was in her court, and yet as the silence went on, a fear grew in him.

'Don't hang up,' he said, surprising himself. 'I just saw your boat go by, I'm here on the levee at the back of the Davis Highway. I called information and got your boat's number. I know you didn't want – I mean, I tried to find you afterward, but I couldn't, and I could tell that you didn't – that you didn't want to be found. So I figured I would leave it at that, I really did.'

He could hear himself lying and added hastily, 'I didn't want to, but I didn't see what else I could do. So when I saw you just now I called a friend who got me the boat's number. I mean how could I not, when I saw you like that.'

'I know,' she said.

He breathed in. He felt himself filling up, his back straightening. Something in the way she said 'I know' brought it all back again. The way she had made it a bond between them.

After a time he said, 'I wanted to find you again. I thought that our time in the elevator, I thought it was . . .'

'I know.'

His skin warmed. It was like a kind of St Elmo's fire running over him, he'd never felt anything like it.

'But –' she said, and he learned another new feeling; dread clutched him under the ribs. He waited as for a blow to fall.

The silence went on. An isolated freshet of rain pelted down, cleared, and then he could see across the wind-lashed Potomac again. A huge rushing watery world, awesome and dreamlike.

'Give me your number,' her voice said in his ear.

'What?'

'Give me your phone number,' she said again.

He gave her his number, then added, 'My name is Frank Vanderwal.'

'Frank Vanderwal,' she said, then repeated the number.

'That's it.'

'Now give me some time,' she said. 'I don't know how long.' And the connection went dead.

The second day of the storm passed as a kind of suspended moment, everything continuing as it had the day before, everyone in the area living through it, enduring, waiting for conditions to change. The rain was not as torrential, but so much of it had fallen in the previous twenty-four hours that it was still sheeting off the land into the flooded areas and keeping them flooded. The clouds continued to crash together overhead, and the tides were still higher than normal, so that the whole piedmont region surrounding Chesapeake Bay was inundated. Except for immediate acts of a lifesaving nature, nothing could be done except to endure. All transport was drowned. The phones remained down, and power losses left tens of thousands without electricity. Escapes from drowning took precedence even over journalism (almost), and even though reporters from all over the world were converging on DC to report on this most spectacular story – the capital of the hyperpower, drowned and smashed – most of them could only get as close as the edges of the storm, or the flood; inside that was an ongoing state of emergency, and everyone was involved with rescues, relocations, and escapes of various kinds. The National Guard was out, all helicopters were enlisted into the effort; the video and digital imagery generated for the world to see was still incidental to other things; that in itself meant ordinary law had been suspended, and there was pressure to bring things back to all-spectacle all-the-time. Part of the National Guard found itself posted on the roads outside the region, to keep people from flooding the area as the water had.

Very early on the second morning it became evident that while most areas had seen high water already, the flooding of Rock Creek had not yet crested. That night its headwaters had received the brunt of one of the hardest downpours of the storm, and the already-saturated land could only shed this new rainfall into the streambed. The creek's drop to the Tidal Basin was precipitous in some places, and for most of its length the creek ran at the bottom of a narrow gorge carved into the higher ground of Northwest district. There was nowhere to hold an excess flow.

All this meant big trouble for the National Zoo, which was located on a sort of peninsula created by three turns in Rock Creek, and therefore directly overlooking the gorge. After the hard downpour in the night, the staff of the zoo congregated in the main offices to discuss the situation.

They had some visiting dignitaries on hand, who had been forced to spend the previous night there; several members of the embassy of the nation of Khembalung had come to the zoo the morning before, to take part in a ceremony welcoming two Bengal tigers brought from their country to the zoo. The storm had made it impossible for them to return to Virginia, and they had seemed happy to spend the night at the zoo, concerned as they were about their tigers, and the other animals as well.

Now they all watched together as one of the office's computers showed images of Rock Creek's gorge walls being torn away and washed downstream. Floating trees were catching in drifts against bridges over the creek, forming temporary impediments that forced water out into the flanking neighbourhoods, until the bridges blew like failed dams, and powerful low walls of debris-laden water tore down the gorge harder than ever, ripping it away even more brutally. The eastern border of the zoo made it obvious how this endangered them: the light brown torrent was ripping around the park, just a few feet below the lowest levels of the zoo grounds. That plus the images on their computers made it ever more clear that the zoo was very likely to be overwhelmed, and soon. It looked like it was going to turn into something like a reversal of Noah's flood, becoming one in which the people mostly survived, but two of every species were drowned.

The Khembali legation urged the National Park staffers to evacuate the zoo as quickly as possible. The time and vehicles necessary for a proper evacuation were completely lacking, of course, as the superintendent quickly pointed out, but the Khembalis replied that by evacuation they meant opening all the cages and letting the animals escape. The zookeepers were sceptical, but the Khembalis turned out to be experts in flood response, well-acquainted with the routines required in such situations. They quickly called up photos of the zookeepers of Prague, weeping by the bodies of their drowned elephants, to show what could happen if drastic measures were not taken. They then called up the Global Disaster Information Network, which had a complete protocol for this very scenario (threatened zoos), along with real-time satellite photos and flood data. It turned out that released animals did not roam far, seldom threatened humans (who were usually locked into buildings anyway), and were easy to recollect when the waters subsided. And the data showed Rock Creek was certain to rise further.

This prediction was easy to believe, given the roaring brown water bordering most of the zoo, and almost topping the gorge. The animals certainly believed it, and were calling loudly for freedom. Elephants trumpeted, monkeys screamed, the big cats roared and growled. Every living creature, animal and human both, was terrified by this cacophony. The din was terrific, beyond anything any jungle movie had dared. Panic was in the air.

Connecticut Avenue now resembled something like George

344

Washington's canal at Great Falls: a smooth narrow run of water, paralleling a wild torrent. All the side streets were flooded as well. Nowhere was the water very high, however; usually under a foot; and so the superintendent, looking amazed to hear it, said,'Okay let's let them out. Cages first, then the enclosures. Work from the gate down to the lower end of the park. Come on – there's a lot of locks to unlock.'

In the dark rainy air, beside the roaring engorged creek, the staff and their visitors ventured out and began unlocking the animals. They drove them towards Connecticut when necessary, though most animals needed no urging at all, but bolted for the gates with a sure sense of the way out. Some, however, huddled in their enclosures or cages, and could not be coaxed out. There was no time to spare for any particular cage; if the animals refused to leave, the zookeepers moved on and hoped there would be time to return.

The tapirs and deer were easy. They kept the biggest aviaries closed, feeling they would not flood to their tops. Then the zebras, and after them the cheetahs, the Australian creatures, kangaroos bounding with great splashes; the pandas trundling methodically out in a group, as if they had planned this for years. Elephants on parade; giraffes; hippos and rhinos, beavers and otters; after some consultation, and the coaxing of the biggest cats into their moving trucks, the pumas and smaller cats; then bison, wolves, camels; the seals and sea lions; bears; the gibbons all in a troop, screaming with triumph; the single black jaguar slipping dangerously into the murk; the reptiles, the Amazonian creatures already looking right at home; the prairie dog town, the drawbridge dropped to Monkey Island, causing another stampede of panicked primates; the gorillas and apes following more slowly. Now washes of brown water were spilling over the north end of the park and running swiftly down the zoo's paths, and the lower end of the zoo was submerged by the brown flow. Very few animals continued to stay in their enclosures, and even fewer headed by mistake towards the creek; the roar was simply too frightening, the message too clear. Every living thing's instincts were clear on where safety lay.

The water lapped higher again. It seemed to be rising in distinct surges. It had taken two full hours of frantic work to unlock all the doors, and as they were finishing, a roar louder than before overwhelmed them, and a dirty debris-filled surge poured over the whole park. Something upstream must have given all at once. Any animals remaining in the lower section of the park would be swept away or drowned on the spot. Quickly the humans remaining drove the few big cats and polar bears they had herded into their trucks out of the entrance and onto Connecticut Avenue. Now all Northwest was the zoo.

The truck that had delivered the Swimming Tigers of Khembalung headed north on Connecticut, containing the tigers in the back and the Khembali delegation piled into its cab. They drove very slowly and cautiously through the empty, dark, watery streets. The looming clouds made it look like it was already evening.

The Swimming Tigers banged around in the back as they drove. They sounded scared and angry, perhaps feeling that this had all happened before already. They did not seem to want to be in the back of the truck, and roared in a way that caused the humans in the cab to hunch forward unhappily. It sounded like the tigers were taking it out on each other; big bodies crashed into the walls, and the roars and growls grew angrier.

The Khembali passengers advised the driver and zookeeper. They nodded and continued north on Connecticut. Any big dip would make a road impassably flooded, but Connecticut ran steadily uphill to the northwest. Then Bradley Lane allowed the driver to get most of the way west to Wisconsin. When a dip stopped him, he retreated and worked his way farther north, following streets without dips, until they made it to Wisconsin Avenue, now something like a wide smooth stream, flowing hard south, but at a depth of only six inches. They crept along against this flow until they could make an illegal left onto Woodson, and thus around the corner, into the driveway of a small house backed by a big apartment complex.

In the dark air the Khembalis got out and knocked on the kitchen door. A woman appeared, and after a brief conversation, disappeared.

Soon afterwards, if anyone in the apartment complex had looked out of their window, they would have seen a curious sight: a group of men, some in maroon robes, others in National Park khakis, coaxing a tiger out of the back of a truck. It was wearing a collar to which three leashes were attached. When it was out the men quickly closed the truck door. The oldest man stood before the tiger, hand upraised. He took up one of the leashes, led the wet beast across the driveway to steps leading down to an open cellar door. Rain fell as the tiger stopped on the steps and looked around. The old man spoke urgently to it. From the house's kitchen window over them, two little faces stared out round-eyed. For a moment nothing seemed to move but the rain. Then the tiger ducked in through the doorway.

Sometime during that second night the rain stopped, and though dawn of the third morning arrived sodden and grey, the clouds scattered as the day progressed, flying north at speed. By nine the sun blazed down between big puffball clouds onto the flooded city. The air was breezy and unsettled.

Charlie had again spent this second night in the office, and when he woke he looked out of the window hoping that conditions would have eased enough for him to be able to attempt getting home. The phones were still down, although e-mails from Anna had kept him informed and reassured – at least until the previous evening's news about the arrival of the Khembalis, which had caused him some alarm, not just because of the tiger in the basement, but because of their interest in Joe. He had not expressed any of this in his e-mail replies, of course. But he most definitely wanted to get home.

Helicopters and blimps had already taken to the air in great numbers. Now all the TV channels in the world could reveal the extent of the flood from on high. Much of downtown Washington DC remained awash. A giant shallow lake occupied precisely the most famous and public parts of the city; it looked like someone had decided to expand the Mall's reflecting pool beyond all reason. The rivers and streams that converged on this larger tidal basin were still in spate, which kept the new lake topped up. In the washed sunlight the flat expanse of water was the colour of caffe latte, with foam.

Standing in the lake, of course, were hundreds of buildings-become-islands, and a few real islands, and even some freeway viaducts, now acting as bridges over the Anacostia valley. The Potomac continued to pour through the west edge of the lake, overspilling its banks both upstream and down whenever lowlands flanked it. Its surface was studded with floating junk which moved slower the farther downstream it got. Apparently the ebb tides had only begun to draw this vast bolus of water out to sea.

As the morning wore on, more and more boats appeared. The TV shots from the air made it looked like some kind of regatta – the Mall as water festival, like something out of Ming China. Many people were out on makeshift craft that did not look at all seaworthy. Police boats on patrol were even beginning to ask people who were not doing rescue work to leave, one report said, though clearly they were not having much of an impact. The situation was still so new that the law had not yet fully returned. Motorboats zipped about, leaving beige wakes behind. Rowers rowed, paddlers paddled, kayakers kayaked; swimmers swam; some people were even out in the blue pedalos that had once been confined to the Tidal Basin, pedalling around the Mall in majestic mini-steamboat style.

Although these images from the Mall dominated the media, some channels carried other news from around the region. Hospitals were filled. The two days of the storm had killed many people, no one knew how many; and there had been many rescues as well. In the first part of the third morning, the TV helicopters often interrupted their overviews to pluck people from rooftops. Rescues by boat were occurring all through Southwest district and up the Anacostia basin. Reagan Airport remained drowned, and there was no passable bridge over the Potomac all the way upstream to Harper's Ferry. The Great Falls of the Potomac was no more than a huge turbulence in a nearly unbroken, gorge-topping flow. The President had evacuated to Camp David, and now he declared all of Virginia, Maryland and Delaware a federal disaster area; the District of Columbia, in his words, 'worse than that'.

Charlie's phone chirped and he snatched it to him. 'Anna?'

'Charlie! Where are you!'

'I'm still at the office! Are you home?'

'Oh good yes! I'm here with the boys, we never left. We've got the Khembalis here with us too, you got my e-mails?'

'Yes, I wrote back.'

'Oh that's right. They got caught at the zoo. I've been trying to get you on the phone this whole time!'

'Me you too, except when I fell asleep. I was so glad to get your e-mails.'

'Yeah that was good. I'm so glad you're okay. This is crazy! Is your building completely flooded?'

'No no, not at all. So how are the boys?'

'Oh they're fine. They're loving it. It's all I can do to keep them inside.'

'Keep them inside.'

'Yes yes. So your building isn't flooded? Isn't the Mall flooded?'

'Yes it is, no doubt about that, but not the building here, not too badly anyway. They're keeping the doors shut, and trying to seal them at the bottoms. It's not working great, but it isn't dangerous. It's just a matter of staying upstairs.'

'Your generators are working?'

'Yes.'

'I hear a lot of them are flooded.'

'Yeah I can see how that would happen. No one was expecting this.'

'No. Generators in basements, it's stupid I suppose.'

'That's where ours is.'

'I know. But it's on that table, and it's working.'

'What about food, how are we set there?' Charlie tried to

350

imagine their cupboards.

'Well, we've got a bit. You know. It's not great. It will get to be a problem soon if we can't get more. I figure we might have a few weeks' worth in a pinch.'

'Well, that should be fine. I mean, they'll *have* to get things going again by then.'

'I suppose. We need water service too.'

'Will the floodwaters drain away very fast?'

'I don't know, how should I know?'

'Well, I don't know – you're a scientist.'

'Please.'

They listened to each other breathe.

'I sure am glad to be talking to you,' Charlie said. 'I hated being out of touch like that.'

'Me too.'

'There are boats all around us now,' Charlie said. 'I'll try to get a ride home as soon as I can. Once I get ferried to land, I can walk home.'

'Not necessarily. The Taft Bridge over Rock Creek is gone. You'd only be able to cross on the Mass. Ave. bridge, from what I can see on the news.'

'Yeah, I saw Rock Creek flooding, that was amazing.'

'I know. The zoo and everything. Drepung says most of the animals will be recovered, but I wonder about that.' Anna would be nearly as upset by the deaths of the zoo's animals as she would be by people. She made little distinction.

Charlie said, 'I'll take Mass. Ave. then.'

'Or maybe you can get them to drop you off west of Rock Creek, in Georgetown. Anyway, be careful. Don't do anything rash just to get here quick.'

'I won't. I'll make sure to stay safe, and I'll call you regularly, at least I hope. That was awful being cut off.'

'I know.'

'Okay, well . . . I don't really want to hang up, but I guess I should. Let me talk to the boys first.'

'Yeah good. Here talk to Joe, he's been pretty upset that you're not here, he keeps asking for you. Demanding you, actually – here,' and then suddenly in his ear:

'Dadda?'

'Joe!'

'Da! Da!'

'Yeah Joe, it's Dad! Good to hear you, boy! I'm down at work, I'll be home soon buddy.'

'Da! Da!' Then, in a kind of moan: 'Wan daaaaaaaaaa.'

'It's okay Joe,' Charlie said, throat clenching. 'I'll be home real soon. Don't you worry.'

'*Da!*' Shrieking.

Anna got back on. 'Sorry, he's throwing a fit. Here, Nick wants to talk too.'

'Hey, Nick! Are you taking care of Mom and Joe?'

'Yeah, I was, but Joe is kind of upset right now.'

'He'll get over it. So what's it been like up there?'

'Well you see, we got to burn those big candles? And I made a big tower out of the melted wax, it's really cool. And then Drepung and Rudra came and brought their tigers, they've got one in their truck and one in our basement!'

'That's nice, that's very cool. Be sure to keep the door to the basement closed by the way.'

Nick laughed. 'It's locked Dad. Mom has the key.'

'Good. Did you get a lot of rain?'

'I think so. We can see that Wisconsin is kind of flooded, but there are still some cars going in it. Most of the big stuff we've only seen on the TV. Mom was really worried about you. When are you going to get home?'

'Soon as I can.'

'Good.'

'Yeah. Well, I guess you get a few days off school out of all this. Okay, give me your mom back. Hi babe.'

'Listen, you stay put until some really safe way to get home comes along.'

'I will.'

'We love you.'

'I love you too. I'll be home soon as I can.'

Then Joe began to wail again, and they hung up.

Charlie rejoined the others and told them his news. Others were getting through on their cell phones as well. Everyone was talking. Then there came yells from down the hall.

A police motor launch was at the second-floor windows, facing Constitution, ready to ferry people to dry ground. This one was going west, and yes, would eventually dock in Georgetown, if people wanted to get off there. It was perfect for Charlie's hope to get west of Rock Creek and then walk home.

And so, when his turn came, he climbed out the window down into the big boat. A stanza from a Robert Frost poem he had memorized in high school came back to him suddenly:

It went many years, but at last came a knock,
And I thought of the door with no lock to lock.
The knock came again, my window was wide;
I climbed on the sill and descended outside.

He laughed as he moved forward in the boat to make room for other refugees. Strange what came back to the mind. How had that poem continued? Something something; he couldn't remember. It didn't matter. The relevant part had come to him, after waiting all these years. And now he was out the window and on his way.

The launch rumbled, glided away from the building, turned in a broad curve west down Constitution Avenue. Then left, out onto the broad expanse of the Mall. They were boating on the Mall.

The National Gallery reminded him of the Taj Mahal; same water reflection, same gorgeous white stone. All the Smithsonian buildings looked amazing. No doubt they had been working inside them all night to get things above flood level. What a mess it was going to be.

Charlie steadied himself against the gunwale, feeling so stunned that it seemed he might lose his balance and fall. That was probably the boat's doing, but he was, in all truth, reeling. The TV images had been one thing, the actual reality another; he could scarcely believe his eyes. White clouds danced overhead in the blue sky, and the flat brown lake was gleaming in the sunlight, reflecting a blue glitter of sky, everything all glossy and compact – real as real, or even more so. None of his visions had ever been as remotely real as this lake was now.

Their pilot manoeuvred them further south. They were going to pass the Washington Monument on its south side. They puttered slowly past it. It towered over them like an obelisk in the Nile's flood, making all the watercraft look correspondingly tiny.

The Smithsonian buildings appeared to be drowned to about ten feet. Upper halves of their big public doors emerged from the water like low boathouse doors. For some of the buildings that would be a catastrophe. Others had steps, or stood higher on their foundations. A mess any way you looked at it.

Their launch growled west at a walking pace. Trees flanking the western half of the Mall looked like water shrubs in the distance. The Vietnam Memorial would of course be submerged. The Lincoln Memorial stood on its own pedestal hill, but it was right on the Potomac, and might be submerged to the height of all its steps; the statue of Lincoln might even be getting his feet wet. Charlie found it hard to tell, through the strangely shortened trees, just how high the water was down there.

Boats of all kinds dotted the long brown lake, headed this way and that. The little blue paddle boats from the Tidal Basin were particularly festive, but all the kayaks and rowing boats and inflatables added their dots of neon colour, and the little sailing boats tacking back and forth flashed their triangular sails. The brilliant sunlight filled the clouds and the blue sky. The festival mood was expressed even by what people wore – Charlie saw Hawaiian shirts, bathing suits, even Carnival masks. There were many more black faces than Charlie was used to seeing on the Mall. It looked as if something like Trinidad's Mardi Gras parade had been disrupted by a night of storms, but was re-emerging triumphant in the new day. People were waving to each other, shouting things (the helicopters overhead were loud); standing in boats in unsafe postures, turning in precarious circles to shoot three-sixties with cameras. It would only take a water-skiier to complete the scene.

Charlie moved to the bow of the launch, and stood there soaking it all in. His mouth hung open like a dog's. The effort of getting out through the window had reinflamed his chest and arms; now he stood there on fire, torching in the wind, drinking in the maritime vision. Their boat chugged west like a vaporetto on Venice's broad lagoon. He could not help but laugh.

'Maybe they should keep it this way,' someone said.

A Navy river cruiser came growling over the Potomac towards them, throwing up a white bow wave on its upstream side. When it reached the Mall it slipped through a gap in the cherry trees, cut back on its engines, settled down in the water and continued east at a more sedate pace. It was going to pass pretty close by them, and Charlie felt their own launch slow down as well.

Then he spotted a familiar face among the people standing in the bow of the patrol boat. It was Phil Chase, waving to the boats he passed like the grand marshal of a parade, leaning over the front rail to shout greetings. Like a lot of other people on the water that morning, he had the happy look of someone who had already headed out for the territory.

Charlie waved with both arms, leaning over the side of the launch. They were closing on each other. Charlie cupped his hands around his mouth and shouted as loud as he could.

'HEY PHIL! Phil Chase!'

Phil heard him, looked over, saw him.

'Hey Charlie!' He waved cheerily, then cupped his hands around his mouth too. 'Good to see you! Is everyone at the office okay?'

'Yes!'

'Good! That's good!' Phil straightened up, gestured broadly at the flood. 'Isn't this amazing?'

'Yes! It sure is!' Then the words burst out of Charlie: 'So Phil! Are you going to do something about global warming *now*?'

Phil grinned his beautiful grin. 'I'll see what I can do!'

Acknowledgments

Many thanks for help from Guy Guthridge, Grant Heidrich, Charles Hess, Tim Higham, Dick Ill, Chris McKay, Oliver Morton, Lisa Nowell, Ann Russell, Mark Schwartz, Sharon Strauss, Jim Shea and Buck Tilley.